white rose painted red

Petal and Thorn Books is an imprint of Thorn House Publishing Inc

Copyright © 2025 Elena Lawson + Blake Lawson

All rights reserved. No part of this publication may be reproduced, stored in a retrieval system, or transmitted in any form or by any means without the prior written permission of the authors except for the use of brief quotations in a book review.

This is a work of fiction. Characters, incidents and dialogs are products of the authors' imagination and are not to be construed as real. Any resemblance to actual events is strictly coincidental.

Cover Design: The Pretty Little Design Co.

Editing: Rumi Khan

Proofreading: Leslie Morgan

white rose painted red

BLAKE & ELENA LAWSON

Playlist

"RUNRUNRUN" Dutch Melrose

"No Mercy" Austin Giorgio

"Shadow" Livingston

"Sugar" Sleep Token

"Dizzy" MISSIO

"Control Freak" New Medicine

"Empty" Letdown.

"Funeral" Neoni

"Here Come the Wolves" Lola Blanc

"God" Jake Daniels

"Breathe" Lø Spirit

"Jaws" Sleep Token

"Bottom Of The Deep Blue Sea" MISSIO

"Masterpiece" Sam Short

"Rule #34" Fish in a Birdcage

"Madhouse" Nessa Barrett

"Vicious" Bohnes

"Nail polish" Holywatr

"Surprise!" Livingston

"Trouble" Camylio
"Yes & no" XYLØ
"River" Bishop Briggs
"APHRODITE" Ethan Gander
"Damn Those Eyes" Ashley Sienna
"Love Me Dead" Ludo
"Like You Mean It" Steven Rodriguez
"You Put a Spell on Me" Austin Giorgio
"The fruits" Paris Paloma
"Shameless" Camila Cabello
"Gravedigger" Livingston
"Angel" Camylio
"MONSTER" Chandler Leighton
"Siren" Kailee Morgue
"Cinderalla's dead" EMELINE
"Kiss Me You Animal" Burn The Ballroom
"Go To War" NOTHING MORE
"Alkaline" Sleep Token
"Beautiful Crime" Tamer

add to Spotify

A note from the authors

There is a dog in this book. Her name is Ellie. We want you to know straight off that nothing bad is going to happen to her. In fact, she will be spoiled and loved by all the men in the why choose—even the one who proclaims to 'not like dogs' at the start—however, someone did hurt Ellie in the past. This is mentioned very briefly, and the person responsible absolutely gets what they deserve.

Okay. We good? Awesome.

You may now continue to read the full list of trigger warnings.

Triggers

Assault, grief, gun violence, murder, mental illness, PTSD, alcohol use, parental abandonment, explicit language, and sexual content. It also contains remembered/not on-page mentions of parental illness/death, childhood trauma and abuse, domestic violence, drugging, abduction, torture, and rape. Featured kinks include praise, sharing (no MM), DVP, pierced peen, mild domination, dirty talk, biting/marking, and face/throat fucking

1

RUN, BABY, RUN

AURORA

The windshield wipers thump as they try to keep up with the torrential downpour, matching the throbbing in my temple.

A whine comes from the back seat, and I glance in the rearview at my Aussie girl, her blue and brown eyes staring accusingly at the rain spraying into the car.

The passenger window in this shitbox has been stuck in the down position for miles, but we can't stop. Not yet.

"It's okay, Ellie," I say. "We're going to be okay."

I lift a trembling hand to my cheek and wince when my fingers brush the fresh cut there. "Everything's going to be okay."

Now that there's no adrenaline burning away the pain, I can feel everywhere that bastard touched me. The sting in my cheek. The gnawing pain in my ribs. The thick ache every time I swallow.

With a shaky breath, I turn up "Alkaline" by Sleep Token. It filters through the car in familiar, soothing notes but does little to dull my racing thoughts.

Between the complete and total lack of streetlights out

CHAPTER 1

here and the rainwater absolutely flooding my windshield, I can't see shit on these mountain roads. If it were any other night, I'd have already pulled over, but I have to keep going. The more distance I put between us and Jesse, the better.

Jagged rocks rise from the darkness on my right, and I grip the wheel tighter, fighting to keep us between the lines I can barely make out on the rainwashed road.

My gaze returns, for a second, to Ellie in the back seat. I almost lost her tonight, but never again. I don't know what I would've done...

That's a lie, I do know.

I swallow hard, banishing the thoughts before they can sink their claws in.

We got away. That's all that matters.

Turning, I reach back to pet Ellie. "It's just water, Ellie girl. We'll be in Boone soon."

In the college town, surrounded by people my own age, it'll be easier to blend in. Harder for him to find us.

I try to make out a road sign as we pass, but I don't recognize the names of the places, and the nearest one is still at least sixty miles away.

"At least I hope we'll be in Boone soon," I mutter to myself, gripping the wheel tighter as I adjust myself in the seat, sitting higher to get a clearer view of the road.

My phone's GPS has been sketchy in this weather, and I'm not sure I took the right exit a few miles back. For all I know, we could be going back the way we came. I shudder. I've been the only one out here for a while, and the farther I go, the narrower the road gets.

It doesn't help that the cell service just keeps getting shittier and fucking shittier.

Was it the right call to head into the Blue Ridge Mountains instead of going to Charlotte? That's where all my friends live, but thanks to Jesse, I haven't talked to them in over a year. Charlotte would probably be the first place he goes to look for me anyway.

And my parents' place is out of the question.

Ellie nudges her nose into the back of my arm, trying to come up front again as I drive into another steep bend.

"Ellie, you have to stay back there."

I turn to gently push her back into the seat, knowing she's only trying to help. She can always sense when I'm on edge.

Forest replaces the guardrails that warned of a steep drop to my right, and I sigh, letting myself relax a little as one song blends into the next on my playlist. When the opening notes of "Shelter" begin to play, the pelting rain softens beneath the cover of long-limbed trees. A small smirk tugs at my lips at the serendipitous timing.

"See, Ellie? That's better."

Ellie barks a call of warning just as we clear a sharp turn and my headlights illuminate something big and dark on the road.

Oh god.

There's someone right in the middle of my lane!

"Shit," I yell, slamming on my brakes, but between my bald tires and the slick pavement, I can't keep control of the car and we skid straight toward the giant idiot.

His head whips in my direction, piercing eyes wide as they catch in my headlights.

No. No. *No.*

"Watch out!" I shout, grinding the brake pedal down so hard, I'm surprised it doesn't go straight through the rusted-out floorboard.

I scream as his body hits the hood of my car with a sickening thump and rolls violently into the windshield and over the roof, cracking glass and denting metal.

Through the rearview, I watch the shadow of him hit the road in a motionless heap and nauseating dread roils in my stomach.

Ellie barks, snapping my attention back to the road.

A thick lump lodges in my throat, choking off my scream as the other shoe drops.

"Oh fuck!"

My hands want to lock on the wheel, but I force my right arm out to protect Ellie from being thrown as I brace for the second impact.

The front end of my car impales the back of a sleek black vehicle parked at the side of the road, hurtling my body forward. The airbags deploy, slamming me back into the seat so hard my breath rattles in my lungs and my ears ring.

Blinking hard, I ignore the sting of the reopened wound in my cheek and the bone-deep ache starting to pulse in my forearm, shoving back the deflating bag with shaking, numb hands. Ellie's name forms on my lips, but no sound comes out as I gasp for air.

Finally, mercifully, I drag in a ragged breath, filling my lungs with exhaust smoke and hot metal. I cough hard, turning in my seat, my right arm blindly reaching into the back. "Ellie?"

She steps unsteadily back up onto the back seats from the footwell, pacing the cramped space as she whines. I run my hand over her gray-speckled fur. It doesn't look like anything is broken. I don't see any blood. She's just scared.

She's okay. *She's okay.*

My pulse evens out as I thank whatever gods will hear me for saving my Ellie girl twice in one night.

She pushes her cold nose into my palm, sniffing, checking to see if I'm okay, too.

"I'm alright, Ellie."

At least, I think I am.

Eyes burning, I peer through the steam rising from my engine, finding a black Dodge Charger with a busted back end.

Oh my fucking god.

My eyes jerk to my side mirror, searching the dark road behind us.

The guy!

I fumble to grasp the handle to push open the door and get out. Ice-cold rain wets my hair and clothes in seconds.

"Ellie, *stay.*"

I blink, squinting in the dim red glow of my taillights, trying to find—

There.

My throat constricts as I take in the shadowed lump twenty feet from me.

The man groans, and I could cry with relief at the sound.

Holy fuck, *he's alive.*

"Don't move!" I blurt, rushing over to him on shaky legs. "Your back or neck could be broken. Fuck, I'm so sorry. I lost control of the car."

The rain starts to let up, and I kneel in my ripped jeans on the wet asphalt next to him.

His dark hair is plastered to his forehead, covering his left eye. I reach over to him, trying to get it out of his face with trembling fingers.

His head lolls to the side.

Please be okay. Please be okay.

CHAPTER 1

I gasp when his blue eyes open and fix on me, and like a punch to the gut, I can't breathe.

A steady stream of blood flows from a deep cut on his brow, carving a path past a jaw sharp enough to hone steel. It streaks down his tattooed neck in a river of watered-down red and pools in the collar of his worn leather jacket.

Head wounds always bleed more, I tell myself.

It's not that bad. It's *totally* not that bad.

He bares his teeth, bracing himself as he tries to sit up.

"I don't think you should move," I repeat in case he didn't hear me.

He shakes his head, and I notice more tattoos adorning the skin there. From his temples all the way around to where his skull meets the pavement like a Greek crown branded in black ink—visible through the close-shaved hair on the sides of his head.

He lets out a wet cough, and I tear my eyes away from the intricate whorls of ink, tracing a path down his pierced nose to his mouth, praying he isn't coughing up blood.

The man's lips are cut and bleeding at one edge, but he doesn't seem to have any visibly major injuries. His lips twist down into a sneer as he finally manages to push himself all the way up.

"*Think,*" I mutter, mostly to myself.

What am I supposed to do?

I half wonder if I should just throw myself off the cliffside now or wait until after help comes.

I'm not insured, which means I am wholeheartedly fucked.

My breaths catch on a tight feeling in my chest and it feels like the air I'm pulling hard into my lungs isn't getting where it needs to, and my head spins. I breathe harder. Faster. Trying to soothe the tension in my chest.

Squeezing my eyes closed, I'm able to clear my racing thoughts enough to see what actually matters.

He's hurt.

I desperately pat down my jeans for my phone and remember it's still in my car.

"Shit. I—I need to call an ambulance."

Before I can get to my feet, he snatches my wrist, jerking me back down. "No," he growls, coughing again. "Calm the fuck down."

"Seven, what the hell happened?" The baritone voice echoes off the rocks, and my stomach drops as two men emerge like dark shadows from the tree line.

They rush around the side of the car I crashed into, and I scramble back to my feet as they approach.

"I'm so sorry," I start. "I swear, I didn't mean to hit him. I tried to brake, but he was—"

Before I can finish, the bigger guy of the two rushes past me, knocking into my shoulder hard enough that I almost fall on my ass. I clench my jaw but say nothing as they kneel next to the guy they're calling Seven.

The smaller one reaches to examine the cut on his forehead, but Seven slaps his hand away with annoyance pinching between his brows. "Elijah, I'm fine."

The giant ignores Seven's protests, jerking down the collar of his jacket, patting him down for injury. "You were hit by a fucking car, Sev."

"I said I'm fine, Atticus," Seven snaps and pushes him back, but the rough movement has him cursing, his torso hunching inward. He reaches for his side, and the silver rings on his tattooed fingers glint in the moonlight. "Just bruised."

His blue eyes drift to me. I swallow hard, my teeth beginning to chatter as the cold wetness seeps into my

CHAPTER 1

bones, lending a sharp chill to the dread already pooling in my gut.

Atticus lurches to his feet and turns, towering over me with his dark eyes narrowed.

"What the hell is wrong with you?" he seethes.

I bite my tongue, resisting the urge to wrap my arms around myself. To cower.

"It really was an accident. The road is just so...so fucking slippery, and he was standing right in—"

He steps closer into my bubble and the sentence breaks off as he bends his six-and-a-half-foot frame down to snarl into my face. "Have you been drinking?"

"What? *No*. No, I haven't, like I said, I didn't see—"

"Back off her, Atticus," Seven says, brushing dirt from his jacket. "She tried to swerve. She's lucky she didn't drive into a damn tree. I'm fucking *fine*. Can't say the same about the car, though."

Atticus lets out a frustrated growl as he turns to inspect our cars.

My ancient Ford Focus is worse off, with the blue hood crumpled and the engine still steaming. I doubt it will even run after this. It's probably a total write-off.

Sleep Token still filters through the speakers, filling the quiet of the night.

At least that part of the car still works, I think bitterly.

Atticus runs a hand over the neatly trimmed beard that defines his square jawline, and I see blood and dirt caked into his knuckles, no doubt from the rough pat-down he gave his friend.

"It's not that bad," the other guy, Elijah, says, his tone clearly aiming to calm his friend. His eyes flit to me as he extends a hand to Seven, who takes it, letting his friend pull him up to his feet.

Elijah pushes damp, dark curls away from his face, streaking ruddy dirt across his forehead. "Are you hurt?"

It takes me a second to register that he's talking to me. I blink, taking stock. My neck is stiff as hell, my chest and forearm burn, and there's a dull ache forming in my temples, but other than that...

"I think I'm okay."

"Is that yours?" Atticus asks, turning his heated stare my way as he inclines his head to something interrupting the dark surface of the road.

"*Shit*," I mutter, my shoulders sagging as I spot a very familiar bra, and then a band tee, and then a couple errant socks, *and my fucking vibrator.* The items, now drenched and dirty, lead to where my cheap-ass suitcase is upturned on the side of the road, the rest of its contents piled in the mud. It must've been flung out of the busted passenger window when I hit their car.

I want to scream. Or cry. But instead, I drop my head back and sigh. Of course.

Of. Fucking. Course.

I trudge over, snatching the items from the road with my teeth clenched tight and the burn of unshed tears stinging in my eyes. How fucking embarrassing.

I toss it all into the case and try to zip it up, but every time I do, the zipper just comes apart at the other end. I give up, lifting the whole damn thing and chucking it back into the passenger seat of my car with a vulgar sound in the back of my throat.

One of the guys murmurs something to another, and I close my eyes for one blissful second, pretending they didn't just watch me shove eight pairs of soggy panties into my bag.

The one who should be on his way to the hospital lifts

CHAPTER 1

his brows, his head cocked to one side like he isn't quite sure what to make of me.

I realize, seeing them all standing there in the dark, that I really shouldn't have turned my back to them at all. I'm alone out here. I was too busy thinking about whether the guy I hit was all right and if they were going to call the cops, that I didn't register the potential threat.

Atticus strides over, and I step back, closer to the car, to Ellie who barks from the back seat, pushing her nose against the glass. She's a good listener, but if this guy comes any closer, my command for her to stay in the car won't stop her from trying to protect me.

He roughly pushes a few wet strands of hair from his forehead where they escaped from the soaked bun of dirty blond hair atop his head. Between the hair, the short beard, his insane height, and Scandinavian features, he looks like a damn Viking god. And not the fun, trickster kind. *No.* The kind that raids and pillages. A warrior.

Dangerous.

His expression shifts, something like recognition in his hooded, brown eyes as they carve a path over the injury on my cheek and down my neck. I cross my arms over my chest, gripping opposite elbows like a shield. The cut and bruises could just as easily have come from the crash, so I don't bother trying to hide them.

Besides, I'm done covering for Jesse.

"What are you staring at?"

The muscles in his jaw tense when he cocks his head to one side, his stare intensifying even more until I feel like I'm under a fucking microscope.

"What are we going to do about you?"

2

A DEAL IN THE DARK

AURORA

"I don't have insurance," I blurt, biting the inside of my cheek until I taste copper on my tongue. "Or enough cash to pay you for the damages."

God, I am *so* fucked.

Tears burn my eyes as the whole-ass situation sinks in, and this time, I can't stop them. I reach up and unclasp the white gold necklace around my neck, holding it out to him in my palm. It's the only thing I have left that's worth anything at all.

"It has to be worth enough to fix your car. Here, take it."

Atticus ignores my offer, letting my hand hang in the air until I lower it to my side.

He glances over his shoulder for a silent exchange with the other two and then focuses back on me as they come to stand with him. Together, they form a wall of muscle wrapped in shades of black, blocking me in against the passenger side of the car.

"Do you have any cleaning experience?" Atticus asks.

My brows knit together.

CHAPTER 2

"We're looking to hire a maid. The job pays well but we haven't had many applicants because we're so remote."

Wait, what?

"The position also offers live-in accommodations," he continues as if this is totally normal, while the other two remain silent.

"You're offering me a job? After I hit that guy and smashed your car?"

This is the weirdest way I've ever been propositioned for a job. But honestly, cleaning up after Jesse for a year should be considered a decade's worth of experience as a housekeeper. And I *do* need a job.

And a place to stay.

Besides Ellie and one small suitcase full of old clothes, I have nothing.

At least we had the car to camp out in until I could find better shelter, but now even that is basically totalled and I don't have the money to get it fixed.

Right now, calling my situation desperate would be putting it very fucking mildly.

Atticus lifts his brows with impatience. "Do you want the job or not?"

"I..."

Flicking my gaze between the three men, I size them up, and gulp. They aren't your typical twenty-something dudes. They're tall and muscled and look like the universe has already shown them her teeth.

I know how to handle dangerous men. I've been doing it my whole damn life. But I am not about leaving one shit situation just to jump right into another one. Not this time. It's not just me I have to think about anymore. I have Ellie. She deserves a good home. A *safe* home.

"Your other option is getting the authorities involved. Your choice."

Atticus says it with a shrug as if he didn't just make it impossible for me to say no.

My chest tightens again, and it's a struggle to breathe as I try and fail to consider my options. None of them are good. But that's not exactly new. Tonight, I ran without really thinking through any sort of long-term plan, aside from putting as many miles between us and Jesse as possible.

From the car, Ellie barks, drawing our attention. She jumps out from the driver's side door with a growl, her head lowered as she makes her way around the car, sensing my distress.

"Ellie, no!"

Seven reaches down to pet her, and I almost shout at him not to touch her, but then he chuckles as she sniffs the back of his hand.

A brilliant smile spreads across his face, and the rebuke dies in my throat as Ellie licks his knuckles and he crouches to scratch her under the chin with a wince.

"And who is this? What's your name, sweet girl?"

Hearing him say 'sweet girl' does something to my insides, and I fight to keep the surprise off my face.

To my shock, Ellie lets out a happy whine, pressing into his touch.

"I thought she hated men," I say under my breath, watching her go to the other two, sniffing them both with her tongue lolling out.

The sight melts my heart and makes me relax a fraction. She hated Jesse and any of his guy friends. For damn good reason, too. They were *not* good people.

She moves back between Seven and Elijah and sits

down, her tail dragging over the wet asphalt as she regards me stoically. I tip my head at her in question, and she barks at me the same way she does when she wants my attention. And maybe it's the dumbest thing I'll ever do, but the ugly truth is that I have nowhere else to go.

Curling my fingers around the necklace in my palm, I bend to one knee, telling Ellie to come. She bounds over, pushing her head into my chest.

"You better be right about this, Ellie girl," I whisper into her damp fur before looking back up at Atticus. "What's your pet policy?"

"Is she trained?"

"Better than most men." The words fall out of my mouth before I can catch them, and I press my lips tight, holding my breath. *Fuck.*

But I see the ghost of a smirk on Atticus's face before it's gone, and he clears his throat to hide his amusement. "Well, you got the job, Miss...?"

"Bellerose. Aurora Bellerose."

3

WHO HURT YOU?

SEVEN

The high beams illuminate the ancient pines hedging in our gravel drive as Atticus pulls through the front gate and it yawns shut behind us.

Every fucking bump jars my battered rib cage, but I've been through worse.

I meet Eli's eyes in the rearview and catch his smirk. I shake my head at him, nostrils flaring, knowing exactly what the fucker is thinking.

He figures I've got nine lives. If that's true, then I still have a few left to spend before my card is punched.

Aurora asked several times about me going to the hospital, saying I could have internal bleeding, but I know what that's like, and nothing in me says I'm dying. I might have a cracked rib or two, but it's nothing that won't heal on its own in time.

"This road isn't on the map," Aurora says from the back seat, and I can hear the questions in her words, the ones she isn't asking.

Where are you taking me?

What are you going to do with me?

CHAPTER 3

Normally, I'd have those answers, but this time, I don't have a damn clue what Atticus is up to. I do know one thing, though: we weren't looking to hire a cleaner a couple hours ago. Atticus's clean freak ass is enough to keep the whole place military clean even without the threat of sergeant inspections.

When I glance over my shoulder, a bolt of heat ricochets up my neck. I grit my teeth through the pain, my gaze locking on to the girl in the back seat, her face illuminated by the glow of her cell phone. She taps and slides her fingers over the screen, zooming in on an offline map.

She's trying to track where we are. Clever girl.

Only, this house isn't on any GPS, and the coordinates it gives for fifty miles around are bogus, thanks to the cell jammer Atticus installed last year. Our phones can work with it, but no one else's will

I open my mouth to give an ominous reply but Atticus beats me to it, offering the simple, boring truth.

"That's because it isn't a road. It's our driveway."

She lifts herself higher in her seat, trying to see farther ahead, but from here the road still looks dark and endless. It will be for another minute.

"We like our privacy," I say in a low tone, feeling my lips pull up into a smirk when she can't hold my gaze for longer than a few seconds before looking away.

She pushes a hand into the fur on the nape of her dog's neck, giving her a comforting scratch that I think is more intended to calm her own nerves than the pup's. She's been dozing between Aurora and Eli for miles now.

Funny, I seem to recall mentioning on several fucking occasions that I wanted a dog only to be shot down by Atticus. The guy actually shuddered at the thought, grumbling about 'pet dander' and 'dirty paws'. But of course *now* he's pet-friendly.

There must be something he wants from this girl.

Even all cut up and bruised, with wet hair and running mascara, she's absolutely stunning. But I know Atticus better than to think he'd bring a woman, with a fucking dog, into our house just to get some pretty pussy.

Aurora's attention goes back to her phone just as the screen turns dark, flashing with a battery symbol before dying completely. She clutches it tightly, and her throat bobs in her slender neck.

"Do you have a phone charger in..." Her words trail off as we reach the front yard of our cabin.

We call it that because of the rustic feel of the timber and stone frame, but as her lips part in awe, I realize it's like calling a large caliber rifle a fucking pocket pistol.

Atticus's watch connects to the house, and it lights up inside as he puts the 'borrowed' Dodge into park.

"What the fuck?" Aurora mutters under her breath.

Elijah chuckles, and she glances at him, blinking as if she just realized she said the words out loud.

By the time Aurora is out of the car, Atticus has already retrieved her mangled suitcase from the trunk and shut it again before she can see the evidence of what resided there an hour before she ran me over.

I incline my head to the crimson stain on the top right corner of her suitcase, and Atticus quickly rubs it away with his sleeve.

"Oh. Thanks," Aurora says, reaching out to take it from him, but Atticus doesn't hand it over, stalking right past her with a grumbled, "I've got it."

Her dog bounds behind him, stopping next to the door with a soft bark. The beep of Elijah putting his thumb to the

CHAPTER 3

digital lock makes Aurora flinch, but as the door swings open, she follows her dog inside as if in a trance.

From here, she has a good view of the cabin's layout.

In the high-ceilinged entryway and living room to our left it's all exposed beam, warm colors, and wide-paned glass. To the right is the dining room we never use and the stairway to the basement.

Straight ahead is the main staircase that leads to the couple of upstairs bedrooms and behind it is the hall that feeds deeper into the cabin, through the kitchen, and out past Atticus's office to the gym and garage.

The dog's nails click on the mahogany hardwood as she goes straight for the furniture in the living room, sniffing around the low couches and carpet until Aurora calls her back.

"Hey, come here, girl. We have to clean your paws."

Atticus's brows lift in surprise. "Grab her a rag, would you, Sev? And, Eli, there should be clean sheets for the guest room in the hall closet upstairs. I'll get the stitch kit."

Aurora reaches a hand out like she might stop Atticus from leaving, but he's already long gone.

"My...bag," she says under her breath, and I realize Atticus still has the filthy suitcase. He's probably going to put it into quarantine.

"Be right back," Eli offers with a smile for Aurora as he rushes up the stairs. I feel more than see her eyes shift to me and then away as she folds herself onto her knees to busy herself comforting her dog.

I run to grab a rag from the kitchen and come back to see she hasn't moved an inch.

"What did you say her name was?" I asked her on the road, but I don't think she ever said.

Aurora tips her head up, and I fight a smirk at how

fucking delicious she looks on her knees. A blush rises on her high cheekbones as if she understood exactly how I was looking at her.

"It's, *um,* Eleven," she replies, taking the rag from me to quickly clean off Eleven's paws before straightening to her full height.

"Eleven?"

"Yeah, it's from *Stranger Things*. But mostly, I just call her Ellie."

"What's *Stranger Things*?"

She peers up at me, a knot between her brows like she thinks I might be from a different dimension. "You've never heard of *Stranger Things*?"

My smirk fades as I take in the dark bruise on her temple. It stands out in vivid violet against her olive skin. Beneath it, across her cheekbone, is the cut I noticed earlier, but now, in the light, I can see it's more than a bit of split skin.

That shit was carved in with a knife. The edges are too perfect. The line is too straight. Before I realize I've done it, I have her chin between my fingers, angling her face more into the light.

She jerks away, but not before I catch the bruising over her collar. The unmistakable marks of fingers where they squeezed too tightly along the right side.

"Who hurt you?"

She takes a half step back, her lips pulling up in a false smile meant to misdirect me as she scoffs. "I don't know what you mean."

I wave a hand toward the wounds with a derisive snort. "You have fingerprint bruises on your neck."

My eyes return to them, and I swear I see her pulse

CHAPTER 3

jump. She's so damn thin I notice, too. Like she hasn't eaten a proper meal in weeks.

Who is this girl? And who the fuck looked at that face—lips made for sinning and eyes like a doe's—and chose violence?

She shakes her head at me as if I don't know strangulation marks when I see them.

"It must've happened in the crash. Probably from the airbag, or maybe the seat belt or something."

"Mmm," I reply, letting her spoon-feed me her bullshit, knowing damn well no one can make a victim talk until they want to.

When she meets my eyes again, she sees something there that makes her pause.

For a heartbeat, I wonder if she's decided to be honest. If she'll give me a name to cross out for her.

I wait, noticing the ring of honey-brown around her pupils and the gold flecks littered across her jade irises. She breaks eye contact first, and I nod to myself at her choice to remain silent.

Fair.

She doesn't fucking know me.

Reaching out, I pinch the hem of her Pink Floyd tee, rubbing the damp fabric between my fingertips, watching as her hands curl into fists at her sides.

"You're wet," I say, and her cheeks flush. I lift a brow, smirking as I wonder if her thoughts went to the same dirty place mine did. "I'll grab you something dry to sleep in."

"That's all right, I don't need you to—"

"Wasn't a question."

"Okay, all set." Eli descends the stairs, eyes darting between Aurora and me with a question in them neither of us answers.

"Are you hungry? Thirsty?" Eli asks, and I leave him to play chaperone, my fucking ribs and joints protesting each step I take upstairs to my bedroom.

The lights in my closet flick on as I open the doors, illuminating rows of gray and black fabric, dark-wash denim, and fine suits that once belonged to Eli's dad. I pull out a pair of gray drawstring sweatpants from a dresser drawer in the center island, where I keep my shit for working out.

She should be able to cinch them tight enough to stay on her narrow waist. I grab one of my plain black tees as well. It'll be like a dress on her, but it'll work.

I head for Elijah's dad's old room. He doesn't stay here anymore, and since it's the only other room in the house with a proper bed, I assume it's what Atticus referred to as 'the guest room'. As if we ever have guests.

When I pass the stairs, Eli is on his way up with two silver mixing bowls from the kitchen. One empty and one filled with kibble that must've been in Aurora's bag.

He must've left her upstairs in the room to get settled while he grabbed it out of her bag for her.

"I can take them to her."

He eyes me for a second but passes them over. "They're for the dog."

"Eleven," I tell him.

His brows wrinkle.

"The dog's name—it's Eleven."

"Seriously?"

"Yep. Together, we make a whole convenience store."

Eli snorts, but when I turn to leave, he stops me with a serious expression. "Did you see the bruises on her neck?"

"I did."

He lowers his voice as if she can hear us from all the

way down the other end of the hall. "Those aren't from the crash."

"Clearly."

"She say anything to you about where she was coming from? Or heading to?"

I shake my head, starting to walk away. "But I intend to find out."

"Hey, meet us in the garage. We need to close those cuts," Eli calls after me, and I wave the dog bowls in a noncommittal gesture to tell him I heard him.

It can wait.

4

HOW ABOUT A LITTLE FUCKING GRATITUDE?

SEVEN

Using a knuckle to knock, I push open the door to Julian's old room with my elbow.

For a second, I think she might've decided not to accept Atticus's completely out-of-character offer of hospitality and bolted. The room is empty. Freshly made bed untouched. No evidence of her anywhere.

Until a faucet turns on in the en suite, and I hear the shuffle of feet and paws on the other side of the door.

It's already open a crack, so I push it wide with the toe of my boot.

She picks fragments of glass out of her hairline and a frown pulls at her lips. Eleven notices me first and sits up, her tail thumping on the white marble floor.

The sound draws Aurora's attention, and she jumps as her gaze catches mine in the mirror.

"For the dog," I say and step more into the large bathroom, forcing her to step aside as I lean over the counter to fill the empty bowl with water and set it on the floor with the food.

CHAPTER 4

Eleven goes right for it like she hasn't had water or food in days, and I have to wonder if whatever fuckwit hurt this girl also hurt this dog, and that feeling in my veins tightens. Grows hot. Insistent.

I clear my throat.

"These are for you," I say, pulling the clothes from under my arm.

"Right. Thanks."

Eleven wags her tail almost violently as she eats, pausing to give me a lick of thanks before going right back to it. I don't miss how Aurora's jaw tightens or how her eyes shine as she watches her dog happily eat and drink her fill.

A knock sounds at the door, and Aurora's gaze finds Atticus over my shoulder. When my eyes meet his in the mirror, there's a muscle flexing in his jaw, and he's frowning.

If there's one thing Atticus fucking hates, it's being kept waiting.

"We need to get you patched up, Sev."

He turns to Aurora. "When you've had a chance to settle in a bit, Eli can patch you up, too. From the front entryway, you go through the living room and past the library. His room is at the very end of that hall."

She shakes her head. "Um, that's okay. I'll be fine. I'm not even bleeding anymore."

Atticus raises a brow at her. "That cut needs closing. If you leave it, it'll scar pretty badly."

She gives him a polite nod, but I don't think she'll be going to pay Eli a visit.

That's all right. We can do it in the morning.

I drop a heavy hand on Atticus's shoulder. "Lead the way. I think Aurora's too polite to tell us to get the fuck out."

How about a little fucking gratitude?

"No, I'm—"

"It's okay." I toss her a wink, shoving Atticus out the door. "I've got you."

Atticus grumbles under his breath as we head out to the garage.

The big med kit's already pulled out and on the counter when we get there.

Elijah leans against the tool locker, arms folded over his chest as we shut the door behind us.

"What the fuck, Atticus? We need a house cleaner, really?"

I head to the sink to get cleaned up enough for Eli to stitch me back together. "And since when are you cool with dogs in the house?"

Atticus pulls the antiseptic spray from the kit and gets the other supplies ready for Eli, so he doesn't have to grasp as much with his right hand. "I'm not."

I wash off as much dirt as I can, the cool water and the sting waking me up enough that I know I won't sleep after they're done fixing me up.

"Okay, I'll bite." I flick the water off my hands and take a seat. "Why let her stay, then? We both know you'd rather eat a dick than let someone else clean."

He flexes his jaw. "I'm still working on it."

"Working on what? Not being a neat freak with a—"

"No. There's something..." He trails off. "I'm not sure if it'll work yet. Just trust me. I think maybe we can use her."

Use her?

Use her for what?

I can think of a few ways, but I doubt any of my *uses* are in the same neighborhood as Atticus's.

"Do you think she suspects anything about what we were doing out there?"

CHAPTER 4

"Super subtle subject shift, bro."

"We all have blood on us," Eli replies, taking the bait. "And grave dirt."

He's right, though. Everything we're wearing will need to be burned. Except for my jacket. I'll die in this thing. Even if it is a fucking petri dish of foreign DNA that could see me convicted for at least six murders.

"If she noticed anything, she wouldn't have come with us. She didn't get a good look at you two until after you came to peel me off the pavement. If she saw blood, she probably thought it was mine."

Eli sighs and rubs his forehead. Scars litter the back of his right hand, and his ring finger will forever have a slight bend to the left. Every time I see the evidence of what he did—what he had to do—to get back to us, I remember there's still so much work to be done.

So much more DNA to add to this jacket.

And how we don't have the time to be wasting on a girl Atticus decided might be 'interesting'.

His gaze turns to me, annoyance in the slant of his brow. "Did you really have to shoot the guy, Sev?"

What kind of question is that?

"Fucking right, I did."

I push the hair back out of my face as Elijah comes over with some alcohol-soaked gauze, resigning himself to silence while Atty and I have it out.

"It's more warning than most get when they threaten my fucking family."

If I hadn't shot him, the others might not have scattered. The only regret I have is that the fucker kicked the bucket in the trunk five minutes after we stuffed him in. We didn't even have a shot at questioning him first because my tired ass nicked his femoral artery with the shot.

How about a little fucking gratitude?

Atticus shakes his head. "You could've shot somewhere less lethal. Kneecap. Foot. Fucking shoulder."

"Hey, excuse the fuck out of me for keeping you both alive. I wasn't thinking about questioning him when he pointed a gun at your head."

He glares at me. "Lower your voice. She might hear you. And sit back down so Eli can stitch you up."

I hadn't even realized I'd stood, but I let myself sink back against the counter, clenching my teeth as Eli starts to dab the gauze on the stinging gash in my head.

It was always *why did you have to kill him, Sev? Did you really have to shoot him nine times, Sev? Was paralyzing him actually necessary, Sev?*

How about a little fucking gratitude?

Atticus pinches the bridge of his nose and sighs. "Whatever. Doesn't matter now. It's done."

"We need to wipe down the car and ditch it," I say, unable to keep the acid out of my tone now.

Atticus rips the band out of his hair, setting it loose around his face in a mess of damp gold and copper. "Yeah. I got it. If the girl asks, we had it dropped off for repairs."

He runs a hand over his face, betraying how exhausted he really is. "Eli, I told her you would help her with first aid after she gets cleaned up. She might come by your room, so take the kit with you."

With that, Atticus stalks off.

"She won't come," I add after he's gone. "Just get some sleep. We'll see if she'll let you touch her tomorrow."

Eli nods once, his gaze darkening as he pulls the hooked needle out of the kit and threads it.

"Ready?"

He passes me one of the small bottles of whiskey we

CHAPTER 4

keep in the box, and I twist off the cap and drain it in one swallow before lobbing it into the trash bin.

"You kidding? This is my favorite part."

5
WAKING UP IN WONDERLAND
AURORA

I meant to go see Elijah. I really did. Not for him to clean and dress my wounds, though.

He seems like the least intimidating of the three to ask for a phone charger, but sitting down on the bed in Seven's silky T-shirt and baggy sweats for a 'quick sec' led to at least five hours in a total coma.

It's impossible to tell without the clock on my phone, but judging by the light filtering into the room, it isn't long after dawn. The house is still quiet, save for Ellie making little sounds that tell me she needs to tinkle and the soft scrape of her claws on the door.

"Give me a sec, Ellie," I whisper, gesturing for her to back away as I climb from the warm bed and pad across the floor.

Soundlessly twisting the handle, I peek out into the hall. It's dark. Doesn't seem like anyone is around.

"Okay, the coast is clear."

I pause before letting her out, noticing the laundry basket on the floor to the left of the door.

Is that my shirt?

CHAPTER 5

I lift the scrap of aged black fabric from the pile, looking for the faded dancing skeletons on the front.

It is mine.

I carefully sift through a few more layers of folded clothing, finding that it's actually full of my clothes. All of it freshly washed, dried, and folded into neat piles. And is that...

My charger.

I snatch up the basket and bring it into the room, plucking out the charger and rushing to plug it in behind the nightstand. I perch at the edge of the bed to connect it to my phone, and wait.

It blinks with the red battery symbol and goes black again.

"Come on," I mutter, bouncing my knee.

Ellie whines, making a soft growl that tells me she's annoyed I've sat back down again.

"All right," I sigh. "Fine. Just let me change."

Really, all I want to do is pull up my location on a map. I have no idea exactly how far I drove from Amherst last night. Or where I let these guys take me.

Elijah. Atticus. Seven. I remind myself of their names. I've always been bad with names, and offending any of these overly muscled, heavily tattooed, and intimidating men seems like it wouldn't be in my best interest.

Elijah seemed chill at least. Sweet, even. I'm willing to bet he's the one who did my laundry.

Atticus seemed like the one to watch. Quick to anger. Short fuse. I'll be careful around him.

Seven...

He equally scared the shit out of me and intrigued me in a way I can't describe. When we were alone in the foyer, I wasn't sure...

Yeah. I'll need to be careful around that one, too.

Fuck, I really hope I didn't make a huge-ass mistake coming here.

Please, I pray to the universe. *Just give me a little break here, would you?*

I pull the first things from the basket I see, jean shorts and my skeleton tee. I've worn neither in years. Jesse did *not* like me wearing short shorts.

He liked me in bright colors. Liked me as a blonde. Liked me *conservative.*

And Jesse got what Jesse wanted.

He thought I threw all these clothes out when we moved in together, but I shoved them into the back of my closet.

They were the only ones I wanted when I left.

For a second, I wonder if I should keep the sweats on. Keep myself covered up. I don't know these guys. What if they're creeps?

I shake my head. You know what? If they are, it'll be better to smoke them out as quickly as possible.

My phone lights up as I change, and I almost trip in my haste to grab it, but recoil as all the messages and missed calls that came in while it was dead light up the screen.

Him.

It will be him.

Just waking up with a mean headache and an even meaner attitude—enraged to find me and Ellie and the car gone.

I tap the 'X' to get rid of all notifications at once and then tap the map icon, but it loads with my pulsing blue dot in the middle of empty gray space. I try to zoom out and a notification fills my screen.

Can't connect to Maps. Try again in a few minutes.

CHAPTER 5

"What the fuck?"

There's a symbol in the top right corner of my screen that I've never seen before, but the lost-looking satellite can only mean one thing: no service.

By the look of it, there's Wi-Fi, but it has a password.

Shit.

I set it back down to charge and slip on my shoes. No problem. I'll just get the password. Easy. Nothing to freak out about. It's fine. Everything is fine.

"Come on, girl. Let's go."

Ellie lets out an excited bark, and I hush her, signaling for her to stay close and be quiet as we creep out of the room, retracing our steps to the front door.

In the light of early morning, it's so much bigger than I thought, and I already thought the place was outrageously massive. The staircase leading down to the foyer is wide enough for at least four people to walk up shoulder to shoulder without stepping on each other's toes.

The decor in the entryway and living room speak of hours spent at estate auctions and in small shops where the price tags give normal people heart attacks. Inspecting a painting by the door, I find I can actually see the individual brush strokes. It's not a print. It's real.

God, actually, all of the art on the walls look like they belong in the fucking Louvre.

Who the hell are these guys?

The heavy front door doesn't make so much as a creak as we step out into the crisp morning air and I sigh as the first rays of sunlight kiss my cheeks. The long road that I remember Eli saying was actually their driveway winds downward through the trees.

Wasn't there a gate? I think there was. And I didn't see this road on the map at all.

Jesse won't find me here.

I don't think anyone will if I don't want them to.

It's somehow both comforting and disconcerting at the same time.

Ellie barks at me to follow her, tail wagging as she stomps her front paws and takes off around the side of the house, following along a flagstone pathway.

"*Ellie.*"

My rib cage aches with every step, and I *definitely* feel where the airbag punched me in the chest. The skin that was uncovered at my collar is angry and red.

My legs feel stiff, too.

All around, I'm a fucking wreck, but Ellie seems to be completely fine, and it's a more than acceptable trade.

When Jesse kicked her, I thought...

I don't even want to rethink what I thought.

But seeing her bounding through the nettle-covered grass, sniffing every little thing she can get her nose close enough to, makes the pain bearable.

"Not too far, Ellie," I call after her when she starts to get hard to see through the brush.

She's a smart girl. She never goes far, even when she's off her leash, but this is a new place. There could be a drop-off somewhere or bear traps or poison ivy. This isn't our property. Even if Ellie seems to know exactly where she's going as her ears prick and she zooms past me toward the rear of the house.

I sigh, pressing a hand to the ache in my side as I hurry to follow her. I stop dead as I come around the side of the house, finding an oasis in the backyard.

"*Wow.*"

The patio is huge and completely made of stone the color of sand. But even though there seems to be no less than two lounge areas, a dining area, an outdoor kitchen—and is that a sauna?—it's the pool I can't look away from.

It's pristine. A perfect rectangle that looks like it's carved right into the stone. The water is *so* blue and crystal clear.

And Ellie is about to dive right into it with her nettle-covered paws.

"Ellie!"

She stops just short of jumping over the edge, letting out a whine.

"Ellie, *no*."

She sits down with a look in her eyes that tells me she is not impressed with my pool block. I've never seen a dog with such an expressive face. It's almost human. I think that's why Jesse hated her most.

It's why I love her best.

"Thought I heard someone out here."

I whirl, almost slipping down the steps, but he's so quick, snatching my forearm to keep me upright and guide me away from the edge with a sharpness in his honey brown eyes.

"I'm sorry," I mutter as Elijah lets me go and shakes out his hand as if he's hurt it.

His lips quirk up in a half grin. "For what?"

"I was just—I mean, Ellie needed to—"

He lifts a brow, and I know I'm rambling and probably sound like a complete idiot, but I can't seem to make the psychobabble stop.

"You don't need to explain yourself," he says, saving me. "I heard Eleven and thought I'd come see how you slept."

"I'm sorry if she woke you up."

He shakes his head and his deep chestnut hair catches

the light, making it shine with strands of the richest auburn.

"She didn't," he says with an easy shrug.

I don't know how I didn't notice before—how beautiful this man is. His wavy dark hair hangs just past his ears, and the way his olive skin stands out against the relaxed ivory button-down shirt he's wearing makes him look like Italian nobility. But it's his light brown eyes, five-o-clock shadow, and crooked grin that place him firmly in American blue blood territory.

I straighten and quickly wipe the look of awe from my face, trying to divert his attention anywhere else. "Um, this is probably the most beautiful pool I've ever seen."

Stepping closer to the crystalline water, I bend down to dip my fingers in. It's heated to perfection—because of course it is.

"Yeah, Atticus is anal about keeping it pristine."

If it weren't for the very real way my body reacts to Elijah watching me, I'd have to wonder if I actually died on the road last night. Which would make this some strange sort of heaven?

I chuckle to myself as he adds, "If you want a morning swim, I can grab some towels."

Fuck yes, I want a morning swim. But I don't even have a bathing suit, and he's probably just being nice. I bet he's actually really busy. They must have to work hard to afford all of this. Not for the first time, I wonder what it is they do all the way out here, but I feel like now isn't the right time to ask.

"That sounds amazing, but I think I should probably figure out what my jobs are for the day."

Shit. I sigh. "And probably figure out what to do about my car. I can't just leave it on the side of the road."

"Atticus already called the local garage. It was towed there last night."

"Oh."

"Don't worry about the towing fees. The guy who owns the garage is a friend who owed us a favor."

I tuck some loose hair behind my ear, aware all at once that I didn't even brush it before taking Ellie outside. Or wash my face. I probably look like absolute shit. *Great.*

"It's good it's off the road," I reply, trying to nonchalantly drag my fingers through my hair and smooth it out. "But I really doubt it's worth fixing."

I don't bother repeating that I can't afford to fix it anyway.

"We'll get a quote from our guy anyway, then you can decide. Sound good?"

I nod and force myself to stop trying to fix my damn hair.

There's a charged silence between us as Ellie comes padding over to my side and cocks her head at Elijah as if to say, *Why are you just standing there?*

He grins warmly at her. "Think she's hungry?" he asks. "Atticus was starting breakfast when I came out."

Is that an invitation?

"She has her kibble," I tell him, grimacing as I continue. "And if I can just get my suitcase back, I think there were a couple protein bars in there I could—"

"Aurora," he interrupts. "It's just breakfast. Besides, I'm pretty sure Atticus still has your bag in quarantine."

"Oh?"

"He's kind of a germaphobe."

Huh. That actually makes sense. "So that's the vibe I was getting."

"Very perceptive," he praises, and I shiver.

"Come on. I'll give you a quick tour on the way to the kitchen."

I follow Elijah with Ellie on our heels as he leads us back into the house. The moment we enter, my mouth waters from the glorious smell of breakfast cooking. I'm so fucking hungry that I don't think I'll remember any of Elijah's short tour of the main floor later because all I can think about the whole time is *bacon*.

6

FIFTEEN THOUSAND REASONS

AURORA

Ellie runs ahead of us into the massive gourmet kitchen and darts through the space between the stove and Atticus's legs.

I cringe. "Ellie! Come here, girl."

She comes without hesitation, almost barreling into my legs. She might have a firecracker of a personality when I let her loose, but thank god she always listens to me.

Before I can apologize to Atticus for her getting in his way, Seven comes into the room from another part of the house. He has a coy grin on his face despite the stitched-up gash on his forehead, split lip, and swollen eye. In his loose-fitting muscle shirt, I can't help noticing how his tattooed muscles flex when he lifts an arm to grip the doorframe in a BookTok-worthy stretch.

"What's for breakfast?" he asks Atticus, but his eyes are completely fixed on me as he licks his lips.

My mouth goes dry.

"*Not* the new cleaning girl," Atticus quips as he flips something in a pan.

I jerk as Elijah leans down to whisper in my ear, "Don't

CHAPTER 6

mind Sev. He has absolutely no manners. We've tried to train him. No luck."

"I heard that, dickface."

My cheeks go hot.

"It smells incredible," I venture, angling for a subject change as I crouch down to rub Ellie's belly. It makes it a hell of a lot easier to avoid looking at any of them while my face is still on fucking fire.

As Seven and Elijah settle into easy conversation, I wonder if I should be helping. Washing the dishes, maybe? Looking around, I don't actually see anything else that needs cleaning. Everything in this mammoth house looks like it was dusted this morning. The floors are gleaming, save for the little bit of dirt that Ellie brought in on her paws. Fuck. I totally forgot to wipe them off.

"Stay," I tell Ellie and cross the kitchen, going around the eat-in counter and the kitchen island toward the sink, but the instant I cross the imaginary line between the designated eating and cooking areas, Elijah and Seven fall silent.

"Nope," Atticus says without turning around, lifting his spatula in warning.

I freeze.

"I was just going to—"

"Nope."

I look to the other guys, confused.

"He's a mean cook," Elijah says with a strained smile. "Literally."

"No one touches the kitchen," Seven adds. "Atty's rules."

"Don't fucking call me that."

I step back, feeling awkward. "Ooookay."

I'll just fuck right off then.

40

I settle for hovering near the center island where Seven's leaning.

"How are you feeling?"

"Like roadkill."

He smirks at me, looking amused, and even though his words hit me like a sucker punch, something about how he said it, and the playful gleam in his blue eyes, pulls an unintentional laugh from my chest.

He raises one dark brow.

"Oh my god. I'm so sorry—I don't mean to laugh, I..." I bite my lip and try to make my face cooperate with being very demure and apologetic, but it isn't working.

If he'd stop looking at me like that, maybe I could control myself.

"Don't worry about it," he says when I'm ready to crawl into a hole and die. "You have permission to laugh at my misfortune. Everyone else around here does."

The elastic band around my chest releases, and I'm able to breathe.

"Speaking of roadkill," Elijah says. "We need to get you fixed up, too. I'll be right back."

He's up and out of the room before I can ask what he means.

"He's probably talking about that gnarly cut on your cheek," Seven explains, tracing a line on his own face where the cut would be.

Elijah returns after a second with a big black tackle box that has a first aid cross spray-painted over the side.

"If we don't clean that up, it could get infected and leave a pretty bad scar," he says as he sets the box down and starts to rifle through it. He holds up some butterfly closures and an alcohol pad. "Do you mind if I...?"

"I can do it."

CHAPTER 6

"I don't mind."

He pats the stool in front of him, and I sit down, folding my hands awkwardly into my lap. "Thanks."

Despite the fact that he's given me no reason to question his motives, I flinch when Elijah reaches over to carefully inspect the cut.

He immediately stops. "I'm sorry, I didn't—"

"No," I shake my head, fidgeting my fingers. "It's fine. Sorry. Go ahead."

He's so gentle that I barely notice the sting of the alcohol, losing myself in the way his hair falls forward to obscure his view while he works. Until I notice his right hand.

Scars riddle the back of it, and a couple of his fingers don't seem to have set right after whatever happened to him. He flinches as he pries apart a bandage, and something in my chest tightens.

The scars look old, but it's obvious they still cause him pain.

He notices me looking and frowns, making me cast my gaze to the floor and keep it there.

Crap.

Thank fuck it isn't long before he's finished.

Gingerly, I prod the clean, bandaged cut and a sense of warmth floods me. This bitch has always applied her own Band-Aids. I don't actually remember the last time I was taken care of like this. It's...*nice.*

You are so not going to cry right now. Get your shit together.

"You're good at that," I tell him, hoping he doesn't hear the thickness in my voice as I fight to swallow it down.

"Thanks."

It's so easy to feel comfortable next to Elijah that I need to remind myself to be wary.

I can't be giving these guys my trust just because my dog likes them and one of them gave me a Band-Aid for my fucking boo-boo. *Or* because they're all insanely good-looking.

Ted Bundy was hot, and look at what a total psycho that guy was.

Stay smart, Aurora.

Trust no one.

Haven't you learned by now?

"Hey," Atticus calls, and I turn to see him with a pan poised over a metal dish. "I made some extra breakfast for Eleven. Is she allowed to eat human food?"

Wait, *what?*

He made food for my dog?

"Yeah. But you didn't have to do that. I have some more kibble for her somewhere."

In the suitcase you're still holding hostage.

He doesn't reply, making me shift on the stool while he gives the bowl to a happily bouncing Ellie, and then picks up three full plates with ease to hand them to Elijah, Seven, and me, and I think giants maybe shouldn't wear aprons. He looks like a domesticated Ragnar Lothbrok.

I snort and cough to cover the sound, my mouth watering as I take the offered plate.

The breakfast looks like it's meant to be served at a five-star restaurant. Silver dollar pancakes drenched in honey, perfectly scrambled eggs, and *bacon.*

"Oh my god, this looks so good." I almost drool. I take back what I thought about giants wearing aprons. "Thank you."

Atticus just grunts as he turns away to start cleaning.

Elijah lifts a brow, and he and Seven share a look that makes me wonder if something's off.

And I realize Atticus didn't make a plate for himself. "What about yours?"

I really hope he didn't just give me food he intended to eat himself.

"Already ate," he answers without turning around, filling a sink with hot, soapy water as he slings a dish towel over his shoulder.

My stomach growls, but as I pick up a strip of perfectly cooked bacon, I realize I'm not sure I can trust eating it. What if it's drugged?

Fuck. Being around Jesse and his asshole friends has made me so damn paranoid.

I spend three seconds hesitating before the bacon wins and I shove the whole strip in my mouth.

Oh my fucking *lord.*

Seven lets out a low chuckle and when I look up, I want to die. He totally just watched me flavorgasm the instant the bacon touched my tongue.

Awesome.

He suppresses a smirk as he fluidly gets up and comes over with his plate, pushing his own six strips onto my plate despite my unintelligible protests.

"I'm sick of bacon," is all he says in reply, dropping into the seat next to me. "We've been eating it all week."

Atticus grumbles something from over the sink, and the water shuts off.

"So," he says with a note of finality in his tone. "There are a few things we need to cover."

Abandoning the dishes to soak in the soapy water, he pulls a document out of an envelope on the kitchen island.

I chew and swallow faster so I can respond. "Oh, of course."

I try my best to sound eager to hear him out when all I'm actually eager to do is shove this food in my face.

He slides the papers over to me, spinning them right side up.

"We'll just need you to go over this and sign it. If you still want the job, that is."

The words *Nondisclosure Agreement* stare back at me.

"Why do I need to sign this? It's just a cleaning job, right?"

"It's standard. Everyone who works for us needs to sign one."

I keep reading as I jam another strip of bacon into my mouth, refusing to let the weirdness of this put me off my appetite.

Obligations and Confidentiality
The recipient shall uphold strict confidentiality and shall not disclose anything they witness or overhear while at the residence of or in the presence of the Disclosing Party.

A six-month contract...

The recipient must also notify the Disclosing Party if they intend to depart the property for any purpose with a minimum of 12 hours notice...

Um, what the actual fuck?

I open my mouth to question Atticus again, but before I can get a word out, I see it.

The number at the bottom of the last page.

The recipient will receive a remuneration of $15,000 a month for all services rendered during the contract term.

Fifteen *fucking* thousand.

For cleaning?

In my periphery, Atticus shifts.

"Is there a problem?" he asks gruffly.

Is there?

I did have one, but...I forget what it was.

Couldn't have been important.

I mean, fuck, I can do anything for six months if they're going to pay me this much, right?

By spring, I could save enough money to give Ellie and me a real fresh start. My mind conjures images of a big, fenced yard, a full refrigerator, and a car where all the windows work.

Quickly, I flip through the rest of the document, scanning over the text for keywords that could give me pause. But there doesn't seem to be anything else that's overly concerning. Nothing to say that my job might require me to clean in my birthday suit or a skimpy maid uniform. No mention of anything dangerous or sexual.

Other than the bits on nondisclosure and letting them know when I want to leave the property, it appears fairly standard.

"Aurora?" Atticus presses, and I drop the pages closed.

"No. No problem at all."

I smile up at him, and when he extends a pen to me over the table, I take it, and sign my name on the dotted line.

7

T-I-A-L-A-G-G

ATTICUS

I finish wiping down the training bench just as Sev shoves into the room, water bottle in hand, *without* a fucking gym towel.

His bulky black headphones blare music so loudly into his ears that I can hear it from across the space. It makes absolutely no sense to me how he can crack a safe in under a minute with eardrums constantly subjected to that sort of abuse.

"*Hey*," I shout.

He glances up at me, pushing one side of his headphone back. "Two workouts in one morning? Going for a record, Atty?"

He knows it helps me think. He also knows I fucking hate it when he calls me that.

I chuck the damp paper towels into the trash. "Didn't Eli tell you to take it easy for a few days?"

He had at least two cracked ribs and a mild concussion after losing the fight with Aurora's rust bucket of a car last night.

CHAPTER 7

"I am taking it easy," he replies and pushes the headphone back into place, effectively cutting off the conversation and making me grit my teeth. There's really no point in arguing about it.

With Sev, it's like talking to a fucking brick wall once he's set his mind to something.

I pull one of my extra towels from the neat stack on the counter, throwing it at his back when he sits down on the freshly cleaned training bench. He whirls on me with a glare, and I give him a pointed look that says, *At least use the fucking towel*, before leaving.

When I head to the kitchen for some water and a protein bar, Aurora's already there, invading my space just as she's been invading my every thought from the moment I laid eyes on her.

Usually when we have a woman in the house, there's a signed contract involved and she's free game for any of us to use and fuck whenever we want to during the agreed-upon dates. But we haven't had one in a long time. Not since Eli lost interest.

Aurora fills a glass with water from the sink while her dog stands next to her, tail wagging, its tongue lolling out.

With a grimace, I try not to imagine how much fucking drool and pet dander is probably already coating the floors.

If this works out, it'll be worth it, I remind myself.

And if it doesn't, it'll be easy enough to come up with some excuse to fire her.

The dog barks and Aurora spins in a snap, a flush staining her cheeks pink as she takes in my bare, sweat-coated arms and chest.

"*Shit.* Hey."

She collects herself and swallows. "I was just looking for one of you, actually."

T-i-a-l-a-g-g

She backs away a step as I move to refill my water bottle from the proper faucet. "This one's for drinking," I tell her. "The other one's for washing dishes."

"Oh. What's the difference?"

"This one's alkaline. Filtered. With more minerals."

She sips her tap water anyway, unbothered as I rake my gaze over her. She's cleaned herself up. Her blonde hair hangs in damp, loose waves that leave wet patches on the baby blue shirt she wears, making the dark bra below it visible through the threadbare fabric. It's impossible not to notice her curves in the little outfit, even if she is a little thin for my taste.

"What was it you needed?"

"Wi-Fi password?" She says it like a question, waving her battered iPhone at me. "There's no cell service here."

"It's t-i-a-l-a-g-g."

"*Uh*, can you say that again?" she says with a wince. "A little slower."

"Here. Let me do it."

I take the phone from her fingers and punch in the letters.

Take It All Like a Good Girl.

The instant it's in, her phone vibrates in my hand and a slew of notifications from someone called *Jesse* light up the screen. Aurora snatches the device back before I can read them.

She has no idea that just by connecting to the Wi-Fi, I'll have access to anything and everything I want to look at or read on her phone with the click of a few keys in my office. My Linux Precision 7920 always takes it all.

"Looks like someone's trying to get a hold of you."

Her face pales as she shakily tucks the phone into her

49

CHAPTER 7

back pocket without checking any of the alerts. "I'll call her back later."

"Her?"

I eye the bruising over her collar. The cut on her cheek.

Her throat bobs as she casts her gaze away from me. "I was also wondering if there's anywhere in particular you want me to start."

I lift a brow.

In the light of day, her eyes are a lot more green than I thought. Bright and clear and bold, sort of like Seven's except his are blue.

The shade of jade is...

"For work," she explains, and I snap the fuck out of it.

Right. That part. It seemed like a good idea at the time. A plausible cover for keeping her here while I felt her out as potential bait and fleshed out my plan. Now, though, I wish I'd come up with something else.

Though there is one place in the house she could help with.

Eli's studio is like a grotesque scab in my mind. It's been festering there for literal years, but he's forbidden me from touching it.

The new cleaning lady, though...

Eli will be pissed.

I shouldn't.

"There's an art studio," I say, convincing myself that once it's done, Eli will be grateful. The Band-Aid just needs to be ripped off. It's been long enough.

"Do you remember where I told you Eli's room was?"

She grimaces. "Sort of?"

"It's on the main floor. From the entryway, you head left down the hall. There are only two doors past the library that way. Eli's bedroom door is at the end. The other door to the left leads into his adjoining studio. You can find cleaning supplies in the cupboard under the stairs."

"Anything else?"

I shake my head. "It's a total wreck in there. If you can get it done, that's enough for today."

She nods and a whisper of a smile pulls at her lips. Like she's excited about a mess. Who the fuck gets excited about messes?

This may go down in history as the worst idea I've ever had. If it does, the guys will never let me live it down. I sigh and rub at a knot aching in the base of my neck, my gaze falling back to the dog.

"What did you say its name was again?"

"Eleven, but I call her Ellie mostly."

Aurora bends to give her dog a pat on the head, scattering a few strands of white fur onto the floor. "I meant to ask you, actually, are there any, like, animal traps or anything on the property? Poisonous plants, that sort of thing?"

I shake my head. "No. And most of the property is gated, so no predators usually, either."

At least, not of the animal kind.

"Great. It'll be easier to have her outside while I work."

Music to my fucking ears.

"She won't run off?"

"No. She never goes very far."

Eleven stares at me like she somehow understands every word of this conversation and barks as if in agreement with what Aurora said.

Sev was right. She's a smart dog.

As long as her training doesn't extend to the scent detection of cadavers or explosives, we'll be fine.

CHAPTER 7

"Well, I guess I'll go get started. Thanks," she says. "For the Wi-Fi."

When she walks away, I head straight for my office instead of the pantry or the shower. I make sure to pull the door shut behind me before leaning over my desk to wake the monitors.

"Let's see who you are, Aurora Bellerose."

8

NOW IT'S A PARTY

ATTICUS

I navigate through the system to find the backdoor I coded in a few years back. It's only a few clicks and keystrokes before I'm in. The application runs and a new window pops up with a cloned phone screen. Aurora's wallpaper—a photo of her Australian shepherd with a birthday hat and a face full of mud—fills the background, and I grimace.

Tapping the key to switch from mirrored view to ghost mode, I start with the obvious suspect: social media. But she doesn't seem to have any accounts. At least not connected to the apps on her phone. There's no way she's over twenty-two or twenty-three. What twenty-something girl doesn't have social media?

Undeterred, I continue my search, looking for anything that will help me decipher who she is. Where she came from. Where she was headed when she ran into us.

After an hour, I don't have nearly as much as I should, but it's enough to get a general idea.

She's twenty-three. A college dropout. Most recent employment was as a server in a steakhouse in Amherst.

CHAPTER 8

From what I can tell, she doesn't have any friends or family she's in any form of regular contact with. Less than thirty dollars in her checking account. No savings.

And Jesse is not a girl.

I don't waste too much time on their messages. The most recent three were enough to tell me all I needed to know.

Jesse: Do you really think you can just leave like this? I own you, Aurora.

Jesse: You're so fucking pathetic.

Jesse: You know what, maybe I'll just release the little videos we made online. They'll make me a killing.

Sex tapes, maybe?

The math is easy. Bruises on her neck. Driving through a rainstorm in the middle of the night with one suitcase and no money to her name.

Aurora has a shit boyfriend and I don't think she wants him to find her.

It could work.

She could work.

Tabbing to another window, I bring up the portrait I've been staring at for months. Ever since *he* put it up online. I compare the age progression software-generated image with a photo of Aurora from her camera library.

She could definitely work.

Her cloned screen blinks with a new message.

Jesse: Tell you what, if you drop that mutt at a shelter and get back here by dark, I'll let you make this up to me. I won't even punish you.

Oh, he's bargaining now.

Jesse: If you don't, maybe I'll finally make that call to your mommy and daddy. Show them what a bad, bad girl you've been...

Now it's a party

Intrigued, I tap to open the conversation.

What did you do, Aurora?

Jesse: This is one of my favorites. Do you think Mommy and Daddy will agree?

The next message isn't a text, it's a video.

A muscle twitches in my jaw as I take in the image. The contrast of pale skin in a dark room is indecipherable until I hit play.

Aurora moves on the screen and my cock twitches.

She's naked.

Her hair is a mess of gold hanging down her back as she rolls her hips in reverse cowgirl on some guy's cock. Her ass is stained red. A fading bruise covers the lower half of her right rib cage. Her breathing is rapid and shallow as she moves.

The video jars as the one recording it slaps her ass again, so hard she flinches and whimpers.

"Who's my dirty little slut?"

He slaps her again when she doesn't answer fast enough.

"*I am,*" she slurs. Is she drunk?

Somewhere off camera in the dark, another male voice laughs.

Then the one filming twists his free hand in her hair until she's forced to crane her neck back to look at him.

"Damn right you are. Come here."

Her cheeks are stained with mascara. Her eyes are glassy and hollow.

"Who's your daddy?"

"You are," she slurs.

Not just drunk. She's wasted. Possibly on drugs, too, by the way her pupils are dilated. I know the look. I picked up after my dad for ten years before I got the fuck out.

"And you're going to do exactly what Daddy says, aren't you?"

"Y-yes."

"Get over here and take a spin. Aurora won't mind."

"Wait," she slurs. "Jesse, I don't—"

My stomach turns and I think I've seen enough when there's a quick rap on the door behind me. Eli pushes inside without waiting for me to answer and I'm almost not fast enough to stop the video and return the monitors to a blank desktop.

"*What?*"

"Am I interrupting something?"

Did he hear the video?

"Nope. What do you need?"

He eyes my damp workout clothes without bothering to hide the knowing smirk pulling at his mouth.

At least this means he hasn't found Aurora yet. With any luck, she'll have the whole fucking studio done before he can stop her.

Eli looks down the hall, his brow furrowing as he shakes his head at something I can't see.

I hear Seven's music long before I see him.

"What's this? Party in Atty's office? Did my invite get lost in the mail?" Sev leans against the doorframe behind Eli, pulling his headphones off. "What's up?"

Jesus Christ.

"Nothing is up. Eli, did you need something?"

"No, just wondering if you know where Aurora went. I thought she might have been outside somewhere with Eleven, but—"

"Do you need her for something?"

"No, I just wanted—"

Now it's a party

My phone rings atop my desk and I lift the screen to check the caller.

"It's Jack," I tell them before picking up.

"What's the damage?" I ask our mechanic before he can speak.

Having Aurora's car towed off the road was more for us than her. If we left it there, it would be like leaving a billboard on the side of the road with a giant red arrow pointing into the woods. The last thing we need is the local PD investigating the area. I've called in enough favors with their chief in the last few months. I don't need to add another one.

This is what I get for agreeing to a less-than-perfect cleanup after the mess Seven made in Jonesville.

"Hey, Atticus. It's Jack."

As if I don't have caller ID.

"I know."

"Right, well, I had a look over the car. It's like you said—a total write-off. Your lady friend would be lucky to get a couple hundred bucks for it at the scrapyard."

Not surprised.

"Just get rid of it, would you?"

"Normal get rid of or special get rid of."

I think about it.

"Just scrap it."

"All right. Oh! Almost forgot. Do you know if she wants the tracker back?"

"What?"

"Yeah, I thought it was weird, too. I don't know why she'd bother putting a LoJack on it in the first place. The system is probably worth more than the whole damn car."

I pull the phone from my ear and put Jack on speaker. "Say that again."

CHAPTER 8

"*Uh.* The LoJack system is probably worth more than the car?"

"Hold a sec."

I mute him.

"There was a LoJack on her car?" Seven asks, his eyes darkening.

Eli bites his lip. "I don't think it was her who put it there."

"Who then?" Seven asks.

Great. The new cleaning lady comes with a free douchebag.

"I think I might have an idea."

I whirl back to the monitors and bring Aurora's cloned phone back up on the screen.

The guys come around to look, placing themselves behind each shoulder.

"Seriously, Atticus?" Eli complains behind me, but he falls silent as I bring up the message thread with 'Jesse' and he leans over my shoulder to read.

The vibe in the room shifts as they read all the messages on the screen. The threats from this *Jesse*.

"What's the video?" Seven asks in a detached tone. The kind that usually precedes the breaking of bones.

"One no woman would ever want anyone to see, never mind her parents."

Sev takes the phone from my hand. "Seven, what are you—"

"Hey, Jack, it's Seven."

Jack chokes on a reply as Sev brings the phone closer to his mouth. He never really got over seeing Sev covered in someone else's blood and gore that one time we had to drop off two sedans for him to 'special' get rid of.

I can't really blame him. I told Sev the wood chipper

was going to be too messy, but he insisted he'd always wanted to see if it would actually work.

Spoiler alert: it did. But the cleanup was fucking atrocious.

"If anyone comes looking for the car or the girl," Sev hisses down the line. "You send them to us."

"Wait, like, to your house? I thought you said never to give out your address to—"

"If anyone comes," Sev repeats in a threatening tone. "You send them up. Got it?"

"Yeah. Whatever you say, Seven."

The line disconnects and Sev drops the phone into my lap.

"Real fucking smart, Sev," I call after him as he storms away. "Why don't we just invite the whole state of Virginia over? Then it'll be a real party."

Eli gives me a look.

"*What?*"

"Nothing. I just hope you know what you're doing with this girl."

"What is that supposed to mean?"

"She seems like a good person," he says, and then indicates the still-frame video and the crude messages still on my computer monitor. "And she's clearly been through enough."

What he's not saying is written all over his face.

Don't put her through any more.

9

GET. OUT.

ELIJAH

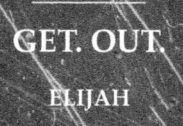

Aurora's room is just as empty as it was twenty minutes ago when I checked. The bed is unmade with the basket of laundry I washed for her sitting atop the rumpled covers.

This room used to be my dad's. He barely stayed with us three months before he took a turn and started needing more care than we could give him, but there's still evidence of him if you look hard enough.

We couldn't quite fill the lines he carved into the walls and you can still see the slight depressions through the dark green paint. And under the bed is a series of angry gouges and lines he scratched into the hardwood with nothing but the prongs of his lamp plug when we stopped letting him near sharp objects.

We really need to go see him. It's been over a month since our last visit.

Guilt compounds like laid bricks in my gut, but they can't stack high enough before that familiar nameless thing that eats away at me from the inside can start chipping them down.

CHAPTER 9

He did this to my father.

He destroyed us.

I blow out a shaky breath and close the door. Ambrose may have broken us, but we'll make him watch while his entire empire falls to ruin, until there's nothing left of what he built. Until he feels just as empty as I do.

And just as shattered as my father.

Pushing the poisonous thoughts away, I resolve to find Aurora.

Atticus said I should leave her alone to work and I will, but I have to make a run into town. I just want to know if she needs anything. Or maybe if she'd like to come with me.

When I went to pull the clothes from the battered suitcase Atticus quarantined in the garage, I couldn't help noticing how little she had. Barely enough clothes to make more than three or four outfits. Nothing warm for the cool evenings. Nothing much I could see as far as food or toiletries.

She's welcome to whatever's in the fridge and pantry, but not everyone wants to eat the green smoothie and heavy protein regimen Atticus has us all on right now. She should be allowed potato chips and nuggets if she wants them, even if Sev and I have to watch her eat them.

I check the other rooms down the hall, listening for her, but she's definitely not upstairs.

Sev is pulling on his boots when I head back down to the main floor.

"You seen Aurora?"

"Still can't find her?" His brows draw together, and if I didn't know any better I'd say that was worry flattening the line of his mouth.

I shake my head.

"I wouldn't worry about it," he decides, shrugging off

Get. Out.

the tension. "She's probably outside somewhere. I'm headed to the hive. If I see her, I'll text you."

"Do you really think telling Jack to send that asshole up here was the right move?" I ask before he can leave, and his blue eyes slide to me with a defiance in them only Seven can achieve.

He scoffs and shakes his head, not giving me a reply before storming out.

I huff out a sigh. The fact he didn't defend it means he isn't sure himself if it was the right move, but what's done is done. If the guy shows up, we'll be forced to deal with him, which is probably exactly what Seven wanted.

There's a reason only a very trusted few have our address.

If Ambrose knew where we lived—well, there's a good chance we wouldn't *be* living anymore.

Maybe Aurora will want to talk about it—about this *Jesse* person. Maybe we can fix her problem before it becomes our problem.

I nod to myself.

Yeah.

That's it.

Since Sev has the outside covered and I've looked pretty much everywhere else, the only places left to check for her now are the library and my bedroom, but I'm guessing Atticus would've already warned her against cleaning those. At least until we know how trustworthy she is.

There are too many things she could find hidden away —or in Seven's case, proudly on display like little trophies of all his many crimes.

Between his jacket and his bedroom, the FBI would have a fucking field day with slam-dunk convictions. But with Sev, we choose our battles.

CHAPTER 9

"Aurora?" I call, pushing into the library. It reminds me so much of my father's study when I was a boy. We set it up the same way, but the heavy antique desk in the middle of the space belonged to my father back then, and when he had the library doors shut, no one was allowed to enter.

I remember the first time I snuck in, trying to make sense of the blueprints and other scribbled notes and documents arranged neatly over the surface of the desk like some puzzle I was beyond understanding.

"Aurora?" I call again, heading back around to my room. I mean, I guess if she were going to start with a bedroom, mine would be the safest. I used to keep a lot of things in my room none of us would want her to see, but not anymore. Not since what happened.

The door creaks as I push it open, finding the space empty.

There wouldn't be much in here for her to clean, anyway.

A long time ago, mine would've been the messiest room in the house. I got like that when I was creating. But now that I can't paint anymore, I get to exist in a space that is free of clutter and half-drunk refreshments.

Silver linings.

I guess I could just grab her a few things from town and—

A soft hum sounds from the door that leads into my connected studio space and my mood instantly sours along with the food in my stomach.

No.

I listen with a tightness in my chest that won't ease, swallowing past the hard lump in my throat.

There it is again, the humming. *Aurora's* humming. The sound of a broom sweeping debris off a wood floor.

Get. Out.

Fury, red hot and slithering, coils around my spine like a fucking parasite.

I'm at the adjoining door without any memory of moving my feet, my fingers poised over the handle I haven't touched in over a year.

My teeth clench as I twist it and shove inside, controlled by the parasitic rage now building in my chest.

It's me. But not me.

I'm not going into the studio. *It* is.

Breathe.

Aurora whirls with a scream from where she's standing facing away from me with a broom clutched tightly in her hands. She pulls out an earbud, her green eyes going wide before she relaxes.

"Oh, it's you." She laughs. "You scared me."

The studio hits me like a five-finger death punch right in the fucking chest.

It's just the way I left it, and yet somehow even worse than I remembered.

There are cobwebs in the corners now and other webs that connect the spaces between the busted easels that are somehow still partially upright in the corner. The remnants of the ones that didn't survive that day are mostly all swept up now. Their bits of sharp, splintered wood in a pile with snapped paintbrushes and flecks of dried paint.

My focus zeroes in on the wide paint stain in the center of the floor. The empty tub is gone, but Aurora hasn't finished scraping the paint splatters from the hardwood yet. My right hand aches at my side, shaking as I pull it into a tight fist that only makes it hurt even more.

An involuntary image of the jagged ivory stone fills my mind and then it's not just the stone.

CHAPTER 9

It's the stone covered in red gore as it's brought down against my hand again and again *and again.*

"Did you paint those?" Aurora asks, completely oblivious to the threatening skies closing in on us. *Can't she feel the electricity of the coming storm?* It prickles against my skin like a thousand tiny needles.

I breathe through my nose, trying to remember why I was looking for her. Trying to grasp onto anything to use as a lifeline to pull me out of these violent waters.

Aurora crosses the room, going to the far wall. The artworks there were scattered throughout the room, most of them destroyed, but now she has them in a neat, gently leaning stack.

"They're beautiful. I've never seen anything like them."

She smiles up at me, but when our eyes meet something falters in her unguarded stare. She swallows. "You're an incredible artist," she continues, but her tone is different. It edges her words in a question I won't answer.

I'm not even sure I can speak.

Was, the parasite hisses in my ear.

I was *an incredible artist.*

Not anymore.

Not after what *he* did to me.

What I was forced to do to myself.

"Get. Out."

I don't recognize my own voice.

"What?"

"I said get out!"

Aurora freezes, the broom still in her hand. I can't make sense of her expression. I can't make sense of why the fuck she's still standing there.

"I—I didn't mean to—"

Her words break off when I stalk over to her and rip the broom from her hands, chucking it across the room.

"*Leave.*"

She recoils from me, her shoulders turning in, eyes filled with a horror that cuts at the rage with claws and teeth, making it want to fight back.

"I—I'm so sorry. I didn't mean to—I should've—i-it's just that Atticus said—" She stops rambling, cutting herself off with a gulp as she lifts her delicate pale hands in a gesture that a distant part of me recognizes is meant to be disarming, but that part isn't in the driver's seat.

Atticus.

That motherfucker.

"Elijah?"

A hollow laugh fills my chest.

Aurora tiptoes around me like I'm toxic. "You know what, I'm just going to—yeah, I'm going to go."

She keeps her eyes so firmly fixed on me that she doesn't see the edge of the stacked paintings before it's too late. She yelps as she trips over them and they fall with a thud, splaying mutilated artwork over the floor in full, unobstructed view.

It reminds me of everything I lost. All the parts of me I will *never* get back.

All my remaining control dissolves, slipping through my fingers like sand.

My pulse thuds loud in my ears, uneven and cold. Distant, like it might decide to give out at any second.

Not again.

I slam a fist against my temple.

Stop. Stop. *Stop.*

I throw my arms out. Something crashes. Breaks.

It feels good so I do it again.

CHAPTER 9

Again.

I don't stop until the cold broken bleating in my chest feels stronger. Until my muscles feel weak from exertion and my thoughts stop spiraling and the parasite detaches.

"*Fuck*," I slump, dropping my head back against the wall, trying to catch my breath, but the smell of paint in my nose makes me want to vomit.

When I open my eyes, my studio is in a worse state than the one I left it in last time.

And Aurora is gone. Long gone. I wouldn't be surprised if she left for good.

Because of me.

Fucking Atticus. I told him I wasn't ready. I fucking *told* him.

My chest burns as I kick a busted easel away from me and drag my hands over my face, hating how they come away wet with the salt of my tears.

The bones in my right hand ache like hell after what I just made it take part in and I force myself to feel the pain. Hold the paint smell in my chest until it doesn't make me want to be sick anymore.

I exhale sharply and push to my feet, ignoring the part of me that wants to chase after Aurora and tell her...

What would I even say?

It doesn't matter. She doesn't know me. She doesn't owe me the courtesy of hearing me out.

I'm probably the last person she wants to see right now.

Swallowing the urge to walk back through the door and lock it for good, I bend and lift the broom from the floor, and start to clean my own mess.

10

STAY OR GO?

AURORA

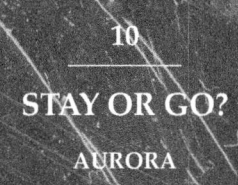

The distant sounds of Elijah trashing his studio chase me through the house.

Fuck.

What should I do?

"Atticus?" I call out in a voice that's pitched too high when I make it to the entryway. "Seven?"

There's another loud crash from way down the hall and I flinch, rushing for the door.

Nope.

I slip into my sandals and notice a metal bat in the corner by the front door. Biting my lip, I consider grabbing it in case I need protection, but the next loud crash sends me straight out the door instead. I pull it closed behind me and bolt down the steps, turning to watch the door as if it could burst open any second.

It doesn't, and I swallow hard, pushing a hand to the heavy beating in my chest as I bend down to catch my breath.

"What the fuck was that?"

Ellie barks, racing over to me from the trees with a

CHAPTER 10

worried whine in her throat. She barrels into my legs, rubbing her wet nose into my belly until I finally bend lower so she can put her chin over my shoulder in her version of a hug.

"It's okay, Ellie. I'm okay."

I can't seem to tear my gaze away from the door as I wrap my arms around her and give her a good scratch. If he comes out here in that rage, with Ellie in his blast radius, I will deck a motherfucker and I won't even be sorry about it.

When I left Jesse and his goons, I promised myself *never again* and I fucking meant it.

The shittiest part of it is that I thought Elijah was the nice one. The one I might be able to trust.

God, I have the worst damn judgement skills known to man.

Ellie pulls back enough to give my cheek a lick and I snort as I wipe off her drool. I don't know how she does it, but every time I'm upset, one of Ellie's 'hugs' always makes me feel better. She's pure magic. Which is why I need to do a better job of protecting her.

It means this is over.

So much for me and Ellie having that beautiful fresh start.

We'll have to find our own way. I scratch either side of her head, giving her a look. "I'm sorry, Ellie. We're going to have to find a new place to crash."

She barks at me, backing away.

"Don't look at me like that. We can't stay here. These guys are crazy."

She barks again, and I sigh.

My gaze flicks back up to the door one last time, trying to imagine staying, but I can't. Even when I consider the pain I saw in Elijah's eyes.

It wasn't like the cruel fury I often found in Jesse's stare. It was this...profound sadness. A rage that felt familiar in a way I didn't want to admit. Elijah didn't want to hurt me, that much I felt pretty sure of, but it doesn't matter if he's a loose cannon. People could still get hurt—intentional or not. Ellie could get hurt.

Then there's the possibility that I'm just making excuses for him. Like I did for Jesse in the beginning.

My jaw tightens.

"Come on, Ellie. Let's go get our things."

She darts in front of me, blocking my path with another bark.

"Okay, stay out here then."

When I move to walk past her, she catches the hem of my shirt in her teeth and gives me a tug in the opposite direction. I gently pull the material loose, but she only nips at it again, tugging hard enough to rip.

"Ellie!"

She backs up a few steps and barks again, turning her head in the direction of the trees she just ran from, before barking again and stamping her paw.

I squint to see into the trees.

"What is it, girl?"

She jumps, turning to the trees with another bark that might as well be a command to follow her.

I rub a hand over my forehead, where a tension headache starts to form behind my eyes. "Ellie, we really need to just—"

She barks again, more insistent.

"You know what, fine."

It's not like I want to go back inside right now, anyway. For all I know, Elijah might've finished with his studio and

CHAPTER 10

moved on to other parts of the house. "Go on, then. Lead the way, you stubborn little shit."

I swear she grins at me before bounding into the trees, staying just close enough that I can see her enough to follow.

I kick at the leaves and sticks carpeting the woods on this ridiculous property. Like, who even needs this much land? They aren't even using it. If I had my own personal forest, you can bet your ass I'd be building myself a little fairy cottage complete with a witchy herb garden and squirrel friends.

What a waste.

Up ahead, Ellie trots through a break in the trees with a yap. I know her little sounds well enough to know it's a greeting and wonder who else is out here or if I'm going to have to destinkify her again because she decided the skunk family living under the neighbor's shed were *definitely* her friends.

Please, I send the plea to any higher power that will hear me, *anything but a skunk.*

That nasty smell lingered in her coat for weeks.

I lift a hand to shield my eyes from the sun as I step through and find a wide clearing carpeted with long grass and clusters of spindly wildflowers. Ellie lets out another yap as she rushes to the little structures in the middle of the space, and the man standing with his back to me as he pulls something out of a tiny house.

My throat constricts. Who the fuck is that?

The man turns to look at Ellie and I see that it's Seven.

I'm relieved at first, but given how the one I thought was the nicest of the three just reacted to me trying to help him tidy up his art room, maybe I shouldn't be relieved at all.

I squint to try to see what he's doing.

There are at least four of those tiny houses that I can see. They're really nothing more than little white boxes atop raised cement platforms with peaked roofs. They match the larger structure that's about the size of a big shed set off to one side.

A buzzing drone fills my ears and I realize what it is with a flinch.

I prayed for no skunks, so the universe gave me fucking bees.

It's a hive, or a colony, or whatever the hell they call it.

Great.

Seven lowers the thing he was checking back into the box with the bees and puts the roof-shaped lid back into place before turning to properly greet Ellie with some pats.

"You're back," I think he says, bending to a knee to give her a good rubdown that she is definitely taking advantage of.

As if he senses me, his head jerks up, eyes latching on to mine with ice in them that melts as soon as he recognizes my face.

"There you are. Eli was looking for you," he calls.

I snort, unable to conceal the still lingering agitation.

"Well, he found me," I say, walking over to them, unsure if I want Ellie near any of these guys anymore, even if she's definitely taken a shine to this one.

We aren't always attracted to what's good for us and I am the painful evidence of that fact. If I never let Jesse take me home that night all those months ago, none of this would've even happened.

I would still be in Charlotte trying to get into that music program at UNC. Still trying to be the good girl my adoptive parents expected me to be.

CHAPTER 10

"Everything okay?" Seven asks as I approach.

I stop when a bee flies right past my face and recoil.

Yeah, actually, this is far enough.

I hate bugs, especially the kind that bite and sting. I can't help but notice how Seven has several of the little fuckers crawling on his black T-shirt, and grimace. He seems entirely unbothered by them, and I realize that I literally just watched him pull one of those thingies covered in bees from one of their hives with his bare freaking hands.

It's official: they're all insane.

"Define okay," I reply, making a hand motion at Ellie. "Come."

She sits down next to Seven defiantly and he pats her head with a smirk, cocking his head at me. "Did something happen?"

Another bee buzzes right by my nose and I reel back, swatting it away just as another one comes for me.

"Ah. Fuck."

Seven catches my hand on the next swat and I didn't even see him come over here.

His rough fingers trap mine with a little squeeze before I can jerk my hand free and he raises his in surrender.

"They're harmless," he says. "If you ignore them, they won't bother you."

"Tell that to the one trying to get in my mouth."

He laughs, and something about it disarms me.

When I lift my hand to shoo another one away, he catches it again. "Ignore them," he repeats. "They won't sting unless you provoke them or threaten their queen."

This time, I'm slower to pull my hand away. How are his eyes so freaking blue?

Damn.

I blink, realizing I'm staring, and swallow, hating that I

can't seem to just make myself turn around and leave. It should be easy. Pivot. Step. Keep fucking walking.

"Well, too bad the same can't be said for your friend," I mutter and almost wish I could stuff the words back in, but this is it. I might've lost touch with the girl I was before Jesse bulldozed into my life and decided I was *his*, the girl who didn't take shit from anyone. But I'm starting to remember.

This is what it looks like when you don't just lay down and take it and I am *done* doing that, no matter the consequences. If Jesse makes good on his promise and uploads his disgusting videos to the internet, so be it. At least I'll be fucking free.

Seven lifts a brow, so I lift my chin. He damn well heard me.

His brows lower. "Do you mean Atticus?"

I shake my head. "No. Not him, the other one."

He blinks. "Eli?"

"He totally freaked out on me," I blurt, wanting an explanation I shouldn't even need. "Atticus asked me to clean his studio and when he walked in, he just..." I throw my hands up.

Seven's jaw tightens. "Atticus shouldn't have done that."

I scoff. "It wasn't Atticus who was smashing easels and kicking holes through paintings."

He flinches.

"Look, all I'll say is that Eli is the best of us, and he'll probably be beating himself up about losing it in front of you for weeks. No, probably months."

"Care to share why he might've felt the need to completely lose his shit?"

CHAPTER 10

Seven runs a hand over the dark hair on the back of his head with a sigh. "It's really not my story to tell, Aurora."

I hate how he says my name.

I'm a shitty liar.

"Fine," I decide, but he makes my choice easy. "Come on, Ellie, we're leaving."

"Wait," Seven says, catching my wrist when I turn to go.

Why does he keep touching me like that?

He drops my wrist when I glare at him. "Just wait."

"Why?"

"Because I don't want you to leave," he says like it's the most simple thing in the world when that couldn't be further from the truth.

I shrug. "I really didn't want to either until twenty minutes ago."

I need that money.

"Look, I can't tell you why Elijah just did what he did, but I can promise you it wasn't without a valid reason. There are things you don't know. Seeing you in there, touching those things, it would've triggered him, and Atticus knew exactly what would happen if Eli found you in there and still sent you in blind anyway. If you want to be mad at someone, be mad at him. Fuck knows I am."

He's telling the truth. I can hear it in his tone. If that's true then *fuck* Atticus. Why the hell would he send me in there if he knew that was how Elijah would react?

What a dick move.

I hesitate and it's like he can sense it.

"Stay," he says. "Stay and talk with me for fifteen minutes. You can ask me anything you want and if it's my answer to give you, I will. Just fifteen minutes and if you still want to leave, I'll drive you to the bus station in Wilkesboro myself."

My teeth grind behind my lips. "Fuck. *Fine.* Fifteen minutes."

11

STING LIKE A BEE

AURORA

The fifteen minutes I'm giving Seven is not for them. It's for me.

For the future I saw for me and Ellie, if I can just survive the next six months working for these strange men in this strange place.

Seven snatches my hand to tow me along behind him, back toward the little bee hives and the shed-like structure next to them.

"Um, Seven, I *really* don't like bugs. Can we just—"

"They're not going to sting you. Just trust me."

That's exactly what I can't do, but I let him lead me to the shed and pray that it's a bee-free zone. It's warm and dark inside and Ellie, who's been following us up until now, sits just outside the door as if Seven has already told her this space is off limits.

"All right." He lets me go, rubbing his hands together before heading for the short counter where one of those bee boxes rests, and all my hopes of having a bee-free conversation are dashed.

He said they aren't going to sting me.

CHAPTER 11

They aren't going to sting you.

I force myself to drag in a calm breath through my nose and attempt to make my arms feel less like they're in the early stages of rigor mortis.

"Fifteen minutes. Go."

Right.

Um...

I rack my brain but can't think of anything to ask as Seven scoops bees that have started to gather on the corner of the box with his hands. *His fucking hands.*

He brushes past me to deposit the bees outside and comes back to start prying a honeycomb-filled panel from the box. It still has a few bees on it and as they start to crawl onto his fingers, he seems to not even notice.

Maybe they really won't sting me.

I start to relax and realize he's still watching me expectantly, but now there's an edge of amusement in his eyes. I cross my arms over my chest.

"Beekeeping?" I ask.

If he'd asked me to guess at a hobby before I saw this meadow, beekeeping wouldn't even have made that list, and right now I can't think of what else to ask to try to understand these men better.

Seven pulls out a long knife and I shoot back a step.

He deftly flips it in his fingers, holding it almost flippantly as he begins to speak. "What? Never seen a tatted beekeeper?"

He starts to scrape something that looks like wax off the honeycomb with the long blade and I see now that it's more of a tool than the weapon meant for decapitation that I first pegged it as.

I give him a look. He said he'd answer my questions.

"All right, all right. I guess you could say it was inherited. The hives belonged to Eli's dad, Julian. I've always had a knack for the work and the bees don't mind me and I don't mind them, so when Julian couldn't care for them anymore, I told him I'd do it."

"So, you and the others aren't related then?"

I didn't really think so, given how different they all look from each other, but I wasn't really sure until he said *Eli's dad*.

"We're not blood," Seven says, cutting away more wax. "But they're my family."

He really does seem to have a knack for it. He sees me watching him and holds out the knife. "Want to try?"

"Oh. No. I'd probably just mess it up."

"I don't think so."

I hide my blush and clear my throat. "You said when Julian *couldn't* anymore. Why couldn't he?"

His lips press into a taut line.

"Not your story to tell?" I guess.

He doesn't answer, finishing with the first panel and slipping it into a metal drum before prying out a second one.

"Okay, then."

New question...

"Is Seven your real name?"

His lips twitch. "It is."

"Really?"

He lifts his brows at me, challenging the doubt in my tone. "Really. I have six older siblings."

"Do they all have numbers for names, too?"

Seems a little...impersonal.

"No."

No? He had six older siblings with normal names, but his parents chose to name him Seven?

CHAPTER 11

"Oh."

"My story isn't a pretty one, Aurora."

Neither is mine.

A knot forms between his brows as he continues his work of scraping wax, not looking at me anymore.

"I'd like to hear it anyway, if you'll tell me."

I'm surprised at how much I mean it. I really do want to know.

Ellie lets out a little groan as she sinks onto her belly outside the door and perches her chin atop her paws, as if she, too, is very interested in this story.

"Sure you wouldn't rather ask about the bodies buried in the backyard?"

I let out a huff of a laugh. "Let me guess, they all had it coming?"

He canters his head this way and that. "Yeah. More or less."

I wait.

Seven nods to himself. "All right. Just remember you asked for it, and I don't need your pity."

My stomach twists.

"My mom's husband wasn't my bio dad," he says. "That's why they called me Seven. Her and my stepdad—if you could even call him that—had six kids together before she was unfaithful. I was the stain on an otherwise perfect family."

My heart hurts already and I'm not sure if I want to tell him he doesn't have to keep going or wait and listen to every word because I want to know if any of his scars match mine.

"My siblings and I went to the same school and lived in the same house, but that's where our similarities ended. They all looked the same. Auburn hair. Brown eyes. They all had big bedrooms on the top floor of the house. Played board games together. Sat on the big sofa in the living room and watched family movies every Friday night. Sometimes, if they had the volume up loud enough, I could almost pretend I was sitting up there with them."

Oh my god.

I'm almost afraid to ask, but the words leave my lips anyway as my fingers clutch the counter behind me. "Up there?"

He clears his throat. "Yeah, my bedroom was in the basement. Actually, the basement was where I lived, I guess. It was unfinished but it had a half bath and a little space where I slept. It was cold, but Annie's old mattress wasn't half bad and I had some blankets."

My hand goes to my throat, fingers tangling with my necklace as I try to eject the image of a little dark-haired boy all alone in a cold cement room having to listen to his family laugh and play without him.

Seven's expression tightens and I drop my hand.

He didn't want my pity, but...*how*?

I'd been through some horrible shit. With Jesse, yes, but long before him, before my parents signed off on the official adoption, there were lots of families whose idea of what a loving household should be massively deviated from what I imagined. But at least those assholes weren't *my* family. Not my own blood.

But then again, my real parents left me at a shelter before I was even old enough to remember their faces, so...

"What about your real father?"

He shrugs. "Never met the guy. Don't even know his name."

"Your mom never told you?"

Another shrug.

CHAPTER 11

"God, how could they treat you like that?"

"You get used to it," he says as if it's no big deal. "And when I was still little, they did let me go with them to events where it would've been weird for me to not be with them.

"For a long time I thought that if I was really good and behaved just...just fucking perfect at those parties, maybe they'd see I could be part of the family. A real son like Alex and Aaron were. After a couple years I realized it didn't matter what I did and I stopped trying. Instead I found some pretty inventive ways to make them hate me even more. Really creative stuff, honestly. I don't know where I came up with most of it.

"I was punished, of course, but my stepdad's belt was no match for the pure joy of seeing the shock on their faces after I did something truly fucking horrifying."

He laughs darkly, eyes gleaming as if he's remembering something particularly inventive.

A part of me wants to ask what sort of things, but I'm not sure I want to know. If he asked me what sort of things I did to my most cruel foster parents and siblings...or imagined doing to Jesse a thousand times, I sure as hell wouldn't tell him. I could barely admit the truth of them to myself.

"Anyway, I started sneaking out when I was about twelve or thirteen," he continues. "Stole a bike and kept it hidden behind the shed out back. I met Eli for the first time by this pond I liked to hang out at in the woods. It was just down this little dirt path at the end of a no-exit road. Fuck, he was such a weird kid back then. All gangly and shit. Always with a pencil or a paintbrush in his hands."

He looks sad now.

"Eli took me back to his place that very first day I met him. I remember looking at the house and thinking it was a castle. Some fairytale place that I made up in my head, and maybe I really went psycho like my brothers always said I would. Eli's mom was—well, she took one look at me, dirty and scrawny like some sewer rat, and told Eli to go grab me some clean clothes and show me where the shower was while she made us something to eat. I went back almost every day after that."

"She sounds like an amazing woman."

"She was."

An ache forms in my chest when his jaw twitches and his eyes leave mine.

Was.

Hadn't he also said something like *until Julian couldn't care for the bees anymore*?

A pang of empathy rings in my chest for Elijah, making it even harder to be objective. Did he lose both his parents? Was that somehow connected to his trauma with the art studio?

"Having Eli's place definitely made it easier when they left."

My brows screw up in confusion, and I think I missed something. "Sorry, when who left?"

He swallows and whatever fleeting emotion I think I see flash over his stark features is gone before I can name it.

"My family. They left when I turned sixteen. I snuck out that morning to hang out with Eli and Atticus at Eli's place. His dad made me birthday pancakes. I still remember how fucking burnt they were—he was a terrible cook—but it was the first time anyone had lit the candles for me and done the whole birthday song thing."

My eyes burned.

"I went home after. My one sister, Annie, she would always sneak me some kind of treat on my birthday. She'd

CHAPTER 11

sit with me on the top step while I ate it. She wouldn't say a lot, but I always looked forward to having that five minutes with her. She was definitely the most *gracious* one about me."

He sighs, adding the next honey-clogged panel to the big metal drum. "But she wasn't there. None of them were.

"Instead of Annie on the top step there was a note with a single word on it that I knew she left for me. *Sorry,* it said. That's it. I found out later they'd had plans to move for months. They went to live somewhere in the UK to be closer to my stepdad's family."

"So, wait—" I blurt, a hot, heavy rage chasing the sadness from my chest. "They just...they just *left* you?"

It strikes a broken chord in me I thought I'd healed from and my hands ball into fists.

Seven nods gravely.

"What did you do after that?"

He lifts his shoulder in a noncommittal shrug that is anything but flippant. There is no way in hell talking about this doesn't hurt him. Is there? I can't talk about my biological family or much of my past without feeling like someone's hollowing out my insides and filling the aching chasm with an echo of old hurts.

"For a while I stayed there in the empty house, in my basement. I don't know why, but I didn't want Eli or his parents to know. I knew they'd feel somehow obligated to take me in and I couldn't stand the idea of that. It was a month before the moving trucks came and the new family who bought the place arrived. After that, I lived on the streets for probably about a year. Found work at a tattoo shop sweeping up and doing piercings for practically pennies."

His lips pull up at the corner.

"Julian and Florence were so mad when they found out," he tells me. "I should've told them sooner, but I was embarrassed, I guess. I still remember Julian's face the day he and Eli showed up at the shop. He told me I was 'coming home with them, goddammit' and I was staying and he 'didn't want to fucking hear a word about it'—and he never swore. Not ever."

Are his eyes glassy?

Fuck.

Fuck.

Seven finishes with the last panel and closes the metal drum with an ominous *clang* that rattles in my bones.

"The rest is pretty much history," he says, turning around without any trace of the emotion I thought I saw a second before as he jumps up to sit on the metal counter next to me, rattling the honey jars atop it.

It takes a massive amount of restraint not to reach out to him.

He doesn't want your pity.

But I just can't imagine anyone ever looking into those eyes and wanting to hurt the bright soul I can feel roiling just below the stormy blue depths.

"What about you?" Seven crosses his arms, leaning back. "What's your story?"

I blink, already feeling my head shake, but I don't fall back to my default response of *Trust me, you don't want to hear it.* Maybe it's because he's looking at me like he already understands. Like he'll listen and not judge. Like he'll hear me, but not pity me. And afterward he won't clam up and come up with some excuse to run as far and as fast as he can.

"I…"

He waits.

CHAPTER 11

It's really only fair. He showed me his scars. I could at least offer a small glimpse of mine.

"Cliff Notes version?"

"I'll take what I can get."

I nod.

"Okay. Well, I was orphaned as a baby. Grew up in foster care until I was about sixteen and the family I was with at the time adopted me."

Seven reaches up to gently push my hair away from the still healing cut on my cheek. "Was it them who hurt you like this?"

My face heats and I let out a hollow laugh. "No. God, no. They're perfect. *Too* perfect. I never really fit in there with them, but I tried to, you know?"

When he nods, I believe him. He probably knows even better than me what it's like to try to fit into a mold that was never made for the shape of you.

When Seven drops his hand, my own fingertips replace his, gingerly running along the perfect slice in my skin where Jesse ran his pocketknife along my cheekbone. "No, this...this was someone else."

"I know."

I search his eyes. They give me permission to say anything. Or to say nothing at all.

"May I?" he asks, indicating the cut on my cheek as he twists open a jar of honey.

I cock my head at him.

"Nature's antibiotic," he explains, dipping his little finger into the jar.

I must still look doubtful, because he lets out a small chuckle and then sets to dabbing a little of the honey onto the stitched gash in his forehead.

When he comes for me next, I turn my cheek for him to apply the honey over my cut in small, gentle pats.

This is so weird.

And yet, somehow, I'm smiling.

"So, what's his name?" he asks after he's finished. "The trash who carved that into your cheek?"

I swallow hard.

"H-his name is Jesse."

Ellie lets out a soft growl from the ground outside and my stomach turns. I shouldn't tell him. I'm not even sure I can say it out loud. And I can't...*I can't* say what he did to Ellie—how he kicked her so hard in the head that for a second I thought she might not get back up. It makes me sick just thinking about it.

It was my fault. If I'd left sooner. If I'd done something to *stop* him...

If.

There's always a fucking *if*.

"You can tell me."

Seven's voice, strong and calm and somehow already completely understanding, breaks the feeble wall I tried to build and before I know it, my lips part and the whole disgusting story is coming up like vomit.

I purge Jesse in waves, telling Seven how we met. How I let him get in my head and assert himself over me like a black shadow. I tell him how Jesse changed me, crafting me into the image he wanted to see. The perfect girlfriend with every bolt and cog and thought and strand of hair meticulously chosen to create this "Aurora doll" I no longer recognized when I looked in the mirror.

"It all happened so fast that by the time I realized it, it was too late to get out. He's in this sort of gang. They run

CHAPTER 11

drugs and weapons sometimes. When I tried to leave, he started threatening me. It wasn't anything I wasn't used to, honestly. I can handle myself. But I helped them this one time with an arms deal—Jesse didn't really give me the option to say no—and he still has proof that could get me into trouble."

When I get to the parts about his jealousy and his... *appetites*, I almost stop but the words keep coming out like Seven's pulling them from my soul like a fucking trauma twister that's too strong to not get swept up in.

I tell him about the times Jesse drugged me and then filmed me with him.

And with his friends.

And even though I'm horrified at the words coming out of my mouth, it's like I can't turn off the faucet he's opened up inside of me.

"When his threats to turn me in to the cops stopped working, he started threatening to share the videos he had online and...and with my parents. He owned me, and he knew it. He reminded me all the time. 'I *own* you, Aurora, *I own you*'."

I shudder and an angry growl clambers up my throat.

"And the amount of times I wanted to just fucking—"

I cut myself off before I admit my one last visceral, dirty truth, my hands shaking as I try to control the snarl on my lips, swallowing my rage and the burning tears trying and failing to escape my eyes.

"Anyway, the important thing is that I left and I will *never* go back. Even if he does try to ruin my life, at least I'll be free of him."

Seven's hooded eyes are dark as they fall from my face to my neck and drop lower to caress my curves like he can see the other bruises I'm hiding under my clothes.

He doesn't say anything. *Why isn't he saying anything?*

Fuck. I just admitted to a crime. Full-on admitted I'm a criminal. I am so stupid.

The energy around him shifts as he slides from the counter, and I drop my head, a hot blush crawling up my neck.

I flinch when he places his hands on my arms, making me look back up. "You are so much more than that pathetic fucking excuse for a man could ever deserve. You know that, right?"

My jaw clenches.

What?

"You don't even know me."

"Not yet," he agrees. "But I see you."

His hard eyes hold me captive for long seconds until finally, mercifully, he releases me.

"If you stay, I can promise you that he won't be able to hurt you anymore."

"You can't promise that."

His eyes flash with cold fire.

"I can."

Seven ducks his head as he steps past me to exit the honey shed and stoops to give Ellie a little scratch as he starts to walk away. She jumps up and the little traitor pads along behind him like a lovesick puppy, leaving me alone with the bees.

"Hey! Where are you going?" I call after Seven.

"To carve out a name."

He turns to face me but continues walking backward. "Stay here as long as you want. And, Aurora?"

I bite my cheek.

"I really do hope you decide to stay."

12

RAGE & REGRET

ATTICUS

I *should've come earlier.*
My teeth grind as I linger in the hall outside Eli's room. When I heard the distant sound of something smashing on the other end of the cabin this afternoon, I knew I fucked up. And if I wasn't a hundred percent sure, the frantic way Aurora called my name all but cemented that fact.

But by the time I was across the house, Aurora was already outside, and the smashing and breaking down the hall had only intensified. I went to stop him before he could hurt himself but he was finished when I reached the studio door, and I couldn't bring myself to open it.

Not when I heard him let out a choked sob on the other side.

He wouldn't have wanted to see me when he was like that.

I thought he'd come charging after me to ream my ass out in no time, and I waited for it, but he didn't come.

Seven didn't, either.

That made it worse.

CHAPTER 12

So much worse.

Fuck.

I knew Eli wouldn't like it, but I didn't expect his reaction to be quite so...

I'm supposed to protect them. It's literally my only fucking job. Too bad I can't protect them from my own damn stupidity.

"I can see the shadow of your big-ass feet under the door, Atticus." Eli's voice is muffled through the panel of wood.

I clench my fists and drop my head as I turn the handle and step inside.

Eli's sitting on the edge of his bed with his elbows resting on his knees. I don't miss how the door to his studio has been left ajar. I can't remember the last time I saw it open.

Even though the light is off inside the studio, I can smell the wood cleaner and see how the floor is free of debris.

"I hope you're happy," he says in a hollow croak.

"Eli, I..."

He lifts his head. There are dark rings around his eyes and he's paler than I've seen him since when we first got him back.

A weight settles on my shoulders. On my chest.

"I never should've sent her in there like that."

"No. You fucking shouldn't have."

"And I should've respected that you weren't ready yet."

He nods, interlinking his fingers and squeezing them in a way that must hurt. Like he wants the pain.

"Eli—"

"Don't."

He falls silent, and I hate it. I want the old Eli back. I want him to shout at me. Tell me how much of a dick I'm being. I want him to use his fancy vocabulary and tear me a new asshole with it.

This phantom version of him rips my goddamned heart out.

"Aren't you glad it's done?" I ask, only because it'll piss him off. I need to stoke the slow-burning coals in his bitter stare back to a full fucking blaze. I at least have to try. "If I didn't send that girl in there—if I didn't do something about it—"

He jumps to his feet, leveling me with a wrathful glare that gives me hope.

"She could've been hurt!"

"I didn't know you'd go apeshit on her."

He shoves me hard, and even though I hate seeing him upset, inside I'm relieved to see the fire in his eyes.

"You damn well should've!"

There he is. Yes. Get angry.

Feel it. Feel something!

"You know what the fuck I went through, Atticus. You know what he did to me!"

His throat bobs, and whatever relief I felt five seconds ago drains away.

My stomach twists, and something like bile burns in my throat.

"*You know what he did*," he repeats, and I'm sure the whole fucking house can hear him. "And you did it anyway."

There's a lump in my throat that's making it hard to talk. Hard to get out the words I've never been good at saying. So Elijah uses his instead.

"You can be such a selfish fucking prick, you know that?"

I bet that feels good. I wait for more, knowing it's in

CHAPTER 12

there. Knowing I deserve it. But he stops and turns around with a heavy sigh.

"Elijah, I'm sorry."

He whirls, cocking his head at me. The rage is still there, still simmering, but dying by the second.

"It's not just me you owe an apology to."

"I'm not going to apologize to her. I don't even know h—"

"Yes," he snaps. "You are. This is *your* fault. I'll take the rap for my part, but you can damn well own yours, too."

I clench my teeth. He's right. And if it means he'll forgive me for being such an inconsiderate prick, then I'll beg her forgiveness if I have to. I'd do anything for my brothers.

"Fine. I'll apologize to the girl."

A vein in his temple jumps as he sits back down on the edge of his bed and roughly pushes his rumpled hair from his face.

"Feel better?"

He scoffs, shaking his head.

"That's the worst fucking part, Atty. I *do* feel better. Now that it's done, it's like this weight that's been pushing on me...suffocating me..."

He pushes on his chest for emphasis, and I know what he means because I feel that weight, too.

"It's gone."

"But there's a new weight there now." His brows lower. "Because of your compulsive need to have everything around you in perfect fucking order, I scared the shit out of Aurora. God, I was a complete asshole to her. I don't even recognize the person I was when I came into this room and saw her..."

I want to tell him that she'll probably forgive him and

that it doesn't really matter, but it's clear it matters to him, so I keep my trap shut.

"What can I do? Do you want me to talk to her?"

"Fuck no."

Eli sighs again.

I rack my brain for another solution. Something to fix the mess I made. "Maybe I could—"

"Just get out, man," he says in a low tone that's like a punch to the gut. "I'm done talking to you."

13

ITALIAN COLD CUTS WITH A SIDE OF DOUCHEBAG

SEVEN

A urora didn't leave in the middle of the night like I thought she might.

I know because I couldn't fucking sleep after everything she told me. The girl had it rough. And not just with this Jesse fucker, but with everything she had to endure before him. I couldn't imagine the foster care system would be a safe place for someone with a face like hers.

By dawn I assumed if she were going to run away she'd have done it already, and by nine in the morning I knew where Jesse worked, who his friends were, the town where he was born, and even where he bought his six-pack of bud every night before heading home. I also predicted the hour of his death, and figured I was only off by anywhere from twenty-four to forty-eight hours.

What I *should* have been doing while using all of Atticus's super fun and highly illegal surveillance programs was getting myself good and fed. I fucking forgot that it's Wednesday. One of three days every week that Atty has us fasting until one in the afternoon. He insists its good for us,

CHAPTER 13

but tell that to my rapidly dropping blood sugar levels and steadily fucking rising impatience.

From the back windows, I can see Aurora still netting leaves from the pool. I don't have the heart to tell her there's no need. Atticus bought a robot pool vacuum and it'd have done the job for her within the hour. But she's only out there because she doesn't want to be in here. I can't blame her.

"Is she still out there?" Eli comes up behind me, peering out the window with a sigh as he leans a forearm against the glass to watch her. "I still think I should talk to her."

I shake my head. We already talked about this. Aurora needs to feel in control. "And I still think you need to wait for her to come to you."

From the corner of my eye, I see his jaw tic as he clenches his teeth. Knowing Elijah, every second she avoids him is another second spent in his own personal hell. He hates conflict. But he hates being the guilty party even more.

"You're probably right."

"I am."

"Atticus is making lunch."

I twist to look at him and find the tension still clear in his expression. In the knot between his brows and the flat line of his mouth.

He and Atticus had it out last night, so the air is thinner between them, but it still isn't clear.

In the end, Atticus got what he wanted at Eli and Aurora's expense and he knows damn well it was shitty of him to do.

There was some good that came out of it, though. Eli cleaned his studio spotless. That's where I found him after my chat with Aurora. A zombie with a fucking broomstick.

Italian cold cuts with a side of douchebag

At least he let me help him.

I was going to have a word with Atty myself but Eli wanted to talk to him alone. By the shouting I heard coming from the studio, I knew he was doing a damn good job of letting him have it without my help.

"How'd it go with Atticus last night?" I ask.

Eli shakes his head. "He knows he was wrong, but..." He sighs. "I'm still fucking angry about it, Sev. He should've asked. He should've fucking waited until I was ready."

"He should've," I agree. "But when has Atticus ever been patient?"

"This was different. He knew—he fucking knew how it would affect me. But, honestly, I think I'm more mad at him for sending Aurora to do his dirty work. She could've got hurt, and I..."

I nod as he trails off.

He would never have been able to live with himself.

There isn't any fucking excuse, which is why I chewed Atticus's ear off about it again this morning before the house woke up just for good measure.

He really does seem to get how badly he messed up—how much worse it could've been—but it doesn't change the fact that he did it. I love him like he's my own blood, but I wish he'd *think* a little more before he does shit that might affect the rest of us.

"Are you glad it's done, at least?"

The studio has been in shambles since not long after we finally got Eli back.

He drops his head. "Of course, I am."

And that's the rub, isn't it? If Atticus hadn't forced him, Eli might never have been ready. When we were finally done in his studio, there was a conflicted peace in his crum-

CHAPTER 13

pled stare instead of the ever-raging war where he was both enemy and ally.

I grip his shoulder. "Come on. I don't know about you but I could eat a whole damn horse."

Eli lets me tow him to the kitchen, where Atticus has all the ingredients out for his famous Italian cold cut sandies, Eli's favorite lunch.

I toss Eli a Gatorade from the fridge and grab one for myself, earning a sharp look from Atty since it's still five minutes to one, but he's smart enough to keep his trap shut for once.

I'm still guzzling it back when we hear the kitchen door open and Aurora steps through with Ellie on her heels. She freezes just inside the doorway, her keen jade eyes flicking first to Eli and then to Atticus's back where he's bent over the counter, carefully placing slices of salami onto beds of lettuce like I'm not three seconds from shriveling into a prune.

"Oh," Aurora chirps, letting her gaze fall before turning back the way she came. "Sorry, I'll just—"

"Wait!"

Eli really just can't help himself.

Aurora pauses, chewing her lip as she looks at him sidelong through her lashes.

"Um, are you hungry?" Eli asks. "You can have my sandwich."

"You need to eat," Atticus says without turning.

"Dude, shut the fuck up," Eli snaps back and then flinches when he remembers our audience.

I had no idea lunch was going to be this entertaining.

"Eli, I'm already making her, her own sandwich, man."

"No, really, that's okay. I'm not very hungry. I'll just keep work—"

Italian cold cuts with a side of douchebag

"I'm sorry," Eli says, stopping her from leaving a second time. "I shouldn't have shouted at you and I feel like a total asshole for behaving how I did. I promise you that's not me and it won't happen again."

Aurora's throat bobs.

"Will you let me make it up to you?" he pushes when she says nothing, but his offer seems to have intrigued her or at least made her curious enough to hear more.

"Yeah," I add, jumping in to help him out. "Eli was thinking you might want to do a little shopping. Grab some new clothes? Maybe get your hair done."

When she lifts her gaze, her eyes burn into mine. She knows why I offered that. She told me when she got roped in with Jesse and his gang she'd just gone 'menty B blonde', and when she mentioned she was thinking of changing the color, he wouldn't have it. Apparently his brand of asshole only dated blondes and said she'd be ugly with any other color.

I circle my shoulders back, trying to coax the excess rage to roll off.

"Yes," Eli says animatedly. "We actually know a great stylist and she'd be more than happy to take you on short notice. It's a bit of a long way away, but I'm sure she'll fit you in, if you want."

Aurora looks absolutely dumbstruck and it makes me wonder how long it's been since someone did something nice for her, and I hate this Jesse fucker just a little bit more.

"That's—wow. I mean, that's really nice of you to offer but I don't..." She pushes a lock of hair behind her ear. "I don't really have much money right now."

"That's okay. Atticus is going to give you an advance on your first salary," Eli tells her with a glimmer of mischief in

CHAPTER 13

his eyes that I whole-fucking-heartedly approve of. "Aren't you, Atticus?

Atty grumbles out a noncommittal reply, slapping slices of meat onto Aurora's sandwich.

"That would actually be great, but I'm sure I can drive myself into town and get everything I need as soon as I'm able to pay for the damage to my car."

I flinch. "Yeah, about that...our mechanic said it's a write-off."

Her face falls.

"Actually," Eli is quick to correct me. "I called Jack back, told him to go ahead and do whatever he needs to fix it. It might be a while—the damages were pretty bad—but he owes us a favor, so no worries on the cost."

He doesn't owe us shit and Eli will see to it that Jack is paid well for his time, but Aurora doesn't need to know that. We can afford it.

Her face screws up. "Really? He's not going to charge me?"

I shake my head. "Nope. But since it'll be a minute before he does the repairs, you should let us take you."

Eli does that thing with his eyes that always has the ladies eating out of his palm and I know that Aurora is fucked.

"It's really no trouble," he says in that endearing way only Eli can.

Fuck, I haven't heard him sound like this in a while. He's been too in his own head to care about what anyone else thinks since everything.

"We can get whatever you need."

Aurora chews her lip again and I imagine what it might feel like to run my teeth over the place where hers are. How she would taste.

"Well, Ellie is getting low on kibble."

"So, that's a yes then?" Eli confirms.

She hesitates, then nods. "Yes. That would be really great. Um, thanks."

"How about Friday?" I ask.

"Whatever works for you guys."

Atticus drags a serrated knife sharply through Aurora's sandwich and piles the two pieces onto a plate, shoving it across the island toward her. "Here."

"I…" Aurora starts to protest but seems to think better of it, crossing the floor to the kitchen island.

Eli gives Atticus a glare for the ages.

His nostrils flare and his jaw hardens, but when Aurora reaches for the plate, he pinches the other end to stop her taking it and running away.

"Sorry," he says, and she scrunches her brows at him.

"For?" Eli pushes.

Atty's lips flatten into a hard line. "For asking you to clean Eli's studio knowing he wouldn't be cool with it. That was shitty of me, and I'm sorry."

It sounds like he's reciting words from a fucking cue card, but it's probably the best she'll get. Atty doesn't usually apologize at all and I've never heard him apologize to someone who wasn't in this family. Baby steps.

He flicks his gaze to Eli for approval and gets the faintest nod.

"Judging by the way Elijah reacted, I'd say you should really be apologizing to him," she snaps, and then immediately pales as if she didn't mean to say the words out loud.

Atticus stares openly at her with harsh lines in his forehead while I try to hold in a snort. He's doing a job of trying to look angry, but I know him well enough to see that he's a little impressed, too.

CHAPTER 13

"What did you just say to me?"

"Atticus," Eli warns, and Atty's lips press shut.

"I'm, uh," Aurora stammers. "I'm just going to go eat outside. Thanks—for the sandwich."

Eli's ears turn red, but he has the decency to wait until she's fully out of earshot before opening his mouth. "Do you always have to be such a dick?"

"Do *you* have to be such a fucking tryhard?" Atticus plates up our sandwiches and drops Eli's in front of him with a clatter. "It was shit of me to send her into your studio and I fucking apologized, but don't forget: the girl is a tool. Nothing more. Don't get attached to her."

He's one to talk. I've seen the way he looks at her. My skin bristles and I have to shove down the urge to bite his head off, sinking my teeth into my sandwich instead.

Eli says something to himself under his breath that I don't catch.

Before I can finish chewing to tell Atty that I'm not sure I'm cool with using Aurora for anything she doesn't want to be used for, his phone chimes.

It's the tone we chose for the motion sensor at the entry to our private drive.

Oh *shit*.

He's early.

Begrudgingly, I set down my Italian cold cut and brush breadcrumbs from my fingers onto the floor as I move next to Atticus. He brings up the feed, and we watch a car I recognize from Atty's surveillance program stop at the gate.

I know who it belongs to and I grin as heat coils up my spine like a burning snake, making me shudder.

"Seven," Atticus hisses when I snatch his phone and jam the button to open the gate, allowing the car through.

"Oops," I say, louder than I mean to as the anticipation plays with the rage in my chest. "If I'd known douchebag was on the menu, I'd have brushed my fucking hair."

14

SWING, BATTER, BATTER

SEVEN

I'm already halfway to the front door when Atticus finally clues in and shouts after me to wait.

I snatch up the metal bat by the front door as I exit, giving it a good twirl to test the weight. The world outside is a brutally beautiful shade of pulsing crimson as I step into the sun and the car comes to a jarring stop at the base of the main drive.

The man himself exits, leaving the car door ajar as he storms up the drive and I inhale deep, filling my lungs with the scent of dead man.

"Where is she?" he screams, and I can't fucking wait to hear him scream louder.

"Seven!" Atticus shouts somewhere behind me, and I give the bat another good spin as Eli joins him, shouting my name, but in my delirium their voices are like cheers from the bleachers.

Seven! Seven! Seven!

"Is she fucking in there? Is my fucking girlfriend in there?"

"Seven!"

CHAPTER 14

They're pumping me up, their applause motivating me, injecting heat and delicious tension into every muscle. Every vein.

I'm halfway to Jesse when he starts shouting again.

"Aurora!" he roars, and I *will* erase her name from his vile lips. "Aurora, get out here!"

"Hey, batter, batter." My own low voice sounds foreign, echoing like an announcer in a stadium as I test the bat one last time, swinging it up to press a kiss to the cold metal.

Jesse seems to finally see the bat. See *me,* and he slows his walk. "Who the hell are you?"

Your worst fucking nightmare.

I imagine his hands on her throat. His fists against her body. His knife on her cheek.

"Swing, batter, batter, *swing.*"

My body coils for the strike and I get one delicious glimpse of the fear in his beady eyes as he rushes to reach into the back of his jeans for a weapon.

Too late.

The metal connects with bone, making the most beautiful sound in all of existence.

And he knocks it out of the park!

My chest heaves and it takes a second before the red haze in my vision can clear enough for me to see him, like a curtain drawing open to reveal the final act.

Staggering and dazed, Jesse's jaw is unhinged and pushed off into an unnatural angle as dark red blood falls down his chin and broken teeth scatter to the earth.

Fuck, that felt good.

There's straight fire in my blood, begging for another swift release that can only come with the breaking of bones and the claiming of souls.

"P-pfeease," Jesse mumbles through his busted teeth,

still fighting to stay on his feet, making him a more challenging target as he lurches and sways.

"Only because you asked so nicely," I mutter, rushing him with another swing of the bat until his head rings like a bell and the ricochet of the hit reverberates up my arms like the sweetest heroin. Hot liquid splatters over the right side of my face like a sexy slap.

Behind me, a decidedly feminine voice lets out a short gasp and I pivot.

Aurora's hands fly to her mouth and the instant my eyes meet hers, she bolts back into the house, almost tripping over the doormat in her haste to get away. Ellie barks after her, but doesn't follow, instead coming down the steps with a feral growl in her throat as she carefully approaches the spasming form of her person's abuser laying in the driveway.

I put a sticky hand to my forehead, squinting past Eli and Atticus for any sign of Aurora inside, but she's long gone. I tip my head up to the sun and let out a heavy exhale as it warms the blood on my cheeks.

It's always a shock the first time.

She'll be all right.

The rage that'd been singing a violent chorus in my veins takes a softer outro as my body sags.

Atticus rushes down the drive to where I stand next to Jesse, but I throw out the bat, pressing it to his chest to stop him. "Don't touch him."

Eli catches up and I give him a hard look. "He doesn't deserve your help."

Eli's face twists as he looks down at the sad, crumpled man at our feet.

Atticus shoves the bloodied bat away from his chest

CHAPTER 14

with an angry snarl and wipes his hand over the stubble on his face.

Ellie growls at Jesse, parking herself far enough away that she's safe, but close enough to have a front-row seat, and fuck if that isn't a great idea.

"Where the hell do you think you're going?" Atticus bellows after me when I start to walk away. I wave the bat in a noncommittal motion before going up the steps and back into the house.

I take another quick look for Aurora, but she's still nowhere to be seen. Either she ran straight out the back door or she's up in her room. Either way, my bloody face is not the one she wants to see right now.

I make my way to the kitchen, depositing the bat by the back door in favor of grabbing a stool from the island and my plated sandwich from the counter. I carry them both outside, ignoring Atticus's protests as I push the stool legs into the gravel a couple feet from where Jesse is slowly dying on the ground, and park myself atop it.

"Are you serious?" Atticus demands.

I take a large bite and talk around the mouthful. "Don't ruin the show for the rest of us, bro."

There's a vein about to pop out of Atticus's thick head as he gets control of himself. "You know what, Sev, you can clean up your own fucking mess this time. Do *not* ask for my help. By the time I come back out here tomorrow, I do not want to see any trace of *that* on this property. You hear me?"

"Loud and clear, lieutenant."

I give him a little salute. Really, I just want him to leave me in peace to watch this fucker die nice and slow while the blood pools in his fractured skull. I don't want to be distracted and miss the second the light leaves his eyes. Someone should watch it.

It should be her. It should be Aurora out here seeing justice served, but she isn't ready yet and that's okay.

I'll be her proxy.

"She told you?" Eli asks in a small voice once Atticus has left.

I swallow. "She did."

He nods quietly to himself. "I should check on her."

"You should. Go." I already know she won't see him, but he's ruining the moment, and I don't want to miss another second of this fucker's suffering.

Jesse gurgles unintelligibly, his dazed eyes pleading for help he won't find here.

Now he knows what it's like to be made small. To feel powerless.

It takes longer than I thought it would.

By the time the light starts to leak out of Jesse's eyes, I'm long finished my sandwich, and the sun is low on the horizon, bathing him in shades of angry orange.

I grin, leaning down on the stool at the same time Ellie lowers her head and lets out a soft growl, as if she, too, is wanting a closer look as Jesse pulls in one last ragged breath.

Her growls stop the instant the oxygen leaves his lungs for the last time.

"You hear that, girl?" I ask her. "That's the sound of justice."

15

WHAT NEEDS TO BE DONE

ATTICUS

Why do I always have to be the bad guy? I pull my gun from the safe beneath my desk and kick it shut, falling into the seat at my desk to check and load it before leaning back and setting it in my lap. Swiveling to my monitors, I bring up every camera feed we have. They don't cover the entire property, but they do cover the entire perimeter around the house and the entrance to our drive. It's enough that I'll be able to see if she tries to make a run for it.

The weight of the sleek metal in my lap makes me fucking antsy and it's going to be a study in patience to stay here and watch the feeds instead of working off the extra energy in the gym. It's a poor substitute for a warm cunt and the prearranged agreement that I can do whatever I want to it, but I respect Eli too much to parade a naked woman through this house before he's ready.

Because of it my focus is shot, my patience is nonexistent, and I swear my dick's about to dry up and snap off.

My leg bounces beneath the desk as I double-check that the motion sensors are all switched on and their sensi-

CHAPTER 15

tivity is turned all the way up. It means I'll get an alert for every squirrel and bunny rabbit that comes within a hundred feet of the house, but it's better than missing something.

I sigh heavily, watching Sev drag the corpse of Aurora's ex-boyfriend around to the garage at the side of the house, leaving an ugly trail of red the whole way around the building that he better fucking get rid of.

The world lost one more abusive fuckhead today and I'm not going to lose any sleep over that, but what I *will* lose sleep over is the fact that Sev killed the bastard right in front of Aurora. He didn't even attempt to hide it. Almost like he wanted her to see.

But that's Sev. Spontaneous. Reckless. Every moment of his existence balanced at the tip of a hairpin trigger you don't ever want to be on the wrong side of.

He's also the reason Eli and I are still breathing, but fuck if I'd ever tell him that. It would only justify his complete inability to step back and think for two fucking seconds before jumping straight to pulling a knife or a trigger.

He may be the reason we're alive to keep fighting the good fight, but he's also the reason we've lost more than one opportunity to get the vengeance we're owed after what happened to Eli.

Sev drops Jesse's legs when he reaches the back of the Jeep and pulls a pack of cigarettes from the inside of his jacket, lighting one up.

Motherfucker.

Every time I confiscate his stash, the bastard just replaces it.

As if he can somehow sense I'm watching him, he throws a middle finger to the camera above the side door and inhales nice and deep. I roll my eyes and grit my teeth,

What needs to be done

checking the rest of the feeds for the third time since I turned them on.

"She won't come out," Eli says, and my hand goes straight to the gun in my lap before I register his voice. *Fuck*. I didn't even hear the door open.

I push myself into the desk, trying to conceal what I'm holding in my lap. Of course he chooses now to start talking normal to me. It only took Sev sending another soul to hell for him to bury the hatchet. Noted.

"No shit. She just watched Sev rearrange her boyfriend's face with a baseball bat."

"*Ex*," Eli corrects me, as if it fucking matters.

I snort.

"What are you doing?"

"What does it look like?" I snap, indicating the feeds filling up every available inch of monitor real estate. "Someone has to make sure Maid Molly doesn't go running straight to the first fucking badge she can find."

There's a pause before he finally says, "She won't."

"No?"

"Just a feeling, but I really don't think she'll rat."

I click to expand a feed when it blinks red with an alert and find it's just Sev exiting the garage with a hatchet, a gallon of bleach, and some wire cutters. "You'll forgive me if I need a little more than your gut instinct to help me sleep tonight, Eli."

"What are you going to do if she tries to run?"

I don't answer. I don't like that he's even asking. He knows what I'll do. It's what I have to do. What I will *always* do to protect us in the ways that Sev can't.

I'm not foolish to think something like an NDA could keep her quiet.

I'd make it quick. She wouldn't even see me coming. She

wouldn't have to be any more afraid than she already is. Just one bullet to the back of the head. *Bang*. Lights out. I don't relish the idea of it. She might've been the perfect bait. The opportunity we've been waiting for to finally settle the score.

But I will always do what's best for *us*. For my family. My brothers.

"Atticus?" Eli presses, and my stomach twists.

"What does it matter? You said it yourself she won't run."

"Don't hurt her."

I may not have a choice.

"I'm serious, Atticus. I'm still fucking pissed at you for pulling that shit with my studio, and if you hurt her..."

"Then let's hope you're right, because if I am, I won't have a choice and you damn well know it, Eli."

After several long seconds, his footsteps retreat down the hall.

I lift the gun from my lap and rest my forehead against the cool barrel with a sigh. I really fucking hope he's right, but even if she doesn't run now, how can we trust her? And after what she just witnessed, how can we ever let her go?

16

PANIC ATTACKS & PASTRAMI

AURORA

I tiptoe down the hall, listening for even the smallest sounds as my bare feet leave warm hardwood and step onto the cooler tile in the kitchen. I need water. And food. And possibly a lobotomy to cure my insanity, but I can worry about that later.

I thought about going out the front first, down the steps, to the spot where I watched Seven swing a baseball bat into Jesse's head.

Is he still there? Is he alive? Is he dead?

Right now Jesse is Schrodinger's Cat, and I like him that way. As long as I don't go and look he can be both, dead *and* alive. The box can stay closed and I can stay in the dark. I can go on telling the rational and irrational thoughts in my head to shut the fuck up and focus on the things I *can* control.

I was able to make myself stop hyperventilating in the bathroom.

Now, I can make my throat less dry.

I can stop the incessant rumbling in my stomach.

And once I've raided enough food from this fridge to

last me a couple days, I can decide if running away from a house full of psychos who know my legal name is a good idea or not. That last problem is one to examine in daylight while properly hydrated with a full stomach, right?

One step at a time.

Glass bottles in the door of the fridge rattle when I open it and I hiss, slapping a hand over them to settle them back into place. They're filled with something green and separated and I'd be willing to bet my first month's salary—that I will probably *not* be getting now—that it's some disgusting green smoothie, courtesy of the control freak.

I won't be taking that. I shove some lettuce out of the way, digging toward the back to find half a liter of chocolate milk hidden there. It takes some more rooting around before I also have a chunk of what looks like good cheddar cheese and a paper-wrapped wad of meat that says *Atticus's Good Pastrami - DO NOT TOUCH* in messy permanent marker.

My mouth waters. He won't notice if a couple slices are gone.

I push my spoils into the crook of my arm and let the fridge fall shut, my smile dying on my lips when the door closes to reveal a dark shadow watching me from the opposite side.

"Fuck!"

I drop everything, and the carton bursts, spreading cold milk over my bare feet and the floor.

Seven flicks on the dim amber light beneath the stove hood and I sag with relief, until I remember. Not because I'm suddenly letting myself think about it but because he is absolutely riddled with the evidence of what happened this afternoon.

He's wearing the same leather jacket he was the night I

hit him on the road, and it doesn't look much different now than it did then. Covered in dirt and blood, except this time it's not his. There are still remnants of dried blood splatter on his cheek and when he lowers his hands, there's more black soil in the cracks of his knuckles, under his fingernails.

I swallow hard and back away a step, almost slipping on the spilled milk.

"Hungry?" he asks with a lifted brow, as if this is a perfectly normal weekday evening, and turns to wash his hands in the sink. "Give me a sec, I'll grab the mop. Didn't mean to scare you."

I step back again.

Seven peers at me over his shoulder, his gaze narrowing on my face as he finishes scrubbing the dirt from under his fingernails. "You don't need to be afraid of me, Aurora."

Shit. I have to know now. He just had to come in here—had to make me see him. The truth of what he did is written all over him in red and black and now I have to open that fucking box.

"Is he..."

My voice sounds so small.

Seven turns off the faucet and fingers an ivory cloth from a hook next to the stove to dry his hands and lean against the counter. He tosses his head to throw his dark hair away from his brow.

"Is Jesse..."

He cocks his head. "Dead?"

I nod.

Seven comes closer and I scramble to put the kitchen island between us, my heart a wild flutter in my chest. He only smirks as he holds the kitchen towel up in a wave.

CHAPTER 16

"White flag," he says in a joking tone, as if this is funny, and bends to wipe up the chocolate milk.

It's like I'm frozen in place, trying to see him over the island, needing to keep him in my sights. I shift to the right, moving back around to the side of the counter just as he finishes a lazy cleaning of my mess and tosses the soaked towel into the sink, rising to his feet.

"You didn't answer my question," I find myself saying.

Seven works his jaw, holding my stare. "Would you be upset if he was?"

Upset?

Am I upset?

Wait, am I?

My teeth clench.

Why did he have to ask that?

"Aurora?"

I shake my head. More at myself than in answer to his question because no, I am not upset. I am whatever the opposite of upset is and it's fucking terrifying.

Don't think about it.

Don't think about how you feel better. Safer. *Free.*

Think about how that makes you a terrible person instead because that's what a normal person would be feeling right now. A normal person would feel sad and angry and guilty and scared and a million other things that are not relief.

"It doesn't matter."

Seven reaches into the cupboard and fills a glass with water from the normal tap despite the fancy 'drinking water' tap being right next to it. He takes a couple long swallows before refilling it and holding it out to me. "You look thirsty."

I shake my head and he sets the glass down on the

counter with a sigh, and it dawns on me that I am standing here in this kitchen with chocolate milk getting sticky on my toes while talking to a *murderer.*

"Seven, you...you *killed* him."

He grunts in simple agreement and his silent admission makes a whole new line of realization crowd my already overcrowded thoughts. I have to throw a few out to hear the new ones, and I'm not sure anymore if I'm prioritizing correctly or throwing out the right ones.

I push a hand to the twisting ache in my stomach. "Oh god. Wait, when I told you—I didn't think you would... Holy shit—you're going to go to prison and—and your whole life is ruined now and it's all because I told you what he—"

"Hey, Aurora, stop. It's okay."

I snap back to the present moment when his hands grip me, making me look at him. Seven smells like grave dirt and leather and sin and I'm powerless against the soothing effect it has on my nervous system the instant it enters my lungs.

"No one is going to prison," he says, his blue eyes wide and warm with the amber light on them in the dark. "And my life isn't ruined. Maybe the opposite, actually."

I don't understand. "What?"

I get the feeling I'm missing a very large piece of a puzzle I didn't even realize I was trying to build, but instead of trying to find it and make it fit, I want to break all the other pieces apart instead.

Break and run.

So then why can't I move?

Why the fuck am I still here?

"This is crazy," I say through my teeth. "*You're* crazy. You just murdered my— You know what? I need to go."

CHAPTER 16

My skin itches and I'm pretty sure if I stay here with him for another second, I will spontaneously break out into hives or combust but either way it will not be nice.

And nice girls don't have mental breakdowns in front of murderers.

Seven's warm hands fall away but his voice catches me before I can move.

"Before you do, can I ask you something?"

I frown.

"What were you about to say out at the hives?"

A sneaking cold fills my arms and I shiver against the chill.

"You said 'and the amount of times I just wanted to...'"

Kill him, my brain fills in the blank, eager to please, and a sour taste fills my mouth. I snap my jaw shut.

"Okay," he says cautiously. "Then let me ask you something else. Do you feel unsafe right now?"

I almost laugh. I want him to define *unsafe*.

From him?

Or from my own mind? My own thoughts? My feelings?

By the guarded way he's watching my face for any hint of something I'm not saying, I think he wants to know if I'm afraid of *him*.

"Should I?" I ask.

"Do you?" he presses.

"No?"

"Is that a question?"

I draw in a taut breath. "No. I don't."

He bites his lower lip, tipping his head as if trying to analyse me in a different slant of light. "But you do feel something. I can see it here."

Seven lifts two fingers, pointing at the knot between my eyes.

"You're...angry?" he guesses.

Am I?

I'm not even sure I know my own name right now.

His fathomless eyes widen infinitesimally, as if he's just figured out the emotion on my face—and the reason behind it. But how could he, when I haven't even let myself think it yet?

"Aurora, tell me why you're upset."

It comes up like bile, acidic on the back of my tongue, the truth trying to claw itself free from the prison where I keep it. It might feel good to say it, and if I were going to give voice to the darkest part of my own shadow, why not offer them to the psychopath who just murdered a man and somehow seems more calm than I've seen him since we met?

He wouldn't judge me. He couldn't.

"You can tell me."

I believe him.

"It should've been me who did it," I spit, and gasp out a sob as I let myself feel it. *Remember it.*

Every time I came *this fucking close* to hurting Jesse, to *ending* him. Hovering above him when he was passed out drunk with the pillow between my white-knuckled fists, ready to press down and *hold*.

The time he left his skinning knife on his nightstand after sharpening it and I stayed up all night imagining how I might use it to hurt him while my own bruises ached from the places he hurt me.

"I almost did...so many times..."

But it wasn't just Jesse.

No.

The worst part was knowing that the dark thoughts weren't born from his cruelty. They came much earlier.

CHAPTER 16

When I was eleven and had my first abusive foster dad. He liked for me to sit on his lap in his recliner in the corner of the living room, the darkest part of the space. I wanted to hurt him, too, but I settled for taking the long cooking knife from the kitchen to the recliner until it was beyond repair.

When I was thirteen and had foster parents who starved us to the point of death and then used food as a means to get us to do whatever they wanted...I never saw what went on behind the door in the basement, but I would've if I hadn't started adding household cleaners to their favorite soda to make them sick enough that they couldn't get out of bed for months and had to give up all the kids they took in.

"I knew if I stayed there any longer, I wouldn't have been able to stop myself, and I'd be the one staring down the barrel of a life sentence right now."

My chest heats.

"It's part of why I left. After he hurt Ellie, I should've—"

My teeth are two seconds from cracking.

It would've been worth it.

"It should've been me." The certainty in my tone shakes me to my core, because I mean it. I should've killed Jesse fifty times over and I *am* angry. I'm angry that I didn't have the courage to hurt him right back and damn the consequences because some people...*some people fucking deserve it.*

Seven stares at me like he's seeing me for the first time, scoffs, and then looks away.

I open my mouth but no words come out.

He laughs hollowly, shaking his head as he brushes past me to leave the kitchen.

My stomach turns. I want to call after him, but there's a dam in my throat. It strangles me silent as my fingernails bite into my palms at his icy rejection.

He pried it out of me. I *let him* pry it out of me. What did I think was going to happen? I just showed him my true color and he was disgusted by the shade of black he found.

I blink against the burn in my eyes, mentally berating myself for being so honest. I sag against the counter, closing my eyes, knowing there is definitely no way I am going to stay here now.

"Hey."

My eyes snap open to see Seven coming back, holding something in his hand as he approaches like a cat might approach a startled mouse. I don't like the way his knowing eyes dart between mine, finding the pain I'm not fast enough to hide there.

He stops in front of me, lifting the baseball bat between his hands in offering. Confused, I look down at the battered, dirty metal and stop breathing when I see...letters. Letters scratched into the bat with something sharp. By the look of the blood in the grooves, it was scratched in before Seven ever swung it.

The vicious lines carve out a name.

AURORA.

17

LUCKY NUMBER SEVEN

AURORA

"It *was* you, Ro," Seven says as I trace a finger over the lines that spell my name as if in a dream or maybe the sweetest nightmare.

My heart is a kick drum thumping in my chest. So loud I'm not sure I've fully heard him until his words catch and my lips part on a shuddering inhale, lungs aching for air.

It was me.

In this small way, it *was* me.

Because I told Seven. I poured my truth on him and he grew into the fist of my justice.

My skin feels hot and there's a mosh pit in my stomach and when I look up at him, I find the same violent clash of emotion that I feel mirrored in his eyes.

There's still dirt on his cheek. The blood of my enemy splattered along the triple seven tattoo on his neck. And fuck if he isn't the most beautiful monster I've ever seen.

"I promised you if you stayed he wouldn't be able to hurt you anymore." His voice is low, barely more than a breath, as his cheekbones flare. "I keep my promises, Ro."

CHAPTER 17

My thighs squeeze and Seven's hot gaze travels to my lips.

Before I can second-guess it, I shove the bat from between us.

It rings against the tile when he drops it.

There's a snarl on his lips when he moves in like a shadow, crowding me against the counter, gripping the back of my neck to tip my mouth up to his. His kiss is hard, so hard it grips all of me in its electric vise, squeezing, twisting, breaking, *burning*.

"Fuck," he pants against my lips, shivering as he pulls me tight to him with a fist in the back of my shirt. When I moan, it's an animal sound in the back of my throat that he swallows, prying my lips apart to sweep in and taste me with a merciless flick of his tongue.

My breath hitches and Seven growls in response, whirling my body to press me into the solid surface of the refrigerator. I grasp for anything to hold on to, catching the door of the fridge as he runs a hand down my side.

Oh god.

"I knew," he says breathily between claiming kisses. "I knew from the moment I saw you."

His fingers catch under my thigh, hitching my leg up, opening me for him to press his cock against my core, drawing another half moan, half cry from my chest.

"I knew you were *more*."

He thrusts his erection against me through our clothes, jarring me and the refrigerator. We shift to one side and I gasp as it opens under my hand. Seven swallows that sound, too, heedless as I grip onto the shelves inside the fridge, searching for a handhold as he tangles his body with mine, worshiping me with his hands.

Condiments and other items drop, break, and splatter

as I fight for something to hold on to as Seven moves his mouth from mine to kiss a path down my throat, onto my chest. My shirt is ripped into two so he can continue his torturous descent between my breasts and down my stomach. He slows only to press two soft kisses to the bruises on the side of my rib cage. Almost sweetly. It's enough for a bubble of emotion to swell in my chest like a deranged, lustful sob.

"Never again," he mutters against my skin, so softly I barely hear him, and when he looks up at me from the space just below my belly button, I know I'm completely and utterly fucked. It hits me with the sort of terror that should only be reserved for convicts on death row, because that's what I see in his blue, blue eyes.

My own death. Wrapped in black ink, eyes studded with Hades's blue fire, lips made for sinning, and hands like branding irons as they squeeze and caress my skin.

I'm nearly beyond noticing the mess when a jar of green smoothie smashes at our feet and Seven lifts mine from the danger of being cut on the sharp glass, throwing my thighs over his shoulders as he kneels.

"The glass," I gasp. "You'll get hurt."

I feel his smirk against my lower belly and hear glass crunch under his knees as he settles in the mess and angles my hips with rough intention.

Fuck. *Fuck.*

I find a handhold on a fridge drawer just as he hooks his fingers into my soft sleep shorts and yanks them down with hurried movements.

My breaths come hot and hard. Every second he drags it out feels like a millennia and soon we'll run out of time and I'll turn to dust in his hands if he doesn't put out the flames.

"S-Seven," I stutter between breaths, shaking as he

CHAPTER 17

maneuvers my shorts and panties, pulling them from one leg entirely to hang uselessly on the other as he grins up at me from between my legs.

"That's my number, baby," he croons wickedly. "Let me show you why it's lucky."

When his gaze drops to my bare pussy, I clench my teeth. Every muscle in my body is coiled and ready, like a finger poised over a trigger, and once he pulls it...

This weapon will kill every remaining ounce of sanity I've been clawing to keep for so long I don't remember what it's like to let go.

As if he reads my mind, Seven lifts my hips high enough to feel his breath fan over me, coaxing the flames higher. "I've got you," he says. "*Let go.*"

I nod, and his expression shifts as the warmth of his mouth closes over my pussy. I moan, gripping the shelves of the refrigerator tighter, and his eyes soften and almost roll as he gets his first taste of me.

Seven drags his unholy tongue through my folds, flicking it against that spot just *there* and it's the gunshot I knew was coming, but it hits so much harder than I thought possible. The ricochet scatters reason to the wind like a buckshot and I move against him, needing his friction.

He replaces his tongue with expert fingers, rubbing me as he watches me come undone for him through hooded eyes. "So fucking wet for me, Ro. So fucking sweet."

He sucks me into his mouth again, pressing his fingers to my entrance, and there's a moment when I acknowledge that the same hands that killed a man—that killed Jesse—are about to enter me and it turns me on so fucking much that I have to wonder if I've gone insane.

But maybe I already was to begin with.

Seven pushes into me with one finger, then with two, stretching me, and it's all happening so fast.

It's crazy. Chaotic. Completely out of control in a way that I am utterly powerless to stop as he fucking *groans* against my pussy, the vibration of the sound rolling over me like a tidal wave that leaves goosebumps in the wake of its destruction.

I'm caught in his undertow, and drowning, I think, doesn't sound like the worst way to go.

He pushes in a third finger and before I know it, I'm there. Gasping for air. *I can't fucking breathe.*

I can't think of anything but the orgasm ripping through me as I tremble and cry out, coming so hard the edges of my vision black out and every muscle locks.

Seven continues to fuck me with his fingers and tongue through the release, and I squeeze around him, spasming against the fullness of his three digits inside of me. When he pulls away, he licks his lips before swiping the back of a hand over his mouth.

"You're so fucking pretty when you come."

My core tightens as he shifts, hands gripping my ass to hold me up as he rises from the floor and pulls my legs around his waist and buries his face into the crook of my neck, breathing me in.

"Tell me I can fuck you," he says, his voice hot and husky against my neck, more of a demand than a question, but he could ask me for anything right now and I'd be powerless to say no.

"Please." He punctuates the word with a thrust of his hips, making me feel him against my dripping core.

I moan. "Yes."

Seven lifts me infinitesimally higher. High enough so that my ass is able to rest on the shelf inside the fridge as he

CHAPTER 17

unzips his jeans with frenzied motions, pulling himself out. My mouth waters when I see him. Thick and long, cut with a vein that I desperately want to trace with my tongue.

He gives himself a firm stroke before grabbing my hand to drag it between us, replacing his hand with mine, guiding my fingers to stroke him until he's shivering beneath our joined touch.

I slip my thumb over his wide tip, gathering the perfect bead of precum there to rub onto his underside in tight little circles as he starts to thrust into my hand. He grows impossibly bigger, even harder as he throws his head back and steps forward, tipping his hips to line himself up with my pussy.

A strangled sound I don't recognize comes from my own chest as he nudges my entrance and I take in every inch of him between us, finding ink over his base that spreads up to where his Adonis belt disappears beneath his shirt.

He's *much* bigger than any man I've ever had, but it doesn't scare me. It's a challenge, and I fucking accept.

I angle my hips, pressing against him enough that his tip dips into my warmth and even that pressure is enough to unravel me all over again.

I growl as I yank him to me, taking what I want from him this time, tasting myself on his lips as he deepens the kiss and thrusts into me. The pain brings everything into startling clarity. Makes it real. So vividly real that I scream into his mouth.

Seven doesn't give me time to adjust, I don't think he can. His fevered kiss and labored breathing and the way his muscles are tight and shuddering where my hands press against him tell me he's lost in me just as much as I'm lost in him and it makes me feral for more.

He uses me as an anchor with one hand on my hip and the other clutched around my shoulder, pushing me onto him as he shifts back and slams harder into me with a primal sound in the back of his throat.

The fridge rattles and shakes, more items cascading onto the floor as he fucks me, each thrust coming faster than the last, harder as he slams his hilt against me. He's doing something I'm not used to. With each thrust is a slight flick and roll, his hilt hitting my clit in the perfect punishing rhythm to make me come.

I've *never* come from a cock alone. Didn't think it was possible. But when my orgasm builds, I chase it, thinking about how good he feels. Not just his cock, but *him*. The connection between us is bright. Completely electric in its intensity.

This man killed for me. He walked right into my nightmare and murdered my demon.

He barely knows me, but he heard my story and he decided that my enemy shouldn't get to keep breathing and he *did* something about it. He kept his promise. And that deranged part of me that stayed when I needed to throw out my crowded thoughts wants to show him how grateful I am.

The fridge smashes against the wall and the counters, clanking like it might come apart as he fucks me into it.

"You're so fucking tight."

When he pulls back to look into my eyes, I show him how close I am and his face goes beautifully, tragically taut. His full lips part and his brows draw together, but he doesn't stop. "That's it, Ro. I need you to come on my cock. Please. I need to feel it. I need to—"

He cuts himself off with another groan that comes out through his clenched teeth.

CHAPTER 17

Oh my god, he's going to come.

My face flushes hot and I explode on his cock.

"*Fuck.*"

Seven's lips trap mine in a brutal kiss as he fucks me through my orgasm, denying himself as long as he can. The sensation races through my body like a thousand hands squeezing and twisting and pulling in a symphony that is equal parts pleasure and pain until I'm crying at its intensity.

Seven gasps out a strangled sound against my mouth and pulls out, fisting his cock as if strangling it when his hot cum spurts onto my belly. This time when our lips part, he drops his forehead to mine and our quick breaths mingle in the air as he runs a thumb along my jaw. I taste the salty tang of his seed as the warm digit runs down the middle of my lips and I suck it inside, wanting to get a better taste.

He sighs, resting his forearms on either side of my head against the shelves like he isn't ready to move away just yet. When he speaks, his voice is a sultry whisper against my neck and I can feel his smile in the words. "I'm so fucking glad you hit me with your car, Aurora Bellerose."

18

WHAT A FUCKING MESS

ATTICUS

Seven's back already? It's barely one in the morning.

I click to zoom into the camera feed, watching Sev come in the back door.

He couldn't have gone very far to get rid of the body if he's finished already.

Unless he half-assed it. *Again.*

I take another swig of the power smoothie on the desk, checking the rest of the cameras. I haven't seen Aurora try to leave at all and she's only touched her phone a total of three times.

Once to google the symptoms of shock.

Once to google if it's illegal to know about a crime and not report it.

And once to type out a message to someone named Chris asking if her room is still free, only to erase it before sending.

I make a mental note to watch communications with 'Chris' since it seems she's deleted the majority of the chat history and I can't get it back.

Surprisingly, there have been no attempts to call the

CHAPTER 18

authorities. The Wi-Fi calling feature would allow it if she tried, which is why I need to be diligent. They wouldn't be able to triangulate the call, but I'd need to cut it off before she could say anything that might lead them to look for us.

The local PD is in our pocket, but I don't need any bigger fish biting at the bait of a mysterious untraceable call from a frantic girl squawking about murder.

I push away from the desk and tuck my M18 into the back of my waistband before going to meet Sev. If that corpse is anywhere on the property or in the surrounding area, he can damn well go dig the fucker back up and plant him somewhere else.

We said no more corpses within a fifty-mile radius after the other night and we all fucking agreed.

I stop dead when Aurora comes around the corner into the kitchen, tucking myself back into the shadows of the hallway, careful not to make a sound as I watch her.

She digs around in the fridge, tension in the way her shoulders are hitched high and the way she jumps every time she makes a sound.

First she pulls out the carton of chocolate milk Sev thought he was hiding from me in the back of the fridge, then...

Is that my fucking pastrami?

The almost ninja level silence of Sev's footsteps reaches my ears and I realize Aurora hasn't heard him.

I open my mouth to say something before she can be surprised, but think better of it.

This is better. I need to see how she's going to react.

Carefully, I tug the M18 from my waistband and check that there's a round in the chamber.

The kitchen is the last place I want to do this, but if she completely loses it...

It'll be best to just get it over with.

Aurora gasps when she finally sees Sev, and I grimace when the offensive sound of the carton hitting the tile and milk splattering all over my freshly cleaned floor reaches my ears.

I wait for the inevitable scream. For her fight-or-flight response to kick in. I'm genuinely curious which it will be.

But seconds pass, and she does neither.

Their hushed conversation is too low for me to hear more than a few words, but it seems more or less calm.

Surprised, I peer around the corner to see them just... talking. Even if Aurora is trying to keep the kitchen island between them as Sev grabs the clean white kitchen towel from the hook, waves it around, and bends to sop up the spilled...

Seriously?

I turn on my heel, not even trying to be quiet as I stalk back to my office before I can lose my shit.

"There is a fucking *arsenal* of cleaning supplies and disposable cloths under the sink, but no, you just have to use the white fucking towel," I mutter to myself, tucking back into my office with a heavy sigh.

I swear it's like he wants to piss me off lately.

I sit down hard at my desk and shut my eyes, steepling my fingers against my lips while I take in several calming breaths, consoling myself with the fact that Aurora seemed more or less all right.

But that's fucking weird, isn't it?

My eyes flick open and my fingers fly over the keyboard, ready to do another deep dive into her phone's history. There has to be more there for me to find. If I could just get my hands on all her deleted chat history, that could give me some insight.

CHAPTER 18

Why delete it to begin with?

It isn't just her conversation with 'Chris'. There's evidence of deleted messages in most of her text conversations.

Who does that?

People who have something to hide.

I'm just about to run another ghost bot through her messenger to try to spook out anything recently deleted, when a metallic *clang* rings through the main floor of the cabin. I shoot to my feet and race to the door, but don't rush out, pausing to listen first instead.

Part of me wants to see if Sev will handle this without me.

He handles any threat against us with unwavering, unflinching action. It's so ingrained that it's a reflex for him. One we've been trying to temper.

But with her...

He's different.

She's not some asshole bent on hurting us. She's just a girl. A girl with trauma scars that might be a close match to his own. Someone who's been hurt and needs protecting.

He wouldn't have killed her ex if he didn't care about her.

And that's a terrifying thought.

The gun in my waistband feels hot against my back. Heavy.

I reach for the door handle and hear a new sound, one that makes me freeze.

Was that a *moan?*

As quietly as I can, I twist the handle, opening the door just an inch. Enough to better hear what's happening way down the hall.

What a fucking mess

Glass shatters and I almost rush in, but stop. There it is again. That sound.

Aurora moans loudly and there's a rattle and a *bang*.

No fucking way.

I listen harder, and hear her cry out. Not in pain. No, definitely not in pain.

The sound of shattering glass punctuates her next cry of pleasure and I clench my teeth so tight they squeak from the pressure.

What the *fuck*, Sev?

My skin heats, itching as I clench my fists, and my knuckles pop.

I told him. I fucking told him I had a plan for her.

And he goes and kills her ex and fucks her in the same twelve-hour span.

Something slams loud enough to echo down the hall. It slams again.

More glass breaks.

The rhythmic rattle and *smash* of something being rammed into the wall again and again and again has me pacing the small space inside my office, breathing smoke and spitting fire.

Fuck.

"*Fuck.*"

My dick responds to her next moan and that's fucking *it*. I will not allow myself to be attracted to this girl.

She chokes on another moan and I imagine those pouty lips parting, her eyelids lowering over crystalline green eyes.

I grip the edge of the door, ready to wrench it open and break up what's happening in my fucking kitchen, but I can't.

I can't go rushing in there because despite the very

rational part of my brain that's screaming *hell no*, my dick is now harder than stone. Growling to myself, I jerk my hand free of the door and curl it into a fist, breathing through clenched teeth.

Come on, get it together.

I grip my erection roughly, but that only makes it worse and I snatch my hand away as if burned.

"Okay. You got this. Fucking get rid of it."

My hands go to my head, as if I can slap some sense back into myself, but all I manage to do is tear some loose hair free from where it's tied back as I curse under my breath.

I recall my training. The rigorous bullshit I put my body and mind through when Florence finally passed away and I couldn't stand to be in the house where she still haunted the halls. Where I could see the ghost of her in Julian's eyes as he taught me how to read blueprints. In Sev as he self-destructed. And in Eli who didn't do anything but paint for months, throwing himself into his work to cover up her loss.

Florence's last words to me fill my head, bringing clarity I desperately need.

"I'm so glad they have you, Atty. I know you'll take care of them. I know you'll do whatever it takes to keep them safe."

When I became an absolute menace, high-strung with anger and control issues that I couldn't temper, it was Eli who suggested I put the energy into something useful before I drove myself mad. And since I'd just completed my certificates in cybersecurity and digital forensics to better help Julian with the family trade, I made the perfect candidate to work in intel for the Marines.

The training was grueling. The rules strict. The sense of

What a fucking mess

structure, no matter how hardcore, gave me back at least partial control of my mind.

Remember. Your. Training.

Already, the need starts to abate.

With a gun in my hands and my boots on the ground, I learned quickly that it wasn't about the weapon or the armor, but the man. It's all a mindfuck and if I was able to find my way through it from inside, I could get through anything.

I could *do* anything.

Even come home after a tour in Iran and face the worst.

Breathing to a count of nine, slow and measured, the tension in my chest eases, but the tension *elsewhere* winds tighter and starts to ache, bringing the rage right back to the forefront just in time for the song of Sev and Aurora's fuckfest to hit its crescendo.

Motherfuckers.

I wrench the door open and storm down the hall, holding on to that rage because if it slips for even a second, I know what will try to replace it and I'm not sure I can deal with the problem twice.

Sev's body blocks most of Aurora's from view, but only because she's *inside the motherfucking refrigerator.*

A puddle of god knows what combination of fridge contents, slowly spreads over the tile in a flood of horrific green-brown, interrupted by sparkling bits of broken glass and floating peas.

Aurora gasps when she sees me, but Sev doesn't so much as flinch, turning his head just enough to peer over his shoulder at me with a maniacal grin. "Hey, Atty. Hope you didn't want a snack."

Aurora's eyes widen over Sev's shoulder, her lips press

CHAPTER 18

tight, and I'm confused by the look on her face until it turns red and she lets out a stifled sound that turns into a laugh.

She's...laughing?

"*Sev*," his name comes out in a lethal hiss as Aurora continues to laugh, dropping her head against Sev's shoulder to hide her face. She tries and fails to contain the sound that's starting to border on madness.

"You good, Ro?"

Aurora nods against his shoulder, still shaking with the spasms of her laughter.

"Sev," I repeat. "A fucking word?"

"Right. Yeah. Give us a sec?"

"Now."

"I heard you, man," he snaps back, and I don't fucking like his tone. It softens as he whispers something to Aurora, carrying her over the broken glass to the safety of the hardwood beyond their blast radius.

"Okay, crazy-pants, you go have a nice long shower," he tells her as he sets her down. "I'll take care of this."

Aurora can't get away fast enough, clinging to the scraps of her shirt as if they are doing anything to cover her perky tits or the bouncing peach of her ass as she sprints from the kitchen.

Sev turns to face me, pulling his jeans up as if he's completely unaffected by the fact that they are absolutely *disgusting*. "If this is about the mess, I'll clean it up."

I stoop to pick up my pastrami from the floor and it drips with green smoothie, the red paper wrapping disintegrating until it falls back onto the floor and splashes fucking pig slop onto my socked feet.

"Fucking Christ, Sev. What the hell were you thinking?"

His violent blue eyes narrow. "Me?"

What a fucking mess

"Yeah, you, asshole. We don't even fucking know this girl. We can't trust her. And here you are acting like...like..."

"Like what, Atticus? Fucking say it."

Heat rushes up my back. "Do you have feelings for this girl, Sev?"

"And if I do?"

I lower my voice. "Then I'd fucking remind you that she is *part of a plan*—"

"What fucking plan?" He pushes back from the island and stands taller, reminding me that beneath his very human exterior, Sev is a hand grenade one finger pull away from detonation.

And he's aiming his wrath at me...*because of her.*

I scoff, shaking my head at him. He's never been like this with the other women we've brought in. He's never been this agitated on anyone else's behalf except for ours.

"I never should've brought her here." I say the words under my breath, but he hears me, and stiffens.

"Too late for that, bro."

A muscle in my jaw tics as he roughly pulls several bottles of cleaning spray and the disposable cloths from beneath the sink and slams them onto the counter.

Dammit.

I am not handling this well. I open my mouth to try to change tack, hating how his energy is diluting my rage.

Shoving a loose strand of hair back from my face, I sigh. "Sev, I just mean that—"

"Unless you want to grab a mop and help me, I suggest you get the fuck out of my face."

19

AM I MISSING SOMETHING?

ELIJAH

"This feels wrong."

Atticus leans with his forearm against the fireplace mantle in the living room, rubbing his thumb with his first two fingers like he found some offensive dust there. Seven's music blares through his headphones from where he sits in the biggest chair across from me, tapping his fingers against the armrest to the violent beat.

"Doesn't this feel, like, intervention-y?" I try again, wanting to chuck the paperweight on the table next to me at Atty's head but abstaining because he didn't kill Aurora last night.

She didn't try to leave, but knowing Atticus, he would've considered every possible scenario and came up with exactly none that didn't end with some kind of risk to our safety if he let her live. But still, he allowed it.

So either she's slowly crawling under his skin, like she's started to burrow beneath mine—unlikely—or he listened to me for once.

I lean over my knees, massaging the tension out of my hand. "Maybe I could just go up there and talk to her first?

CHAPTER 19

She isn't going to like coming out of her room right after waking up to find all three of us waiting for her here in the living room at the bottom of the stairs. We've scared her enough in the handful of days she's been here, already."

"We can't just leave this untouched, Eli. She's a liability."

His dark brown eyes slide to Seven for the fourth time since he entered the room, narrowing like he holds Seven personally responsible for all of this. And I mean, that's fair, but also if Aurora's douchebag of an ex-boyfriend hadn't come here ranting and raving and just let her go like he should've, it wouldn't have happened.

I'd say it's fifty-fifty. Both the douche's fault and Seven's.

I still don't know what Jesse did to have Sev want to bash his brains in but if Sev said the guy deserved it, I have to believe he did. He doesn't kill people for nothing.

It means that Aurora must've told him enough for him to feel the need to keep her safe. Which is new.

The women we used to share before everything happened had all been pretty, but Sev never cared to learn any more about them aside from how far they'd let him push his cock down their throats or whether or not they'd be opposed to a little primal play out on the property after dark.

When we hear Aurora's door open upstairs, Atticus moves to the seat next to Seven's and Sev cuts his music, pulling his headphones down to rest on his neck.

I'm up in an instant, straightening my button-down shirt and shoving my hands deep in the pockets of my jeans as Ellie's paws click down the stairs and Aurora's soft footfalls follow.

She freezes in place when she hits the bottom step and

sees me, her eyes flicking to Seven and Atticus behind me as her throat bobs.

"Good morning." I try for some normalcy, but my own voice sounds ridiculous to my ears.

Idiot.

Good morning?

What the hell else are you supposed to say? 'I'm sorry Seven killed your shitty ex. Are you planning to go to the cops or are we cool?'

Jesus.

"Uh…" she stutters as Ellie rushes over to push her wet nose against my hand. I give the pup a small pat before she makes a beeline straight for Seven, going up on her hind legs to lay her upper body on his lap with a bark.

"Good morning to you, too, pretty girl," he croons, roughing up the fur around her face.

"Sorry," Aurora says, sidestepping the living room to head for the front door. "I was just— Ellie needs to, um— Ellie, come on, girl. Let's go pee."

Ellie obediently jumps from Seven's lap, bounding to the front door just as Aurora opens it.

"Hold up," Atticus says. "We need to talk. Can you have a seat?"

Aurora's grip on the door turns viselike as she slowly pushes it closed after Ellie is through. She's getting paler by the second, and she seems to be purposefully avoiding looking at Seven. He must've really freaked her out.

She's probably still in shock.

And we're ambushing her.

"Maybe this can wait." I cut a look toward Atticus, but he isn't having it.

"No. We need to address the obvious…*concerns*."

"Do we, though?" Seven asks, and the way he's looking

at Aurora, like this is all one big joke, makes me want to punch him. "You're good, right, Ro?"

Ro?

When she finally looks at him, he winks at her.

I slap the back of his head. "Seriously, man?"

"Dude, what the fuck?"

"Be a little more apologetic?"

"For what? Taking out the trash?"

"Seven," Atticus warns.

My chest heats, but the fire fizzles out quickly. She doesn't need to see us arguing right now.

Stay calm.

Stay calm.

"Look, we know what happened yesterday might've been..." I can't think of the right word.

"Let's just cut to the chase," Atticus finishes for me. "We need to know if you're going to go blabbing about what happened to the first uniformed fuckhead you can find."

Her lips part in surprise. "How do you know I haven't already called the police?"

I wince, but Atticus only smiles at her. It isn't a nice smile. It shows all his teeth, and she sees it for the threat it is. I wonder if she has any idea that he knows exactly what she does and doesn't do on her phone.

He probably disabled her location services and her ability to make outgoing calls the instant he went back into the house.

"She won't," Seven says.

"I wasn't talking to you," Atticus growls.

"Come on, man. I cleaned up my messes—both of them—you should be giving me a gold fucking star."

Atticus's jaw flexes. "And the fridge? It's completely fucked. The door doesn't even shut properly now. Why don't you tell Eli what you got up to last night after burying your sins, Sev?"

Aurora goes impossibly red and her eyes drop like stones to the floor, and I am *definitely* missing something.

What the hell happened last night?

I squint at Seven. "What's going on? What did you do to the fridge?"

"Nothing, I might have just broke it a little when I was grabbing a midnight *snack*."

"Um, can I just ask one thing?" Aurora blurts, her arms stiff at her sides.

"Of course you can," I rush to say, not realizing I've started to move closer to her until she backs away a small step. It feels like a slap.

"Are you going to kill me?"

I remember Atticus in his office last night. The gun in his lap he was trying so hard to hide from me. I swallow. "Why would you think that?"

Her eyes dart between me and Atticus, avoiding Seven even though he scoffs at her question as if personally offended.

"Well, you guys are—what? Mafia or something? Isn't that what the mafia does with loose ends?"

"We aren't mafia."

"Why does everyone always think that?" Seven adds.

"Serial killers, then?"

Now it's my turn to smile. "No. We aren't serial killers."

"Depends on your definition," Seven corrects while picking something from his teeth, and Atticus kicks his chair.

He pushes to his feet and stretches. "Are we almost done here? We have plans."

"What the hell are you talking about?" Atticus sighs.

CHAPTER 19

"Eli owes Ro an apology and he already made an appointment with Céline for her hair."

Fuck, I forgot. I did manage to get Céline to agree to the last-minute slot for Aurora.

She raises her brows and I hold my hands up. "If you're not up to it, I can cancel," I offer. "We can take you another day."

She blinks. "This is the weirdest morning I've ever had. Is no one worried about the fact that he just killed someone?"

Atticus and I share a look.

Atticus shrugs first and I wonder if he picks up on the fact that she's asking if *we* are worried about it when actually, she doesn't seem all that worried or sad about it at all.

I suppose if the person responsible for what happened to me were to meet the business end of Seven's bat, I wouldn't exactly be upset about it, either. Only angry that he didn't suffer more.

"What about the fact that people could come looking for him? And what if he told someone where he was going?"

Atticus sucks his teeth. "Already dealt with. But if you think someone's coming, a little heads-up might be nice."

"He has friends who might."

"Are they anything like him?" Sev asks.

She nods. "Some are worse."

"Sounds like a party."

God help us.

"So," Sev claps his hands together. "Should we get going? It's a long way to the salon."

Aurora gapes at him and it takes her a full five seconds before she can force out a response. "Um. You know what, I'm a little tired, maybe we could go another—"

"You can sleep on the way," Seven offers.

"We aren't done talking here."

Seven crosses the room and takes Aurora's hand in his. "Sure we are."

She lets him lead her to the door and when he kicks her sandals over to her, she slips her feet into them with her bottom lip caught between her teeth and *yeah,* I am definitely missing something.

Something similar to jealousy twists in my gut.

She still hasn't pulled away from him. She's still holding his hand.

Did they…

No way.

"Wait, what about Ellie?" Aurora says, taking the sweater Seven offers her but not putting it on. "Can we bring her?"

"It's really far," Sev says. "Better if she stays. Atty will watch her, won't you?"

"No, I will n—"

"Great, that's settled," I interrupt him, clapping a hand on his shoulder, eager to get out of here before Aurora changes her mind. A quick trip to one of the best places on earth may be exactly what she needs, and I want to give it to her.

"Thanks, man," I add pointedly, squeezing his shoulder.

I'll get Sev to explain to me what I missed on the plane, but whatever it is, I'm guessing it's the reason she's not hyperventilating or calling the cops. Which means it's a good thing, right?

Besides, this way I get to make up for being a giant asshole the other day.

"I really don't want to leave Ellie," Aurora pushes. "If you don't have time to—"

"It's fine," Atticus says through gritted teeth, giving me

a look that says this better make us square. "I'll feed her and play fetch or whatever."

If he thinks watching her dog is enough to make anything even remotely square between us, he's mistaken, but it's a start.

"Do you have the black card?" I ask.

His lips press into a flat line, but he pulls out his wallet, fingering the glossy black metal card from the first slot.

When I go to take it, he doesn't let it go, instead leaning in and lowering his voice. "You keep your eyes on her at all times. Hear me? Ambrose has a lot of contacts in the city. Stay out of the art district and come right back after the salon."

I flinch at the mention of his name.

"I said I'd take her shopping, too."

"You can just take her shopping in Boone."

The disgust must show on my face. As if I would subject her to the likes of Old Navy or TJ Maxx. No. This is a proper apology and it comes with a proper apology budget and a higher thread count than fucking *two*.

He lets me pluck the card from his hands. "You could come with us if you're so worried."

"Fuck no. I have better things to do than watch her spend our money."

I can't think of anything right now that would make me happier, but to each their own.

"Like what?"

"Like playing fetch, apparently."

I hear Seven and Aurora talking in hushed tones by the door and decide I'm done waiting for him to tell me exactly what he wants that involves this girl.

"When we get back, I want to know what you're planning with her."

Am I missing something?

I need to decide if I'm willing to be involved in it. There isn't much I wouldn't do to destroy the man who almost destroyed us, but I'm not sure I'm down with using this girl anymore.

"Yeah," he agrees. "When you get back."

"Try to relax a little," I tell him. "You'll get wrinkles."

I rush to catch up with Sev and Aurora at the door and this time she doesn't flinch when I come near. She smirks when I lean down to whisper conspiratorially in her ear, "Let's find out if this has a limit."

Feeling more playful than I have in months, I slip the black card into her hand. Her mouth opens in a little 'O' and something stirs in my chest. Something I thought I lost in captivity.

"Are you bribing me?" she asks.

"Is it working?"

She lets out a small, nervous laugh that I immediately want to hear again. "I guess that depends on what the limit is."

20

DUCK, DUCK, GO

AURORA

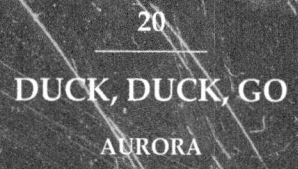

I stoop to pet Ellie, whispering to her to behave for Atticus while Seven brings the car around.

"You sure Atticus will be okay with her while we're out?"

I'm still not sure I'm comfortable with it.

Elijah smirks down at me and Ellie. "Yeah, he'll be fine. Don't tell him I said so, but I think he secretly loves dogs. Animals in general, actually. Not the messes they make, but..." He shrugs. "I'm willing to bet he'll have her doing some kind of new trick by the time we're back and I can guarantee she'll be the best fed dog in the state. He takes any kind of responsibility obscenely serious."

"I can see that," I agree, thinking about Atticus's general demeanor and the way he seems to need to be in control of the situation at all times, even if it's just cooking breakfast.

Elijah gives me a strange, questioning look and a lump forms in my throat.

Please don't ask about last night.
Please don't ask about last night.

CHAPTER 20

Please. Please. Please.

He parts his lips to speak, but is interrupted when a gunmetal gray Jeep crunches over the cobblestone, speeding around from the garage to the front drive.

"Oh! I forgot to ask about your other car," I say, quick to try to bring up something else to talk about. Literally *anything* else. "I hope the repairs on it weren't too bad. I could use some of my first salary to—"

"It's fine," Elijah interrupts me. "It was—uh—a rental, actually. We returned it and paid for the damages already. It wasn't that bad."

"Oh."

The driver's side window rolls down and Seven rests his arm on the frame, leaning out with a mischievous look on his face that makes my belly flip and my cheeks heat until I'm sure I can't hold his gaze for another second without bursting into flames.

"We going or what?"

I swallow, pressing one last kiss to Ellie's head. "You be good," I tell her again. "Stay."

Seven slaps the side of the Jeep and I hurry to catch up to Elijah as he holds the passenger door open and looks at me expectantly.

"Oh, that's okay. You can have the front," I offer, but he only shakes his head and sweeps his arm dramatically.

"Today is about you. I insist."

I chew on the inside of my cheek, finding Seven waiting with his lower lip between his teeth as he revs the engine and pats the seat next to him.

"Don't worry, Ro. I'll take it slow."

The way he says it drips with innuendo, and my core tightens as I slip into the seat and buckle in before I can make this any more awkward than I already have.

Duck, duck, go

If Elijah still doesn't know what happened last night, a couple more comments like that and he'll be able to guess on the first try.

I don't notice the ducks until the seat belt clicks audibly into place and Elijah slips into the back seat behind me.

The entire dash is filled with little rubber ducks squatting in a neat line from one end to the other. Ducks that look like pandas. Ducks with aviator sunglasses and crowns and visors and cowboy hats.

"Um?"

I reach out to pick up the one directly in front of me, but it's fused to the dash with some kind of sticky silicone. When I slide my questioning gaze to Seven, he's grinning at me broadly. "Sick, right? I've been trading ducks for years and these are the cream of the crop."

Now that he says it, I think I have heard something to do with Jeep people and ducks before but I've never actually seen it with my own eyes.

"They're...cute."

Elijah lets out a soft chuckle from the back seat and Seven shakes his head, giving him a glare without any real bite to it through the rearview.

"It could be worse," he says as he pulls away from the house and jams the button on the stereo to connect with the Bluetooth on his phone. "I could collect teeth. Or bones."

"You *have* done that."

"Well, I don't anymore. Now it's ducks."

"A vast improvement."

A strange smile worms its way onto my lips as my brow wrinkles. They can't be serious, can they?

"This one's my favorite," Seven says, indicating a duck

with a bandana covering most of its face, a black cowboy hat, and an old-fashioned pistol.

I look over the rest and smirk. "Mine, too."

The first notes of one of my favorite songs filters into the cabin and my lips part. "You listen to Sleep Token?"

"So do you," he says in answer, and snorts when I look at him in confusion. "It was playing in your car when you hit me."

I flinch and he reaches over to pat my thigh. "All is forgiven, Ro."

"Do you mind if I turn it up?"

He presses a button on the steering wheel to turn it up before I can, filling the Jeep with "Jaws" as we pull out onto the main road. I let the music bring me a sense of calm, feeling the tension in my shoulders ease and my restless legs release into the cushioned seat as one song shifts into another I like, and then another I've never heard but immediately love by someone called Livingston.

Taking in the remote mountainous scenery, I sigh and it quickly turns into a yawn.

"We're almost there. Don't fall asleep yet," Elijah says from the back seat.

I turn to face him. "I thought you said it was pretty far."

We've barely been driving for twenty minutes.

His eyes crinkle when he smiles. "It is."

He looks past me out the windshield and when I twist back around in the seat, we're turning onto a narrow road with a tall chain-link fence running along it. On the other side is an open space with long paved roads and a large building at one end.

Hangar, my mind supplies.

It's a hangar.

There's sunlight glinting off a small plane just outside of it.

"Surprise," Seven says, lifting his brows playfully.

My heart slams in my chest. "You can't be serious?"

"*Dead* serious."

"Especially about good fashion and even better hairstyling," Elijah agrees. "Did you think we'd take you to the nearest Great Clips and have a quick shop at TJ Maxx?"

I blink and Elijah makes a show of looking hurt. I get the feeling he's trying really hard to make this easy for me. To make it *normal*. Unlike Seven and Atticus, Elijah seems genuinely worried—not about my going to the cops or anything like that—but about *me*.

I can see it in his eyes, how he's waiting for me to snap. To break down and start screaming and begging for them to let me go. And I remember that he doesn't know about my past. Where I came from. What I've been through. Not like Seven does. And even he has only scratched the surface. I'm no stranger to fucked-up shit.

"Please don't tell me you're afraid to fly," Seven says, and for a fleeting second I find real concern in his eyes and I think if I said yes, he would turn the car around right here and now, and it makes my throat burn just thinking it would be that simple.

"No," I answer finally. "I'm not, but this is insanely excessive for a hair appointment."

"If it makes you feel any better, Sev left his jacket in Amsterdam this one time and made us all turn around *midflight* to go back and get it."

"And Céline is the only person any of us trust enough to let near our throat with a straight razor."

"You did say you're not mafia, right?"

CHAPTER 20

Elijah laughs, but I'm serious. "If not that, then what is it that you do, exactly?"

"If we told you that," Seven says, his voice low and husky as we pull through the main gates and drive toward the plane. "We'd have to kill you."

"Seven," Elijah hisses, and I wait for the jolt of panic that should come, but it doesn't.

"He didn't mean that," Elijah rushes to say as Seven puts the car into park.

Seven doesn't agree with him, but the way he tosses me a wink before stepping out of the Jeep makes it almost impossible to stop the surprised smile from tugging at my lips.

"Let's go!" Seven calls, whistling in greeting to the guy carrying a briefcase onto the private plane who has to be the pilot.

Elijah opens my door for me and extends a hand to help me out. This time, I take it.

"Where are we going?"

"Do you want to ruin the surprise?"

I'm not sure I can take any more surprises and Elijah seems to see that written on my face.

"It's okay, I can tell you. We're going—"

"No," I rush to say, sensing his disappointment. "It's okay. I do like surprises. Or, at least, I'd like to like them."

He gives me a sad smile and his grip on my hand tightens just a little as if to say he understands before he lets it go. "If you change your mind, let me know. I'll even show you the flight path."

I console myself with the fact that we can't be going too far since I don't have my passport with me, and last I checked you need that to enter another country.

Duck, duck, go

I let him lead me to the short set of stairs where Seven is already waiting at the top.

"This is crazy."

I don't realize I've said it out loud until Seven chuckles, and says, "If you think this is crazy, you ain't seen nothing yet."

21

FEAR OF FLYING

AURORA

"Everything set?" Elijah asks Seven as we board the plane, and the stairway starts to close up behind us with a metallic whir.

"Yeah. All set."

It smells like clean leather and opulence and that's exactly what I find as a panel slides open to reveal the cabin. Plush cream-colored leather seats with endless leg room. Soft lighting and an even softer carpet. There's an actual *couch* and a flat-screen TV in the back. It's like a mini living room. If there weren't seat belts on the seats, I could almost believe I just walked into someone's million-dollar tiny home.

"We're behind schedule," Seven says. "Want to grab a seat? It's just for takeoff, then you can move around."

Seven takes the first seat, closest to the front. There's a chair across from him, but when Elijah takes the one on the opposite side of the walkway, I pick up on his tension. How his fingers fumble with the belt. His whole vibe is just...*off*, and I realize that even though *I'm* not afraid to fly, Elijah definitely is.

CHAPTER 21

"You good, bro?" Seven asks him, confirming my suspicion, and even though Elijah makes a show of smiling and waving him off, I can tell it's mostly for my benefit. He's trying not to make it a big deal.

I slide into the seat opposite Elijah. "*Sooo*," I say, elongating the word. "Why take me somewhere we need a plane to get to if you're afraid of flying?"

"It's just takeoff and landing," he says.

Sev scoffs.

"It's *mostly* just takeoff and landing," Elijah laments.

Is he blushing?

His Adam's apple bobs as the pilot says to prepare for takeoff and the plane starts to move.

"It's a pretty rational fear," I offer. "Better than being afraid of bugs or snakes. Most aren't even venomous."

Elijah pushes his dark chestnut hair from his face and smiles tightly as the plane turns onto what I assume is the runway and stops as the engines prepare for takeoff.

"Any...other fears?"

"Too many," I admit. "What about you? Anything besides planes?"

His white-knuckle grip on the armrests tightens as we start to move fast and my stomach hollows.

"Elijah?"

He licks his lips, blinking, trying to think through the panic in every tense line of his face.

"Cages," he blurts as the wheels race over the runway and the nose of the plane tips up to touch the sky. "Being... locked in. Not being able to get out."

In my periphery, Seven shifts in his seat and his jaw tightens, making me wonder if there's something more to Elijah's answer than what it appears on the surface.

Fear of flying

I make myself pull my focus back to Elijah as we lift into the sky.

"Want to hear something really stupid?"

He nods, closing his eyes tight.

"When I was a kid, I was afraid of bathtub drains."

His eyes pop open. "What?"

"Yeah. One of my foster brothers told me that there were snakes that lived in the drains and if the water didn't go down fast enough that they'd be able to slither right up and get me before I could get out of the tub."

"No," he says, horrified. "That's so mean. How old were you?"

I shrug. "I don't know. Maybe, like, five or six. But don't worry, the jerk got what he deserved."

"Oh yeah?"

I nod.

The plane levels out and when Elijah sighs, my job is done. At least for now.

"Thanks," he says softly after a minute. "For um..."

"Distracting you?"

"Yeah. That."

"Anytime."

The seat belt light overhead turns off and I unbuckle immediately because much like Elijah, I don't like the feeling of being trapped in one spot. Seven does the same and heads for the couch, lifting a remote from a console in the arm to flick it on.

"Want to watch something? There's Netflix."

It's strange, I swear I was dead tired thirty minutes ago, but now I'm not sure I could sleep even if I tried to.

"Sure."

I join him on the couch, making sure to keep a natural distance between us that Seven immediately notices, but

CHAPTER 21

thankfully, he only lifts a curious brow and says nothing. It was awkward enough this morning with Atticus. I don't know why I didn't think about being overheard last night. But it was probably because I was too busy being railed into Atticus's good pastrami to care.

When Seven holds out the remote to me, I take it, watching the big red N light up the screen.

"Do you want to join us?" I ask Elijah.

"Good luck with that," Seven says before he can reply, but he eats his words when Elijah's belt clicks off and he rises unsteadily to his feet.

I take it Elijah doesn't usually leave his seat after takeoff and I grin at him as he carefully crosses the floor and gingerly folds himself onto the cushion next to me.

"What are we watching?"

"Oh! You said you've never seen *Stranger Things*, right?" I ask Seven, but I remember him saying that. "Want to try it? It's really good."

"Sure."

"It's where Eleven got her name," I explain to Elijah.

"Then we definitely have to watch it."

I put it on and settle in the seat, not realizing until after the opening that I'm stuck on a moving plane fifteen thousand feet in the air with a man who murdered my ex and another man who trashed his art studio right in front of me...and somehow I feel safer than I ever did when I was with Jesse.

The tension in my limbs melts away, and I think maybe I'll just close my eyes for a few minutes.

When I open my eyes, it's to see what definitely *can't* be one of the last episodes of season one come to a close and the credits start to roll.

"Oh my god." I jump from Seven's lap as if shocked,

wiping at the damp spot at the corner of my mouth, realizing my feet are up on Elijah's lap, shoes off.

"Hey, you okay?"

Elijah's hand touches the small of my back and I jolt up from the couch, remembering the drive to the airstrip. The private plane with the mysterious destination.

Right.

Right.

I shake my head. "Shit. Sorry, I—"

"Here, have some water," Elijah offers, standing now, too, but keeping a low center of gravity that tells me he'd much rather be sitting.

I take the stubby little water bottle he offers me, trying to calm my racing heart. When I twist the cap, I take note of the seal breaking and know it's safe to drink. I sit back down and guzzle it in one go.

"Fucking great show, by the way," Seven says. "Eleven is a total badass."

"I didn't mean to fall asleep," I say as I twist the cap back on, still a little mortified. "How long has it been?"

Judging by the crick in my neck and the fact that they're almost done an entire season of the show, it has to have been a *lot* more hours than I think it has.

Are we still in the air?

"Seven hours, give or take. It's perfect timing, actually, we'll be landing soon. Here," he says, taking the empty bottle and passing me a seat belt that was tucked into the seat. "You should buckle up."

Still a little sleep-drunk, I peer out the round window across the cabin and see something sparkling in the dark.

City lights.

But there's something amidst them. Something tall and shaped like...

CHAPTER 21

My blood spikes with adrenaline.

"Holy fucking shit," I gasp. "Is that the Eiffel Tower?"

Seven chuckles next to me.

Elijah lifts my hand from my lap and presses a chaste kiss to the back of it with a wicked gleam in his eyes. "*Oui, cheri. Bienvenue dans la ville lumière.*"

Seven snorts. "Show-off."

"Have you ever been to Paris, Aurora?" Elijah asks in English, but I'm still blushing from how his perfect French accent affected me.

"Paris? *The* Paris?"

There's no joke in his steady stare. This is really happening. *He's serious.*

"But...I don't have my passport."

"I have all our credentials," Seven says, patting the right breast of his leather jacket, indicating an unseen pocket within.

Did they take it from my suitcase?

Do I care?

Paris.

That's *Paris* outside.

I seriously consider the possibility that I actually died in the car crash on the mountain road and this is all just purgatory playing tricks on my mind.

Jesse? *Dead.*

Job with massive paycheck? *Got it.*

Best sex I ever had? *Triple check!*

Trip to Paris with no spending limit?

Someone fucking pinch me.

22

LIKE OLD TIMES

SEVEN

The downstairs room at Céline's never changes. Old recliner chairs with a chess table between them. A bar along the far wall. The artwork we gave her decorating the walls. All of it drenched in subdued amber light. And not a window in sight.

How many nights did we spend hiding out in this very room before Atticus could figure out a way to get us out of this city without being seen?

I chuckle to myself. Too many. But Céline never minded. She fed us good wine and even better food while we waited it out.

Her children passed in a freak accident as teenagers, and even though she wouldn't admit it, we knew Céline liked having people to care for and fuss over. It helped that she was a wizard with a pair of scissors and made the best crepes this side of the Seine.

Swirling the fine French wine in my glass, I eye Elijah over the chessboard. He's contemplating his next move, but I've already decided mine, and there's no way he can win this match.

CHAPTER 22

"It's useless," he says, sitting back in his recliner with a huff. "No matter what I do, you win."

"How about we play something else?"

His dark brows draw. There's only a chessboard here, but I have a different sort of game in mind.

"Like what?"

"A game where we can both win."

"I don't like that look in your eyes."

I grin and pull my phone from my pocket, flicking to the browser window I've been saving since we first came up with the idea of taking Ro to Paris.

"It's on display," I tell him, my blood already buzzing as I slide the phone to him across the table.

His jaw tenses and for a second, he doesn't pick it up.

Pick it up.

Come on, man. Pick it up.

After another second's hesitation, he lifts the phone and taps the screen to brighten it, the flat line of his mouth softening as he sees the prize.

It's a Van Gogh. *Three Figures near a Canal with Windmill.* Eli's been wanting to get his hands on it for as long as I've known him, but it's never been on display and the collector who owns it keeps it locked up tight enough that it was never worth our time to try to get it. Especially since it isn't worth half of what our usual targets are.

This piece would be more of a passion job. An easy two-man job.

Eli's gears turn as he looks at the gallery invite I went to great pains to set up.

"We can't," he says finally, and hands me back the phone.

"Why the hell not? This might be the only chance to get it."

His expression sours. "Not with Aurora here."

As if that's any inconvenience. If anything, she'd help our cover, and he damn well knows it.

We won't get caught. We never do.

It's an excuse. And a shitty one.

"If you're still not ready then just say that," I blurt before I can stop myself, and instantly regret it from the hurt that crosses his face.

We haven't done a proper job since he came back. We've focused all our energy on toppling the empire of our enemy. *That,* he could do. But he was still completely unwilling to do something for himself. For *us*.

Just because he can't replicate the art anymore doesn't mean we need to stop collecting it.

Fuck, I miss it.

I miss *us.*

"It's not that."

"Then what is it?" I press.

"It's too risky. We know he's looking for us. Besides, Atticus wouldn't like it."

I fall back in my chair and lift my gaze to the brocade ceiling with a heavy sigh. "Atty isn't here, Eli. *We* are."

Silence.

When I drop my eyes back to him, a pang of guilt lances my gut.

"You know what, forget I said anything. I'm sure it'll be on display again someday."

"But probably not at *La Tante Sophistiquée*. There's almost no security there."

There he is.

"You have a point," I whisper, embodying the devil on his shoulder that I've always been.

"*If* we did this..."

CHAPTER 22

"Yes?"

"If there's any risk or security has changed since the last time we were there—we leave it."

"Since when do you back down from a challenge?"

"Sev," he warns seriously.

"Fine. Fine. Yes. Agreed."

He nods. "And it has to be up to her. If she doesn't want to go, we don't go. This trip is for her. Not for us."

I want to ask why it can't be both, but I won't argue with him anymore. Truth be fucking told, I'm just glad he agreed.

I knew something had changed. I could sense it from that first night she came to stay with us. A shift in him. A thirst for life I thought he lost when he lost his ability to paint.

No. Not lost—*taken.*

Suppressing the rage that always surfaces when I think about what he's been through, I nod my agreement. "Deal."

We spend the next thirty minutes going over the plan in case Ro is cool with a detour into the art district, pulling out the go bag Atticus started keeping here a couple years back to see all our gear still inside and intact.

It really feels like old times as I pass Elijah his small tool kit, slide a blade into my boot, and secure a Beretta to my waistband while tucking a Glock into my jacket pocket.

I'll need to pick up something a little more...refined to wear in the shopping district while we're there, but other than that, we should have everything we need.

Fuck. I really missed this.

The beaded curtain down the hall rattles and shifts, signaling the return of the women, and I kick the go bag beneath the table and pull my shirt down to cover my other blade, which I've had holstered since we left home.

Like old times

Céline steps through first. Her short auburn hair bobs as she bounces on her heels with a rare smile on her lips as she clears her throat for our attention.

"May I present Miss Aurora Bellerose," she says in her familiar French accent, giving each of us a knowing look. "For your viewing pleasure."

Ro awkwardly steps into the space and pushes a lock of dark hair behind her ear.

Not a fan of the spotlight? Too bad...she fucking *glows* in it.

Eli is on his feet first, straightening his blazer jacket. "Wow."

She's cut a couple inches off so her hair now falls just past her shoulders with blunt cut ends. The dark brown she's chosen complements her skin so much better than any shade of blonde ever could. But it's not just the hair that's screaming *goddess*.

Céline has had her change into a sexy little ivory silk dress with a modest slit in the thigh. She's even given her sparkling earrings to wear and a pair of strappy heels to go with it. The perfect outfit for an outing at an upper-class art exhibit in an old *pied-à-terre,* just as I requested.

All eyes will be on *her*, and not on *us*.

"Do you like it?" she asks Eli, fiddling with her hair with worry in her eyes that shouldn't be there. "Céline said I could keep the dress. Is it too much for shopping?"

"Not at all," Eli replies. "The dress is beautiful. *You* are beautiful."

She's unable to hold his stare, her eyes dropping to the carpet.

My turn.

"You did great, Céline," I say as I push from my chair and stalk over to them. "As always."

CHAPTER 22

"You sure you boys don't have time for me to give you a little trim? Look at this mess."

Céline ruffles my dark hair with a tut.

"Next time," I tell her, stooping to give her a peck on the cheek. "I promise."

"*Soon*," Céline demands, already starting to leave the room. "You can pay on your way out."

I roll an impossibly soft lock of Ro's dark hair between my fingers, drawing her gaze up.

Fuck, I love it when she blushes.

My cock thickens, and I grit my teeth. I don't notice the small near growl of a sound that leaves my chest until her lips part in surprise and her eyes narrow in a fuck-me stare that I will absolutely make good on.

It was fast and frantic before. Unplanned. Next time, I want to take it slow.

Taking her hand, I give her a twirl, taking her by surprise so much that she laughs and nearly stumbles in the heels, but I've got her.

"Stunning," I declare.

"Yeah?"

"Definitely."

"Thanks. Hey, do you think maybe we could call Atticus again? I just want to check that Ellie's still okay."

She's already had us call him once and text twice since her phone died, but she can bother Atty as many times as she needs to. I hold my phone out.

"Wait, it's probably late there now."

"Early," Elijah corrects. "Very early. But don't let that stop you."

"Maybe just text him again? Please?"

I do. Demanding a photo of a very happy dog at his

earliest convenience before saying, "Done," and watching her visibly untense.

I wrap my arm around her shoulders, and love how she fits the space there perfectly. "Hey, would you mind making a quick stop at an art exhibit after we're through shopping? There's an artist on display that Eli's been wanting to lay eyes on for a while."

"It's your day," Eli answers before she can, coming to stand next to me and shove his hands in his pockets. "If you're not into it, I can go another time."

"No, I'd love to go, actually."

I can't stop smiling.

"I've never been to an art show, and, I mean, we're in Paris, so...isn't that what you're supposed to do?"

"You heard the lady," I say, squeezing her and starting to lead her out. "It's go time, bro."

23

A WORK OF ART

ELIJAH

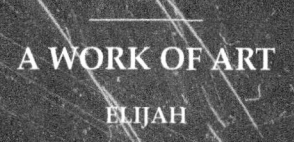

I can't believe we're leaving *Triangle d'Or* with only three bags. Even Sev spent more than her on his new designer jeans, crisp white shirt, fine indigo-black blazer, leather belt, and matching Derby shoes.

He looks sharp as hell and ready to blend in with the well-dressed clientele at *La Tante Sophistiquée*. The whole ensemble makes the tattoos around the sides of his head and down his neck look avant-garde and artistic rather than alarming.

Aurora barely scraped the surface of the black card's limit despite my insistence that she should get whatever she wants.

"Are you sure this is enough?"

I peek into the Saint Laurent bag as I take it from her and find only a couple of simple black shirts wrapped in monogrammed paper.

"Those shirts are worth more than every article of clothing in my suitcase," she replies with a pained look.

I try not to seem disappointed, but it's hard. I wasn't kidding when I said we should try to find the card's limit.

CHAPTER 23

Even considering that I had the service staff at a few of the shops pack up anything she seemed interested in for me to pick up later, it still wouldn't be even *half* of what I was prepared to spend.

"She's not used to this, man," Sev mutters to me as Aurora slips into the back seat of our hired car and thanks the footman in bad French for opening the door.

Sev is right. Every time I swiped the card, she flinched.

"It's just money," I mutter back.

"Not to her."

I'm reminded that unlike me, Sev and Atticus didn't grow up knowing wealth and privilege.

I pause on the sidewalk. "What do you mean?"

I genuinely want to understand.

Sev runs a hand through his hair. "I don't know why I didn't think of it before but I'm pretty sure she thinks letting us buy this shit for her comes with strings."

"What? No. This is me making up for being a monumental douchebag the other day. And, honestly, now it's also to make up for the fact that you murdered that piece of shit, Jesse, right in front of her."

He shrugs. "All I know is there's a good chance she thinks we're going to expect some kind of repayment. And she doesn't strike me as the type to enjoy being indebted to anyone."

I sag and Sev claps me on the shoulder before going to join Aurora in the car.

"We should go," Aurora calls to me from the open door. "We'll be late for the gallery opening."

A work of art

Aurora's face lights up the instant we enter the gallery, and watching her appreciate the art is sweeter than stealing it could ever be.

It was easy to distract her while Sev checked us in under our aliases.

And when she refused to hand my overcoat to the coat check, I was surprised at the tremor of gratification that fell down my spine.

She pulls it tighter around her shoulders. It's big on her, but somehow she makes it look elegant paired with the dress. I can't remember a time when a woman has worn any of my clothes, I'm not sure if any have. Atticus likes to mark his women like that—and in many other ways—but I never saw the allure.

At least not until right now.

Aurora catches me staring and cocks her head as we press farther into the space.

I blink and look away, adjusting the collar of my shirt a little too hard, making the top button pop.

Her gaze snags on the bit of exposed skin at my throat and her own bobs in response. I undo two more buttons when she looks away, earning myself a raised brow from Sev as he joins us in the main atrium to view the first piece.

We've only lifted art from this location once before, and that was almost four years ago now. They had no concrete suspects for the theft, so no reason to be recognized, but they *have* upped security since.

There are cameras in most of the corners now. And two security guards wander slowly through the exhibit, positioning themselves along the walls for several minutes at a time before moving on.

It's a scenario I'm intimately familiar with, even if we are a little rusty.

CHAPTER 23

Sev was right.

This will be easy.

"What do you think?" I ask Aurora as she takes in a landscape by Camille Corot with wide, curious eyes.

She blinks and shakes her head. "I'm not sure. I guess I don't really know what I'm supposed to think."

"There's no wrong answer."

I wait as she purses her lips, considering.

"I like it," she says finally. "Especially the way the light hits the water."

"It's brilliant," I agree.

"It's sad, though," she adds, her gaze narrowing.

"Why do you say that?"

"Um, I'm not sure...god, I really know nothing about art."

She shrugs, laughing nervously as more people begin to fill the space, eager for their turn to look at the piece, but I don't budge.

"Should we..." She points to the next piece, her eyes flicking to those waiting for us to move on.

I take her hand without thinking about it and tug her gently back. "Don't worry about them. I want to know why you think it's sad."

My chest squeezes while I wait for her to look again and watch her expression shift as she feels the art. Analyzes it.

Fuck, she's so beautiful.

And it's not the new hair color or the pretty dress or the fact that she's wearing my coat. It's *her*. In my peripheral, Sev watches me watch Aurora with a knowing smirk and the spell breaks.

I clear my throat.

"It's the colors, I think," Aurora whispers finally. "They're all a bit...gray. Muted. And the light is...*cold*."

A work of art

On his way past me, Sev leans in to quickly whisper, "She has the eye," echoing the words of my father.

When he met my mother, it was in a gallery not so unlike this one. They talked of art and while looking at a piece by Vermeer, he knew she had the eye. The story goes that after they left that gallery, he never had eyes for anyone else.

Losing her was the first big blow. The start of his downfall that I only sped up. I never should have agreed to meet the demands of his double-crossing partner. I was trying to save his legacy, but I should've known better.

Fool me once, shame on you.

Fool me twice...

I know it's my fault, but I'll spend the rest of my life working to right all the wrongs it caused if I have to.

It occurs to me that this little detour is just that—a distraction from what we should truly be focusing on. I give Sev a nod that says he should begin. The sooner we're finished here the sooner we can get home and finally find out what Atticus is planning.

Sev nods back and swivels to begin a slow, calculating walk of the collection. He'll find the piece we're after and probe the surrounding area for security threats and weak points.

If we do this right, Aurora won't even know it happened.

24

GRAND LARCENY IN PARIS

AURORA

They're up to something.

I fiddle nervously with my necklace as Elijah leads me through the gallery exhibit. Ahead of us, Seven moves like a shadow, pausing to look at several pieces. But his interest doesn't seem genuine. Either he really doesn't care for art at all, or something else is going on here.

They keep glancing at each other in this way that tells me they're communicating without the need for words. And Elijah has clocked every security guard and camera in this entire room. I don't think anyone else has noticed. He's really smooth about it, but standing right next to him, chatting with him, it's hard to miss every time his gaze wanders.

My mind comes up with several unlikely theories as to why they're being sketchy as fuck, but the truth is I still don't know these guys. Who they are. What they do. They said they aren't mafia and I'm starting to believe that, but then what?

What is it Seven seems to be looking for? Are they meeting someone here? Maybe an exchange?

CHAPTER 24

Is it dangerous?

Am *I* in danger?

Elijah smirks at the next piece, letting out a small scoff that draws my attention back to him as Seven moves down a dim corridor from the main space into what I assume is another room of the gallery.

I follow Elijah's line of sight to the painting in front of us, confused at his reaction. It's a nude portrait with soft shades of blue in the background that complement the woman in the painting's pale, perfect skin.

"Not your type?" I ask, admiring the model's shapely curves. I had curves like that once—before Jesse and all the bullshit that came with him.

Elijah shakes his head, leaning in close. "It's a fake," he whispers conspiratorially.

"How do you know?"

"It's messy work. The forger tried to age it. You can see that the paint is cracked. The canvas material is in too good of shape. Amateur move."

"You seem to know a lot about art."

Even though there's a small smile pulling at the sides of his full lips, there's pain in his eyes when he answers. "It was my whole life," he replies, massaging the scarred flesh on the back of his right hand.

"Does that hurt?"

He blinks, releasing his injured hand with a bob of his throat as if he didn't realize he'd unconsciously begun to massage it.

"Sometimes. The repair surgery made it usable, but it never really stopped hurting."

We move to the next piece, but I can't shift my focus to the whorls of spring green and muted yellow. "What...what happened?"

A muscle in his jaw flexes and when a few more long seconds pass in tense silence, I regret asking.

"Sorry. It's obviously not my business."

"It's not that," he rushes to say. "I want to tell you."

When his warm honey brown eyes meet mine, I can see that he means it. There's a depth to his stare that screams with brutal honesty, and if I don't look away, I might be sucked down into that golden abyss, so I save myself from drowning, tearing my gaze from his.

I can't afford to feel anything more for this group of men than I already do, and besides, after what happened with Seven...

Well, I don't think he'd appreciate finding out that I might be just a little bit attracted to his best friend, too.

"But?" I press, wandering to the next piece with him following close behind.

"But I'm not sure if I should."

What does that mean?

Elijah's attention shifts to something behind me, and I turn in time to see Seven jerk his chin down the hall.

"Come on," Elijah whispers, sliding his hand into mine to gently pull me toward the next room. "This room is getting busy. Let's see what's farther in."

I don't miss the abrupt shift in attention or change in subject, but I don't point it out, curious to see how this plays out even though my pulse is fluttering.

The next space is smaller. Much smaller. With raised platforms in all different sizes, glass-encased paintings perched atop them on display. It makes the tighter space almost maze-like, and for a second, we lose sight of Seven behind a taller display before he comes back into view, pausing in front of a small piece set on a lower platform near the back.

CHAPTER 24

He moves away to look at the next one, making space for me and Elijah to see the painting he was just looking at.

It's small compared to most of the others. About magazine-size with a simple but elegant gold filigree frame.

It's three people standing by a canal, with a windmill far in the distance. Everything is in shades of gray and black, making it feel really quiet and a bit somber. The three figures look like they're blending into the background, adding to the gloomy vibe of the scene.

I can't exactly describe why, but I love it.

The way Elijah is looking at it, I can tell he loves it, too. His expression is near reverent. How someone devout might look at religious artifacts or the Pope himself.

Seven coughs, and Elijah's head snaps up.

His hand, now clammy, releases mine in favor of pressing lightly against my lower back through my borrowed coat. Confused, but not wanting to draw attention to us, I let him guide me to look at a painting near where Seven is standing.

"Excuse me for just a second," Elijah says in a low tone and shifts to stand next to Seven. I can't hear them, but I can see their lips moving. See Elijah nodding.

What the fuck is going on?

My skin prickles, and I take a cursory look around the room, tracking the few people in here with us. There are only four including the guard by the corridor to the main atrium. The other way out is a plain black door with a sign that says *DO NOT ENTER, DOOR ALARMED* in both French and English.

No one else in here looks like someone an artist and a killer would be meeting in a gallery on a Friday night. I swear there's a punchline to this joke somewhere, but I can't find it.

"Ro," Seven says in greeting, bringing me back to where I'm standing as he places himself inconspicuously next to me to look at the large piece in front of us. "Having a nice time?"

I peer around him to find Eli, and see him wandering through the other paintings, but he doesn't seem to really be looking at any of them like he was in the other room.

"Ro?"

"Hmm?"

"I asked if you were having a nice time."

"Oh. Yeah. It's, um, all really beautiful."

"This one's a Goya," Seven tells me, indicating the piece we're meant to be looking at. "It's worth about five million."

That gets my attention. "*What?*"

I look at it again.

It's morbid—with a pair of dead rabbits arranged in a sort of cross shape. It leaves a hollow feeling in the pit of my stomach. Despite the content, it's worth more money than most people see in their entire lives.

I wonder how Seven knows that. *Why* he knows that. And my gears turn some more.

"Do you know a lot about art, too?" I ask, trying not to sound too interested.

"A bit," he replies with a smirk and a shrug, his eyes flicking to Elijah in the corner so fast I almost miss it.

I turn to see what he was looking at, but he wraps an arm around my middle, pulling me into his side. "Don't look."

Adrenaline rushes up my back, and I shiver. "Seven, what's happening?"

"Do you really want to know?"

We turn to view the artwork behind us, but I'm not

CHAPTER 24

looking at it, and neither is Seven. His electric blue eyes are zeroed in on the guard by the corridor just as the man moves from his post to stride back toward the atrium.

Seven coughs, and then grins at me.

My knee-jerk reaction is to look toward Elijah, and I almost do, but he lifts a hand to caress my cheek, drawing my attention back to him. "Uh-uh," he says. "Eyes on me, Ro."

The pad of his thumb brushes along my jaw, setting flame to the adrenaline flooding my veins. "We don't want to draw attention to him while he works. He's a little rusty at the moment."

My lips part.

While he *works?*

I'm having trouble remembering why I should be wary as Seven drops his eyes to my lips.

Fuck.

His hand around my waist squeezes, and a small breathy gasp escapes me. When he pulls his lower lip between his teeth and leans in, my thighs press together, and I start to wonder if I care if he takes me right here on this gallery floor in front of all these posh Parisians...

Then I hear the heavy booted footfalls of the guard returning and panic jolts me out of the trance he has me in.

Elijah.

Without thinking, I cough and see a shifting movement in my peripheral as Elijah deftly rises to his full height and pivots to look at another piece.

Seven's warm touch drops from my cheek and his shifty eyes search mine.

"Good catch." He lifts a curious brow at me. "But I had it."

Grand larceny in paris

And I get it now.
Elijah is stealing the artwork.
Art worth millions.
Right under the noses of everyone.
They really are certifiably insane.

25

A PERFECT FIT

AURORA

How are they so calm? There are other people in the room with us. Other people who could see. Four of them. They meander through the exhibit, taking long moments to appreciate each piece. Seven is tracking their movements, too, I notice. Will he alert Elijah if any get too close as well?

But...the other patrons are all distracted, I realize. Each of them is absorbed in the art they pause to admire. None of them are at all interested in what anyone else is doing.

I register that we should also be admiring the art and shift just slightly from Seven's grip to face the dead rabbits again, cocking my head as if I'm trying to see it from a different perspective when I sense the security guard's gaze lingering on me.

Seven's squeeze at my hip tells me I'm doing well, and I flush with pride.

"You're doing so well," he whispers to me in a husky voice. "Keep watch on the guard. I'm going to get another angle."

A zap of anxiety races through my nerves, but before I

CHAPTER 25

can argue, he's already gone, wandering slowly toward another piece at the other end of the room.

The guard!

My attention snaps back to him, worried I could've missed something as my stomach drops.

He watches the people in the room, but I can tell from his demeanor that he's not taking this job very seriously. He sighs and fidgets, shifting his weight onto his other leg as he does one more sweep of the room, his gaze catching on me again.

Caught staring, I force a smile and drop my gaze. I should move, I realize. I've lingered at this morbid piece for a little too long.

As an older couple moves away from the next piece, I take their place, keeping the guard in my peripheral vision, my blood buzzing with anticipation.

He doesn't seem to notice Elijah near the back of the room. Mostly because I doubt he can see him from there. Elijah is bent low, fiddling with something on the base of the glass enclosure. I guess he must've noticed that the guard wasn't paying attention, too, and decided to keep working despite his presence.

It dawns on me that I am aiding and abetting theft. Wait, not just theft. This isn't like the time me and a few of the other kids in my grade-ten class jointly stole at least two hundred bucks' worth of junk food from the Aldi downtown. This is grand larceny.

And I'm no longer a juvenile delinquent who is likely to get off with a slap on the wrist.

But then again, I did already fuck a killer and fail to report him to the appropriate authorities, so what's a little grand larceny in Paris?

My mind buzzes as if my every thought is laced with

speed, and I relish the sensation. Like the feeling of being chased, that moment when you're just a whisper from being caught and everything goes beautifully, dizzyingly *taut*.

I shiver.

The security guard turns to do his next patrol back to the main atrium and I clear my throat loudly and see Seven cast his stare over the rest of the patrons before clearing his throat as well.

When Elijah's head pops up again, I think he must've done it because he walks swiftly toward Seven, flicking out the back of his blazer jacket over a familiar gold frame tucked into the back of his pants.

I move to meet them, and Elijah's eyes flash with vivid life as they rake over me. "Well, I was going to make some excuse as to why we needed to leave but..." He lets the sentence trail off.

"You should've just told me," I mutter back, feeling his hand close around my wrist, and I realize how much faster I'm walking than they are and force myself to slow the hell down.

"Nice and easy," he says, echoing the mistake I already realized.

I lift my chin and force myself to walk slower, matching their easy pace back down the corridor. Seven tips his head to the guard as he passes us and I figure between the handful of people in the gallery room and the guard, we have anywhere from two to five minutes before someone notices there's a painting missing.

My heart is a jackhammer against bone beneath my rib cage, but it's not fear. Not exactly.

It's something new, but also familiar. Something powerful and thrilling. Something that makes me

CHAPTER 25

remember the version of myself that liked to push against limits. The free spirit caged by a society where it never quite fit.

As we pass through the atrium and back out to the coat room, I smile at the attendant at the door and thank her in bad French again before stepping outside into the crisp night air. The soul-deep vibration of confidence that comes from walking between Elijah and Seven should be bottled and sold as a street drug because it is absolutely fucking intoxicating.

The car pulls up on cue, and I have to assume one of them must have told the driver we were coming out. Wow. They really are a well-oiled machine.

We slide into the back, Elijah first, me second, and Seven last, sandwiching me into the warm cabin of the luxury Mercedes.

The driver pulls away from the curb and into the sparse traffic, and I'm unable to sit still.

My ears are ringing. The adrenaline still coursing through my veins has my legs shaking and I can't remember the last time I felt so...so fucking alive.

It tastes like *power*, bold and electric, but there's an undercurrent of something else that I didn't expect: trust.

It's just as exhilarating as it is terrifying.

I want to stick my head out the sunroof and howl like a fucking wolf. But instead, I clamp my hands on my knees, trying—and failing—to steady them.

God, when was the last time I smiled like this? Not forced, not polite, just...real.

As our driver blends in with the other vehicles in the busy street, the security guard from the gallery room in the back appears at the threshold of the door. He scans the sidewalk as he shouts at someone next to him, causing a scene that draws a crowd of curious tourists.

He doesn't look at us. He has no idea we're in this car.

My lips split into a grin and the tiny hairs along the back of my neck stand up, prickling at the triumph.

Oh my god. We're really going to get away with it.

Elijah gives the driver instructions in perfect French, and when the divider rolls up to separate him from us, I drop my gaze to Elijah's lower back.

He's sitting forward in the seat, careful not to crush the prize tucked into the back of his pants.

"Let's see it, then," I say, barely recognizing my own voice for how fucking excited it sounds. I earn myself a raised brow and a smirk from Elijah, who pulls out the artwork carefully, resting it on my knees.

It's heavier than I thought it would be for something so small. And so much more beautiful this close up. But maybe it's like how a drink tastes better when it's free. *Or stolen.*

I run my fingers over the gilt frame with my heartbeat loud in my ears.

The rush is almost unsettling in its intensity, like something clawing its way to the surface after being buried alive for so long it's forgotten how to breathe.

"When did you know?" Elijah's question brings me back to earth.

"A couple minutes after we went in," I answer honestly. "I didn't know exactly what you were doing right away, but I knew something was off."

He and Seven share a look. Elijah seems mortified, while Seven seems entirely unsurprised.

"I don't think anyone else noticed, though," I add, hurrying to soften the blow.

CHAPTER 25

Elijah shakes his head, laughing quietly to himself. "So, you aren't upset?"

Upset?

Oh. Because they made me an accomplice to theft?

Right.

That would make most people upset, wouldn't it?

"I wish you would've told me. What if I did something to ruin it?"

"I knew you wouldn't," Seven says with a level of absolute certainty I don't think I've ever had with anything in my entire life.

"How?"

He shrugs. "Call it intuition. You just *fit*."

I remember the puzzle I'd been fighting against building in my mind, piecing together these men and their motives and my feelings for them. Maybe I wanted to tear apart the pieces instead of finishing the puzzle because I was terrified to see the final image. To lay myself down as the final piece and find a perfect fit.

I'm pulled from my own tumultuous thoughts when there's a distinct shift in energy in the back of the car. Confused, I glance between Seven and Elijah, finding them both sitting a little more rigidly. Seven leans closer to the window, looking intently at something in the rearview. Elijah cranes his neck to look out the back windshield.

"Black sedan," Seven says.

"I see it," Elijah replies.

"Is it the police?"

I swivel to see what they're seeing, catching sight of the black sedan about five cars behind us just as it weaves into our lane.

"No," Elijah says, his voice low and dangerous to match his darkening expression, and my teeth clench. "It's worse."

He massages some tension out of his scarred hand, inhaling shakily, his entire body hard. I want to back away, but instead, I find myself reaching out, wanting to soothe the rage-tinted pain in his eyes. When I set my hand cautiously on his thigh, he immediately snatches it up, gripping it tightly.

Seven growls beside me. "How the hell did they find us?"

"It doesn't matter," Elijah says ominously.

I swallow hard, not liking the sensation that's replacing the exhilaration still singing in my veins. "If it's not the police, who is it?"

"We need an escape route," Elijah says, speaking directly to Seven, ignoring me. "*Now*."

Seven hammers the side of his closed fist on the panel separating the driver from us, shouting for him to stop the car in French.

He shoves the passenger door open and steps out before the car has even come to a complete stop.

"One escape route, coming up."

26

BLOODTHIRSTY LEATHER

SEVEN

Behind us, the dark sedan pulls closer, weaving through the thick Paris traffic as I shove out of the hired car and circle it.

The driver saves me having to rip him out of his seat, kindly opening the door and stepping out to argue with me in rapid-fire French.

"Seven!" Eli shouts from the back seat.

I turn to see what's got him yelling and my teeth clench when I lock eyes with one of the goons stepping out of the sedan thirty meters back, his hand reaching for something on the inside of his jacket that he'll regret ever touching.

"*Desole*," I bark, pushing the driver out of the way as I slide into his seat and shut the door in his face, gunning the engine.

The traffic stops me almost immediately and I slam my palms on the steering wheel, glancing in the rearview to see one goon split into two, both of them weaving through the vehicles in perpetual standstill. They'll be on us in seconds, and I'd really rather not traumatize a bunch of Parisians tonight. There's a kid in the car next to us, for fuck's sake.

CHAPTER 26

I know what that sort of thing can do to a child.

The driver catches up, banging on the window, shouting loudly as he tries the handle. If the guy hasn't called the cops, I can bet all our asses someone in a neighboring car has by now, and we don't need to deal with that on top of everything else.

"Fuck it," I mutter, cranking the wheel. "Hold on."

Laying on the horn, I drive the car up onto the sidewalk, scattering tourists as I gain speed to get to the break in traffic ahead at the intersection.

"Move!" I shout, honking again as more people jump out of the way. We clip the edge of a bistro table outside of a boulangerie, and Aurora gasps as it sails high into the air, crashing down somewhere behind us as I swerve to avoid hitting people.

"Who is it?" she shouts over the rev of the engine as I cut off the driver at the head of the line in the intersection, getting us out in front of everyone else. "Who's chasing us?"

I want to tell her. I really do. But knowing that the same sadistic fuck who kept Eli under lock and key for almost two years and now wants all three of us dead is just around the block might not sit so well with her, even if murder and grand larceny did.

"Someone you don't want to meet," I answer, speeding to get to the next intersection, taking a right-hand turn, not even realizing until we're on Rue de Maubeuge that I've unconsciously started to head in the direction of Céline's. If I can lose the tail, we can hide out there for the night and make a run to the airstrip in the morning.

"What the hell is that supposed to mean?" Aurora demands indignantly, twisting in her seat to try to lay eyes on them.

"Did we lose them?" I ask.

"I think so," she says. "No. Wait. They just took the turn. Nine or ten cars back."

"Damn."

"Someone needs to tell me what's happening."

In the back seat, Eli's phone rings. "It's Atticus," he says, and silences the ringer.

"We'll call him back. Keep eyes on them. I'll try to lose them at Place Blanche."

My phone vibrates in my pocket and the *Jaws* theme song ringtone blares in the car as I ignore Atticus's call and take the next right. I honk incessantly as I speed along the narrow shoulder of the road to get ahead of the slowing cars.

"Shit!" Aurora curses when a metal post scrapes along the side of the car, throwing sparks onto the road behind us in a wave of fiery orange.

My phone rings insistently in my pocket, distracting me just enough that I nearly hit the idiot pedestrian trying to cross in the middle of the goddamned street.

Jerking my phone free, I smash the answer call button, and then the speakerphone button, dropping the cell into my lap. "A little busy right now, bro."

"You went to the fucking art district?"

I was wondering how long before he traced our phones and figured it out. Honestly, I thought he'd be quicker about it.

"Yeah, about that—"

I jerk the wheel, bouncing the car back up onto the sidewalk to pass a parked van before jarring us back onto the road. "You want the good news or the bad news first?"

He mutters something unintelligible before growling through the receiver, "What happened?"

CHAPTER 26

"Well, you know that Van Gogh Eli's always wanted to get his hands on?"

"Jesus fucking Christ."

My grip tightens on the wheel as we squeeze between two city buses, and the tires scream as I take a hard left.

"What was that sound?" Atty shouts.

"He did great," I tell Atticus, ignoring his question. "It was just like old times, man. You should've seen him."

Silence on the other end of the call. That shut him up.

"So, that was the good news. Bad news is we have a tail."

"Is it police? I still have that contact at the préfecture de police. I'll call—"

"It's not the police, Atty."

"We didn't see them until they were already tailing us," Eli adds from the back seat, and I can picture Atticus's expression, face reddening, gears turning behind his eyes as he tries to think through what we should do.

"How close?" he asks finally. "How close did they come? Close enough for them to swipe anything from your phones?"

I flinch. We haven't been being as careful with our phones lately, but that's because we haven't fucking done this in a while and usually leave them at home when we're trying to intercept and destroy any and all of Ambrose's US deals.

"I don't think so," Eli answers him, sitting forward in the back seat.

"Fuck," Atty says as I take a short, narrow one-way street to another road, hoping our tail wasn't close enough to see the move.

"I thought you said our shit couldn't be cloned?" I ask, turning onto the next road only to slam on the brakes as we hit an impenetrable wall of traffic. I throw it into reverse, but a fresh wave of traffic blocks us in from behind, and I curse.

"I said it would take a really advanced system to—you know what, never mind. Even if yours are safe, *hers* isn't. Now, assuming you didn't lose the girl in Paris, she's still with you?"

"Present," Aurora says from the back seat as if he were taking fucking attendance, and I smirk at the light in her eyes when they meet mine in the rearview mirror. She's amused by this.

"Great. That's just fucking great. I'll wipe all the data I can, but you'll need to go dark. Do *not* go to Céline's. Do not—"

"Why not Céline's?" Eli interrupts.

"Aurora's location data will show you were there this morning."

"Is she in danger?" Aurora asks with concern in the lines of her face and I know that Céline has already made an impression on Ro.

If they hurt Céline, I will use her fancy scissors to cut away pieces of them until they look like human fucking doilies.

Eli leans in close to her side to comfort her, whispering words of assurance while I scan the traffic all around us, looking for a familiar car or two familiar goons. We're barely moving. If this traffic doesn't clear up, we won't be able to stay here.

Eli reaches forward through the divider and takes the phone from my lap, holding it closer to his mouth. "We don't even know if they swiped any data, right?"

"No, but just to be—*fuck*. Did they see her? Did they see Aurora?"

CHAPTER 26

"What? I don't know, why?"

"Because if they did—" He chokes himself off, and I remember his plan. She was part of it, and judging by the frustration in his voice, them seeing her now, with us, would ruin that plan.

"Why does it matter if they saw me?" Aurora asks, confused and still trying to keep eyes on our pursuers.

I still don't think I'm down for using Ro to exact whatever plan Atticus has cooked up, but what if she wanted to help? She could want to, couldn't she?

I don't know what to say to her, so I reply to Atticus instead.

"I'll take care of it."

"No, Sev, leave it. We'll find another way. It doesn't matter."

I don't answer. He won't like it.

"We should go," Eli says, and I don't know if he's talking to me or to Atty, but Atty is the one who answers.

"Right. Go dark. No usual places. Do not contact me unless it's completely safe. Lose them and head straight for the airstrip. I'll let Troy know to expect you and be ready."

"Got it," Eli says.

Atticus exhales loudly before he speaks again. "And, Seven...?"

He can't say it, but I know what he's thinking. He can't lose Eli again. He can't lose me, either. For all his cold indifference and insufferable control, the fucker knows damn well he can't live without us.

"I know," I say in answer to his unspoken question. "I'll get us home."

I reach back and take the phone from Eli, ending the call while I put the car in park in the middle of Paris traffic.

"Ro, your phone?"

Her throat bobs as she pulls it from Eli's coat pocket and hands it to me. I turn it off at the same time I turn off mine and Eli turns off his own. When I hand it back to her, she clutches it tightly between white-knuckled fists. "Don't turn it back on," I tell her. "No matter what."

She nods tightly, and I pull the Beretta from my waistband and the Glock from my jacket, holding the latter out to Eli through the divider.

"Oh fuck," Aurora says on a breathy exhale, her arms pulling in tight to her body as if she can protect herself from what's about to happen, but that's my job now.

Eli hesitates, his expression darkening.

"You got this, man," I tell him. "Just like old times, remember?"

He hasn't had to use a gun since he came home. I've made sure of it. But right now, he may not have a choice.

Come on, take it.

He glances at Aurora and his nostrils flare.

Finally, he snatches the Glock, checking the mag before reloading and chambering a round as if it's easy when I know it's anything but.

I nod. He nods back.

I'm up and around the car in seconds, pulling Aurora's door open and reaching a hand inside to help her out.

"We're just leaving the car here?"

I scan the traffic behind us, but this time I'm hoping I find them. If we lost them, I won't be able to fix the little problem we created tonight, and I'm nothing if not a problem solver.

My attention snags on a car way back by the intersection. I know it's them when one of Ambrose's men steps out again, gesturing to where we are. I grin. *Perfect.*

"Stay close to me."

CHAPTER 26

The trunk pops, and Eli reaches inside to grab the bags.

"Seriously?" Aurora says in astonishment. "Leave the clothes."

"No way. This was why we came."

He slides the Van Gogh into the largest of the bags, compiling everything of Aurora's into that one tote before slinging it over his shoulder. He tosses me my jacket, and I quickly shuck off the Hermès blazer and leave it in the street, sliding into the blood-thirsty leather.

"We've got to move."

Ambrose's men are coming.

"Oh my god, is that them?"

Eli follows her line of sight, snatching her hand when he sees them. "I got her. Lead the way."

27

A WELCOME DISTRACTION

ATTICUS

The three small blue dots on the map of Paris flicker and disappear from my monitor screen, and I shove away from my desk, pushing to my feet.

"Fucking idiots."

As if summoned by the curse, Aurora's dog comes padding into my office, sitting by the door with its tail wagging over the floor.

"What? What do you need?"

Eleven barks.

"Not now."

Think, I will myself. What can I do?

I already fired off a message to the pilot and to Céline, telling one to get ready and one to get out, just in case. I can't believe their fucking stupidity. Why risk it? What was the point?

Eli can't replicate the Van Gogh, and it's not like we have a proper collection to add it to anymore. Everything, save for the handful of pieces still on the walls of this house, was taken by Ambrose when he double-crossed us.

They just *had* to poke the proverbial fucking bear.

CHAPTER 27

I never should have let them go to Paris.

Shoving my hands through my loose hair, I struggle for a full, unrestricted breath.

They'll be fine.

They're always fine.

Except for the one time Eli walked out and didn't come back for almost two goddamned years.

My chest constricts again and I am about three seconds from losing my mind. I remind myself there's nothing much I can do from here. I have a last known location, but not much else.

Eleven barks again, and I ignore her, going back to my desk.

I push the chair out of the way, preferring to stand over the monitor as I type out a quick message on the secure server to my contact in the *préfecture de police*, letting him know their approximate last known location and to stay out of it unless they want blood on their hands. He won't help them. That's the limit. But this—keeping his men out of the fight and busy elsewhere—this he'll do.

After I hit send, I need to let the energy out. If I don't, I'm going to fucking lose it.

In my head, I'm already calculating the number of hours it should take for them to get to the airstrip, for the plane to take off, and for them to land, and drive home.

A wet nose pushes into my hand, lifting it from my side.

Nine hours max, I think. If they aren't back in nine hours, I can start properly worrying.

Nine hours.

I can do nine hours.

Eleven whines, echoing my distress as I unconsciously pet her head.

"Want to go for a run?"

It's either that or try to jerk off until I can calm my racing thoughts and the last time I did the latter, I wound up picturing Aurora's face when I came, so that's *out*.

Ellie barks again, her heterochromic eyes lighting up as her paws scrape against the floor in a sideways leap of excitement at the word 'run'. I grit my teeth at the new scratches in the hardwood, and sigh.

"All right, all right, calm down. I'm coming. Go on."

She races from the office, and I listen as her claws scratch and scrape over the floors as she darts like a bat out of hell to the front door.

In all the chaos raging in my skull, I make a mental note to add one of those puppy nail files to my online cart. There are already new food and water dishes in there, a big dog bed, a few toys and treats, kibble, and some contraption to pick up her shit from the property.

Aurora's been doing an okay job of that herself, but we're running out of compost bags because of it.

Stop thinking about her.

Cloths! Right, I need to get cloths, too. So she can stop using my good ones to wipe Eleven's paws.

Doggy shampoo would be good, too.

Jesus, at this rate, I'll be picking up the whole goddamned pet store to bring home with me when I go to pick up the order this afternoon.

I meet Eleven at the front door and bend to change into my running shoes, grimacing when she excitedly licks my face and starts to canter her paws on the floor like every second is an eternity of waiting.

"Patience," I hiss, determined to train this word into her. It has to be the twentieth time I've said it since Aurora and the guys left. I give her a look and repeat the command. She licks her lips, closing her panting mouth to

CHAPTER 27

sit in a state of mock calm, her twitching ears giving her away.

"Good girl."

When I'm finished with my shoes, I pull off my shirt and hang it by the door.

"Ready?"

I know I am. My skin itches with the need to move. To *do* something when there is nothing I can do to help them.

The metaphorical knife twists in my stomach and I remember my promise to myself when we weren't sure if he'd ever let Eli go.

If they don't come back, I'll hunt down every last one of Ambrose's men, saving him for last. I will find his hideaway, and even if it kills me, I will fulfill Eli's promise to his father. Only then will I kill Ambrose. And only after he's dead will I let myself follow my brothers to the afterlife.

Eleven barks, letting out an almost frantic keening sound that makes me think she can sense the dark path my thoughts wandered down.

"It's okay," I tell her, hating how I'm soothed as I stroke her forehead. I said I'd take care of the thing, but truth be told, she's been a welcome distraction. Even if cleaning up after her and keeping her entertained kept me from seeing where my brothers were headed until it was already too late to stop them.

"They're going to come home," I decide. "No one gets to wring their necks but me."

She makes a throaty sound of agreement and I drop my hand.

"Now, let's have that run."

28

NO MORE MISS PERFECT

AURORA

I follow Elijah's movements as he leads me through the stopped cars in traffic toward the sidewalk, keeping low in an attempt to remain unseen.

"Seven, stay low," he hisses at Seven ahead of us, who doesn't seem at all concerned about trying to lose our tails.

Every step I take carries me farther from the dark-suited men in pursuit of us, but it also feels viscerally like another step I'm taking away from myself. Into this hellscape—or is it dreamland?—these guys have dragged me into. If I'd had any idea that *this* was where accepting the cleaning job and signing that NDA would lead, would I have done it?

There's a war of opposing thoughts racing through my head, and I have no idea which side is right. They all blend into a sea of gray areas and is *wrong* really wrong if it feels this right?

My senses sharpen as we race into an alleyway off the main road, and alarm bells ring in my mind.

"Shouldn't we stay where there are lots of people?" I whisper-shout to Seven as he leads us deeper, to where the alleyway narrows and forks off in two directions.

CHAPTER 28

"No." He looks up and down each way, and his hesitance makes me sharply aware of every passing second in a way that has me vibrating on my feet and clenching Elijah's hand tighter.

He winces, and I let go as if burned, remembering his injury. "Fuck, I'm sorry."

"It's fine," he says in a rush, reaching out to me with his other hand instead.

Seven squints down the alley to the right. I see the moment some recognition sparks in his mind and hear the music maybe just a second later than he does. It's a bar. Or maybe a club.

He leads us right to the painted back exit. The red tint is scratched and chipped in places, scrawled over in permanent marker and graffiti. He pulls the handle, and it sticks.

Locked. *Fuck*.

"Fuck," Seven echoes my thoughts, spinning in a circle to see another route out of here, but this alley dead-ends and there's no guarantee there's a better way out if we turn around. Bouncing on his feet, Elijah squeezes past him, setting the shopping bag down as he goes to his knees on the asphalt.

He pulls a small kit from his jacket pocket and opens it to pull out two long silver pins. I smirk. It's been a minute, but I had pins that looked a lot like that once. I'd almost forgotten. The same pervy foster dad who liked to have me on his lap in the armchair in the living room *also* liked to keep a key lock on my bedroom door. That lock rarely opened after I took the butcher knife to his chair, so I had to learn to open it myself.

The hairpins were barely strong enough for the job, but I made them work. If I'd had the shining silver picks Elijah has, it would have made things a whole lot easier.

No more miss perfect

"Hurry," Seven says, and his husky, dangerous tone rattles down my spine in a way that makes me shiver. "If they saw us come down here, they'll be on us in minutes and I don't like this alleyway for a fight."

He raises his gun, readying himself in case the men pursuing us come around the corner.

"Damn it," Elijah curses through gritted teeth. I notice how his hand is shaking, how he pauses to stretch it out, and how his breaths are coming heavy.

"Let me." I bend to my knees next to him, ruining the satin dress as it scrapes against the rough, dirty asphalt.

His brows come together, and he hesitates for only a second before releasing the pins still dangling from the lock and shifting out of the way.

"What is she doing?" Seven asks roughly.

"Do you want to get in or not?"

I take one steadying breath and then pick up the pins. The lock isn't exactly like the one I practiced on all those years ago, but it's like riding a bike. I fumble the latch once, twice, but the third time comes with a satisfying *click* and I pull the pins free, pressing down on the handle. The door swings in, and a waft of warmer air gushes out with the music.

Seven looks me up and down appreciatively, biting his lower lip in a way that makes my cheeks heat. "Fuck, that was hot."

Elijah tucks the pins back in his kit with shaky fingers and picks up the bag, a muscle in his jaw ticking. I'm about to tell him it was harder than a normal lock when I catch sight of the first suited man coming around the corner of the alley not more than twenty feet away.

"Move!" I shout, dragging Elijah into the dim hall on the other side of the door. Seven extends his arm, firing two

CHAPTER 28

shots as if the weapon is an extension of his flesh. But then his arm jerks back, and his normally aloof expression twists with cold rage. My ears ring as he follows us inside and shuts the door behind himself, locking it just as fists pound on the other side.

"Got one," he says breathlessly, sagging for a moment's rest against the door as it shakes against him from the assault on the other side.

"You've been shot."

It isn't a question, but still, my eyes race over him to see if it's true.

There's a hole in his jacket. Almost unconsciously, I reach out, and the tips of my fingers find blood on the leather.

"Motherfucker put a hole in my jacket."

"Shit, Seven, how bad is it?" Elijah demands, dropping the bag to pull Seven's jacket back and reveal the wound. He wrenches the collar down, looking at the back of his shoulder. "It went through."

"Great, so there are two fucking holes in my jacket. I wish I could kill him twice," Seven grits through his teeth, and I barely hear him over the thump of the music. He jerks his shoulder from Elijah's grip, giving him a serious look. "It's fine. I'm fine. We need to go. There were more of them."

The banging has stopped, which means they must be looking for another way inside.

I raise my voice to be heard as the song from the bar down the hall crescendos. "How many more?"

"Five. Well, four now."

The casual murder admission takes longer than it should to sink in, and all I can think is, that's one less person chasing us, and I'm glad.

Fear and anticipation clash in a battle of wills as my focus sharpens. Every breath feels wasted without action.

Seven tugs a short, hooked blade from his waistband and grips it in his free fist, using it to gesture at the hallway ahead. "We need to move. They might try to go around."

"Aurora should stay," Elijah says, and I can't stop the shock from parting my lips as I look at him, dumbfounded.

"What do you mean I should stay?"

"I don't think they got a good look at you," he says. "You can blend in with the other people in the bar. They want *us*. They don't care about you." He shifts his stare to Seven. "We can lead them away from her."

A muscle in Seven's jaw flexes and I scoff.

"Fuck that. You are *not* leaving me alone in Paris."

Quickly, I bend to tear the lower part of my dress away. It takes some doing, but the satisfying *rip* of the fabric comes after the second attempt. "Get your arm out."

Seven does as I ask, cursing to himself as he tugs his arm free of the sleeve of his jacket and I wad up one end of the strip of satin and press it tight to the wound, winding the rest around and under his arm twice before tucking the other end through the bind and tying a knot. Holding it in place, I lean in to pull the knot tight with my teeth.

"Can you still use that?" I ask him, pointing at the gun.

His brows rise. "Why? Can you?"

"I can."

He looks doubtful and this is just wasting more time.

"My adoptive dad is a collector. We went to the range every Saturday before I moved out."

He and Elijah share a look.

"Have you ever used one to kill a man?" Seven asks.

"No."

"Think you could?"

CHAPTER 28

There's no time to think. "If I had to."

He flips the gun into my waiting palm. "Good. Because you might have to."

It feels like a bomb in my hands, and I blow out a breath as I check the clip, check that the safety is on, and conceal the weapon inside the lapel of Elijah's overcoat, silently thanking Chris for dragging me to the range with him every goddamned Saturday even when I didn't want to go.

He'd hate that I might break his number one rule tonight.

It's his calm voice in my head as I spin on my heel and press farther into the building, toward the swaying red lights, the drone of conversation, and the swell of the loud music.

Never point your weapon at someone, Aurora. We're connoisseurs, not killers. Remember that.

I was always disappointing him. So this would just be the cherry on top of the disappointment pie.

"Sorry, Chris," I whisper to myself, something like freshly poured resolve solidifying in my veins, bringing with it a rush of confidence as I leave my self-restraint at the door. "I'm done playing perfect."

29

THIS GIRL IS FULL OF SURPRISES

ELIJAH

Sev follows Aurora toward the buzz of the club down the hall like an obedient dog, and honestly? I don't blame him.

Who *is* this girl?

Grunting, I lift one of the two cone-shaped cement door stops along the wall and set it down heavily in front of the back door. It's heavy as fuck and the ache in my hand worsens from gripping the curved rebar handle, but I pick up and move the other one, too, placing them both to block the door for good measure. It won't stop them if they get it unlocked, but it'll slow them down some.

I shake out my hand and hurry to catch up with Sev and Aurora as they cautiously slink along the wall and peer into the open space at the other end of the hall.

I knew she had fire in her from that first moment I saw her, but she's come a long way from that rainwashed girl on the highway: alone, nervous, and desperate.

And still she hasn't stopped surprising me. Sev's right. She does fit. Better than I ever dreamed. And I *did* dream.

CHAPTER 29

From the first night Atticus brought her in, she's starred in nearly every one of them.

I haven't felt anything like what I feel around her in longer than I care to admit, and I can't stop imagining how her lips would taste. Dreaming of the sounds she would make if I touched her just right. I've had to take care of the problem myself almost every morning, unable to leave my room until I relented and pictured her face while I fucked my own hand.

But the last dream was different. Terrifying. *Tempting.*

I dreamt of painting her. She lounged naked on the old settee in the library, lamenting about wanting a snack while I got the curves of her body just right.

I used to dream of painting. Of color and texture and the feel of a brush between my fingers, but not anymore. The dream had woken something in me, and I couldn't stop imagining what colors I might use to capture the greens and golds in her eyes.

After tonight, I know without a doubt it would take at least nine different hues to get them just right. Maybe more. And capturing the way they gleamed when we left the gallery would be damn near impossible. A challenge that I would have happily accepted if I'd met her just a couple years sooner.

My teeth grind as I catch up to them, wondering why they haven't gone into the club until I find what they're looking at.

It's not a bar. Not a club, either.

Patrons sit sipping cocktails and picking at tapas, cheering and laughing in a bustling dark room as they watch the stage.

A shirtless man with a painted-on mustache and painted-on suspenders kicks high with a dubious look in his kohl-lined eyes as women in bejeweled dance costumes and feathered headdresses flock around him, moving in time to the music.

It's a fucking cabaret.

"Follow me," Sev says to Aurora, giving me a meaningful look before slipping into the main space and promptly disappearing into the shadows running along the right side of the room. I look for the exit as I follow them, finding a thick red velvet curtain across the floor that has to be it.

I'm ready to get out there and make a run for it when Sev deviates. From the corner of my eyes, I pick up a quick movement as he snatches something from a low table in a VIP nook carved into the wall. The group of revelers don't notice at all as they clap and cheer, conversing in French.

Sev pulls Aurora behind the beaded curtain of the next VIP section, and I follow them into the darkness of the unoccupied space.

"What are you doing?" I hiss.

"We took too long," he replies. "They'll have both exits covered by now."

I get his meaning without the need for explanation. We are going to have company no matter which way we go, and it could get ugly. My pulse picks up, faltering as it slips out of rhythm and I breathe deep to try to bring it back into sync.

Sev brings the bottle he stole from next door to his lips and takes a small swig before rubbing the back of his hand across his mouth and handing it to me.

"Here."

I take it without looking at the label, hating that I need it. Every deal of Ambrose's that we've ruined over the past two years has come with a stiff shot of whiskey before and

CHAPTER 29

after. Just enough to take the edge off. Make my hands stop shaking. Keep the bullshit anxiety at bay.

Tipping the bottle back, I take one long swallow of the foul-tasting liquor and nearly gag as I force it down my throat. The instant I pull it from my lips, it's ripped away and my eyes go wide as Aurora takes a swig of her own, grimacing as she pulls the bottle away and makes a face that somehow manages to look cute even though she's clearly disgusted.

"God, that's awful," she says, mock gagging as she passes the bottle back to Sev, who's stopped trying to hide his amusement and, you know, for someone with a bullet hole in his shoulder and his gun in the hands of a woman he barely knows, he's shockingly calm. I hate him for that —his ability to never take anything seriously until there's no other option—but it's also why I love him.

"If they're blocking both exits, what do we do?" Aurora asks. "Can't we just call the cops?"

She seems to realize how stupid that would be before we can reply, her gaze dragging to the bag containing approximately two point five million dollars in stolen artwork in my left hand, and the gun in my right.

"Anonymously," she adds. "We could call them anonymously."

"They won't help us," I tell her. "It's a deal Atticus made a long time ago. They won't get involved."

Her brows draw and for a second I think she might ask something else, but then her gaze drops. "Okay, so we pick an exit and, what? Run?"

"We go out the front," Sev says, leaning in closer to be heard over the next act coming onto the stage to a roar of raucous applause. "It's Paris on a Friday night. It'll be busy and they may not want to risk the added exposure if they start firing rounds into groups of tourists."

"And what if they don't care?" My throat contracts around the words. After all the bricks we've thrown through the windows of Ambrose's empire since I got free, what if he's finally decided anything is worth the risk to eliminate us once and for all.

Or worse, bring me back to that room, put a brush between my fingers, and force me to paint until they bleed.

I can't do it again. I *won't*.

Sev drops a hand onto my shoulder, making me look him in the eye. "If they don't care, then neither do I, bro. We're getting home."

Sev's face betrays a rare moment of vulnerability, giving a glimpse into the darkness he keeps leashed just below the surface. It burns there like blue fire and I know it would take the devil himself to stop him from making good on his promise.

"We should go," he adds. "Now, before they can fucking multiply."

"What if we get split up?"

"We won't."

"We might."

He lets out a sound that's half groan and half growl. "You remember where the metro is on Rue des Abbesses? It's two blocks over, near Église Saint-Jean. We meet there."

I nod.

Aurora double-checks the safety on the gun she's hiding inside my coat.

"Don't pull that unless you have to," I warn her, and she gives me a funny look that I don't get until she scoffs and says her next words.

CHAPTER 29

"So I shouldn't start waving it around as soon as we get outside? I really thought that was a great idea."

Sev's lips part in surprise, but it's me who laughs as I take her arm and guide her to turn around, leaning in close to whisper in her ear.

"Such a smart-ass," I croon and feel her shiver against me.

When she tilts her head back to reply, I can't help but notice the tiny amount of space between our lips and wish I could erase it from existence. "Made you laugh, didn't I?"

I smirk, but the reality of the situation sinks back in as we excuse ourselves past a busy table, making for the red curtains. A waiter comes to ask if we need anything, blocking our path, and I shake my head.

"No parle Francais," I say in horrible French that hurts me to spit out.

"You do so," Aurora whispers in a mock accusatory tone as we hurry to the exit. "And it's fucking *hot*."

My cock twitches in my pants and I wish she would say more, but I can't afford to be distracted right now. Not with her safety in our hands and our enemy outside. "Stay close to us, okay?"

She reaches back to squeeze my arm in reply, and I decide that if anyone attacks this girl outside, I will have absolutely no problem putting a bullet between their eyes.

30

DANCING REAPER

SEVEN

Without thinking, I reach to pull back the heavy red curtain, and a snarl curls my lips. The ache in my shoulder is fucking real.

It's not exactly like I'm a stranger to being shot. It's happened a handful of times and, if I'm honest, I'm not even sure Eli would count this one bullet hole as another strike against my nine lives. I've been hit far worse. At least he won't have to dig this bullet out. That fucking sucked last time. Or at least what I remember of it sucked; I passed out before he could pry it out of my back.

Since I'm already fucking here, I hold the heavy-ass velvet curtain back to let Aurora and Eli pass through. Without me telling him to, he maneuvers himself in front of Aurora, keeping her between us almost reflexively and even though it's not the right time, my mind is already coming up with a few other scenarios where she would work beautifully sandwiched between me and Eli.

After the shit she did tonight: helping with the heist at the gallery, picking a lock, and handling my weapon, I have the biggest fucking hard-on for this girl. And I don't think

CHAPTER 30

there's a goddamned thing she could do or say to us right now that would change my mind.

"Ready?" Eli asks her, his hand, steadier now than before, clasped around the handle of the large metal door leading to the street.

Of course there are no fucking windows, so I guess whatever's waiting on the other side will just have to be a surprise.

As soon as Aurora nods, he pushes outside, rushing to fall in line with the pedestrian traffic outside on the street.

Eli and Aurora swivel their heads, scanning the crowd ahead while I look behind us.

We're more exposed than I'd like out here, but within a few seconds, we catch up with a larger group of tourists, sticking close to their heels.

Two shadows peel off from a smaller group behind us, and I clock the one on the right as the fucker who ruined my jacket. Facing forward, I stay as tight to Eli and Ro as I can, using the reflective windows of the shops and restaurants on the street to track my prey.

The one on the right edges closer, shouldering through the people between us while the other one keeps his sights set on Eli and Ro ahead of me. I whistle to Eli to warn him as I slow down, waiting for the ugly asshole behind me to catch up.

I let him come real close, knowing—or at least convincing myself—that he won't cause a scene if he thinks he can do this clean.

Too bad for him I no longer share the sentiment, and I never intended to let any of them get back to Ambrose alive. Especially not with the possibility of them having seen Aurora's face. We're already targets, I won't let her become one, too.

Not when going to the art district was my idea. I won't carry that, and if I kill them, I won't have to.

One plus one equals motherfucking two.

The business end of a gun presses to my lower back and the reaper in me grins. "Keep walking," he says in a heavy French accent. "Don't make trouble and—"

I pivot, gripping the barrel of his weapon, flicking out my blade at the same time to drag it across this wrist. He releases his hold on the gun with a curse that turns to gasp when I flip the blade and drive it up in a quick arc, burying it between his fourth and fifth rib.

I clap him on the back, not even feeling the injury in my shoulder anymore, thanks to all the adrenaline rushing through my veins bathing every second in electric glory.

"Whew, maybe you shouldn't have had that last drink, *mon ami*," I say, unable to keep the manic glee from my voice, but it probably only adds to the facade that we're just two revelers on the streets of Paris who had a little too much fun at the bistro around the corner.

He gasps, choking on his own blood as I search the crowd for his real comrade. He's up ahead, gaining on Eli and Ro as they round the next corner.

Time to ditch the dead weight.

"Come on, buddy," I groan, mostly carrying him now as I set him down against the wall in the alley beside us. I click the safety on his gun and tuck it into my waistband.

Panting, I jerk my blade free from his chest cavity and wipe it on his crisp white shirt before pulling the flap of his jacket to lay over the mess.

"You stay here," I say, patting the top of his balding head while I pocket the blade. "I'll bring the car 'round."

I take off after Eli and Ro, knowing that if there were a couple goons at the back door, they'll have taken the longer

CHAPTER 30

way around and be in a position to cut them off in less than a block, if they used one of the covered passages.

I think I see them up ahead, Eli dragging Ro through the streets, making a beeline for the metro as quickly as he can while casting furtive glances at the guy still tailing them.

Two down. Three to go.

When Eli turns again, I catch his stare and jerk my head ahead, telling him to keep moving. I got this. Unable to help myself, I do a little hop-step-spin that would've made Florence proud, earning myself some cheers from the surrounding crowd.

"*Vas-y*, Mick Jagger," someone calls as they pass me, and I eat that shit up, wondering if they'd cheer if they knew I was about to unalive the guy a few meters ahead of them.

I don't know why Eli and Atty wouldn't let her teach them how to dance. Not only did it make her so fucking happy, but it got me so much pussy through my teens and early twenties that I could've died a happy delinquent by twenty-two.

I'd have to show Aurora, and as I imagine it, I bite my lip, doing a little waltz on the spot, not sure if I'll ever be able to picture anyone else between my arms again.

Shit. Ambrose's man notices that I'm tailing him and makes the very regrettable decision to speed up in order to get closer to Ro and Eli instead of coming back here to handle this like men.

I sprint after him, weaving through the weekend revelers like a wraith.

He's too close.

I just had to get carried away back there. Fuck.

"Eli!"

He spins, eyes widening at the guy practically within

arm's reach behind Ro, then at me, chucking my blade with everything I have, and probably fucking up my ravaged shoulder in the process. It buries itself awkwardly in the fucker's back, the curved blade not the ideal type for throwing. His cry of anguish is overshadowed by the misfire of his weapon as it goes off with a lethal bang, and all fucking hell breaks loose.

31

BABY'S GOT A GUN

AURORA

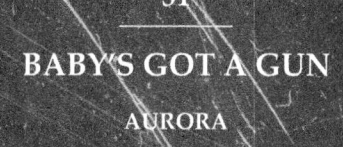

The shot echoes around us, ringing in my ears as the people on the street rush in every direction, trying to get away from the shooter, but most don't seem to know who it was or where the danger is.

Someone knocks hard into my shoulder and my hand comes away from Elijah's. Another hit and I'm on the damp ground, trying to get back to my feet as bodies move in waves of chaos all around us.

"Aurora!" Elijah shouts through the cacophony of noise, but it sounds like he's looking in the wrong direction. His voice moves farther away as he calls for me again, "*Aurora!*"

The heel of a boot comes down on my little finger and I curse, sucking in air through my teeth as I push to my feet and swivel my head, trying to catch sight of Elijah or Seven amid the throng of people.

In the distance, sirens pierce through the raucous sounds of stamping feet, panicked voices, and screams. The lights paint the tops of the ancient buildings in flashing blue as they draw nearer, angling to try to push through the

CHAPTER 31

traffic that's at a dead stop now as people abandon their cars in favor of running away on foot.

"*Elijah!*"

I grab his arm, but the man who spins to face me with wide, fear-filled eyes isn't him. "Sorry," I mutter as he jerks his arm away from me and makes a beeline for the intersection.

I dodge out of the path of a couple running straight for me and almost trip over the dead guy in the street. He's face down, with a hooked blade jutting from his back. Seven's blade. Quickly, I drop to a knee and grip the handle to pry it from the guy's back.

He jerks and lets out a wet, weak groan. "Shit!" I fall backward onto my ass, dropping the gun and scraping my palms against the pavement.

The guy gasps and splutters.

Oh god.

I've seen dead people before. Once on the street when I was a sixteen-year-old runaway. And once when Jesse showed me the severed head of a double-crossing drug dealer to get me to cooperate with his demands. But I'd never seen someone actually *dying*.

The noises coming from his throat are making my own thick, causing my stomach to roll.

Swallowing, I fight a gag, feeling the sticky blood now coating my palm where it holds Seven's blade.

Oh god, what am I doing?

I look around, but as the last handful of people bolt for literally anywhere else, I don't see him. It feels wrong to just leave it, so I give one good tug and jerk it free.

Ugh. So gross. I pocket it and look up and down the street, struggling to see through the still thinning crowd.

An older woman muttering something that sounds like a prayer shrieks when she sees me, and I realize I forgot to reconceal Seven's gun when I picked it back up.

"Fuck," I tuck it into Elijah's coat and grit my teeth, kicking off my heels to abandon in the street, hissing when the cold cement kisses my toes. Where the hell are th—

There!

I rush for the narrow alley where I saw the flash of movement, following the sounds of muted thuds and grunts to find Seven brawling with one of the guys who was chasing us.

He ducks to avoid a blow to the face, catching sight of me with wide eyes as I bounce on my feet, trying to amp myself up to help him. The gun he gave me won't be any good here, I might hit Seven, and I'm not even one hundred percent sure I can make myself pull that trigger.

"No!" Seven grunts, landing a hard blow to the guy's stomach before taking one to his ribs. "E-Elijah," he gasps out between punches. "Go. Up the street."

Something zaps in my veins, and I shift to turn around with fresh ice in my blood. The panic in his voice is contagious, and it grips my heart in a vise.

"I got this. Go!"

Remembering the blade in my pocket, I draw it out. "Seven! Catch!"

The hooked blade catches the light, and he smirks as I throw it. He catches it easily and I don't stay to watch what happens next even though I'm worried he could be hurt.

I trust him. He's got this. He said *go*, so I'm going.

I race back the way I came, veering to follow the sidewalk farther up the street where we'd been headed.

Elijah, where the hell are you?

CHAPTER 31

My heart pounds hard in my ears, beating like a drum in my chest as I race faster, the torn shreds at the hem of my dress snapping around my legs like violent whips.

The people who'd been in the street rush down the block to the right. My eyes dart through the crowd, trying to find a familiar head of rich brown hair, but I don't see him.

Down the opposite street ahead to my left, there's the clatter of metal on cement and I gasp, rushing forward, gripping the rough edge of the wall to slingshot myself around it.

Elijah stands in the middle of the vacant street with his hands raised, palms out, his gun on the sidewalk far out of reach. The suited bastard standing in front of him has his weapon raised, his back to me.

Far beyond Elijah, Seven barrels into the street from an alleyway. He sees the threat at the same time I do and starts to run, shouting, his voice raw and scraping and stabbing straight into my chest as he calls Elijah's name.

He won't make it in time.

"I won't beg," Elijah says as I slip the gun from inside the coat, and my throat goes dry.

My hand trembles as I lift it, needing to wrap my other hand around the grip to steady it enough so I don't miss and accidentally hit Elijah or Seven.

A wave of soul-twisting dread floods into my heart like acid, but worse than that is the rush of power as I realize that I *can* fire.

"Eli!" Seven roars.

Oh god.

Goosebumps flare up my arms as if electrified by the gun. I blow out a shaky breath, forcing them to steady as I rush forward on bare feet, flick off the safety, and take aim.

I can't miss.

Just a little closer. If I could just get within twenty feet, I could—

The guy with his back to me laughs at Elijah, his shoulders square off, and his arms tense.

I run.

"No!" Seven howls, and it's the gut-wrenching fear and rage in his voice that makes me ready.

The fucker adjusts his grip. "Courtesy of Ambrose De La Ro—"

Finally, he hears me, shifting on his feet, but he's too late and I'm *more* than close enough.

He spins to face me, and I don't hesitate.

The gun kicks in my hands and I feel the rattle of it down to my toes as a back spatter of red mists over my chin and chest. The echo of the shot rebounding from the stone buildings all around us.

My heart stops.

Everything stops as his body pitches forward, the hole in the back of his head a garish crater of burgundy.

He falls onto his face, and Elijah's eyes go wide as he takes me in. "Aurora?"

He says my name like he isn't sure it's really me, and, to be honest, I'm not sure it is, either. *I just killed...*

I've seen and done and been through a lot of shit, but I've never...

The gun in my hands is suddenly heavy and I let it fall to my side, remembering to breathe.

Seven's erratic footfalls silence as he skids to a stop next to Elijah, gripping him hard around his shoulders. He pants loudly as he looks Elijah up and down before roughly pulling him in for a hard embrace.

CHAPTER 31

I can't say why, but watching them makes my throat burn. Makes my eyes sting.

"I'm okay, Sev. I'm good. I'm good."

I feel like a spectator at a show I didn't order tickets for. A ghost on the sidelines of the living. A statue unable to move.

When Seven releases Elijah and his eyes meet mine, my solid stone exterior cracks. And when he strides over to me, every one of his steps echoes the beating of my heart.

As his hand comes up to tightly grip the back of my neck, drawing my forehead to his, I feel more than I have ever felt in my entire miserable life.

"*Thank you*," he says through his teeth, and I don't think anyone will ever be more grateful. It comes off him like a wave of energy with no place to go, hitting me in the chest like an iron fist.

As our foreheads come apart, he gives me a tight nod, and his gaze falls to the gun still gripped in my hand. He reaches for it, taking its weight, allowing me the precious seconds I need to let it go. Once I do, he nods again, and I force myself to relax my shoulders, fighting the shifting tides in my stomach. Hating how my hands feel empty and my feet unsteady once the weapon is out of my reach.

Elijah comes to stand next to Seven, shoulder to shoulder, his warm gaze tracking every minuscule shift in my expression. "My guardian angel," he says on a breath, his lips quirking at the corners into a sad version of a smile. "I owe you my life."

"You would've done the same," I find myself saying.

"Yes," he replies as if it were obvious. "I would've."

"We need to get off the streets."

Seven glances up at the blue lights still flashing overhead, the sirens getting nearer. They're coming from the opposite direction now too—the way they said the metro was. I assume Atticus's contact can only do so much to stop his officers from getting involved when there's an all-out gunfight happening right in the streets of the 18th arrondissement.

"This way," I say, remembering the flood of people headed down that way. "If we go quickly, we can blend in with the crowd."

"Wait." Elijah rushes to grab the toppled shopping bag from the ground, snatching a black T-shirt from inside of it before throwing the strap over his shoulder.

"May I?" he asks, holding the shirt to my face, and I remember the blood. I let him clean it as best he can, wiping the soft fabric over my chin, neck, and the tops of my breasts. When he's finished, he reaches up to get rid of one final drop near the corner of my mouth, brushing it away with his thumb. The warmth of his touch draws a shiver from my bones.

Seven holsters his gun and zips his jacket up over the mess of red on his shirt. "Hate to break this up, but we need to move." He indicates the street ahead. "We'll follow you, Ro."

I nod, and lead them the way I saw all the people go. We rush across the street, keeping our heads down to avoid being seen by the police officers still trying and failing to get through the standstill. But by the jarring beams of white light flicking across the cars, I think some are now on foot, which means we'll have company soon if we don't hurry.

It feels good to move, even better once we clear the intersection and I can push myself into a run, feeling the chill night air wash over my skin.

The stampede of people I saw are all but gone now, and

CHAPTER 31

I curse to myself until I spot a party bus down the next street. It begins to pull slowly away from the curb, and I rush to catch it, banging on the door to make the driver stop.

I have no idea where it's going, but it'll get us away from here, and that's a start.

The doors open, and the driver asks me something in French that I don't understand. Elijah squeezes past me to answer him and steps inside, towing me behind him.

"Fucking psychos out there, man," Seven says to the driver as we pass him and head straight for the back of the cramped bus. Whispers follow us and people dressed for a night of dancing clear a path as if they can sense the danger emanating from us in radioactive waves. Maybe they can.

We grip the overhead handles, standing in a tight circle as the bus begins to move. Each of us looks at the other, something passing between the three of us that makes me stupidly giddy, to the point where I think I might actually laugh, but I swallow the sound and give them a knowing smile instead.

When Seven takes my hand, I let him, and without thinking, I reach for Elijah's. He looks at it a second before slipping his fingers down my palm, twining his fingers with mine.

"I'm sorry," he mutters, and I frown.

"For what?" I whisper back.

"For bringing you into this. We never should've put you in danger."

I squeeze his hand in mine lightly, conscious of his injury. I don't know what to say to that, because, truthfully, I don't know how I feel. My whole worldview has been shaken, and I'm not sure how everything fits back together anymore. But I'm finding myself hoping that my broken pieces somehow fit with theirs.

Yes, if they hadn't brought me here and we hadn't stolen that artwork, none of this would've happened but…I don't blame him. And I don't blame Seven, either.

As I lean into Elijah's side and he takes my weight, letting his chin fall on top of my head, I hope he knows that I've already forgiven him.

32

GUARDIAN ANGEL

ELIJAH

"What are you at now?" I ask Sev as I slip the suture needle through his skin, stitching up the exit wound in the back of his shoulder. "Four lives left?"

"You kidding? This shit doesn't even count."

Aurora lifts a brow, ready with scissors in one hand and a fresh bit of gauze in the other for when I need them.

"We figure he's got nine lives," I tell her. "Like a cat. If this counts, which I think it should, then he's down to just four."

Her amused smirk twists into a wince as she comes to the realization. "One of those was from me, wasn't it?"

"Forgiven," he says as I pull the sutures taut and knot the thread. My hand aches as I finally release the tweezers and stretch out the nerve endings. The guy Aurora took out fucked it up bad when he managed to disarm me.

I take the scissors from her with a soft thank-you and snip the end of the thread before beginning to bandage the wound. We've already dealt with the entry wound, and he insists that he isn't injured enough anywhere else to warrant me fussing over him.

CHAPTER 32

I offered to check Aurora's feet since she'd been barefoot all night, but she'd already cleaned them up in the small bathroom at the back of the jet, shrugging it off as just a few shallow scratches.

"There." I pat the bandage on Sev's shoulder for good measure, making him let out a growly sigh.

"Ow?"

"Just *had* to do a job in Paris."

"Hey, I just put the cards on the table, bro. You didn't have to pick them up."

"I—" I stop myself before I can say any more. There's no point in arguing. He's right. I could've said no. I should've. But I didn't. And now Aurora will need to live with the choice she made tonight to save my life for the rest of hers.

"It's your turn," she says, bringing me back to the present as the plane hits a soft patch of turbulence and my stomach drops.

"I'm not hurt. I'm fine."

Despite my reply, she still kneels in front of me, her eyes lifting to mine with a knowing look.

"Liar."

I clear my throat and sit back, forcing myself to focus on what she said instead of how it feels having her looking up at me like this.

"Your hand."

She reaches for it, and as her fingers brush over the raised silver and fleshy pink scars, I pull away.

Her big eyes find mine again. "Trust me?"

My teeth clench behind my lips, but when she reaches for my mangled hand a second time, I let her take it.

"I can tell it's bothering you," she says, almost to herself as she starts to carefully knead her thumbs into my palm.

The sweet relief is almost instant and I sag into my seat,

letting my eyes close just for a second as she tests how deeply she can massage the aches without causing pain. For a few months after surgery, I had to have Atticus give me hand massages just to get through the day without painkillers.

"Is this okay?"

My breathy exhale is almost a moan. "That feels incredible."

Fuck. She's way better at this than Atticus was. Or maybe it's just because it's *her*.

As I blink my eyes back open, it's to find Aurora with a slight smile on her lips. The grin is at odds with the little knot of concentration between her brows, as she carefully works the base of each finger before switching back to broad sweeping movements with her thumbs that feel like heaven.

Sev parks himself in the low sofa along the wall to the left of the cabin, lounging with his uninjured arm slung over the back and one leg up as he watches Aurora. Watches me.

I try to ignore him, instead focusing on the relief that every rounded sweep of her fingers brings me.

The knot between her brows deepens as she works, and I can tell she's holding in so much. So many questions she deserves answers to.

The sight of her with the gun raised comes back into my mind, and I remember how she'd looked as the body of Ambrose's thug fell to reveal her.

Ivory satin dress splattered with red. Hands trembling. Eyes wide and wild. Face pale. Not breathing. Hauntingly captivating.

This girl—this angel—saved me.

"I don't think I've properly thanked you," I whisper,

CHAPTER 32

feeling my Adam's apple bob hard in my throat. "For doing what you did."

Her fingers freeze on my hand for an instant before starting to move again. She won't look at me, and I don't blame her, but I hate it.

I've already apologized, but I'll do it a thousand more times, in a thousand different ways, if that's what it takes. "I promise this won't happen again."

"Don't make me promises you can't keep," she says quietly, but the words are loud in my head, each one a knife twisting in my gut.

She's right. "Are you okay?"

She sighs. "I don't know. How are you supposed to feel after committing grand larceny and murder on the same night?"

"Depends on the person," Sev says, injecting himself into the conversation as he pulls the cork top out of a small bottle of scotch with his teeth and takes a little swallow. "I'm angry as fuck about that goon getting the jump on Eli, that came way too close, but as far as eliminating the threat? I feel like a million bucks."

He takes another swallow, and I give him a look that says to slow down before he fucking bleeds out.

"That's five less assholes in Ambrose's arsenal."

"Not helping," I tell him, but Aurora shakes her head, and I think maybe I'm wrong.

She laughs. "That's the thing. I'm not sorry. I don't regret it. If I didn't pull the trigger, he would've, and you'd be dead."

I can see her gears turning in the way her focus narrows on my hand as she continues massaging on autopilot. She still doesn't look at either of us as she continues. "Maybe this makes me a shitty person, but I don't care that he's dead…because it means you're not."

My stomach flips and I lean forward to close my other hand over hers, and finally, mercifully, my angel looks up at me.

"It's okay to not be all right," I assure her, needing her to know that neither of us expects her to be composed and collected. We don't need her to be strong.

Her brow furrows. "Is it okay that I am all right?"

My lips part, and I search her eyes for any hint that she might be lying—putting on a front because she feels like she has to, but there's nothing false in her sharp emerald stare.

She's so much stronger than I ever gave her credit for, and I'll be the first to admit that I absolutely misjudged her.

After a moment, I nod. "Yes. It is."

Her full lips pull into a small smile and there it is again —that feeling. Like the earth under my feet is unsteady; like being fifteen thousand feet off the ground and knowing that if you start to fall, there's no safety net to catch you.

But maybe crashing and burning wouldn't be so bad if it was with her.

Aurora bites her lip and looks away, slipping her hands out from mine to continue massaging my injured one. I don't move to sit back in my seat, instead studying the curve of her face close up. My chest tightens as my gaze lands on the thin line that I hope won't scar on her cheek. She'll still be just as beautiful with it, she would be no matter what. But I can't stand the thought of her carrying any trace of the coward who gave it to her, being forced to have a constant reminder of the past she didn't deserve. I know what that's like.

CHAPTER 32

I let my gaze trail down her delicate cheekbones to her jaw. Her neck.

She's washed away what remained of the blood, and her old bruises are almost healed now. I note the elegant way her neck curves down to her shoulders. How her collarbones rise and fall with each breath. I'm consumed by the urge to touch her, imagining how soft and sharp she would feel at the same time.

If I could properly capture the way her tiny hairs stand upright as my gaze drags over her flesh. It would require whisper-soft paint strokes. And the lighting would have to be just right.

"She's stunning, isn't she?"

Sev's low voice brings me out of my head and I blink as if coming out of a trance to find Aurora blushing violently, dropping her head even lower so I can't see her expression.

"She is art in its purest form," I say without hesitation, and her face tips up in surprise.

Steeling myself for the possibility of her rejection, I pull my injured hand from hers and sweep her dark hair back from her face so I can properly admire it, tucking the strands behind her ear.

"Stunning, indeed," I confess when she doesn't pull away, the tortured thing in my chest aching for acceptance.

"Imagine the masterpiece we could create together, the three of us," Sev says, his voice rich with intent, and the implication of his words goes straight to my fucking cock.

"You should see how she tastes," he adds, and Aurora's breath hitches as we both whip our heads around to look at him.

He grins coyly at her, swirling the little bottle of scotch between his fingers.

"I've seen how you look at him," he says.

Aurora stiffens, and for a second, I think he must be wrong. She hasn't looked at me in any sort of way. Not that I've seen. Not the way I've seen her looking at him.

"No, I didn't—" she blurts, stumbling over her words. "I didn't mean—it's just—"

"Ro," he says, stopping her. "It's okay."

She reels from his response. "What?"

Sev pushes the cork back into the scotch bottle and leaves it on the floor when he leans over his knees. "He's my fucking family. My brother in every way that counts. There's no one I'd rather share you with, and I'd never deprive him of someone that makes him happy."

I'm about to tell him to shut up, worried he's going to talk her into doing something she'll regret. But when Aurora turns her attention back to me, there's a fire burning in her stare, and I forget how to speak.

"There's light in his eyes again," Sev continues, and I want to hide from the truth he speaks, but I don't. "And you're the one who put it there, Ro. I'd never dream of taking that away...as long as it's what you want, too."

Aurora bites the inside of her cheek. She's nervous, but there's a spark beneath it, desire flickering in her eyes that she's trying to keep hidden.

She doesn't know we've shared before, but this is different. With the women Atticus brought in, it was always prearranged and pre-agreed to. They offered themselves to be shared. Signed off on what they were cool with and what they weren't.

This is...natural. And there's a part of me that isn't sure I want to share this girl. That part wants to take her all for myself.

But as Sev eases off the sofa and sinks to his knees behind her, reaching out to run his fingertips over the back

CHAPTER 32

of her neck, she melts into his touch. Her eyes get heavy and her lips part, and I want this for her. I want her to have everything she wants, and if that's Sev, too, then I'm glad it's him and no one else.

Because Sev is right. My brothers are the only men I would share anything with. I pity any other man who tries to touch her from this moment forward.

Aurora lets out a soft sound as Sev curls his fingers around the back of her neck, easing her forward until there are only inches of space between my face and hers.

His voice is nothing but a rumble of sound when he says, "Taste her, brother."

My angel blinks her eyes open, looking at me through a haze that I can feel starting to cloud my own vision. I would give anything to taste her. To show her my appreciation for what she did for me today. To apologize for any and every bit of wrong I've done since the moment I met her. But first I have to know.

I brush my knuckles along her jaw and feel her shiver under my touch in a way that goes straight to my cock. "If this isn't what you want, say the word, Angel, because I'm about three fucking seconds from losing all self-control."

Her cheeks turn scarlet and her eyes widen at my words, sparking when Sev presses a kiss to her back. He begins to untie the strings at the back of her dress and she gasps and sighs.

The sounds she makes are even better than I imagined.

"Go on," Sev urges her. "Tell him how much you want us both."

I hold my breath. Sev flicks his hooked blade out of his pocket and slices through the delicate laces at her back.

"Yes," she breathes out as what remains of her dress loosens around her. "I want you."

My resolve snaps and she barely gets out the last word before I tilt her chin up and crush my lips to hers. Aurora moans into my mouth as I steal the air from her lungs, letting her oxygen breathe new life into my wearied soul.

Her lips are soft and smooth, sugary sweet in a way that has me starving for more.

I pull the straps of her dress from her shoulders as Sev works to get the rest of the destroyed satin from her body, my lips never leaving hers. *Fuck*, they're so soft. A perfect fit, like they were made to be on mine.

The rhythmic thudding in my ears is echoed down below, where I'm already hard as steel for her, my cock pushing insistently against my leg. With every electrifying second spent touching her, hearing the song of her pleasure, I only crave more, more, *more*.

And I know I'll never feel sated with another woman again.

33

WINGARDIUM APADRAVYA

AURORA

When Elijah kisses me, my center of gravity shifts and the world flips on its axis. But here in this black sky are some of the brightest, warmest stars.

He makes a sound against my lips like a shuddering moan, and oh, god.

I. Am. Fucking. *Drenched*.

Seven runs the flat side of his hooked blade down my back, and I must be certifiable because as he follows the path of the sharp metal with his lips, the friction of him ignites my soul as if I'm the flint to his honed steel.

My core tightens, making me tremble as I arch my back, pushing into the metal.

Elijah deepens our kiss, tangling his tongue with mine in a way that makes me wildly feral for him.

What is even happening right now?

The shock of it all takes a back seat to the deviant desire that's so strong I'm drunk on it. As if their every touch, every kiss, is laced with the strongest whiskey.

I never imagined kissing anyone else could feel as right as kissing Seven did, but kissing Elijah does.

CHAPTER 33

As Seven slips his warm hand around my rib cage to glide down my belly, I try not to think about whether this is wrong or right. I've lived my entire fucked-up life in gray areas. Why stop now?

Maybe gray is my favorite color.

His fingertips dive below the thin waistband of my thong, and I suck in a breath, moaning into Elijah's mouth.

He draws back, looking at me through heavy-lidded eyes as if he can memorize every detail of how I look in this moment. I gasp and my back arches violently when Seven's fingers brush against my pussy. Elijah's throat bobs in response as his gaze travels lower.

I shiver under his lustful stare as he begins to explore my body, lingering on the curve of my throat, my breasts, and then lower to the shredded satin dress laying on my thighs until his eyes meet Seven's hand concealed beneath my seamless white panties.

"Spread your legs for me, Ro," Seven whispers huskily against my neck, and I do as he asks, sliding my knees apart against the carpeted floor to allow him better access. He doesn't waste it.

As Seven strokes my throbbing pussy, Elijah admires me like he did the artwork in the gallery earlier. Studying every curve and swell and nook of my body with an entranced expression.

"I want to see you," I tell him, forcing myself to be patient when all I want to do is tear off Elijah's clothes and ride Seven's hand until I come.

Fuck, I want to feel him in my hands. In my mouth. *Now.*

Elijah unbuttons his shirt, revealing the wide expanse of his chest. He's more muscular than I thought. He only seemed less so standing next to the hulking forms of

Wingardium Apadravya

Atticus and Seven. His hairless chest tapers down to tight washboard abs and a glorious 'V' that disappears into the waistband of his belted pants.

He has the body of a rock star. Lean and sculpted. Everything is tight.

"Elijah..." I breathe. "You're so fucking—"

Seven dips his fingers into me, and I forget what I was about to say as I collapse forward in a whimpering moan, catching myself on Elijah's thighs. No, not just his thighs. Beneath my left hand is a distinct bulge. It runs down his inner thigh, solid and long.

My mouth waters as I run my hand down the length of it, trying to find where it ends.

When Seven starts to fuck me with his fingers, I feel another erection press against my ass, and I can't wait anymore. I grip Elijah's belt buckle and undo it, sliding the end through the clasp to find the zipper and button beneath.

My heart races as he helps me, lifting his hips for me to yank the material down in one swift motion. His cock springs free as his pants fall to the floor.

Elijah's erection stands tall and proud, a mountain with a silver peak. "Is that..."

I've never seen a pierced cock before. At least not in real life. I've heard of the usual suspects. Jacob's ladder. The Prince Albert or whatever. But this is different.

"It's called an apadravya," Seven murmurs in my ear, and it sounds like something from Harry Potter. I bet it feels as magical as it sounds.

"He let me do it last year," Seven continues, and my cheeks heat.

"You pierced his cock?"

His breath fans over my neck, just below my ear, and

CHAPTER 33

my pussy clenches in response. "I did. Took it like a champ, too, didn't you, Eli? It's the piercing that offers the most intense female pleasure."

He kisses that sensitive spot at the nape of my neck, and that, coupled with the promise of his words, makes me hot all over.

I lick my lips as I trail my fingertips up his thighs, teasing him as I slowly edge closer to his cock, watching his burning gaze follow my touch. Fuck, I'm not sure if I'm torturing him or myself at this point.

He leans back heavily, his hands clutching the armrests as his eyes lock on to mine.

The instant my fingers brush him, he tenses, letting out a sound that's pure pleasure tinted with something like pain.

"You'll be the first one to try it," Elijah admits in a tense whisper as I draw my hand up his shaft to touch the piercing.

The first one? Didn't Seven say he did this last year? Has Elijah not been with a woman in that long?

Something about that turns me on even more. That I get to have this 'first' makes it...special. *Makes it mine.*

"Fuck," Elijah growls as I rub the pad of my thumb over the base of the piercing, his knuckles turning white where they grip the armrests.

The piercing is a bar, I realize. It goes straight through his wide tip from top to bottom, and two ball fixtures adorn each end. I just know one of these would perfectly hit my g-spot no matter what position he fucks me in.

I wonder how it would feel in my throat.

Wrapping my hand around his length, I peer up at him as I suck his tip into my mouth, feeling the smooth metal ball roll over my tongue. He pants raggedly, his hips flexing beneath me as his smoldering brown eyes fill with savage hunger.

He lets out another throaty sound, and it's like music to my ears. So deep, so fucking raw, and I can't wait to hear it again and again *and again*.

As I take him deeper, his head drops back, his body sagging as he breaks eye contact and makes that sound again.

"*Holy...fuck*," he growls out, and I fucking love how much he responds to me. I take my mouth off of him for a second to get a better angle, but the sight of precum gathering on his tip sends me right back down.

I suck it off, tasting the sweet and salty tang of him as it mingles with the distinct taste of metal. I'm already addicted to it, hungry for every drop he'll give me, moaning around his cock.

"Easy there, Ro," Seven says, halfway snapping me out of the trance I'm in. "Eli's a little out of practice, and we want to make this last."

I look up at Elijah, and there's a knot forming between his brows. I continue to slide my mouth up and down his length, hoping to erase it from existence as I reach back to touch Seven. His quick fingers snatch my hand and pin it to my back, drawing another gasp that's muffled around Elijah's cock.

Seven's right. Elijah is wound too tight and every flick of my tongue and gag of my throat is just winding him up tighter for his release. But I can't seem to make myself stop, not wanting to let go of this moment. Revelling in the sounds Elijah's making and the way I'm making him squirm.

It takes Elijah another moment to respond to Seven's

CHAPTER 33

caution, but then he pulls himself free of my mouth with a hiss, as if it pains him to do it.

"Get her onto the sofa," Elijah orders breathlessly, and Seven grunts as he lifts me easily from the floor, despite his injured shoulder, and carries me with a firm grip on my pussy and his other arm around my waist until he has me seated between his legs on the sofa.

Elijah inhales deeply before pushing himself to his feet to kick his shoes and pants fully off. He crosses the short walkway of the moving jet and drops to his knees in front of me.

Seven's hand leaves my dripping pussy just as Elijah settles himself between my legs. He hooks his fingers into the straps of my thong and pulls them down my legs before prying them open.

He pauses to drink me in, licking his lips when his gaze settles on my pussy. "Those lips are the most delicious shade of pink."

I shudder as Seven settles himself against the backrest, pulling me down until my back meets his chest. He runs his palms over my breasts, and my nipples peak hard against his touch.

"Lift her hips for me, Sev," Elijah says, and Seven shifts, grabbing me tight around the hips to seat me on his lap instead of on the seat between his legs.

His rock-hard cock presses insistently into my lower back, and he shivers against me as I move my hips, trying to create friction through his pants. *God, why is he still wearing pants?*

His grip on my hips tightens, and when I tilt my neck to see his face, I find his head tipped back, expression slack as he lets himself enjoy the feel of me against him.

It's pure fucking magic, this connection between us all.

Like an ancient song, all the right notes played in just the right ways to create a harmony unlike any heard before.

I cry out in surprise as Elijah's mouth closes over my clit. He moans against me like I taste better than the sweetest wine, and his fingers dig into my thighs to keep them open for him.

Seven moves back to touching my breasts, and when the fingers of his left hand trail up my sternum to my throat, I suck in a breath at the double-edged blade of fear and anticipation that twists in my chest. He caresses my neck, his touch light and probing as if he's hyperaware of every micro reaction I give him as his fingers fit into the places where violent ones grabbed and squeezed not long ago.

I close my eyes, letting the caress of his touch lull me away from the initial reaction of panic to something else. Something that feels a little like trust and a lot like a sense of control I've never had but always craved.

I lift my chin, allowing him better access to my throat, and he squeezes just a little in response while the fingers of his other hand work my nipple, and Elijah flicks his tongue against my clit.

Seven releases my nipple and places his fingers to my lips. "Open."

As my lips part, he pushes two tattooed digits into my mouth, and I suck on them, twirling my tongue around them until he tenses beneath me. But this isn't for him, I realize when he withdraws and uses the glistening fingers to tease my nipples again, increasing the pleasure as they glide easily over my pebbled skin.

Seven uses his grip on my throat to angle my head sharply sideways, stealing the whimpering sound from my lips with a hard kiss.

CHAPTER 33

My toes curl as his grip loosens on my throat, turning back to a languid caress that makes me shiver. His blue eyes burn into mine. "Do we feel good, Ro?"

"Y-yes," I croak, struggling to find my voice with the stampede of sensations running rampant all over my body, forcing my nerve endings to spark and spasm.

This is everything I need. Everything I've ever wanted but been too afraid to ask for. And I don't care what sort of person it makes me, but I can't think of anything better than being fucked by both of them right now. I ache to feel them move inside me. To taste them on my tongue. To feel the press of them deep in my throat until I can't breathe.

I want this. I want this so bad *it hurts.*

Elijah does some devilish fuckery with his tongue and my body convulses, my thighs squeezing against his head, making him have to hold me open for him to eat me alive.

Seven grinds his erection into my backside harder, twisting my nipple at the same time Elijah sucks me hard into his mouth, and I'm going to fucking detonate any second.

"There it is," Seven says with a coy smirk. His gaze slides to Elijah between my legs, and he says, "Don't you dare stop, brother. Our girl likes that."

Elijah sucks me into his mouth again, repeating the movements of his mouth and flicking his tongue over and over again until I'm writhing on Seven's lap enough that he has to hold me down for Elijah to finish his feast. His arms become bars against me, not constricting, just heavy and strong and *hot.*

My breaths come in little gasping pants as Seven devours every flicker of my pleasure with his piercing gaze.

When Elijah pushes two fingers into me, it's seconds before my body squeezes tight, clenching and fluttering

Wingardium Apadravya

and arching and fucking singing for them as I come undone. I don't try to hold back my voice, letting it rip out of me in a raw, animal sound as I come hard and Elijah licks me through every pulsing, spasming moment of it.

Seven releases me, his chest caving in on a heavy exhalation as if he'd been holding his breath. My head rolls to the side, and I blink through the haze in my eyes to find Elijah lifting his head, licking my glistening release from his lips with a slow, satisfied smile.

"My turn," Seven says in a dangerous whisper, and I know I'm in for the ride of my fucking life on this jet.

34

MILE HIGH CLUB

SEVEN

As Eli rises, he reaches for Ro's hands, pulling her to her feet. He steadies her when her legs don't seem to want to cooperate, and I decide to make it my mission to make sure she'll need to be carried from the jet back to the Jeep when we land.

I grin, getting up to take Aurora from Eli and give him a jerk of my chin to tell him to sit down in my place. He catches on to the plan quickly, sliding onto the sofa. His dick ready and waiting for her, and harder than I think I've ever seen him before.

Ro twists in my arms, her gaze getting heavy again as it drops to Eli's dick. She doesn't need me to coax her this time. She is no longer cowering into herself, away from what she really wants. She's coming out of that place as we give her the room she needs to grow.

And watching her climb on top of Eli and take what she wants makes me so fucking hard for her.

I start to undo my jeans, restricting the use of my fucked-up arm as much as I can as I yank them down one-handed to take my cock in my fist.

CHAPTER 34

Ro positions herself, straddling Eli's hips with the tip of his cock a breath from her entrance. She leans in to kiss him, and his arms come around her bare back, where her dark hair sways over her pale flesh. He guides her down onto him, his grip tightening and hips flexing as she swallows every inch of him with her dripping-wet pussy.

Only once she's fully seated does she breathe, a rasping, choking sound that's muffled against Eli's mouth.

I bite my lip so hard I taste blood, unable to give them any more time than I already have. Needing to touch her. I kneel on the sofa next to them, turning her face to mine for another kiss. As our lips part, she starts to grind against Eli, drawing tense sounds of strained pleasure from his chest as he buries his face into her tits and grits his teeth at how fucking good she feels.

Soon, I tell myself. *I'll be back in that sweet pussy soon.*

I've never been good at being patient.

"Is it okay?" Eli asks her between pants, lifting his gaze to hers. He doesn't mean his size. By now he knows I've fucked her, and if she can take me, she can take him, since we're roughly the same length and girth. No. He means the apadravya. Honestly, I'm curious, too. It's a piercing I'd been wanting myself, but a hard one to pull off without help, and the guys didn't want to go near my junk with the mean-looking bit of surgical steel.

Ro grinds harder against him. "So fucking good. It's hitting...just...the right..." She gasps. "...spot."

Ro groans, and it's almost a growl. So sexy coming from her lips. I'm so wrapped up in watching her expressions that she surprises the hell out of me when her hand brushes mine where it's wrapped around my cock. I release myself, letting her take me into her palm. I moan when she squeezes me, giving it a tug. I don't realize what

Mile high club

she wants at first until she looks at me with those fucking eyes.

Like a siren's. I could drown in them.

"Let me taste you," she moans, and I growl in response.

She rolls her hips against Eli, fucking him even more into a frenzy as I shift closer on the sofa.

Ro leans in, eagerly opening her mouth for me, and I shift to bring myself level with her gorgeous lips.

"I want you to fuck my mouth," she says just before my dripping tip touches her lips. She punctuates the words with a quick flick of her tongue, licking the precum from my slit, making my balls pull tight and a curse come out through my teeth. "Don't hold back."

She doesn't have to ask me twice. I take her face in my hands, feeling the hinges of her jaw spread wide as I feed my cock to her. When her lips close around me, my grip tightens, and I'm not sure I'm any better off than Eli in the not-coming-too-early department because...

"*Fuuuuuucckk.*"

The way she teases the underside of my cock with her tongue is nothing short of expert, and I need to remind myself who the fuck I am, because I am definitely not a two-pump chump. And our girl deserves at least a few more orgasms before we're through tonight.

The jet hits a patch of turbulence, and I catch myself on the back of the sofa, but not fast enough to stop my cock from pushing harder to the back of her throat. She lets out an audible gag that I feel like a silky flex against the head of my cock.

I pull my hips back, but Ro stops me, clutching the hem of my shirt to pull me in closer as she relaxes her throat and pushes out her tongue to take me deep.

"Oh, baby," I croon, stroking her jaw as she pulls me

CHAPTER 34

into her tight little throat until I see stars. "That's so good, Ro."

Her moan vibrates against my length as she holds me there, her half-closed eyes rolling back in ecstasy. She likes this as much as I do. Fuck. *Fuck*.

I lose it. My grip moves to the back of her neck, and I angle her down, thrusting deeper until she gags around me and her saliva drips onto my legs. Against my fingers on either side of her neck, her pulse flutters like the wild beating of a sparrow's wings. When I release her, air rushes into her lungs in a great, gasping inhale.

Ro looks at me through slitted eyes, licking her lips in a way that has me utterly entranced as she shivers with Eli's cock moving inside of her.

"Do that again," I moan.

Her grin widens as she opens her mouth for me, taking me into her mouth again, deliberately slow this time. Making me feel everywhere her tongue touches me as I slip past the dam at the back of her mouth and she relaxes her throat for me.

I hiss as her throat constricts around the head of my cock. It pulses and shudders as she gags on it. Her eyes roll back in sweet ecstasy and fuuuuuck...

"You're the most beautiful damn thing I've ever seen, Ro."

I hold myself there with her wrapped around me for another moment before allowing her the oxygen she needs as she drags in a breath, her tits heaving with the motion. She feels so good it should be outlawed. Illicit.

This, right here, is the real test of man.

I thrust against her tongue, against the wall at the back of her throat, fucking her mouth like she asked me to, fighting like hell to maintain control and losing the battle with every pump of my hips.

When she squeezes her eyes shut, and I know she's about to come, I clench my teeth and thrust deeper to feel her flex around me as she shatters around Eli's cock.

Eli squeezes his eyes shut and bares his teeth as his grip on her hips tightens. As her movements become stilted and erratic, he guides her, using that bruising grip on her hips to force her to continue fucking him through her orgasm, making it last as long as it can until he can't take it anymore and we both let her slump into a limp, breathless heap against his chest, my cock popping out from her mouth.

"Oh g-god," she stammers, her voice raspy and eyes watery as Eli wraps his arms around her trembling body and holds her to him. "Fuck."

He kisses the top of her head and meets my eyes as he rests his chin where his lips just were. The look says so much more than he ever could with words.

Ro might've saved his life tonight on the streets of Paris, but she's saving so much more than that, and I will never take it—take her—for granted.

I step down from the sofa, sacrificing my own desire to allow Eli and Ro this moment, but Ro reaches out to me, half dazed, her fingers curling around my wrist. "Stay."

My gaze flicks to Eli, and the bastard smirks at me, and I wonder if he's thinking what I am. Our girl isn't satisfied yet, and I have never been more up for a challenge than I am right fucking now.

Ro pushes herself up from Eli's chest, biting her lip as she glances between us. Leaning down, I brush the damp strands of hair from her cheek. Her gaze drops to my still rock-solid cock, making it jump.

CHAPTER 34

And as much as I would love to get back in that perfect mouth, I think I have a better idea.

"Tell me what you want, Ro," I whisper against her lips, curling a finger under her chin.

Her throat bobs, and she hesitates to reply.

She seems...nervous. Self-conscious?

No.

No, no, no.

There's no need for that.

"You won't get any judgment here."

"You won't," Eli echoes, running a hand over her back.

Her lips part, and I find curiosity in her eyes. I see how she wants to believe us, and I hate the uncertainty.

I guess we'll just have to show her.

"You don't have to hide your darkest desires from us, Ro," I whisper. "But that's okay, we'll unravel them...*slowly*."

Her eyes widen.

I nod to Eli. "Go on, turn her around."

As he lifts her, I help swing her legs around until she's settled in reverse on Eli's lap, and he eases his cock back into her.

Now that she's facing me, I have the glory of watching her bite her lip as her pretty pussy swallows every inch of him back into its warmth.

From the way she watches me through hooded eyes and the way her teeth scrape along her lower lip, I think she knows what I'm planning. And I think it's exactly what she was too afraid to ask for.

Eli and I have never shared like this before. He nods to me over Ro's shoulder, coaxing her to settle back against him as I lift her legs over the tops of his, spreading her wide before going to my knees to get the right positioning.

"W-what are you doing?"

"Oh?" I tease, running my palm over my cock. "Is this not what you wanted, Ro?"

Her jaw clenches, but she doesn't deny it.

"Have you ever had two?"

I'm dying to know, and even though I won't judge her if she says yes, I'm praying she says no, because I want this first. I want to see her face when she's filled with both of us and know that no one else has seen her experience it.

She shakes her head. "Have you?"

I lift a brow and suppress a chuckle.

"I mean, have you both done this before?"

"No, Angel. Not this, exactly," Eli mutters against her temple, running his hands down her sides until they grip her hips to hold her in place. "First time."

She shivers at his words as I reach for her lips.

"Open."

Ro obeys like such a good girl, opening wide for me to slide my first two fingers past her lips. "That's it, get them nice and wet for me, baby."

She tips her jaw up, coaxing my fingers deeper into her throat as she lures a soft growl from mine.

"Good girl," I tell her, using her saliva to lube up my cock, stroking it languidly as she watches and moans.

Our girl's getting impatient, but there's no way I want to risk hurting this pretty pussy. She's going to have to have a little patience. As it is, there isn't even a whisper of a gap where she's closed around Eli's solid width.

As I line myself up, she whimpers, reaching for something to hold on to, her breaths coming quicker with the anticipation as a curse falls from her lips.

"Ready?"

She nods feverishly. "*Fuck*. Fuck, yes. Do it. I want—I want to feel you both."

CHAPTER 34

Gripping my base, everything tightens and squeezes as I press my wide tip to the space just above Eli's cock, creating an opening where there wasn't one a second ago. A breath shudders out of me as I push in hard, needing to plant my hand on her thigh to steady myself as her sweet pussy makes room for me.

Her hand slaps against my shoulder, nails biting down as she cries out.

"Does it hurt?" Eli asks, the words strained as he feels what I do, the tightest fucking squeeze my cock has ever had. It feels fucking...*amazing*.

Ro lets out a broken sound and I force myself to wait for her response, when all I want to do is drive so hard into her that she sees stars.

"It h-hurts so good," she manages through panting breaths, clawing at my arm, trying to pull me in closer. "D-don't stop."

I slide in another inch, letting her adjust for only seconds before pushing in a little more.

"Holy fuck," Eli mutters, throwing his head back.

I look between us, grinning when I find the whole head of my cock buried in her cunt.

"Almost there, Ro." I dip my head down, nudging her nose with mine. "Just another few inches."

"*What?*"

"Shhh," I croon. "You can take it."

The lightning in her eyes meets the fire in mine, and I know we're going to make the perfect fucking storm.

She nods, gasping to breathe as I lean over her, wrapping my right hand around the back of her neck to hold her there, with her eyes locked on mine. I want to see it.

I dig the toes of my boots into the rug and slide my cock the rest of the way inside of her. She gasps, and her eyes go sharper than razor blades before softening, slackening, and *watering*.

Does she feel this pressure? It's fucking *divine*.

This is my altar. Right here, on my knees with my cock inside of her, I submit to the religion of Aurora Bellerose.

When I start to move, rocking myself into her, she closes her eyes and presses her mouth to mine, moaning into all my empty places until they're bursting with everything that is *Ro*.

The sweet, musky scent of her is in my lungs. The vision of her burned into the backs of my eyelids. The feel of her imprinted on my skin more permanently than any tattoo could ever be. It's been a while since I felt this level of obsession starting to take root.

Eli and Atticus sanded down the sharpest edges of my worst obsessions over the years, but this? This grows fangs and claws along with the roots that dare anyone to try to rip them out.

"Seven," Ro groans my name between kisses, and I need her to say it louder. So every motherfucker in this world can hear. They need to know who they'll have to answer to if they dare touch her.

I fuck her harder, filling her as much as she can be filled, manic with my thrusts as I give in to the animal. The primal thing that always wants to chase. To claim.

This time, it wants more.

It wants to keep her.

Ro screams her pleasure as tears roll down the apples of her cheeks.

"Shit, Sev," Eli grits out behind her, and I know he's a goner.

When Ro realizes it, too, she curses, rushing to her own release with a series of gasping, whimpering sounds that

CHAPTER 34

send me hurtling to the edge right along with them. The chain reaction sets fire to every one of my fuses as I thrust into Ro harder, quicker, hearing the sounds of my own ending pouring from my lips.

Fuck. She needs to come. *Now.*

I reach between us and press on her lower abdomen, feeling myself thrusting into my own palm through her belly as I increase the sensation for her.

"Oh fuck," she croaks. "It feels so full. I'm...I'm going to—"

Her words break off on another primal cry.

"Please," she whimpers. "Please, please, *please*, I need to —I need—"

Eli gasps at the same time as I fan my fingertips over her clit, and she fucking *explodes.*

Ro's body bucks violently, her back aching as she comes...and Eli and I pour into her. I growl through my teeth as her pussy shudders around us, milking out every last fucking drop of our release as we collapse into each other. I lay my head on her chest.

An unfamiliar sort of peace loosens the places I didn't even know were still wound tight.

Her heart hammers against my cheek, loud and strong. Limitless.

35

THE PERFECT CAMOUFLAGE

ATTICUS

They should have been back four hours ago.

If they weren't held up and got out when I fucking told them to, they would've been through that door by dinnertime. I stop pacing to grip the ledge above the fireplace, glaring at the mantle clock atop it as if, by sheer force of will, I can stop it from slicing away the seconds.

They just *had* to go to the art district. Had to try to pull off a fucking job in Paris without me. It's been over a goddamned year since Eli's done a job. *A year*, and they thought that now—with that girl—was a good time to take it up again?

Hot air pushes from my lungs, and my nostrils flare as if I could really breathe fire.

But Eli did it...

The voice in the back of my mind has the audacity to sound *glad*. We've been trying to get him back in the game for a while now, but he was never ready. Never willing.

Now, though, despite the shit timing and the even worse circumstances, he *was* ready.

You should've seen him, Sev said, and I wish I had. He's

CHAPTER 35

been a ghost behind these walls for too long now. Here, but not here. Alive, but barely breathing.

It's *her*.

I hate it, but I know it's true.

Something about her being here is changing things, and even though I fucking *hate* change, if she can bring even an ounce of peace to Eli's soul, I can't stand in the way of that. But damn if it might absolutely ruin all my perfectly-laid plans.

The second hand on the old Breguet mantel clock just keeps fucking ticking. I remember when Sev stole it from that private gallery showing in London. I was so fucking angry. We were there for a Botticelli, and it was hard enough to pull off the job without security suddenly being on high alert because it appeared someone stole a four-million-dollar clock. To be fair, he didn't know what it was worth.

Where Eli and I were only ever interested in the art—stealing it, collecting it, replicating it, and selling those replications to the highest bidder—Sev had the eyes of a goddamned pirate. Always hunting for treasures. Unable to say no to anything that gleamed gold or sparkled with diamonds or precious gemstones. His room is a testament to his sticky fingers. A veritable treasure trove of stolen goods and other *souvenirs* that would see him locked up for life.

Fuck. He better be okay. They had better *all* be okay.

Even her.

The second hand reaches the twelve, and the minute hand ticks into the next hour. 9:01 p.m.

If they aren't here by ten, I'll have to do something. I told our pilot to go dark, but there are ways I can reach him if I have to. At least to make sure they made it to the airstrip. If they didn't, I'll charter another flight, pick up their trail from the art district, and do whatever it takes to find them.

I can reach out to my contacts in the French police and the military and get—

My phone chimes in my pocket, and I almost drop it in my haste to get it free. I jam the notification that says there's movement at the front gate at the same time Ellie comes streaking into the living room, crashing into the front door with an excited yap. She jumps up, barking loudly.

"Ellie," I hiss. "Ellie, *hush*."

The fucking video app won't load the feed on my phone. "Fuck."

Ellie whines but does as I tell her. I flick off the lights, pull my gun, and plant myself next to the door, peering out onto the dark drive just as headlights jar across the window.

I blink into the brightness, keeping out of sight as I force my pulse to slow and steady, feeling hot power swelling in every muscle. I'm not sure it's the Jeep.

Eli and Sev wouldn't give up the location of this house for anything, but the girl would. She'd have been able to give Ambrose's men enough to go on to find it. I never should've let them take her off the property.

Eleven whines again, and I give her a look, pointing at my side. She comes to sit next to me, but won't stop tapping her paws, making tiny sounds of tortured anticipation in the back of her throat. "Quiet."

Outside, a car door opens, then running feet take the stairs three at a time. I guide Ellie back into the shadows and square my stance in front of her, flicking off the safety. Breathe in.

CHAPTER 35

Lights out, motherfucker.

The door chirps, and something in my chest crumples as the cabin's security mechanism picks up Eli's watch and unlocks automatically.

"Atticus?"

The door swings in, and Eleven almost knocks Eli over as she rushes past him out onto the drive.

"Shit," he curses when he sees me, eyeing the gun in my hand, but I'm already lowering it. Already jerking him in for a rough hug that makes my fucking bones ache and the muscles in my back tense and burn.

"You fucking idiots," I growl, but I can't let go. *I thought...*

Jesus fucking Christ, I don't even want to remember what I thought.

A muscle in my face twitches as I force myself to let him go, setting the gun down on the short table by the door to flick the lights back on and get a good look at him. My stomach sours as I take in the blood.

"Hey, it's okay. I'm alright."

There doesn't seem to be any on his skin, but it's spattered over the collar of his jacket. On the shirt he's wearing underneath. Gripping him by the elbow, I turn him around, searching for wounds.

"I said I'm all right," he repeats, tugging his jacket free of my grip. "We're okay."

Just as he says it, Sev steps up into the house, setting a bag with a gold frame sticking out of it by the door.

There's a fucking hole in his jacket.

"Bull*shit* you're all right. What the hell happened?"

I reach over and jerk the side open, finding a bandaged wound in Sev's shoulder. "You were shot?"

I immediately look for other injuries, but he seems to have none. He's pale, though. Too pale.

"I'm good, Atty." He gives my shoulder a squeeze. "We're all good."

"You were fucking shot, Sev," I repeat, scrubbing my hands over my face. If that bullet was just a few inches lower. A few more to the left.

God fucking dammit.

"It went through. It's fine."

"It's...*fine*?"

The air is hot in my lungs.

"*What. Happened?*"

They share a look.

"Someone better start talking."

So help me, if one of Ambrose's men saw Aurora and got away, this whole thing will have been for absolutely nothing, and I'll have no one to blame but my own damn self for bringing in an outsider.

I hear Eleven before I see her. She pants happily as she chases Aurora into the house.

The girl who's been nothing but trouble since I brought her here stops short when she sees me, and I'm surprised at what I feel when our eyes meet. I'm not sure what to call it.

Is it *relief*?

I remind myself that she's part of a plan and decide that's where the relief comes from. If something happened to her, we wouldn't have this golden opportunity to get our vengeance. To take back what was stolen from us.

I clear my throat, unable to keep my gaze from tracing the lines of her. She doesn't appear to be injured, but there's something different about her. The Aurora that just walked through this door is somehow not the same one who walked out of it yesterday.

CHAPTER 35

I suppose being party to a major crime and witnessing what I can guess is at least a few more murders will do that to a girl.

But then why does she look...*alive?* Like she's glowing from the inside. She even offers me a tentative, close-lipped smile as she brushes a strand of hair behind her ear. It's dark, I realize. She must've had Céline color it for her.

It looks good. A little too good.

Even all messed up like it is now, with what looks like dried blood sticking some pieces together in the front. The shirt and jeans must be new. They reek of luxury, and the way they hug her curves should be a sin.

And I really need to stop looking.

"Um, hey," she says, and I realize the seconds have turned into a minute, and I haven't managed to drag my eyes from her.

I push the door shut behind them and turn my attention back to Eli and Sev. "Would anyone mind telling me what the fuck you were thinking?"

"Can we do this in the kitchen?" Sev asks, but he's already kicked his boots off and is headed that way. "Ro's starving, and so am I, honestly. Did you make dinner?"

Did. I. Make. Dinner?

I'm going to throttle him.

Eleven jumps up for more pets from Aurora, and she laughs, scratching her around the ears. "I know, girl. I missed you, too."

She jumps down and comes straight to me, wagging her tail with a whine, looking at Aurora and back at me as if to say, *Look, she's back. I told you she'd be back.*

I've never met an animal more expressive or smart than this fucking dog. It's almost unnerving. "I know," I tell her. "I see that she's back."

The perfect camouflage

Eleven lets out a bark and races into the kitchen after Sev, and I remember she left her new stuffed chicken down the hall in my office. She barely put the fucking thing down since I gave it to her. Aurora follows her dog, and I watch her go, not understanding where the rage went. It was hot and tight in my veins a few seconds ago.

"Come on," Eli says, moving to follow them. "We'll talk in the kitchen."

"Send Aurora to bed. *We* need to talk, just us."

Eli pauses, and his shoulders go up. Down. He sighs.

My teeth clench.

"No," he says. "She stays."

The sound of my teeth grinding is loud in my ears as I stalk after him into the kitchen where Sev is already making a mess on the island, pulling out the fresh jars of pickled things I bought to replace the ones he broke, crackers, the honey pepper jelly he made last month, and a couple bricks of cheese.

"Like the new fridge," he says around a mouthful of smoked Gouda. "It's bigger than the last one."

He carves a slice of the Gouda from the brick and passes it to Aurora, who stacks it onto a cracker with some of the pepper honey and shoves it in her mouth with a pickled pepper.

She makes a face at how good the cheese is, and I refrain from saying that I bought it specifically to make my smoked bacon mac and cheese, only because I am still not sure where I misplaced all the frustration I felt five fucking minutes ago.

They're home. *Alive*. Safe enough to piss me off by making a mess in my spotless kitchen and eating my expensive-ass cheese like it's generic-brand cheddar.

"Glad you like it," I tell Sev. "It's the Lexus of refrigera-

CHAPTER 35

tors. Cost you over ten grand. Paid extra for same-day delivery."

He chokes on his cheese, but he doesn't really care how much I took from his account to replace the old one. And he'll actually be impressed that I took the initiative to find the most expensive refrigerator known to man just to try to teach him a lesson.

"For that price, it better do the grocery shopping, too."

I don't tell him that it does automatically notify me when we're low on staple items, but only because I am the only person in this house who would appreciate that function, and who gives a fuck about the new fridge right now?

Eli slides onto the stool at the island, smiling broadly at Aurora when she passes him a spicy pickled bean.

Something happened.

Something more than what left blood on their clothes. I can see it. There's a comfort between him and her that wasn't there before. An ease that should only come from knowing someone a hell of a lot longer than he's known *her*.

I look to Sev, who raises a brow at me, then back to Eli.

"Do I have to drag it out of you?" I snap, finding that misplaced rage exactly where I left it, right in the pit of my stomach. "What happened?"

"It was Ambrose's men," Eli confirms with another heavy sigh.

"Fuck."

"We handled it," Sev adds.

My fists clench.

"They're all dead."

"All of them? You're sure?"

"I'm sure."

He says it easily, with that lazy grin that the bastard has

practically trademarked, and there she is next to him, munching another cheese pickle cracker monstrosity like he's telling me the square root of pi instead of admitting to multiple murders.

The first one I could understand. Jesse hurt her. I'm sure there was some part of her that wanted him gone. A part of her that felt protected by what Sev did. But this?

She was cool with *this*? Cool with art theft? Did they tell her they were in France illegally, too? Are we sharing all the trade secrets now?

The sense of betrayal twisting in my chest is ugly and dark. They didn't ask me. They didn't clear this with me. They didn't involve me in it at all. They ran a whole job, albeit a small one, with this girl.

This stranger who is eating all my fucking cheese.

"You should know," Seven adds, indicating Eli with the brick of cheese still in his hand. "She saved Eli's life."

"I'm sorry, what?"

It takes me longer than it should to understand what he's telling me. Aurora casts her gaze away from me, awkwardly shrugging as she sets down the cracker she was about to deface with a mixture of pepper honey and pickle.

"It's true," Eli answers, reaching over to put his hand on her thigh and squeeze. "One of Ambrose's men had the jump on me. If Sev hadn't given her a gun—"

"You *what*?"

"Shut up. And *listen*," Sev hisses.

I clamp my jaw shut, nostrils flaring, as I force myself to let Elijah finish and disregard the fact that Sev gave an inexperienced girl, who we don't fucking know, a live weapon.

"He had the jump on me," Elijah repeated. "And I think it's safe to say Ambrose doesn't want me back. Not alive, anyway. The guy leveled his gun on me and said some shit about Ambrose sending his regards...I thought I was fucking dead."

He lets out a shaky breath and I feel it rattle in my own lungs.

Then he laughs. "But then the gun goes off and I open my eyes and...I was still alive. Ambrose's guy falls away with a hole in his head, and there she is. My guardian angel."

My lips part, but no words come out. I try, but I can't find them.

Aurora took a life for him?

When I look at her again, *really look*, I see something I failed to before, and guilt hollows my gut.

She protected him.

I'm supposed to protect them. It's my job. I promised Eli's mom before she passed. I swore I would do whatever it took. No matter what. *I swore it.*

I wasn't there last night to do my job, but she was.

"Is that true?" I ask her, and it's not that I don't believe it. Sev and Eli wouldn't lie to me.

I want to see her face when she replies because I need to know why. She doesn't even know us. Not really. This girl has no idea what Ambrose did to us. Why him and every single one of his followers deserve nothing but nine millimeters of lead and a shallow grave.

Her throat bobs as she looks up and nods.

"Why?"

Her brow furrows.

"Because it felt like the right thing."

I detect no lie in her words. Though there is an uncertainty in her eyes, and I'm not sure what it means. But I'm going to find out.

Not right now, but soon.

The perfect camouflage

I want to know exactly what makes this girl tick. No. I *need* to know because I get the feeling she can either be our perfect weapon...or a fucking time bomb if not handled correctly.

I go around the kitchen island and pull her into a hug before I can think better of it.

She lets out a little gasp, and I ignore the fact that she's either too stunned or still too put off by me to return the hug.

She smells like Eli's favorite cologne and sex, and now I know why he isn't catatonic from his confrontation with Ambrose's men. I guess I can thank her for that, too. I would if I didn't think that getting into bed with our Trojan horse was an absolutely terrible fucking idea.

"Thank you," I tell her seriously as I pull away. "Thank you for saving him."

Aurora blinks up at me, still stiff and confused. "Um. Yeah. You're welcome."

Could it be possible that I was completely wrong about her? When I peer into her eyes, I find a sharpness there I never noticed before. Or had I ever really looked?

I thought Aurora Bellerose was a pawn to be placed and moved. Sacrificed to our advantage if necessary.

Could that have been a camouflage?

Was she really something else underneath the weak-seeming, sweet exterior all along? Something stronger and able to make a lot more moves than one?

"Look at us all getting along," Sev says, freeing me from the hostage situation of Aurora's suddenly unwavering stare.

I step back and clear my throat as he takes another bite of Gouda right off the damned brick. "Isn't this nice?"

36

RESISTING THE GRUMP

AURORA

Atticus snatches the brick of cheese from Seven's hands and turns to take a cutting board from the cupboard and a knife from the block, muttering about Seven being a 'fucking animal', and the 'thirty-dollar chunk of Gouda'.

Ellie's claws click over the tile as she rushes back through the kitchen with something in her mouth. "What do you got there, girl?"

Her entire back end sways with her tail as she trots over to me and jumps up to set the toy in my lap. It's a stuffed chicken. A funny-looking one with a long neck and googly eyes. She barks, nudging the chicken for me to pick it up.

I raise a brow at Atticus. I didn't have time to pack up any of Ellie's things when we ran, and she definitely never had a deranged chicken toy.

His lips press into a taut line as he sets to cutting the fancy cheese into perfect, uniform slices, that Seven picks up to eat almost as fast as he can cut them.

Ellie jumps down and pads to the wall along the other side of the kitchen, nosing the elevated dog dishes there.

CHAPTER 36

My neck twinges with a sharp ache when I jerk my gaze back to Atticus too quickly. He bought her new dishes? And a toy?

Something in my chest aches, and I swallow hard against the feeling. "You didn't have to do that."

"It's nothing. I got her a bed, too. I put it in your room."

He says it like it means nothing, when that couldn't be further from the truth.

"And there are some plain white rags by the door for her paws and one of those poop scooper contraptions with the bags built-in."

Ellie comes back over to take her chicken back from my lap and lies on the floor next to Atticus's feet to pull at its neck. What happened to him not liking dogs?

"Oh, and they only had one small bag left of her kibble at the shop in town, but they're ordering more. I'll grab it next week. Between that and the raw diet stuff I grabbed for her to try, it should be enough to last until it gets here."

I blink, and wonder if I misjudged him. He's always come off as the cold and distant one. The asshole of the three, for sure. But how much of an asshole can he really be if he did all this for Ellie? Not just the basics of food and stuff to clean up after her, but also a bed and toy?

I open my mouth to say something, but I don't know what. No one's ever done anything to take care of her but me. He still isn't looking at me and I take the opportunity to study him in profile. His prominent chin and cheekbones. His full lips. There's a pull in my chest and before I can pause to analyze it any further, Elijah nudges me with his elbow.

"Told you he takes any kind of responsibility very seriously," he whispers, making Atticus scoff and Seven laugh out loud.

I clear my throat and excavate the appropriate response. "Well, thanks."

The words come out awkwardly.

"For taking such good care of her," I add. "You really didn't have to do all that. I would've got her everything she needed as soon as I got—"

"Don't worry about it. I had some time to kill while I was waiting to see if these two idiots were going to get you all killed."

"Sorry to disappoint," Seven says, carefully rolling his injured shoulder with a wince. "Close call, though."

"It's not fucking funny, Sev," Atticus says in a low monotone. "You know damn well it isn't."

That wipes the grin from Seven's face, and he finally sits down on one of the stools at the island. "I know, man."

He claps Atticus on the back. "Sorry."

Atticus heaves a hard sigh as he slices the last bit of the cheese and sets down the knife to go and wash his hands, and I get the feeling he's only doing it so he can turn away from the rest of us. I don't think he's the type to want to show any emotion. I know a bit about Seven's past, and a smidge about Eli's now, but I wonder about Atticus's. Where he came from. What he's been through to make him so...closed off. To make him feel like he needs to be in control.

"You guys must be tired. You should all get some rest," he says without turning around.

Eli nods as if 'tired' is the understatement of the century, and yeah, I'm fucking tired too, but they promised me answers. Don't I deserve that? I can't keep going on like this, not knowing what the fuck is happening, or who these men are, or the men who are after them. If I'm going to stay here, then I think I have a right to know.

CHAPTER 36

"Ro, you okay?"

"Hm? Yeah. I'm fine, I just..."

I guess it can wait another night.

"Never mind."

"You want answers," Eli guesses.

I nod. "It can wait, though."

He shakes his head, those warm eyes of his holding on to mine like a promise. "I think you've waited long enough."

Atticus turns to lean against the counter, and I don't miss the look he gives Eli. It's a warning. A request for caution. But Eli shakes his head at Atticus, too. "I want to tell her. I want her to know."

Atticus's cheekbones flare. "We still don't know for sure if we can trust her."

"I do," Eli challenges him, and a warmth spreads in my belly. "Can't that be enough?"

Atticus considers Eli for a few beats before nodding. "It's not up to me," he says finally, and that seems to be the end of it.

Eli lets out a shaky breath, and I don't like how he suddenly looks ill. His throat bobs as he pulls his hands into his lap and begins to unconsciously massage the injured one. Imagining what was done to him makes my skin crawl and my stomach twist. Whatever he says can't be worse than anything I imagined. Could it?

His gaze slides to Seven. "Sev?"

"Yeah. I'll grab the whiskey, bro. I think we're all going to need a drink for this."

37

ANCIENT HISTORY

ELIJAH

"Have you ever heard of The White Rose?"

A small knot forms between Aurora's brows. "Sounds familiar, I think."

Seven pours a couple of ounces of whiskey into a glass and slides it to me. I only take a small swallow. As much as I hate talking about it, somehow, this time feels different. That chaotic vibration in my veins and the buzzing in my head, that always comes with thoughts of that man and what he did to my family, are muted. A bit distant. Tolerable without the need to dilute them with liquor.

"The White Rose is a famous art thief."

I swirl the whiskey in my glass.

"*Was*," I correct myself. "He *was* a famous art thief. He's also my father."

Aurora glances at Seven, He already told her a bit about the circumstances that led him to my family. So, she probably already knows his name. Both of the names of my parents.

My angel is now one of only about four people who know the true identity of The White Rose.

CHAPTER 37

"Julian Ashford."

Nothing is known of his wife, Florence Ashford. It was never suspected that The White Rose married a talented artist who was able to forge artwork so precisely that not a single one of her forgeries has ever been discovered, even to this day.

"He was never caught," I tell her. "And neither was my mother. She was a painter. Taught me everything I know about art forgery."

"They taught us, too," Seven adds. "Not to paint. Atty and I were shit at that. But Julian taught me how to crack a safe in under thirty seconds."

"And he taught Atticus how to read blueprints and account for every possible scenario in every situation," I fill in for Atticus, who grunts his agreement.

My parents taught them so much more than that, but those were the areas where they each excelled.

"When my mom got sick, we started helping my dad more with jobs, but we were still young. Inexperienced."

I remember the first time my father brought Ambrose De La Rosa into our house. It felt wrong right from the start. He didn't bring anyone into the house. Not ever. Seven and Atticus were the only exceptions, and they became family. This man, this stranger, was not family. Not even a friend.

"That's when he brought in Ambrose. He was my father's competition. A rival art thief. The two of them had been racing against each other to get their hands on various artworks for years. My father won most of the races, but Ambrose got his hands on a fair few pieces my father had his heart set on."

Atticus snorts. "Remember how Sev almost slit his throat that first time?"

"I thought he was a suit." Seven shrugs. "You know, like

CIA or something, with that slick, all-black getup and the fuckin' sunglasses."

"Too bad you didn't get the knife in before Dad saw you."

I wish he had. Then none of this mess would've happened.

Seven's expression darkens. "Yeah. Too bad."

"Anyway," I sigh. "My dad got it in his head that they should team up instead of working against each other."

"He wasn't in his right mind after we got Florence's cancer diagnosis," Seven injects, sounding like he's trying to make an excuse for Dad's choice, but back then, it did seem like an all right idea. Even if Ambrose seemed like the wrong man for the job. I could look at it objectively.

If the two of them could work together, Dad thought they could double their acquisitions. And with me able to forge the less complicated pieces by then, we could become a money-making machine. But more than that, for my father at least, and his father before him, it was about the *collection*.

And he decided it was his mission to add every piece of art my mother ever wanted to that collection before it was too late. He wanted her to have them all. Like each one would somehow buy more time for her on this earth.

"Were any of us in our right minds?" I ask, looking pointedly at Atticus, who won't meet my stare. As much as I try not to be angry at him for having to leave, I know why he did. Why he had to…after Mom died. I didn't want to fucking be there, either. Everything reminded me of her. *Everything.*

"From that day on, Ambrose and my dad were business partners," I continue even though it's more of a struggle to keep my voice steady with my chest collapsing in on itself.

CHAPTER 37

"We still helped with the jobs, but our roles were *less* than before. Eventually, it got to a point where Dad didn't need us at all sometimes, and we were getting older and able to run smaller jobs ourselves. For a while, it was very lucrative."

"You were already forging art then?" Aurora asks. "How old were you?"

I think back. "I started forging when I was about eighteen."

"Wow."

"Yeah, it wasn't long after I started that it all fell apart."

"How long ago was this?"

My brows cinch together. "You mean when it all started to fall apart? I guess it started right after Mom..."

Her death really did mark the beginning of the end of everything.

"That was six years ago," Seven finishes for me.

I clear my throat and take a swallow of whiskey, giving myself a mental slap to combat the burn in my throat. "Right. Yeah. Six years ago. By then, we all trusted Ambrose. He was a regular fixture in the house. Dad's best friend as well as his business partner. Ambrose lost his wife, too—a number of years before we met him—so, in a way, Mom's passing just brought him and my dad even closer together."

"He was at her funeral, for fuck's sake," Atticus growls.

The vibration starts low, a hum beneath my rib bones that breeds heat from the friction and makes my hand ache.

Fuck.

I won't lose my shit in front of Aurora again.

I'll stop, I tell myself. *If I can't control the panic, I can just stop talking.*

Aurora reaches over and takes my hand in hers, bringing me out of my spiraling thoughts. Her fingers are cool against my skin, soothing the rattle in my bones, forcing me to take a deliberate breath.

I wet my lips and push on. "It was all bullshit. Up until then, my father never told him where he kept our family collection. That's what it was all about for my dad—the legacy of it. My grandad before him was also a *collector*. And before Ambrose, we already had over ninety pieces in our family collection. So many incredible artists. Lots of Monets, Van Goghs, a Rembrandt or two, a Botticelli, a couple Picassos. Even a Da Vinci and a Johannes Vermeer."

"Wait, I know that one. He did *Girl with a Pearl Earring*, right? I read that book back in high school."

I smile. "Yeah. It was in our collection. The one on display at The Hague is my mother's forgery."

She scoffs incredulously, clearly impressed, and it only makes me want to impress her more, but this story doesn't have a happy ending. Not yet, anyway.

Aurora picks up on the shift in my expression and rubs her thumb over the scars on the back of my hand. "You said *was* in your collection?"

"The bastard took it all," Atticus growls. "Every last piece, save for what we had on the walls in the house."

Aurora gasps. "So, your dad told Ambrose where it was?"

"Yeah. Ambrose didn't take it right away. It was a few months before he made his move and then he just… vanished."

"Florence took a turn, then," Seven recalls, and from the faraway look in his cold blue eyes, I know he's reliving it. He's remembering the raw, scraping, bleeding sensation of his guts being ripped out, because it's how I felt, too.

"It wasn't just our entire collection of stolen art, it was my family's legacy," I explain. "It was all my mother's and

CHAPTER 37

my forgeries, too. And her personal work. My father liked to keep it all next to the greats. Told her it belonged there with them. That it was every bit as good, even if some critics thought differently earlier on in my mom's art career."

"*He* killed her," Atticus says decisively. "Maybe not directly, but her heart was broken after what he did. She might've—" He struggles with the words. "She might've been able to hold on for the next round of...of treatment if he hadn't—"

Seven lifts his own glass of whiskey and hands it to Atticus, who takes it and swallows it in one, swiping the back of his hand across his mouth.

"I'm so sorry," Aurora whispers. "I can't imagine what it must've been like to have something so meaningful taken from you like that."

I nod solemnly.

"The fucker wasn't done yet," Seven seethes.

"It wasn't just my mom who was affected by it. Her illness took her within a couple months of Ambrose's double cross." Another longer swallow of whiskey. "Then my dad started to show signs of..."

I don't know how to put it. It was all so disjointed at first. We didn't know what to think. Weren't sure if we should worry.

"Mental distress," I decide. "At first, we just thought it was the grief and it would get better."

"It didn't," Atticus interjects, and Aurora pulls just a little tighter into herself, her shoulders tense, feeling the energy shift in the room. Ellie senses it, too, letting out a soft whine from the floor, where she's stopped playing with her chicken and lays sullenly as she listens.

"At first, the doctors thought it was a temporary psychosis. They said it should get better with time and

Ancient history

treatment. That it was a symptom of losing his wife and wasn't uncommon among the newly widowed. But they didn't know he'd also lost his entire life's work—our family's legacy—all in the span of eight weeks."

"Oh my god." Aurora's eyes turn glassy as she covers her mouth with trembling fingers.

"In a way, we lost them both that summer," Atticus says, toneless. The calm before the storm.

He really needs to go let off some steam.

"Atticus, maybe you should—"

"No, I'll fucking stay."

I take a deep breath. There's no arguing with the stubborn bastard.

We've talked about this—all of it—more than a few times over the last year and a bit since I've been home, but this time feels different. We aren't going over what we know. Or reminiscing. We're sharing our truth with someone else.

Atticus doesn't like his part in this story. He blames himself for what happened next. He has no idea that whether or not he was with us, I still would have done what I did. He wouldn't have been able to stop me once I'd made up my mind.

"It's developed past that now, into dementia. My dad remembers things, remembers us, sometimes, but when he does remember, it's always the art. And it's always Mom. He wants to see it again, the collection. And the pieces Mom painted for him."

"You never should have taken the deal," Atticus says through his teeth.

"What deal?" Aurora asks.

I finish my whiskey and push the glass toward Seven to

CHAPTER 37

refill. This is the part that's harder, because Atticus is right. I fucked up.

"Ambrose reached out to me. He had his cake, but he wanted to eat it, too."

Her face pinches.

"He had Julian's entire collection," Seven explains. "But no one to forge the pieces for him. He could sell the originals off, but why do that when you can replicate them, keep the originals, and sell off the forgeries for the same price?"

Atticus's knuckles turn white where they grip the countertop. "He wanted to take the title of The White Rose. Every fucking petal and thorn. Leave us with nothing."

"So, what?" Aurora asks, struggling to follow. "He wanted you to paint for him?"

I nod gravely. "Yes."

"And Eli agreed," Atticus seethes, pushing off from the counter to pace to the edge of the room and back.

I drop my gaze to the countertop, to the now untouched food littered over its surface. "For a year," I add, meeting Aurora's searching stare, trying to implore her to understand.

"The deal was I'd paint for him for *one* year, and afterward, he'd send me home with my mother's art. I wanted my family's collection back, too, but that wasn't on the table. I was desperate. I'd just lost my mom, and my dad's health was failing. I had to do something. I thought if I could return some of the art to him. Bring a piece of Mom back…"

My throat burns, and I fight to speak through the flames as my eyes prick. "I really thought that if I did, he'd come back to us, too."

"Oh, Elijah," Aurora fights tears of her own, and I quickly wipe at my nose, a hollow laugh on my lips.

"I knew Sev and Atticus wouldn't like it," I say, changing tack.

"So the fucker didn't tell us," Atticus finishes for me.

"Come on, man." Seven shakes his head at him, and the old wound starts to open between them. "You weren't even here."

Atticus's jaw tenses, but he says nothing. He can't, because he *wasn't* there. After Mom passed, he lost the plot. And then when Ambrose double-crossed us, he was a raging bull. We were doing everything we could to get the collection back, but he was driving himself mental with it. Not sleeping. Not eating. Nit-picking everything. Chasing useless theories. Driving us all fucking mad with his obsessive need for everything to be in perfect order all the time.

He'd mentioned a desire to join the military when we were teenagers, so Sev and I pushed him into it.

We all had our vices back then, but I do wish he'd been in the right state of mind to stay. Not having him around much in the beginning of Dad's mental illness made it harder. I know Atticus regrets going, even if he needed to. And I know that no matter how hard things get now, that he would *never* leave again.

Even if it was only a few years ago, the person I was back then was a fucking child compared to the man I am now. I'm sure Atticus feels the same.

We all have our regrets.

Maybe they won't be so heavy once we take our vengeance.

"Why weren't you here?" Aurora asks Atticus, and she must feel me tense because she flinches and asks. "What?"

"Atty here joined the military," Sev says. "What was it? About ten weeks after Florence passed? Just when Julian was starting to really lose it?"

CHAPTER 37

"Enough," I hiss. "That's ancient history. And you know he needed to go."

Seven tips his whiskey back. He really shouldn't judge. Not with the way he flew off the fucking handle after Mom's passing.

He hated that her enemy was one he couldn't see. Couldn't fight. Couldn't *eliminate*. It drove him crazy, to the point where I thought we might lose him to a sort of madness, too. He went out sometimes after the house was asleep and didn't come back until dawn, reeking of whiskey and blood with a new souvenir to add to his own private collection of teeth and bone.

Sev said they all had it coming. That they were terrible men who did bad things to good people. I believed him, but I still had to worry about his sorry ass every night, counting the minutes until he got home.

I wondered if he'd get caught or killed and if I'd end up motherless, fatherless, and brotherless after Atticus left.

But at least Sev always came home. *Always.*

Atticus stops pacing. "I wasn't the only one who left."

I hang my head.

"No. I left a note. Told Sev to take care of Dad. I said I'd made a deal, and I'd be back in a year with Mom's art."

"He gave us no choice," Atticus snaps.

"Because I knew what your answer would be," I snap right back. "And I had to try. You *know* I had to try."

"A lot of good that did."

Aurora brings her other hand to join the first, cupping them over my broken one. "What happened?"

"Exactly what you'd imagine. Ambrose had already proven he was a traitor. I don't know why I expected any different. He brought me somewhere. I don't know where.

He had me drugged and blindfolded to get me there. When we arrived, he put me in a room.

"It was a big room with good light and a nice bed. That's where he kept me. I thought our deal was still on, so I painted. He brought me the pieces he wanted me to forge, and I painted for him every fucking day for a year."

Aurora searches my eyes, and her hands lightly squeeze mine. It feels so good. I don't ever want her to let go.

I brush my thumb over her knuckle. "He didn't let me out of the room. Not once. I had no phone, no computer, no communication with the outside world. When I didn't paint, I slept, took long-ass showers, and read the books one of his guards occasionally brought me. After a while, I realized I needed to keep track of time and started marking the days. When the day came that marked a year, I was ready to go. But that day, Ambrose brought me a new piece to forge."

"He never intended to let him go," Seven fills in the blank.

"I argued with him. I told him I knew it'd been a year, and we made a deal. I tried to reason with him. In the end, I refused to paint until he would let me go."

"What did he do?"

She looks down at my hand in hers, her chin quivering, but she's got it wrong. Ambrose didn't do this to my hand. *I did.*

"He did what he had to do to make me perform for him. At first, he hurt me. Well, not him personally, of course—he never did like to get his hands dirty—he had his men do it. And when that stopped working after a few months, he tried a new tactic. He burned one of my mother's paintings right in front of me. Promised me he would destroy them all, one by one, if I didn't cooperate."

CHAPTER 37

"We tried to find him," Sev tells Aurora. "When we realized what Eli had done, Atticus used his contacts in the military to try to find where Ambrose was keeping him."

"I went as deep as I could, but everything led to a dead end."

"When the year was up, and he didn't come back, that's when we really started to fucking panic." Sev's piercing eyes meet mine, and in them, I can see the hell they went through during those seven months, when they didn't know if I was alive or dead.

"Eventually, I knew I couldn't stay another day—another *second*—in that room. It got to a point where I thought I'd rather die than lift a paintbrush for him one more time, and if he was going to keep me anyway, then Dad would never get to see Mom's work again, regardless. They were careful then, about letting me have sharp things. Things that I could injure others with. Injure myself with. But it was an old building, and there was this marble bench running the length of one wall, and it had a loose bit of stone."

My stomach churns, and a sour taste coats my tongue.

It comes back in a flash of brutal white stone splattered with red.

It broke away from the corner of the bench easier than I thought it would.

"It was heavy. Jagged. I knew it would work."

Aurora draws in a shaking breath. "Oh no..."

The flashback lashes itself at the barricades of my mind. All violence and pain and red, red, *red*.

I shove it away, not realizing I'm shaking until Aurora grips me tighter, trying to steady me. I think it helps.

It helps enough that I can skip the ugliest bits and tell her plainly the only thing that matters.

Ancient history

"Can't paint with a fucked-up hand..." My laugh is anything but joyful. "I made it so he couldn't use me anymore. "

I didn't realize it then, but when I brought that piece of jagged marble down on myself again and again and again, I was also breaking off some part of my soul that I would never get back.

"My mother taught me how to paint, but she also taught me family comes first. Somewhere along the way, I'd forgotten that."

"You didn't know," Aurora says, trying to comfort me. "You did what you thought you had to at the time."

Whether it's true or not, it's no consolation for the truth. "I traded time with my dad that I'll never get back, Angel. And all I had to show for it when Ambrose dumped me at a train station in Philly, was a broken hand and a fucking mountain of regret."

"You're lucky he let you go at all," Atticus says. "He could've killed you."

I'd never tell them, but for a long time after I got home, I wished he had.

38

DADDICUS

SEVEN

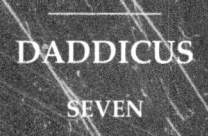

Atty's right.

Ambrose *could* have killed Eli when he rendered himself no longer useful, but he didn't, and we're going to make sure that decision haunts him until the end of his very short, very stressful days.

"We've been working to get our vengeance ever since," I tell Aurora. "But it's easier said than done when your enemy is cunning as a fox and slipperier than an oil-coated eel."

"I wouldn't say he's that smart," Atticus says, stooping to scratch Ellie behind the ears. "Just really fucking good at hiding."

"He has his men do all his business transactions for him," Eli explains, looking more tired than I've seen him in months. Maybe longer. "And we were never able to find the place where he was keeping the art. Keeping me."

"Doesn't mean we won't," Atticus asserts. "We *will* find it. And we will bring it all home."

I push the cork stopper back into the whiskey bottle and sigh. "In the meantime, we've been doing everything in

CHAPTER 38

our power to make Ambrose's life a living hell. Ruining his art deals. Turning his connections in the underground market against him."

Despite myself, I grin. I miss running jobs with my boys, but there's a certain sweetness in causing someone pain who is deserving of it. Even if it's not the sort of pain I'd *prefer* to inflict. Atticus and Eli are right about one thing; as much as I'd like to see Ambrose's head on a pike...

"He should have to watch everything he's built for himself turn to nothing but dust in his hands, just like Julian did. He should have to lose everything he cares about."

Only then should he be allowed to die.

"And so he will," Atticus promises. "If my plan works, we might finally have the in we've been looking for, to take Ambrose down from inside his own network."

My jaw clamps shut and without meaning to, my gaze slides to Aurora.

No.

I won't put her in Ambrose's path. If that's what Atticus is planning, he can fucking forget it. No one is forcing her to do anything. Not while I'm around.

Eli won't go for it, either. We can find our own way.

"About that." Eli's voice drips with tension and something curiously close to malice. "It's about time you told us what you want with Aurora, and how she fits into this 'plan' of yours."

Atticus couldn't look more fucking gobsmacked if I'd actually slapped him upside the head. I purse my lips to hold in a very childish interjection of *Ooooooh shit.*

Yup. He went there. Eli just dropped it right there on the kitchen island, in front of Ro.

Ro twists to look at Atticus, and is that a little bit of

anger in her eyes now? Fuck, I'm just glad I'm not the one on the receiving end of that, though I suspect when she finds out Eli and I knew there was a plan at all, she won't be exactly thrilled with any of us.

"Atticus?" She sounds confused now. A little hurt. I don't fucking like it. "What does he mean?"

"Seriously, Eli?" Atticus mutters.

"Yes, seriously. I'm done playing this game with you. It's time for you to explain why you brought her here."

"I knew the cleaning job was bullshit," Ro says under her breath and then glares at Atticus again. "No one pays a maid fifteen thousand dollars a month to clean a house that's never even fucking dirty. God, how could I have been so stupid?"

"You're not, Ro." I drop a kiss to the top of her head. "He really was going to pay you and try to leave some messes for you to clean."

"How long have you known?"

Ro looks between Eli and me, and I wish I'd just told her the real reason she was here from the fucking start. Why didn't I?

"Since the start," Eli admits. "But Atticus never told us what he was planning. Just that he thought maybe we could..." His face scrunches up. "...*use* you."

She pushes out from the counter and gets to her feet. "Are you serious? Wow. You know every girl loves to hear how she can be fucking *used*."

Ah fuck.

"That's not how it is anymore, and I think you know that," I say, and she stops trying to walk away. Her fists clench and for a few beats, she says nothing.

When she finally turns around, she doesn't look at any of us. Not really. Her face shows only a very strained, prac-

CHAPTER 38

ticed sort of calm. It's a mask I want to pull off. She has a right to be angry, and a part of me wishes she'd let us all have a taste of the fire I can see burning just beneath her placid surface.

"This *plan*," she spits out the word like it's dirty. "It's to take down this Ambrose guy?"

A muscle in Atticus's jaw tics. "Yes."

"Will it mean getting the art back?"

"It could."

"You don't have to—" Eli starts, but Ro silences him with a raised palm.

She grinds her teeth behind her lips, steeling herself before she comes back to the island, but doesn't sit. "I want to hear it."

"And you will," I promise her. "Tomorrow morning. *After* we all get some rest."

Aurora follows my fleeting gaze to Eli, and her lips part when she sees what I see. Taking in the pallor of his skin and the deep circles beneath his eyes. The way he's gripping his knees. How his shoulders are pulled in tight.

He's had enough.

Barring Aurora's catnap on the way to France, none of us have slept in god knows how many hours. This conversation will not be productive or good for anyone if we have it right now. I mean, fuck, depending on what Atticus says, I'm not even sure I can trust *myself* not to deck him.

"No, I want to hear it now," Eli pushes.

I shake my head at Atticus, and he gets the point. "Sev's right, Eli. We all need some rest. Let me collect everything I have so far and show you in the morning."

"All of us," Eli stipulates, reaching for Ro's hand.

I'm more than a little relieved when she lets him take it, twining her fingers with his.

"Yes. All of us."

Eli nods, mostly to himself.

"You should all go get some sleep," Atticus orders, always needing the last word. "And a shower."

"Ooookay, Daddicus," I say sarcastically, trying to alleviate some of the tension in the room. "You're one to talk. Those dark circles under your eyes are bigger than a grave digger's and your stress BO smells like Satan's asshole."

The glower he gives me would be comical coming from anyone else who wasn't a trained killer.

Nah.

It's still funny as fuck.

"Seriously, man." I make a waving motion with my hand in front of my nose and preen internally when Ro struggles not to smile.

"*Daddicus*," she repeats to herself in a restrained whisper, covering her mouth to trap in a snort.

Success!

I thought that was pretty damn good.

"It's making my eyes water," I finish, feeling Atticus's glare on my back as I walk away. "You should really do something about that."

39

MIDNIGHT CIGARETTES

AURORA

I can't fucking sleep.

Ellie's been out like a light since we came to bed, and I just know Atticus must've been playing with her most of the day for her to be so tired. I don't know if I'll ever be able to trust the guy after this, but it's hard to stay angry with him seeing her so comfortable in her new bed. It's absolutely massive and takes up an entire corner of the bedroom. A fancy-looking memory foam thing with raised edges in a fluffy pink cover. It's perfect.

I roll over on the mattress, flicking on the bedside lamp before sitting up to pick through the small pile of items Elijah bought for me in Paris. They occupy the space at the end of the bed. I rip the tag off a long, plain black sweater I found at Versace and pull it over my pajamas. It feels smoother than butter against my skin.

If I were smart, I'd have looked for a bathing suit. A soak in the hot tub outside, or twenty minutes in the steam room next to it, sounds like just the thing right now. But I need some air. Maybe it'll help me think. I suppose I could just dip my toes in.

CHAPTER 39

I bend to retrieve the fallen tag from the floor, trying to ignore the too many zeroes staring back at me with wide, knowing eyes. My fingers brush a rough edge in the hardwood, and I squint to see in the dim light, finding a deep groove that disappears into the shadows under the bed.

Carefully, I run my finger along it, slipping from the edge of the mattress to my knees on the floor. It extends far beneath the bed frame and branches off in either direction. The scratches are too straight. Too deep to have been an accident.

"What the hell?"

I push the bed over a few inches. Then a few inches more, earning myself a chuff from Ellie as she stirs and adjusts her position to go back to sleep.

It's some kind of pattern...

Carved into the floor in violent notches and scrapes.

I push the bed over more, finding a cross and a ring filled with pockmarks. The lighter wood beneath the darker stain makes the spots look almost like stars. Like some constellation I don't recognize. Hercules maybe? Or Virgo? I was never good at recognizing them, but I had an older foster sister once who loved that kind of shit.

Why would someone put it under a bed?

I huff out a mirthless laugh. As if I should expect anything to make sense here. From the moment I stepped foot in this house, my entire world has been flipped upside down and turned on its axis. Jesse's dead. I was just in Paris. I helped steal a few million dollars' worth of art. I'm wearing fucking *Versace*. And, oh yeah, I fucked two criminals in an airplane at thirty thousand feet.

It feels wrong to call them that. They're only a product of what the world made them. Whether it was trauma or legacy—or a bit of both.

Midnight cigarettes

My stomach churns when I think of Elijah in that room where Ambrose kept him. Isolated. Cut off from the world and his family. Utterly alone with nothing but paint and pain to remind him he was still alive.

I try to imagine it, but I can't. I'm not sure if I even want to.

I've been through some shit. I know what it's like to be locked in. Closed out. But not like that. Not for a whole year and seven months. I don't know how he didn't go mad.

A flashback of him smashing easels in his art studio catapults to the forefront of my mind, and I think…maybe he didn't fully evade the madness. I don't blame him, though. How could I, now that I've heard the truth?

Air.

I need some fucking air. I can ask one of the guys about the weird constellation carvings later.

Leaving the bed at an awkward angle so I don't disturb Ellie any more than I already have, I quietly tiptoe into the hall.

The house is silent as I move through its vacant halls. When I reach the bottom of the stairs, I peek down the long corridor that leads to Elijah's bedroom and studio, biting my lip when I find it devoid of light. He might still be awake, just staring at the ceiling in the dark. Somehow, I doubt he's sleeping tonight, either. Not after he had to relive all of his old scars.

He might not want to see me, though.

He might not want to see *anyone.*

Wrapping my arms around myself, I go around and through the kitchen, stopping to make a quick cup of tea with the honey from the hives—I swear the shit is addictive —and take the steaming mug to the backyard with me.

There's a chirp as I unlock the door and exit. Atticus

CHAPTER 39

must have the security system cranked up to eleven. I wait to see if it's going to set off an alarm, but the house remains quiet as I step out and shut the door behind me.

The cool night air brushes against my bare legs, and the thin socks on my feet do nothing to stop the chill of the stone terrace from seeping into my bones. But it feels good. The open space gives me room to breathe, and the cold soothes the uncomfortable tension in my chest.

I sip my tea to get some warmth back into my blood as I walk down onto the pool deck under the bright, full moon. The sky is so clear here, so free of light pollution, that if I had a map, I could probably find any constellation. There's nothing but the sound of the pool water sloshing gently and the din of nature sounds farther in the distance.

It's so peaceful. You'd have no idea that somewhere in these hills, and probably not all that far away, is a dead gangster.

Sure you wouldn't rather ask about the bodies buried in the backyard? Seven's joking words to me at the beehive come back, and I scoff to myself, realizing he probably wasn't really joking. How many others has he buried in the North Carolina mountains?

The scent of tobacco prickles my nose, and I frown, whirling when I hear the crackle and hiss of a cigarette.

"*Jesus.*" My pulse races and a healthy amount of tea sloshes onto the pool deck when I find Atticus lounging in a pool chair behind me. His grimacing face is illuminated in the cherry-red glow of his cigarette as he takes a long drag.

"Nope," he says, his voice muted as he holds in the tobacco smoke and then lets it out in a plume of smoky gray. "Just me. Couldn't sleep?"

He holds the cigarette out to me, and I consider him for a moment. He looks different. It's his hair, I realize. He's never had it loose before. It's always been tied back in a short bun.

It's a lot longer than I thought. Thick and wild. The color of golden wheat with a bit of dark copper laced through it to match his short, trimmed beard.

I close the gap between us and take the cigarette, ashing it before taking a small drag and passing it back. "Didn't peg you for a smoker."

"Didn't peg you for a killer."

I flinch. "Touché."

Of all the thoughts racing through my mind, trying to make sense of themselves, strangely, the fact that I killed a man wasn't even in the top five. I'd barely thought about it at all since we got on the jet to come home. How fucked up is that?

"There's a weird carving under my bed," I say as I exhale, letting the nicotine do its job of calming my nerves.

"Yeah. Julian did it. Fucked up all the walls, too, but we fixed those."

The reminder of what happened to him is like a weight in my stomach.

"Where is he now? Julian?"

"He's back in the old house. The one where Eli grew up. He has a full staff there. Nurses who care for him. A doc that comes to check in once a week. Security. We tried having him here for a while, but he wanted to go back. Said he couldn't see her here."

"See who?"

"His wife, Florence. When he's there, he sees her. He can talk to her. He didn't see her here, and he hated it. When he stopped recognizing us, there wasn't much point keeping him somewhere he didn't want to be if it was going to cause him so much distress."

CHAPTER 39

"Why didn't you go with him? Stay with him in the old house, I mean?"

His face pinches. "We've been trying to dismantle Ambrose's empire for a while now. The only reason any of us are still alive is because he has no idea where we are."

"But he won't hurt Julian?"

From what I understood, Ambrose knows where the old house is.

"Nah. We worried about that for a while, hence the security, but Ambrose already got what he wanted from Julian...and he isn't a threat now. Not with his illness. Eli still worries Ambrose might try to use Julian against us, though."

"Would he?"

"I don't think so. But if there were ever any indication that he might, we'd have Julian moved to a secure location in a heartbeat. Trust me, I don't like him in that house any more than Eli does, but it's where he's at peace and we can't take that from him. It's all he has left."

I want to ask him more, but I don't want to push my luck. This is the most candid Atticus has been with me since I met him. Probably the most he's spoken directly to me since I came to this house.

But judging by the guarded expression on his face, he's not likely to answer many more of my questions. He still doesn't trust me, and that's fine. I don't trust him, either.

Funny how I thought I'd be safe here. So far from everything. So far from Jesse.

When in reality, I might've escaped one prison cell just to walk into another.

A world with the same bars, but a different warden.

The silence stretches between us in the dark. I sip the remains of tea to try to fill it.

Midnight cigarettes

"I should probably head back in."

"Wait."

I turn to face him and his Adam's apple bobs in his throat as he sits up and pats the end of the lounger. "Stay."

"Why?"

"There's something I want to say."

A muscle in my temple flexes as I clench my jaw. There's a lot I'd like to say, too, but none of it is very nice. I can forgive Seven and Elijah for not saying anything because they didn't know Atticus's plan. They probably didn't even know he had one at all when he first brought me here. And I get loyalty between friends. *Between brothers.*

But Atticus? He wanted to use me all along. Even if it might be for a worthy cause, am I supposed to be fucking happy about it?

Because it feels like shit.

I've been used and abused my whole goddamn life. After Paris, I thought this might be the one place where I wouldn't have to worry about that.

And I was wrong again.

"Then say it."

He taps the end of his seat again. "Please."

Something about the way he says it makes me curious.

"It'll just take a second," he adds, his dark brown eyes flitting to mine and holding there.

I sit. "Fine. But only because I owe you for taking care of Ellie."

Not because you asked nicely.

His lips tug up in a lopsided smirk that he erases as soon as he realizes I've seen it. "Yeah. She's a great pup. Smart as hell."

Now it's my turn to smirk. *Don't I fucking know it.*

Atticus studies my face like I'm some puzzle he's still

CHAPTER 39

trying to solve. It makes me nervous. He might find something I don't want him to.

I cock my head, trying to read him right back. What is he playing at?

"Tomorrow," he says finally. "When I go over the plan with everyone, I need you to remember something."

I clasp the mug tighter between my hands as he takes one final drag of his cigarette and pinches off the cherry at the end to snuff it out. He puts the butt in his pocket and blows the smoke away from me, downwind.

"Remember what?"

"I want you to remember that it's your choice."

I feel my face screw up in confusion. "That *what* is my choice?"

"Whether or not you'll help us."

There's a black sea of emotion in his eyes that's too deep and too painful to look at.

I bite the inside of my cheek as I drop my gaze to the small stretch of wooden pool lounger between us.

"The guys..." He trails off. "I can see how they've become attached to you."

It's clear he doesn't like it and I'm surprised when it stings. It shouldn't because I don't care what *Daddicus* thinks.

I don't.

"It could get dangerous, and they might not want you involved."

I'm not sure what to say to that. I'm not even sure if I want to be involved.

I do want to help them, regardless of that being Atticus's plan all along. People like the man who kept Elijah captive—who hurt him—deserve every bad thing coming to them. But it's not my fight. It isn't my legacy that was stolen. Or my family who was taken.

I don't even have a family. Not really.

It's always been just me. And right now, my instinct is telling me to believe Atticus when he says it could be dangerous. Am I willing to risk my life to fight in a war I didn't even have a hand in starting?

I jump when Atticus reaches across the space between us and places his hands over mine where they clutch the empty mug, making a zap of electricity dart up my arms at the contact.

"They're the best people in the world," he says in a low tone. "The only family that has ever mattered to me."

My eyes sting and I don't know why.

"And that...that fucking bastard almost broke us. He *did* break Julian. But I can fix it."

I look up and immediately wish I hadn't. He's set fire to the black sea in his eyes, and I get lost in the flames.

"*With you*," he whispers harshly. "With your help, there's a chance I can set it all right. *Please*. Please let me try. Not for me. *For them*. They deserve this."

I pull my hands from his, leaving the mug between us as I try to block out the way my foundations are shaking. Wonder when the fuck my walls started to crumble.

There's unrestricted passion in his voice that I can't deny, but I wish I could block it out. Fill my ears with cotton.

He loves them. It's what he's saying without saying it. He loves them, and he will do whatever it takes to repair what was broken.

Because they're his family.

Not blood, but brothers all the same.

It's more than I ever dared to wish for myself. The quiet

CHAPTER 39

prayer that the stars never answered for me. And even if my lack of it hurts, I'm so glad Eli and Sev have found that because they do deserve it.

So, I guess I'm glad they have their Daddicus.

Even if he is a rude dickhead with control issues.

Atticus pushes to his feet, snatching up my drained mug to take with him. "You already saved Eli once, and for that, I'll never be able to repay you. So, if you say no, I'll respect it. You can write your own check. Start over anywhere you want. It's your choice. Yours alone."

His deep gaze holds me captive for another moment before he leaves.

As his heavy footsteps retreat back into the house, I regain the ability to breathe. But the hole in my chest and the impossible choice in my lap make it harder than it should be.

I turn around and lay back, looking up at the midnight sky.

I stopped believing in fate and the power of the universe when I was fourteen, sneaking drain cleaner into a bottle of Mountain Dew to poison my foster parents.

We make our own decisions, and good or bad, they define us.

I don't know if I'll make the right one, but I do know Atticus is right. It is my choice to make.

40

HURT/COMFORT

AURORA

I listen for Atticus when I go back inside, but the kitchen and the hall leading to his office are both quiet and still. I wonder where he sleeps. Elijah's room is on the main floor, and I've seen Seven coming out of the room on the opposite end of the upstairs hall from where I'm staying, but I don't have a clue where Atticus' bedroom might be.

During Elijah's tour and while nosing around looking for things to clean, I never saw another bedroom. I'm thinking maybe I'll see if Seven's bedroom light is on as I trudge through to the main entryway. Anything has to be better than staring at the ceiling for another few hours, right?

I should be tired. I really should be, but I can't seem to shut my brain—

Pausing with my foot on the bottom stair, I frown at the light I can see way down the hall. I thought Elijah was asleep.

My throat grows thick.

How could he be after rehashing all of that?

Licking my dry lips, I pad quietly down the hall toward

CHAPTER 40

the light. When I'm close enough, I find it's not coming from beneath his bedroom door, but from the door that leads to his connected art studio.

I almost turn around. What if he's painting? I shouldn't interrupt him if he is. I chew my lower lip, turning away just to turn right back to the closed door again.

Fuck.

I let out my held breath and rap gently on the door. "Elijah?"

On the other side something moves and then soft footsteps rush to the door, opening it wide.

I tuck my hair back and try to look more sure than I feel. "Hi."

Elijah's lips twitch into an attempt at a smile. "Hey, Angel."

Even with the tension still clinging to his face, he looks kind of adorable. It's clear that like me, he tried to sleep. He's wearing nothing but a pair of boxer shorts and the T-shirt he had on earlier. His hair is all tousled and his eyes are sleepy.

"Couldn't sleep?" he asks.

I shake my head. "No. Do you... Would you want some company?"

"I'd love some," he says, stepping out of the way for me to enter the studio.

My stomach flips when I cross the threshold. I really thought I'd never come back in this room—definitely not of my own volition—but holy shit...

"It looks great in here," I can't help but comment. And it's true. Every speck of spilled paint has been cleaned from the floor and the walls. The broken easels and paintbrushes are gone. The paintings, too. It's just a big empty space now with nothing but the massive windows looking out over the side of the property to interrupt the blank walls.

"Yeah, I, uh, I cleaned it all up after you left that day. Well, actually, Sev helped, too."

His voice, even though it's low, echoes in the room. Probably because of the odd shape of it. Like an octagon that's long through the middle.

I notice he's holding his phone in his other hand and wonder when Atticus gave it back. Elijah said he'd have to check them all for spyware before we could use them again. I guess his was clean.

"Well, you guys did a really good job."

He drops his head and lets out a little snort, then seems to remember something. "Hey, come here."

Elijah slips his hand into mine and pulls me to the windows. "Sit right there."

I lift a brow, but fold myself onto the floor and cross my legs, glancing up at him with laughter in my throat. "Now what?"

"One sec."

He rushes back over to the door and shuts it. My belly flutters.

Then he gets the lights, plunging the room into darkness.

No...not quite darkness.

Elijah brushes against my side as he sits next to me and sets down his phone. "I used to love coming in here after dark to watch the stars."

I don't tell him I've just seen them outside on the pool deck. I don't want to ruin this for him. Besides, through the tall, angled glass panes of his studio windows, they look different. Sort of romantic. It really is a great view.

"They're beautiful."

CHAPTER 40

"Yeah. I love it out here. Reminds me of home."

"The house where you grew up?"

He nods. "It's secluded, too. Granted, not *as* secluded, but the stars were always bright there—like this."

Next to him, his phone vibrates and he lifts it to read a message on the screen, some of the tension creeping back over his jawline.

"What is it?"

"My dad," he says. "It's his nurse. He's been lucid for a couple of days now. He's asking to see me."

My heart hurts for him. "Will you go?"

He lets out a shuddering breath. "Yeah. Probably. Last time, I didn't make it before he was gone again. We always try to go when he remembers."

I'm not sure what I can say to ease the hurt, so I decide to just be here. For a long time, we watch the stars together. Just two broken souls wondering where we fit in the universe, then he bumps my shoulder with his and I twist to offer him a closed-lip grin.

He tilts his head, considering me in the moonlight. "You doing okay?"

I frown. "What do you mean?"

I should be the one asking him that question.

"I feel really bad for not telling you sooner," he whispers. "That Atticus had some sort of plan that involved you. I should've told you. Especially after Paris."

How did this turn into him apologizing to me?

"Elijah, I'm not angry at you."

A knot forms between his brows.

"I'm not," I repeat. "I'm pretty pissed at Atticus, though."

Elijah sighs. "He means well."

I make a sound in the back of my throat, and Elijah laughs.

"No, really. He's a brute and a blockhead, but underneath his scowls and muscle, he really has the biggest heart."

Now it's my turn to laugh.

"I'm serious," Elijah says through a chuckle. "You just don't know him like we do. Before everything happened, he was different. Still a bit obsessive with certain things and unapologetic about most things, but he was...*fun*."

"Atticus was fun?"

Now I know he's fucking with me, but still, he nods. "Really. He had this great dry humor that always killed us. And he was always the first one to sign up for a challenge—well, actually, he still is, he's just less obvious about it."

"Huh."

"And he's always there when we need him. Always putting us first. It's why we deal with his grouchiness and his green smoothies and his constant insisting that we fast three times a week. He's done the research, and even if he's annoying about it, Sev and I know he does it all to try to keep us healthy."

I hear what he's not saying as he drops his head and his smirk falls from his lips.

To keep them from getting sick. Like his mom.

I reach over and place my hand on his knee. He covers it with a warm palm.

"Anyway," he says with a deep inhale, looking back toward the stars. "Just don't judge him too harshly yet. Like I said, he means well."

Maybe for you, I want to say, but I don't. Atticus has made no secret of how much he cares for his brothers, but I get the feeling that's where his loyalty ends. It doesn't

CHAPTER 40

extend beyond them and maybe Julian. It certainly doesn't extend to me.

"I'm surprised *you're* not more upset with him for pushing me to come in here."

A muscle flexes in his jaw, and he lifts his shoulder in a half shrug. "I was. I still am, I guess, but it's hard to stay pissed when..." He snorts at himself. "When I'm happy he did it."

I try to understand, and seeing him in here now, so relaxed in the blank slate of a space, I think maybe I get it.

"I'm not sure I ever would've done it on my own. I hate *how* he did it, by involving you, but..." He sighs as he trails off. "It's okay if you don't get it."

"I'm trying to," I offer, and he squeezes my hand.

"How did we get so lucky?"

I don't realize he's talking about me until he slides his gaze to mine again and holds it there until I shiver and the tiny hairs on the back of my neck stand up.

Wanting them was one thing, but the ache in my chest when I look into Elijah's eyes is another. Dangerous. If I'm not careful, it could ruin me.

His phone lights up again and I see the time.

I let out a breathy laugh to break the tension. "God, it's so late." I swallow. "We should really try to get some sleep."

I push to my feet and suddenly don't know what to do with my hands. Where to put them.

Elijah stands, scratching the back of his head. His lips part, but he doesn't say anything as he looks out to the stars and then toward the door that leads to his bedroom, like he'd rather stay here than go back in there.

"Do you want me to, uh, walk you back to your room?"

I hold in a giggle. *Walk me back to my room?*

He cocks his head at me, trying to read my expression in the dark.

I bite the inside of my cheek. "You could," I tell him. "Or if you wanted, I could stay?"

He gestures awkwardly toward his room, blinking as he puts it together. "Like, in my room—er—*bed?*"

There's really no need to be shy. It's been less than half a day since he rocked my world with that pierced cock of his, but that's not what I'm offering here.

"To sleep," I clarify. "Or try to, anyway."

He licks his lips, eyes darting back and forth for an instant while he thinks about it. "Okay. Yeah. If you want to."

I extend an arm. "Lead the way."

He keeps checking back over his shoulder while we cross the studio and he opens the door to his bedroom, like he thinks I might spontaneously vanish into thin air.

Honestly, I might. The last guy I slept in the same bed with of my own free will was Danny Maluco in grade ten. He was a nice boy. Too nice for me.

Is Elijah too nice for me?

It's dark in his room, but I can make out the tidy shapes of simple, gray-toned furniture and bare white walls. It's nothing like how I imagined an artist's room would look and a heaviness settles in my chest.

"What's wrong?"

"Hmm?"

I realize I've stopped walking and shake my head, following him into the colorless space. "Oh. Nothing. I'm good."

Elijah rushes to clear something from the edge of the bed and then pulls the covers back. "Do you need anything? Water or…?"

CHAPTER 40

I shake my head at him, grinning at how fucking adorable he is when he's nervous. "Just get in."

"Right. Okay."

Elijah slips onto the mattress, pushing way over to leave me a huge amount of space in the king bed that I could never fill. I scoot in close as he pulls the covers over us.

When I burrow into his side, he tenses but opens his arm for me to rest my cheek in the crook of it, laying his hand on my waist.

I don't think Elijah has had a woman sleep in his bed for a while, either.

As I settle into him and he into me, the tension I've been holding on to since we got back melts away and the exhaustion I've been trying to find finally hits me.

"Good night, Elijah."

"Good night, Angel."

41

THE PLAN

ATTICUS

Eli comes into the living room with his defenses already up and his expression guarded.

"Hey," he says, his gaze snagging on the file atop the coffee table in front of me before shifting to search the front of the house. "Where's Aurora?"

"Good morning," Aurora says, padding down the stairs behind him. She's been up since six. I know because there was a pot of java that had to be at least two hours old by the time I got to it, sitting half empty in the kitchen.

"Morning," Eli replies, nothing but openness and smiles for her as she comes to give his arm a little squeeze before sitting down opposite me.

If I didn't know any better, I'd say she's been just as anxious to get started as I have.

For a fleeting second, our eyes meet, but she quickly looks away, and I want to know what it means. Does it mean she won't do it? Has she already decided?

"There's fresh coffee in the kitchen," I tell Eli.

"You want some?" he asks Aurora, waiting for her like

CHAPTER 41

he expects her to join him. To take the opportunity to run away from me.

She smiles tightly. "Already had some, but thanks."

"All right, well, I'll be back in a sec."

Eli glances between us, as if he isn't sure whether he should leave us alone together. Maybe he shouldn't.

After our little chat on the pool deck last night, I couldn't get her out of my head. And it isn't just because we need her.

There is something far too familiar in her eyes when she looks at me. I think it's the way I looked at Eli and Sev when they first let me crash their little bromance. When Eli started bringing me home, and I saw what a real family should look like. What I could be a part of if I didn't find a way to fuck it up. If they would accept another wayward misfit with nowhere else to go.

It was fear. Longing. And hope.

A three-punch combo I didn't want to remember the feeling of because I wasn't fucking downplaying it when I said this could get dangerous. I can't afford to care about this girl like that. One of us needs to stay level if this is going to work.

Seven bounds down the stairs just as Eli comes back with two mugs of coffee. "That for me?"

Eli hands him one without a word, and Seven hisses as he burns his mouth trying to drink it before it can cool. So impatient. Some things never change.

"Will you guys come sit down?"

Sev and Eli share a look.

"Sev and I talked about it a bit," Eli says. "We can find a way to get what we want without using Aurora."

They talked about this without me?

"Like we've been doing for the past year?" I snap back.

The plan

"We're still no closer to Ambrose than we were when we fucking started."

"We'll find another way," Seven repeats, and the exasperation is clear in his voice. He knows I'm right.

I can't believe they're dismissing this opportunity before they've even fucking listened to my plan.

"I'd still like to hear it." Aurora's voice is so small that it's nearly inaudible over all the blood rushing to my head. But the tides go back out when I register what she said.

She wrings her hands in her lap and sits up straighter. "If that's okay."

"You don't have to," Eli assures her, his brows drawing together.

"I know," she replies. "I want to."

Sev's brow lifts at Aurora, and a cheeky grin pulls at his mouth. He's surprised. Honestly? So am I. But maybe we shouldn't be.

Aurora Bellerose isn't at all what I thought she was. She's definitely trouble, but she just might be the good kind.

"You heard the lady." I give Aurora a nod that I hope conveys my gratitude. "Come sit your asses down."

Sev parks himself on my right, and Eli drags an armchair closer to sit to my left as I open the file.

Aurora folds herself onto the floor in front of the coffee table to get a closer look at the document at the top of the pile. It's general intel on all Ambrose's legitimate operations.

Just like us, most of Ambrose's money is run through larger public-facing corporations that actually turn a small legit profit of their own. Ours runs through real estate. Ambrose's is mostly traded through cryptocurrency.

CHAPTER 41

Though he does run some through a chain of casinos owned by his family.

"We've talked before about trying to get someone on the inside. But Ambrose's security is tight and he vets his men well. Getting someone in as implanted muscle or security would be next to impossible, but there's another way."

I flip the top sheet over to reveal the next page—where his money goes isn't important right this second.

"You remember Diana De La Rosa?"

It's a full-page image of the woman. Her last known photo before she vanished. In it, she's smiling, but the emotion doesn't reach her eyes. It was taken outdoors, and the sun highlights the lighter strands of glossy brown in her long, dark hair. Makes her oceanic blue eyes bright and clear.

"Is that his wife?" Aurora asks, spinning the image around and lifting it for a closer look. Her brows knit.

Eli taps the photo. "She was abducted," he explains.

"Allegedly," I correct. "She was *allegedly* abducted. It happened a long time ago. Before Ambrose ever met Julian. He never remarried, and he never stopped looking for her. Julian even tried to help Ambrose find her. The authorities in Oregon where she went missing never found any trace of her."

"Okay, so how does Diana have any sort of usable connection to Ro?"

"It wasn't just Diana who was supposedly abducted," I remind him.

I flip to the next sheet. It's a printout of the original newspaper beseeching the public to help find them.

Wife and Two-year-old Daughter of Wealthy Casino Magnate Abducted.

Aurora frowns.

The plan

"The official investigation was closed within a year of their disappearance, but he never stopped trying to find them," I drag the photo of Diana back to the top of the pile. "It was always her, though. Always Diana. Until now."

I flip to the next sheet, another image, and the shift in the room is palpable. Aurora audibly gasps.

"Who is that?" Eli looks between Aurora and the image on the table, seeing what I saw on the midnight highway after she almost killed Seven.

"It's his daughter. Or at least, it's what modern age progression software says she would look like now. A few months ago, Ambrose started putting this image out to multiple PI firms and posted this message on his official social platform."

I show them a copy of his most recent post.

It has the image and a short message.

"It's been exactly twenty years since my wife and daughter were taken from me," I read aloud. "And not a day goes by that I don't think of them. Today, I received this image of what my Delilah would look like from a friend at Harvard. It was created using the most advanced age progression software available on the market. Please, spread this far and wide. If you're out there, Delilah, know that I will never stop searching. #FindDelilah."

42

TROJAN HORSE

AURORA

The similarities are undeniable.

It's not at all like looking into a mirror. The computer-generated woman in the photo has a slightly stronger jaw and a longer, more oval-shaped face. But her eyes look like mine. Same shape. Same shade of green. Her hair isn't the same length as mine, but it is the right color, too. Or at least it is now that I've dyed mine back to my naturally darker shade. There's something in the curve of the nose, too. And in her cheekbones.

Does Atticus really think this is *me*?

I push the image away.

"This can't be me," I blurt, my heart pounding too fast. Too hard. "This girl went missing in Oregon. I was dropped at a fire station in upstate New York. That's the other side of the country."

I am *not* related to the sadistic fuck who destroyed Elijah's family. No way.

My skin feels hot. Tight. Like a million tiny bugs are crawling over me, biting me and pinching me.

CHAPTER 42

Atticus shakes his head, worry in the crease of his forehead. "No, no, no. I'm not saying it's you, Aurora."

I force myself to swallow and press my fingers between my knees until they ache from the pressure. "Then...why...?"

"It *could* be you," he continues. "If we make Ambrose think you're his lost daughter, it could get us the 'in' we need."

"No way he'll go for it," Seven interjects. "He's definitely going to DNA test anyone who comes around making a claim to be this girl. Do you know how many people would love to blink and be a fucking millionaire? There are probably hundreds of women who fit this description lined up for the job already."

"There are," Atticus admits. "Or at least there were when this was first posted in the summer. And you're right. He is DNA testing anyone who he thinks might actually be her. But we have something they don't."

"Which is?" Eli pushes when Atticus doesn't immediately say.

"A contact at the genetic testing facility that Ambrose has been using. A contact who is willing to *adjust* the results of any tests done on Aurora for the right price."

He really seems to know a guy for everything, doesn't he?

"Well, what about her history?" Eli asks. "Ambrose will look into that, too. Trace her back to her actual parents and..."

Eli's voice grows muted as I push the photo of Ambrose's daughter off to the side, sliding the one of his wife a little closer with trembling fingers. I look a little like her, too. My stomach sours as I trace the line of her face. I don't recognize her. For one fleeting second, when I first saw the image, I thought she seemed familiar.

God, how many nights did I spend wishing my mom would come back for me? Wondering if she regretted leaving me behind. If she would look for me someday. I don't even remember her name.

I wonder what actually did happen to this woman and her baby. I'm not sure I want to know.

"Aurora?" Atticus says, and when I look up, I find three pairs of eyes watching me.

"Oh. Sorry, did you say something?"

"You said you were dropped at a fire station?" Atticus asks. "I tried to find more information on your, um, family —the people who gave you up—but it's all sealed. Is there anything Ambrose would be able to find?"

"Uh..." I think, but everything feels disjointed and a little foggy, and I think I really should've had that third coffee, after all. I swallow and try to bring some moisture back to my dry mouth. "Not really. All I know is that I was dropped at Bellerose Fire Station when I was about three. I was left with this necklace and a note."

Eli must notice my shiver because he drags the throw from the back of his chair and hands it to me. "What did it say?"

I pull the plush blanket over my lap. "Not a lot."

Fuck, why does it still sting to remember? *Spit it out, Aurora.*

"It just said, '*Her name is Aurora*' and '*I'm sorry.*' That's what they told me when I went back to ask when I was eighteen. The guy who I talked to was there the night I was abandoned. He said it was a woman who dropped me off— saw her in the camera footage. I don't even know if she was actually my mom."

But I always assumed she was.

Elijah slips from the armchair to sit on the floor next to

CHAPTER 42

me. He takes my hand in both of his, and it makes it hurt more. And less.

Atticus probably didn't find any records because there were none from before that day, and I'm forced to remember it every fucking year on my 'birthday'. It's the day she left me. I was too little to remember when my birthday actually was, and the doctors figured I was close enough to being three years old to just put that date on my new birth certificate.

June fifteenth. Now, I hate that whole damned month.

"She could work even better than I thought," Atticus mutters, and I'm not even sure he realizes he's said it out loud as he begins to flip through the rest of the documents in his file.

"Dude," Seven barks at him, indicating me. Indicating that he's being a callous prick. But I'm used to callous pricks, and, to be honest, I don't want their pity. I don't want the fucking spotlight. But I definitely *do* want them to stop looking at me the way they're looking at me right now.

"Sorry," Atticus says, and I don't miss the way the vein in his temple pulses when he clenches his jaw.

"I never knew my mom, either. It sucks. I get it."

There's a hard bite to his words that makes me believe him. I didn't expect that. I wonder why he never got to know her, but by the guarded expression on his face, I can tell he isn't interested in sharing.

"It's fine," I say, trying to match Atticus's emotionless tone. I wonder how he got so good at that—making it seem like things don't hurt when that couldn't be further from the truth. Maybe he'll teach me someday. "I don't even remember her, and it was a long time ago."

Seven leans forward over his knees to steeple his

fingers, shadows hooding his eyes. "So that was your plan, then? Use her to get us inside?"

I notice how he says *was*. As if he's already dismissed Atticus's plan. I'm not sure why he would. With the guy willing to forge the DNA test, it actually sounds pretty airtight. It could work depending on what they're hoping to get out of it.

"A Trojan horse," Atticus nods to Seven, but he's looking at me now. "If we can get you inside, and if you can get him to let his guard down and *really* make him believe you're his daughter...Aurora, I just need access to his personal devices. His computer or his phone. Something that would have the information we need to find where he was keeping Eli and the Ashfords' collection. Once we have that, you're out. You won't ever have to breathe the same air as that bastard again."

My lips part, but no words come out. There's so much hope in Atticus's warm stare.

It doesn't sound that hard, really. I've played a lot of different roles in my life. Squeezed my whole-ass self into a myriad of different-shaped rooms to fit the whims of whoever held the key.

I know how to handle bad men. How to play into their twisted narratives and keep myself safe. Or at least keep myself alive.

If I do this—put on a new mask and fit myself in that box just one more time—at least some good would come out of it.

"I..."

Eli's grip on my hand tightens. "No."

43

COLLATERAL DAMAGE

ELIJAH

"What do you mean, 'no'?" Atticus asks, cocking his head at me.

I think it's pretty self-explanatory, but it bears repeating if he really can't get it through his head. "No. We aren't throwing her to the wolves."

"That's not what I'm proposing here. I'm saying we—"

"That's exactly what you're proposing!"

"Eli..." Aurora's voice is soft and calm next to me. It should be anything but.

She has no idea what Atticus is trying to sign her up for.

I imagine it, imagine *her* in the same room as Ambrose, and it makes me fucking sick to my stomach. And now in my head it's her in *that* room. The one where I was trapped for five hundred seventy-two days. No windows save for a massive skylight overhead. Forced to turn something she once loved into something she'll grow to loathe with every fiber of her being. Twisting her into a version of herself she won't recognize anymore when she looks in the mirror.

She hasn't even seen my scars yet. All the angry lines Ambrose gouged into my back when I tried to refuse him.

CHAPTER 43

He might not have held the whip, but he was the one who gave the order.

Again. Again. Again.

"You don't know what you'd be risking," I tell her, and the words come out a lot harsher than I mean them to. "You have no idea what that man is capable of. I won't put you in his path, Angel. No fucking way."

"I agree with Eli," Seven says like he's casting a vote. Making it final. Two against one.

Atticus sucks his teeth as he gathers up all the documents and stacks them into a neat pile. "With respect, Eli, it isn't up to you."

His eyes flick to Aurora, and I don't like what I see pass between them. There's some sort of understanding there that shouldn't be. Did he fucking talk to her about this behind our backs? Grease the gears? What did he say to try to convince her?

I turn to face Aurora head-on, trying to appeal to her since it's clear Atticus will not be reasoned with. "I don't know what he said to you, but I promise you it won't be safe. If he were to find out that you aren't who you're trying to say you are..."

I don't finish the thought, mostly because I don't want to give voice to the possibility in case the universe decides to take it and run with it. I just pray she gets the point.

Aurora chews the inside of her cheek, casting furtive glances at Atticus from the corner of her eye. "If Ambrose has been looking for his family all this time, do you really think he'd do anything to hurt them? And if Atticus gets the DNA result to say we're a match—if Ambrose really thinks I'm the daughter he lost—wouldn't he be happy? In my experience, dangerous men are only dangerous when they're *un*happy."

No. She's not hearing me. "Ambrose was like family to my father. *To us*. And he didn't hesitate to take everything from us the second our guards were down. This is not a man you can play. He plays *you*."

I turn my attention back to Atticus again. "We can find another way."

He rolls a reply around in his mouth like it tastes sour and decides to nod instead of spit it out. Smart choice.

"What are you thinking?" Seven asks, and I think he's talking to Atticus, but I find him looking at Aurora. "I don't want to speak for you. You've had enough of that shit."

She's surprised at this, and her expression turns guarded. Uncertain. "I—I don't know. I think it could work."

"But you don't want to do it?" Seven pushes hopefully.

"I didn't say that."

Atticus shuts the file. "She doesn't have to decide right this second."

My back is hot, and my palms grow clammy where they grip onto Aurora's. I let her go to wipe them on my pants, feeling a nauseating vibration begin deep in the pit of my stomach, rattling my defenses. Fighting for release. Making me shudder.

"But it *is* her decision whether she wants to help. It's not mine. Not yours. Not Sev's. *Hers*."

I close my eyes and breathe through my nose, flinching when Aurora places her hand on my back. "Don't you want to get your family's collection back? Get vengeance for what he did to you?"

God, it's like she's already decided. We just haven't told her enough. She doesn't know the whole story. She hasn't seen the extent of his cruelty. Maybe if I show her, she won't be so willing to rush right into his grasp.

CHAPTER 43

I lift the edge of my shirt up to reveal my back, twisting away from her so she'll see. In my periphery, Atticus drops his head. He could never look at it. Seven was the one who had to help me apply the salve to try to lessen the scarring. The one time Atticus tried, he had to excuse himself to throw up.

It's not fucking pretty.

"Oh my god." Aurora's voice is watery. Quivering. I don't dare look at her face.

"It's all I've wanted since the day he took it." I struggle to keep my tone even as I answer her question. "But this is what Ambrose's handiwork looked like when I *inconvenienced* him by delaying forgeries. Imagine what it would look like if he were truly angry?"

His wrath would be without end. He'd kill her. I know he would. Especially if he found out *we* were the ones who planted her there. No one else should become the collateral damage of my father's mistake. There's been enough of that already.

I cringe as Aurora's fingertips brush the scars across my shoulder blades, hating the sound of her soft hiccup and sniffle. "I'm...I'm so sorry, Elijah."

I jerk my shirt down and turn around. "Don't be sorry," I tell her forcefully, reaching up to rub the tears from beneath her eyes, holding her face between my palms. "I won't tell you what to do, but I need you to consider the risk. What Ambrose would do to you would be far worse than anything he did to me if this were to go sideways."

Her chin quivers as she nods and pushes past my hands to wrap me in a fierce hug that makes my chest crack open and *bleed*. Her hands twist into the fabric at the back of my shirt as she clings to me and wipes her tears on my shoulder.

I drop my face into her hair, breathing her in. Sighing. "Take some time. Think about it."

Past her shoulder, I glare at Atticus. He never should have asked her to do this.

"I'm sorry, E," he says with a shrug, as if he's read my mind. "I had to try."

44

TROUBLE

AURORA

I haven't come out of my room since Elijah and Seven left this afternoon to go see Julian. They needed to go check on him. They offered for me to come, but apparently it's a long drive and I didn't want to leave Ellie again. Atticus is staying behind as well. He muttered something about needing to check up on some things and make sure nothing from Paris is going to try to follow us home.

Eli made no secret of not wanting to leave me with him. I think he's afraid Atticus will try to pressure me into agreeing to his plan. He almost didn't go at all because of it. But if Julian is really lucid right now, they shouldn't waste the opportunity to go see him.

From my window, I have an unobstructed view of the pool deck where Ellie lazes on the stone without a care in the world, her belly turned up to soak in the warmth of the sun before it can fully set behind the tall pines.

At least one of us is enjoying herself.

There's a tap at my bedroom door, and I lift my chin from where I'd been resting it atop my folded arms on the windowsill.

CHAPTER 44

"Come in."

The door creaks lightly as Atticus pushes it open and leans against the frame with a wan grin, tapping something against his palm.

"Hey, Trouble."

I snort.

I should be the one calling him *that*. He's the one who had to go and ruin my exit plan, pulling me into something potentially far more dangerous than the shitty situation I left behind.

Atticus steps into the room and lifts the device between his fingers. "Your phone's all clear. Doesn't look like it was compromised."

I take it from him, finding it fully charged and free of notifications. Oddly enough, I didn't miss it. Thanks to Jesse, I haven't had social media in a long time or any sort of regular or meaningful contact with any of my old friends. The only person who texts me on occasion these days is my adopted dad, and I hear from my fucking Duolingo app more than I hear from him. Now, *there's* a toxic relationship.

Hi! I miss you. Do you want to practice your Spanish today?

Aurora, don't lose your 21-day streak!

You made Duo sad. But then we kept learning Spanish without you!

How do you say 'quitter' in Spanish?

All the while his little green avatar wastes away to nothing but dust and bones.

"Thanks."

"Can I show you something?"

Can't he see I'm super busy staring out the window with a case of melancholy?

"Sure, why not?"

Anything's got to be better than sitting here coming up

with a hundred more questions that aren't helping me formulate an answer to the one he wants an answer to. I can't stop picturing Elijah's scars. I don't know how I'll ever get that image out of my head. It's like the lashes are imprinted on the backs of my eyelids, and they're there waiting for me every time I close my eyes.

How could anyone do that to a person?

But Elijah isn't just any person. He's one of the good ones. Thoughtful. Kind.

I don't understand how someone could know him as well as I have to guess Ambrose did, and still be able to do that to him. I thought I'd seen the face of evil, but this guy might take the cake.

I pocket my phone, and Atticus leads me through the house, taking me past the front entrance and through the formal dining room I've literally never seen any of them use, and around to a staircase I've never seen the bottom of.

"What's down there?"

He's already three steps down when he pauses, pushing a loose strand of his bound hair behind his ear. There's mischief in his stare, and it makes my pulse thrum. "Don't you trust me?"

I scoff. "No."

"I guess that's fair."

I don't budge.

"Well, you can go back to staring out the window like a sad old lady if you'd prefer. Up to you."

He bounds down the rest of the stairs without bothering to see if I'm following him.

I bounce from foot to foot. *Fuck.* I'm still angry at him, but our talk out at the pool changed my perception of him, if only just a little bit.

I might not agree with Atticus's methods, and I might

CHAPTER 44

be personally offended at the fact that he would pick any random girl off the street and try to use her for his own gain, but...I get it. Or at least I *want* to get it.

I can only pretend to know what it's like to love someone so much that you'd do anything for them. I always thought that kind of love was fantasy or fiction, but I saw it in his eyes at the pool. He would do anything to get the revenge his family deserves.

Before I can make up my mind whether I want to stay or go, music filters up to me from down the stairs, and like a lure, I am reeled in.

The familiar melody rises in volume with each step I take. It's "Sugar" by Sleep Token.

The quality of the sound is warm, rich, and raw. Different from how I've usually heard it.

I'm at the bottom of the stairs before the end of the first verse, walking through the open door into a bedroom dimly lit with only a single floor lamp in one corner. It smells woody and earthy and warm, like stepping onto a desert plain.

The room is drenched in colors that only reinforce the vibe. Like a moonlit sand dune, it's all darkest navy and softest taupe sand with bits of scorched orange mixed in. And it's spotless. There isn't a single wrinkle in the navy bedding. Not one scratch or scuff on the tobacco leather recliner in the corner.

I almost knock into something next to the door as I turn and I throw my arms out to catch it, steadying the ancient-looking bust of some guy that's perched on a little platform by the door with a wince.

The music isn't coming from this room, I realize, as I blow out a breath. It's farther, past another open door on the other side of the long space. My bare feet kiss the plush carpeted floor of his bedroom as I hurry across and peer through to the next room.

It's smaller than his bedroom but just as dimly lit. At first I think it's a smaller second library, with all the shelves and the low lounger chair pushed off to one corner, but it's not books occupying the shelves. It's records. Hundreds and hundreds if not thousands of them.

Atticus looks up from where he stands next to a record player.

I raise an eyebrow, a slow smile tugging at my lips as I give him a nod of approval.

"I heard you like Sleep Token," he says, his eyes lingering on me with an expression I can't quite read.

When the chorus starts playing, I can't help but wonder if he chose this song for another reason, or if it's just a coincidence.

I really didn't expect we'd have anything in common. Atticus and I are too different.

Apparently aside from being abandoned by our mothers and listening to the same artist.

"My favorite right now is 'Jaws'."

I run my fingers over the edges of the records on the shelf. "Are all of these yours?"

"They are now. Some were Florence's. She had a small collection we used to listen to all the time. I've added to it over the years."

Art *and* music.

"She sounds like she was a cool mom."

"She was." He exhales loudly, pushing his hands deep into the pockets of his jeans. "She would've liked you, I think."

Is that a compliment?

CHAPTER 44

"So, is this you trying to butter me up some more because I don't have an answer for you yet."

He presses his lips into a tight line.

Of course that's what this is...

I pull a couple records off the shelf, finding an old Blink-182 and a special edition Nirvana.

He comes over and takes the Nirvana from my hands, rubbing his thumb over where someone has drawn little stars and diamonds in pen ink around the song "Come as You Are" in the track list.

He puts the record back on the shelf. "No. I guess this is me trying to get to know you."

I'm not sure what I was expecting but it wasn't that.

"Oh."

"I misjudged you," he explains. "And I don't do that often—but, to be fair, most people aren't as good at camouflaging as you are."

Is he accusing me of something? I can't tell, but the air feels thinner. Tight.

"Yeah, well, a childhood spent bouncing around to eight different foster homes makes you learn how to blend in."

I don't mean to sound so defensive, but it's definitely coming out that way.

I might've been 'camouflaging' in the beginning while I was trying to get a feel for these guys—who they were and what they wanted, and most importantly, if they posed any sort of threat. But I'm not anymore.

I'm not sure when exactly it started to wear away. Probably somewhere between Jesse being pummeled to death and what happened between Seven, Elijah, and me on the plane. The only one I might still be wearing a mask for is *him*. Atticus.

And I don't think I want to take it all the way off.

I push the record back onto the shelf, and Atticus grimaces before tugging it back out to put it in what I assume is the *correct* place.

I try not to laugh. He really doesn't handle any type of disorder or chaos very well, does he? That must be hard. Not just for him, but for Elijah and Seven, too.

Much like his bedroom, Atticus always seems to be 'in order'.

He's in peak physical condition that makes him look like some sort of Viking warrior, and I've never seen him dirty. His clothes are always crisp and fresh. Unwrinkled. And he's never without that watch on his left wrist. The only part of him that seems at all chaotic is his hair. He's always fighting to keep it all tied back. I wonder why he doesn't just shave it off.

"You're an enigma, too, you know," I find myself saying. "Seven and Elijah have shared a lot about their history with me, but you—I don't know anything about you other than the fact that your mother left when you were a baby and that…well, that you're kind of a dick."

He blinks at me and I shrug.

He can't deny it's true. I admire his confidence and his strength. And the way he's willing to sacrifice anything—and apparently *anyone*—for his family, but the way he goes about it all definitely keeps him firmly in asshole territory.

"Because I lied about what I wanted from you?" he guesses.

I shake my head.

Wrong.

It's partly that, but now that I know more about Elijah's past, I can't help feeling secondhand rage at Atticus for sending me in to clean Elijah's studio knowing how it could trigger him. He might not have known just how badly it would affect Elijah, but it was still wrong of him to do. Even if Elijah did grudgingly say that he's glad it's done.

"I really don't think you'd have said yes if I'd asked you to help a bunch of criminals take down another criminal right off the hop."

I give him a dubious look. "Hey. I totally might've."

It wasn't a joke, but he takes it as one anyway, his lips faltering into a smile as he lets out a short laugh.

It really does change his whole face.

Up until now, I've grown accustomed to seeing him in a perpetual state of agitation. Whatever the male version of resting bitch face is, he's definitely got a mean case of it. But when Atticus smiles, there's a magnetism to it that I struggle to guard myself against.

The light in his eyes and the dimple in his right cheek aren't helping.

Why do the assholes always have to be so fucking attractive?

Who made that a rule?

He bobs his head this way and that with a doubtful crease in his brow. "Guess we'll never know."

"Guess not."

When the seconds stray too long between us, I back up half a step and gesture to the shelf. To the spot where he put the Nirvana back. "That one was Florence's?"

"This whole shelf was hers."

He takes hold of the lip of wood beneath the records, and there's a sentiment softening his features that I wish I could properly empathize with, but I can't. I don't even have a memory of my own mother to miss.

"We should listen to one."

He stiffens. "I don't—I don't really listen to these ones anymore."

"Don't you think she'd want you to?"

A bitterness purses his lips for an instant before it's gone. "Yeah. She probably would."

He lets his hand fall away from the shelf and the resting asshole face is back. "But she isn't here anymore."

"What about your family? You said you never really knew your bio mom?"

"She left when I was only a couple months old. Couldn't hack it."

"So, who raised you then, your dad?"

"You know what?" He shakes his head, a muscle in his jaw flexing. "I'd really rather not talk about it."

"You said you wanted to get to know me. Isn't it only fair if I get to know you a little bit, too?"

He seems to mull over that, and then nods.

"I don't think I'd say my dad 'raised' me."

What does he mean by that?

He licks his lips, flicking through the records while he talks. "He was a drunk and an addict. If anything, I was the one taking care of him most of the time."

"That must've been hard."

He doesn't reply, but his hand clenches against the shelf.

I wonder if that's why he feels like he always has to be in control now—because he spent so long having everything out of his control.

"Do you still see him?"

His eyes darken. "No. I left when I was sixteen after he OD'd for the tenth time, and I never looked back. I don't even know if he's still alive."

CHAPTER 44

My chest cracks and the wall I was trying to build between us crumbles just a little more.

"Don't look at me like that," he says, and I didn't realize I was looking at him in any sort of way, but now I glare at him with a scowl on my lips. He doesn't need to snap at me.

"Is that where you got your control issues from?"

His lips part and his brows lower.

"Come on, don't look so surprised. You can't tell me the guys haven't called you out on it before."

He scoffs. "No, they definitely have. I'm just not used to anyone else doing it."

"So? Is that why?"

"I don't really know why, Aurora. It's just how I am."

"Kind of a cop-out, isn't it?"

"You think I haven't tried to change it?"

"Have you?"

He scoffs again, getting those lines of agitation in his forehead again.

"Trust me, I have. It's not that easy. There are things that help me manage it, but it never really goes away."

I cock my head. "Things like what? Medication?"

He shakes his head. Pinches the bridge of his nose like he's getting annoyed, but I don't care because I think I just realized why I can't make up my mind about whether or not I want to accept my role in this plan he's cooked up. It's because of *him*. I don't have a good sense of him as a person like Elijah and Seven, and I need to if this is going to work.

"So many questions..." he says in a rough whisper and drops his hand. "*No.* Not medication. Working out helps. Running, too. But sex works best."

I can't hide my surprise as I reply. "Sex?"

"Well, not just regular sex."

I lift a brow and wait for him to elaborate.

"You actually want to know?"

"Yeah, now you kind of have to tell me."

I need to know what the hell 'not just regular sex' means.

"This kind comes with a prearranged agreement—a contract."

"Like that NDA you made me sign?"

He shakes his head again, and is that a smirk playing on his lips?

"There is an NDA involved, but no. It's a different sort of contract. One where the terms of what I want to do—what they'll *let* me do—are all laid out in black and white. When it happens, I don't do anything they didn't already agree to, and they can't say no to anything they did agree to."

"Giving you control," I finish for him, my throat going dry as I imagine what it must feel like to surrender. To submit.

"Exactly."

My core tightens and my toes curl.

This brings a whole new meaning to *Daddicus* I'm not sure I wanted to know.

I'm curious what sort of things would be on a contract like that, but I definitely shouldn't ask. In fact...

"We should probably talk about something else."

His smirk turns wicked. "Why's that?"

"Because I don't want to know what sort of atrocities you like to do to women."

"Oh, I don't think any of them would call the things I do to them *atrocities*."

Atticus watches me carefully, and my face heats under his stare.

What is he thinking?

Say something. *Say something.*

CHAPTER 44

"They probably only let you because you're attractive," I blurt.

He cocks his head at me, narrowing his gaze. "You think I'm attractive?"

"Objectively," I correct, fighting to swallow. "It doesn't make you any less of an ass."

"Well, I think you're *objectively* pretty too, Trouble."

He chuckles to himself. It's a low, throaty sound that would make most women's panties very wet, but not mine.

Definitely not mine.

The album shifts to another song by Sleep Token that I know better, and I pick up the cover, busying myself with reading the track list so I can avoid looking at him.

"I take it you're done with your questions, now?"

I purse my lips.

"My turn, then."

45

BAD HABITS

AURORA

He lets out a long, loud sigh, and it blows some of the sexual tension from the room, but replaces it with a different sort.

"I've got to ask," he says with a guilt-laced grimace. "Have you thought about it?"

My gaze rakes over him. Have I thought about what he might look like under those clothes? What sort of new territory he might discover if I gave him free rein of my body?

"If you'll help us," he adds, and I wish the floor would swallow me up.

Of course that's what he meant. It's the actual reason he wanted to bring me down here. I knew it from the moment I agreed to follow him.

My fingernails bite hard into my palms.

"Of course I've thought about it."

It's all I've been able to think about since this morning.

And I *do* want to help. I think I might've already said yes if it weren't for not feeling like I can fully trust Atticus, and Elijah being so loudly against it. How can I agree to help if Elijah doesn't want me to?

CHAPTER 45

It's *his* family's legacy, after all. It was him who was held captive and hurt. Atticus and Seven would have suffered in their own ways—probably going crazy worrying about him and trying to find him—but ultimately, this feels like Elijah's vengeance, and if he doesn't want me to be a part of it, then who the hell am I to insert myself where I'm not wanted?

"And?"

My mouth is dry and I have to wet my lips and swallow before I can speak. "Elijah doesn't want me to be a part—"

"Eli doesn't know what he's saying. We've been trying to take down Ambrose forever. He'll never find real peace until this is over. *Until it's fixed.*"

I want to ask Atticus if it's *him* who won't find peace until it's over. Judging by the almost manic look on his face, he's the one who can't seem to let go. Maybe it's because he left. He wasn't there to help them while they grieved, or stop Elijah from leaving.

"I failed them, Aurora. I should have been more suspicious of Ambrose. I should've seen what the bastard really was. Fuck, I never should've left, and...and when Eli didn't come home, I should've been able to find him, but I fucking couldn't."

He comes nearer, forcing me to retreat a step as he crowds me in against the shelves.

"Let me try to fix it. Eli's right, it won't be easy, and it *will* have risks, but I will do everything in my power to make sure nothing happens to you."

My skin prickles as the warmth of his scent and body surround me. Making it harder to breathe.

I move to shoulder past him, but his arms come up to cage me in against the shelf.

"Wait," he whispers harshly, the word gusting against

the baby-fine hairs on the top of my head. Was he always this fucking tall? I crane my neck to glare up at him, but his eyes are squeezed shut. "I'm sorry. *Fuck*."

He backs up a few inches, not enough for me to get past, but enough that I stop thinking about kneeing him in the junk.

"I'm not good at this."

"No, you're really not."

He barks out a laugh and looks down at me in a way that makes goosebumps erupt on my skin.

Down, girl.

This one's a bad idea.

Those red flags are *not* a carnival.

Abort.

Atticus trails the tips of his fingers down my jaw.

Stop him.

I should stop him.

"I can see why they like you," he says on a breath that tastes like mint and chocolate on my tongue.

My lips fall open, and he takes the opportunity to run his thumb along the lower one, licking his own like he's imagining how I might taste.

What is happening right now?

My body starts to overheat and I almost melt into the shelves against my back.

"I don't mean to be so pushy." His words are a whisper. A lie. He knows exactly what he's doing, and he's damn good at it. The fucker. "It's a bad habit."

His gaze drops to my mouth and an ache spreads like wildfire in my belly. I clamp my jaw against the sound trying to claw its way out of my chest.

"You don't have to be afraid of me," he says, misreading me.

CHAPTER 45

"I never said I was," I snap back, surprised at how bold my voice sounds.

His eyes spark with amusement as he snatches my wrists from my sides and pins them above me with one hand.

"How about now?" He hums, making me gasp as his other one brushes along my waist, gripping at the curve of my hip. When he leans in close enough that his breath fans over my lips, I shiver.

"Not even remotely."

My lips part, but he doesn't close that tiny gap, instead he holds me there, suspended in time, like he hasn't just tied me to a stake and set me on fire. My chest is hot, and it's making my breaths come fast and hard as I try to breathe through the burning.

"That's not what your eyes are telling me."

I shouldn't be so curious about what that glint in his eye could mean. What he might be able to do with those strong hands of his. I may not be a cat, but curiosity could kill me just as easily. Especially if the look he's giving me is any indication.

In them is a threat, and *a promise*.

Danger, *and desire*.

When he speaks, his lips are so close that they brush mine.

Teasing me. Taunting me. *Testing me*.

"Is that so?"

He nods.

"And what are my eyes saying now?"

His next words are a growl that I feel like claws shredding away my resolve. "They're begging me to stop."

My thighs squeeze; body at war with mind.

"Will you?"

Atticus's lips pull back in a half snarl. "I should."

His Adam's apple bobs and he shakes his head. "I really fucking should."

His head drops, and he steps back so quickly I almost stumble forward, but I'm still caught in his web. Gripping onto the shelves behind me so tight my knuckles crack when I let go. I struggle to catch my breath as Atticus rubs a palm over his mouth.

Fresh oxygen soaks into my lungs, but it's not enough to wash away the scent of him still clinging to the air around me.

"Maybe you should go," he says in a dangerous tone. "I don't want you to do anything you..."

He doesn't finish the sentence, and I'm not sure what to say because I'm not even fucking sure what I want anymore. Less than twenty-four hours ago, I wanted to stab him in the dick. Now, here I am, wanting him to stab me with his dick.

I'd blame biology, but I know it's just plain old insanity.

Where's that lobotomy when I need it?

Might as well stop toeing the line with madness and jump in with both feet.

"If I agree to your plan, do you really think you can keep me alive?"

Atticus whips his attention back to me at the abrupt subject shift. His eyes narrow like he thinks this is a trick.

It's not.

"I do," he says.

"Because you know they'll blame you if you can't."

Hope crackles like embers in his eyes. "I'm aware."

"Then I'll do it."

46

FUCK IT

ATTICUS

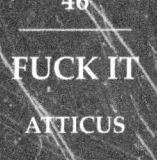

"You will?"

I need her to say it again. Make it real.

"I will."

I eliminate the gap between us in one long stride, crushing her in my arms. "You won't regret it."

The thudding echo of my heart raging in my chest sounds like the drums of war.

This is it. Our chance. And I meant it when I said I would do everything in my power to make sure she gets out of it safely. I don't want to see her hurt.

I tense.

I don't want to see her hurt.

Shit.

Aurora is rigid in my arms and I realize I'm hugging her. I'm *hugging* a girl.

Clearing my throat, I let her go.

"When this is done, you can still write your own check," I offer. "Enough to start over anywhere in the world."

Her expression twists for an instant before it turns placid. But I see it for the mask it is now.

CHAPTER 46

"Or you could stay." It sounds like a question. "If it's what you wanted."

It's what Eli and Sev want. They haven't said as much, but they don't have to. I know them like they're extensions of me, and now I'm starting to figure this girl out, too.

Conversation is the best way to do that. Studying her reactions. Her replies.

Her body language.

I'm fluent in the one it's speaking right now. It's practically my mother tongue.

Her brows lower in question as her thighs press tightly together. "You wouldn't mind that?"

"No," I tell her, watching her throat bob. "I don't think I would mind that at all."

The last song on the record finishes, and the needle skips off the vinyl, whirring as it resets itself off to one side, plunging the room into silence.

Aurora looks at me. I study her.

Heavy breaths. Clenched fists. The tension around her eyes when they meet mine. The plea that cannot go unanswered.

She licks her lips, and my cock jumps.

"Atticus..." My name falls from her mouth in a lustful whisper and there's only so much a man can take.

"Fuck it."

I close the gap, claiming her mouth with a hunger I can't control. Aurora moans as her fingers twist into the front of my shirt, clinging tight.

She tastes like the sweetest poison. Like sugar and sin. She opens to me as I slide my tongue along the seam of her lips, moaning into my mouth. I push in, needing to taste her deeper.

My fingers twist into her hair, knotting tight along her

Fuck it

scalp as I use my grip there and around her waist to lift her legs around me. She locks them tight, making me hiss when her hot center lines up with my raging fucking hard-on. She rubs herself against it, creating a wicked friction that makes me feral for more.

Fuck, I want her. Even knowing it'll bring nothing but trouble.

She feels like hot coals. Tastes like victory.

I push her against the shelf, rattling the records, needing more pressure. Stronger friction.

Aurora drops her head back, and I kiss and suck a path down her pretty throat, leaving my mark just above the delicate chain of her necklace, making her cry out as I grind against her. Her hands delve into my hair, and the band holding it in place snaps. It falls loose around my face as I lick the reddened skin I left on her neck.

Already, I'm imagining fucking her. The feel of her wet heat pulsing around me.

"Fuck, I need to be inside you," I groan, sucking her lower lip into my mouth, running my teeth over it, making her gasp and tremble.

When she reaches to pull her shirt over her head, revealing a thin bralette that's practically see-through, a growl pushes out through my clenched teeth.

She's going to be the death of me.

I skim my hand up her ribs, feeling the swell of her breast against my palm. I tear the fragile fabric away and her nipple pebbles against my touch. I dip my head and suck it into my mouth, making her back arch so violently I have to push her harder into the shelves to keep her steady enough to get a proper taste.

I need her stripped bare. I need to see what else she's hiding under these clothes.

CHAPTER 46

Shifting back to her mouth, I rob another vicious kiss from her lips, holding her tight against me as I carry her out the door and into the bedroom.

Aurora lets out a yelp as I toss her onto the bed, and I'm on her in a fraction of a second, reaching beneath her to unclasp what remains of her bra and chuck it to the floor.

She hisses as I kiss a hot path down her belly to the seam of her yoga pants. She lifts her hips for me to hook my fingers into the soft fabric and drag them down her legs, panties and all.

I kneel over her, pressing myself flush against her naked body as I curl a hand beneath her neck and guide her mouth back to mine. I've never been one for kissing, but she's making me acquire a taste for it, her tongue matching mine stroke for stroke.

I jerk as she buries a hand between us, finding the button and zipper of my jeans. A throaty moan pushes from my mouth as she gains entry, her fingers brushing my swollen cock.

My head drops to her neck, and I bare my teeth as I thrust into her smooth palm. She's so soft. How is she so fucking *soft*?

"*Goddamn*," I grit out through my teeth. "Do you feel what you're doing to me, woman?"

She strokes her palm over me twice more, bringing a wet bead of precum to my tip that she's quick to use, smearing it mercilessly over the head until I'm at very serious risk of losing this game.

I never lose.

Pulling myself from her grip, I snatch up her hands and hold them over her head. *My turn.*

Lifting my head from her collar, I watch her face crumple as I reach low to find her pretty pussy with my fingers. She struggles against my grip, squirming, forcing me to use my right hip to pin her down.

My cock throbs as my fingers brush her entrance. "*Fuck*," I utter. She's so wet already.

Aurora bites her lip against a moan, her expression a mixture of pleasure and pain that's my new fucking favorite.

"Just so you know," she says between gasping moans. "I still think you're a dick."

I hook my middle two digits into her wet heat, making her eyes roll back.

"And I still think you're trouble," I rasp against her mouth, nipping her lower lip between my teeth. "But you might be the good kind."

She flexes and shifts, fighting to regain control, but that shit is *mine*.

With my fingers, I work her into a frenzy, devouring every one of her sounds. Keeping her pinned there while I take control of her body, making her spasm and whimper.

And when I press my palm to her clit, rubbing it while I continue to fuck her with my fingers, she falls apart.

Aurora cries out as she comes on my hand.

Her pussy clenches hard around my fingers still knuckle deep inside her.

I swallow her sweet cries of pleasure as if each one is a pretty pill—the remedy for my affliction. Maybe that's exactly what they are. Aurora might not have signed herself away, but for tonight, I'll pretend that she's mine.

Just this one time.

47

PUSH AND PULL

AURORA

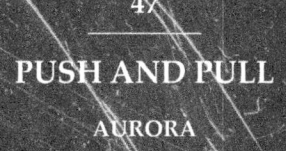

My legs shake when Atticus withdraws his fingers and rises back to his knees.

He stares down at me with a wicked intensity in his hooded brown eyes as they roam over my naked body. His hand lifts to his lips, and he parts them to suck my release from his fingers.

I can't look away as he enjoys the taste of me. As a rough groan vibrates in his chest, and his eyes fall shut.

When they open again, they fixate on me, and his throat bobs as he swallows and drops his still wet fingers from his mouth, bringing his fist to his cock.

My throat goes dry as I follow the movement with my eyes, my breaths coming shallow and short as a deep ache pulses in my lower belly.

"Holy fuck," I mutter, licking my lips as Atticus strokes himself.

Atticus grins darkly, his eyes gleaming as he watches me try to calculate the odds of it fitting.

I watch him stroke himself twice more before the ache of need in my core starts to almost hurt. With a sound

CHAPTER 47

that's half whimper, half moan, I lower my hand to my pussy, trying to find some relief as I move my fingers over my greedy clit.

Atticus watches every one of my movements with rapt attention.

"I can't believe *this* has been under my roof this entire fucking time," he says in a husky growl, showing his teeth as he cocks his head to study the way my fingers move as they dip into my heat to gather more wetness and spread it over myself. I'm still a little sore from Elijah and Seven, but fuck if I don't want to see how much more my pussy can take.

She can handle it, right?

Atticus grins as if he knows exactly what I'm thinking, and he moves so fast that I don't have time to react before he's thrown my legs to one side and grabbed me by the hip to flip me over so I'm face down on the mattress.

A gush of air pushes from my lungs as he splays a hand over my lower back, jerking my hips up from the mattress until I'm half on my knees. He gives my pussy a little slap that has me sucking air in through my teeth. The sting feels good. So good. I lift my hips for him to do it again, arching my back to allow him better access.

"You like that?" he asks just before bringing the flat edges of his fingers down on my aching pussy again.

I moan into the covers, fisting them as his fat tip pushes against my clit.

My core tightens and I brace myself, but he only slides into me an inch before pulling himself out and grabbing the base of his cock to tap it against me. He holds it against my heat, using my folds to stroke himself as he thrusts against them but not into them, drenching himself in my wetness. And *fuck*, it feels so good.

I shudder and groan into the blankets, moving my hips to try to increase the friction.

When he angles himself and pushes into me the second time, he does deeper, and I tense, my breath coming out in a heavy pant as I stretch around him.

"*Fuck*," I moan as the stretching—*the fullness*—becomes too much. The soreness that hasn't fully gone away from Seven and Elijah's double penetration adds another level of sensation I'm not sure I'm ready for.

"I can't," I choke out, but *the pressure*. God, even with the pain, the pressure is exquisite. "I... Atticus—"

"You can," he says in a husky tone that whispers over my skin like a physical touch. "Relax your pussy, Trouble."

I do as he says, or at least, I try to.

"Yeah, that's it," he says in a strained voice as he eases himself into me impossibly deeper. "There you go. Good girl."

Atticus bottoms out inside me, trembling as his thighs slap against my ass. "*Mmmmm*," he growls. "*Goddamn, you feel good.*"

The praise goes straight to my pussy and I clench around him, drawing a strangled sound from his throat that makes me smile into the covers. I slowly roll my hips, trying to get used to the size of him, the *depth*. And every time I move the slightest bit, he seems to hit something new inside of me that makes me flex and quiver.

His hand slips from my back as he pants, letting me continue making my small movements against him. His warm fingers curl around my left arm, pulling it behind my back before doing the same with the right one. Once he has them pinned to my lower back in one hand, he uses the other to reach up my spine to where my loose hair has fallen over my shoulder.

CHAPTER 47

Atticus wraps it in his fist and gives it a tug, jerking my head back so I can look at him while he eases a few inches out of me.

His face twists in pleasure as he bares his teeth and slams back inside, *hard*. I gasp, and he rocks his hips against me to soothe the ache.

"This pussy is ours," he says through his teeth as he fucks himself into me again. "All ours. Do you understand?"

I bite my lip and try to nod, but with his fist in my hair, I can't move my head.

"Do you understand?" he asks again, punctuating the question with another bruising thrust.

"Yes," I croak.

I can't imagine ever wanting any more dick after these three men. I can't imagine any other dick will *ever* measure up again. "*Yes.*"

"Good fucking girl," he grits out, releasing my hair to push my head down against the mattress as he picks up his cruel pace between my thighs. And it's what I crave. It's hard and fast and unforgiving, but so, *so* good it makes my eyes roll back and my body raw with need.

My cries are muffled against his bed as he holds me down and fucks me until I can feel my wetness dripping down my thighs, and it's beyond pleasure. Beyond pain. It's new territory that I can't fucking wait to discover.

And the fucking *stamina* of this man...

Fuck. Me.

"Such a good little slut," he croons, and something about the words snaps me out of the lustful fog he's trapped me in. Because, yeah, right now, I am his good little slut, but I am *not* those women who signed their rights away on the dotted line. I am not a toy to be taken out and used when wanted.

Flexing my shoulders, I'm able to wriggle my wrists from his grip. His thrusts falter as I plant my hands and push back with my hips, taking back my control. I rock my hips into him, bouncing them on his cock how I want to.

Atticus growls behind me, but his hands wrap around my hips and grip them tightly, making each backward thrust of my hips come harder, both of us fighting for dominance. He shifts his grip and jerks me up onto my knees so my back is flush with his chest.

"Is this what you want?" he grunts, catching me under the chin to turn my face to his while his other hand reaches lower, slapping my clit and then rubbing it. I shake in his hold, nodding against the grip of his hand under my chin.

He lets out a throaty laugh, starting to thrust into me again while he works his fingers on my clit and devours every expression on my face while he does it.

I reach up to slide my fingers into his hair, gripping it tight for something to hold on to. It's so fucking soft.

"Such a greedy girl," he says between panting breaths, and I don't correct him, because I *am* being greedy, and I am not fucking sorry about it at all.

My thighs strain and shake as the pressure of his cock and the sensation of his fingers coil me into a frenzy until it feels like I'm collapsing under my own gravity.

"Yes. *Yes,* Trouble."

"D-don't stop," I stutter, gripping everything tight for the fucking supernova that's about to tear me apart.

"I wouldn't fucking dare," Atticus growls, and my cries reach a crescendo as I explode on his cock, my vision splintering into a kaleidoscope of color.

"Oh fuck, *oh fuck,*" I howl as the sensation becomes almost too much, and he grunts as I realize I'm literally ripping his hair out.

CHAPTER 47

I force my fingers to release and fall forward onto my elbows as the last flutters of my orgasm shoot through my core.

I've barely caught my breath when Atticus starts to move again, slow at first, but gaining speed as his hands grip my ass like fucking handlebars.

He curses as he rushes to his own release while burying himself deep inside me again and again and again.

With everything still so sensitive down there, it feels like every thrust makes another microgasm shatter through me until my eyes are watering and every one of my muscles shakes.

When he hisses, I know he's close, and *I want it*. I want to taste him like he tasted me. I want to feel him on my lips.

"Come in my mouth," I demand, my voice a crackling rasp. "I want you to come in my mouth."

"*Fuuuuck*," he groans, and his excitement only winds me up more as he pulls out of me and flips me over onto my back like I weigh less than a fucking doll.

He crawls over me, planting his knees to either side of my head as I lift it to meet him, opening my mouth.

"*Goddamn.*" His voice is almost a snarl as he takes himself in one hand, jerking himself rapidly while he curls his other around the base of my neck, holding me up to feed me his cock.

He throws his head back as I suck him in, twirling my tongue around his fat tip as he pumps himself to full release.

"Ahrg. Fuck, *Aurora.*"

His salt erupts into my mouth, and I drink him down, sucking every last drop from him as his face pinches in glorious ecstasy.

When his eyes finally open and he pulls himself free of

my lips, he looks down at me in troubled wonder. "That was the hottest thing I've ever fucking seen."

I grin at him wickedly, licking the last of his spend from my lips.

"We should probably take a little break."

My brows pull together. "A *break*?"

He nods, his throat bobbing between pants. "Oh, Trouble, I'm nowhere near finished with you yet."

48

THE WHITE ROSE

SEVEN

The sun is setting by the time we make it to the cemetery.

I stretch my back as we get out of the Jeep, carefully rolling my shoulder. The wound is healing nicely, but if I don't keep it moving, it'll stiffen up and hurt ten times worse when I need to use it. The six-hour drive spent unmoving in the passenger seat really took its toll. I should've insisted on driving, but Eli was still pissy from this morning, and I wasn't in the mood for a fight.

"You good, bro?"

He barely spoke at all on the drive.

"Fine."

We all know what that means.

"Weapons," I remind him, and he plucks the short blade from his pocket and then removes the Ruger from his ankle, depositing them into the glove box with my Colt Python. We don't need a repeat of the time Julian had a meltdown and got a hold of Eli's gun. No one was hurt, thank fuck, but I had to use the spare on the back of the Jeep to replace the tire he blew out with an errant shot.

CHAPTER 48

Eli grabs the bouquet of flowers we picked up on the way and starts along the path toward his mother's grave. I follow him past headstones in various states of disrepair, up over the short grassy hill and down to the other side, where the headstones are spaced farther apart, kept company by a handful of old willow trees.

Julian is already there, kneeling in front of the tall marble stone that marks his wife's final resting place. His nurse is off to the side, keeping a respectful distance. Not so close as to make him feel like his every move is being shadowed, but not so far that she can't catch up to him in a few seconds if he has an episode. He must've asked his security detail to wait in their vehicle.

I nod to his nurse as we pass. She's the newest member of his staff. An older woman who reminds me of Céline with her no-nonsense demeanor and eclectic fashion sense.

"Dad?" Eli calls when he's within hearing range, and Julian jerks in surprise, dropping the flowers he'd been carefully arranging around Florence's headstone. His head whips round, squinting against the angry orange glare of the sun to see Eli.

He dusts his knees as he stands, and my mood sours.

He's even thinner than the last time we saw him. Where there used to be densely corded muscle, his dress shirt sags off him like a sheet hung over a line. Just skin on bone. And even in the warm amber glow of the sunset, his pallor is off —the once golden hue that Eli inherited now a sickly shade of greige that doesn't belong.

I'll have a word with the nurse about that. They need to get him outside more. Make him eat.

Julian frowns as Eli steps up to the headstone next to him, and I wait, giving them a moment. We've done this song and dance enough that I know it's better one at a time.

The white rose

Less overwhelming that way. Less chance of him spiraling back into his delusions before we've even had a chance to talk to him.

Julian squints and cocks his head at Eli, who raises the bouquet of flowers to hand them to his dad. "I thought Mom would like these."

Lilies. They were always her favorite.

"Elijah," Julian says finally, the wrinkles around his eyes softening as he recognizes his son. "You came."

"Of course I did."

Julian takes the lilies and bends back to his knees to pull them apart and arrange them amid the roses he brought. "I wasn't sure if you would."

Eli bends to help him, taking half the lilies to help complete the ring-like pattern Julian has started.

The nurse was right. He's more lucid than usual. This is always where he wants to come when he's not in his delusions—talking to Florence's ghost. It worked out for us this time since we wouldn't have been able to go to the house. Ambrose has shown no interest in Julian since he got what he wanted from him, so he's been safe enough to stay there.

But we aren't foolish enough to think Ambrose doesn't at least check in on the old place to see if we'd design to visit. The last thing we need is to lead Ambrose back there. I don't even want to imagine how Julian might react to seeing his face again.

I move up and crouch on Julian's opposite side, fixing one of the flowers that doesn't seem to want to stay put.

He turns to look at me, his shifting gaze narrowing as I pluck the little Eiffel Tower trinket from my pocket and place it atop her headstone. I snatched it while we were at the *Triangle d'Or* in Paris. It was always her favorite place in the whole world, and it's painted red—her favorite color.

CHAPTER 48

Julian watches me suspiciously, and I offer him a grin, turning a bit to the left to tap the triple 7 tattoo on the side of my neck to help remind him.

When I turn back to face him, he's smiling, and a laugh booms from his chest as he reaches over to pull me into a bony-armed embrace that somehow still manages to be fierce. "*Seven*. It's good to see you."

Beyond his shoulder, Eli drops his head, and I grimace.

Julian might not remember why he's angry with Eli, but Eli can't forget. Atticus wasn't the only one who left. Accepting Ambrose's deal meant Eli did, too. For well over a year. Leaving me to hold the fucking bag when Julian's condition started to worsen.

"How's the colony?" he asks when he pulls back, his gaze clearer than I've seen it in the last few visits. "Are they producing well?"

I nod. "Yeah, all good. Hives are healthy. The flow is better than ever."

"Maybe I could come see them soon."

Not far off, the nurse gives a slight shake of her head, overhearing the conversation.

I put a hand on Julian's shoulder and lie through my teeth. "Yeah. Maybe soon."

Julian smiles tightly, hearing the truth I won't say. But I hope he remembers why he can't.

Eli looks at me, and from the way he's working his jaw and the harsh lines between his brows, I know he's thinking about bringing it up. Bringing *him* up. But the last time we tried to ask Julian if there was anything he could remember about Ambrose that might help us, it set him off in a bad way.

We always thought there was more he knew that could

help, but since everything happened, whatever knowledge he might've had has been locked away. Repressed.

I shake my head at Eli. It's not worth it.

It'll only cause Julian more stress.

But I don't think Eli's thinking about that right now. He's thinking about Ro. He's thinking if he can just get his dad to give us *something* to go off of, then she won't feel like she's the only hope we have to put things right.

He doesn't get that she already decided the minute Atticus asked her. I could see it in her eyes. And nothing short of Elijah telling her point blank that he doesn't want her help will stop her. Hell, that might not even do it.

Eli's throat bobs.

Julian follows my line of sight back to his son. "You seem different."

Eli's brows draw together. "What do you mean?"

Julian gives a noncommittal shrug.

"It's probably this girl he's been seeing," I offer with a devious smirk, and Eli rolls his eyes.

"A girl?" Julian's interest is piqued. Eli only had one actual girlfriend back in high school, and that didn't last very long because he preferred to spend his weekends painting and learning the family trade, rather than taking her out.

Eli sighs. "Yeah, Dad. Her name's Aurora. I think you'd like her."

He looks around. "Well, where is she? Did you bring her?"

"No. Not this time. Maybe next, though, if you want."

"You know, I was about your age when I met your mom. Forgot every woman who came before her like that." He snaps his fingers. "She was…"

CHAPTER 48

"An incredible woman," I finish for him when he can't seem to find the right words.

Julian nods sadly to himself, then reaches out for Eli, taking his hand. "Tell me about her. Tell me about this Aurora. What's she like? Is she... Is she..."

Oh shit.

Julian's shoulders twitch as he looks down at Eli's hand in his. At the scars marring the back of his palm, making his pinkie and ring finger a little crooked. Eli tries to pull his hand back, but Julian grips it tighter, hauling him in for a better look.

"What..."

"Dad, it's fine. *Dad*, just let go."

"What...what is..."

I take Julian's shoulders, shoving down the roiling acid in my stomach as Eli finally gets free.

"Hey, he's fine. *He's fine*."

Julian is still looking at Eli and I see the exact moment he remembers. His shoulders go up, and he stiffens under my hands.

Fuck.

"Mr. Ashford," the nurse says, coming to stand a little closer. "I think maybe we should be getting ba—"

"He's fine," Eli snaps. "We're fine."

The nurse backs off, but she's right. The damage is already done.

"Come on, Pops," I mutter, helping him stand by the shoulders. "Let's get you—"

He rips from my hands, grabbing onto Eli with fists twisted into his shirt.

"*Did you get it back?*" Spit flies from Julian's mouth at Eli and when I try to pry him off, he just turns to me instead, pulling hard on my jacket with blown pupils, looking as mad as a bag of fucking bees.

"Florence's art—did you get it? The collection! Did you get it back? Did you... *Did you...*"

"*Julian*," I struggle to keep my tone even with my chest caving in. "Hey, it's all right. You don't have to worry about—"

He jerks away from me violently, and when the nurse tries to corral him, he growls at her, growing big, baring his teeth.

"Did you find him?" Julian demands again, whirling when Eli answers him.

"No, Dad," he says calmly, when I can tell he's anything but. "We still don't have it back."

"I told you," Julian sneers, jabbing his fingers at Eli. "I told you!"

"You told us what?" I ask, stepping around him cautiously.

I give the nurse a look when I see her using a nearby gravestone as a table to ready a syringe from the items in her purse. I shake my head. We can handle this without fucking drugs.

"I told you!" Julian hollers again, his voice breaking, and I steel myself against the sound.

Like it always does, the memory of him *before* hits me square in the chest. Julian was always the most levelheaded of any of us. The first person you would want to go to when you needed advice. The voice of reason. The man who taught me how to crack a safe and wield a blade, shoot a gun, and tend to the hives.

When he's like this, I don't even recognize him, and it hurts to know that he wouldn't even recognize himself, if the man he was before were here to bear witness.

CHAPTER 48

"Oh, the Monets," he cries, gesturing wildly, stepping on the flowers he so carefully placed around Florence's grave only a few minutes ago. "The Picasso! We need to get to the archipelago. We have to get them back! You *said* you'd get them back."

"You mean the Caravaggio? We still have that one, Dad. It's on the wall at the house, remember?"

"No!"

He shoves Eli, and that's when I can't stand idle anymore. My throat thickens as I wrap my arms around Julian, holding him back, holding him steady, completely ignoring the screaming ache in my shoulder as he writhes in my grip.

"Julian, listen to me," I hiss. "We're trying. We never stopped trying. We'll get it all back."

"You said that last time! *You said that last time!* You said...you said..."

"Breathe with me, Julian. *In*—"

"He took my son! *He took my son!*"

He starts to sag in my arms, his breaths coming harder, heavier, as if he can't get enough of it into his lungs to bring oxygen into his troubled mind. I go to the ground with him, still holding on to him, but only so he won't fall.

"I'm right here." Eli kneels in front of Julian. "Look, I'm fine. He let me go."

"*No*," Julian moans, a sob trapped in his throat. "My son...my son never...he never came home."

Eli's jaw tightens, and his eyes darken. *Dampen.*

Julian smacks his forehead with his open palm. "Never came home." *Smack.* "The bells..." *Smack.* "The bells and the birds." *Smack.* 'The boats and the—the boats and—"

Eli helps me get hold of his arms, keeping them tight to his sides to stop him from hurting himself.

"No!"

We're losing him. It's too late now.

"Dad. Hey! *Dad*. It's all right."

When Julian looks up again, he recoils at Eli. "Who... who are you? What do you want? Let go of me! *I said let go!*"

I hold tight, giving the nurse the go-ahead to give him what he needs to be at peace.

I detach myself as she does her work. I can't watch. And I don't relax my arms until Julian fully sags against me and I take his weight.

Eli holds in his pain as he reaches over to push Julian's graying dark hair from his face, and flicks his red eyes to me. "Help me get him back to the car?"

We each take a shoulder, walking Julian down the path in silence as he mutters more nonsense to himself.

"Are you okay?" I ask Eli once we have Julian safely strapped into the back seat with the nurse checking his vitals.

"What do you think?"

Yeah. Stupid fucking question.

Eli sighs and pinches the space between his eyes, as if I don't know he's trying to covertly erase the tears that have gathered there. I pinch the Jeep keys from his pocket and flick them into my palm.

"What are you—"

"Come on. I'll drive."

He's definitely in no state to.

49

TOO GOOD TO BE TRUE

ATTICUS

Something shifts in the bed, and I jerk awake.

My eyes take a second to adjust to the early morning light filtering through my bedroom door from upstairs, but when they do, I relax back into the mattress.

Aurora lets out a small sigh as she settles back to sleep on her stomach next to me. Her arms are pulled in tight, but her right leg is free of the covers she stole in the night.

I follow the line of it up to where it vanishes, and my cock stiffens.

She's the picture of perfect ruin. Her hair is a mess of tangles that fall to cover most of her face. Her lips are swollen and slightly parted. Her mascara blackens the delicate skin around her eyes. And there, just below and to the right of her chin, is the mark I left on her neck, like a splatter of red paint on an unblemished alabaster canvas.

Fuck, my cock vividly remembers the feel of being buried so deep inside of her sweet pussy that she could barely catch her breath. It throbs between my legs, hungry for a second helping of Trouble.

She took me so well, too.

CHAPTER 49

Carefully, I reach over and push the tangles of hair from her face, but she stirs at my touch and I snatch my hand back.

Get control of yourself.

She sighs into the pillow, falling back into a dead sleep.

I tear my eyes from her. I'm not about to watch her sleep like some kind of pussy-whipped fiction-book hero.

The buzzing of my phone snaps me out of it and has me dragging my eyes away from her again. *Fuck.* I should get that.

Slowly, so I don't wake her, I slink from the bed to where I kicked off my pants. If it's Eli and Sev and I don't answer the call, I'll never hear the goddamned end of it.

And what if something happened? We almost always pop into a motel or truck stop somewhere on the way home to get a few hours of sleep after visits with Julian, but usually, I'd have heard from them to let me know they were on their way back by now.

If I wasn't so fucking distracted last night, I'd have already called them to see where the hell they were at.

I swipe my jeans from the floor and pull my phone out. There's a text there from them sent close to four hours ago that says they're on their way, but it's not vibrating.

The fuck?

I search the area, trying to locate the source of the sound. Across the room, Aurora's cell vibrates insistently against the wooden leg of my dresser. I peer at Aurora, but the noise hasn't woken her, and I decide it's a testament to my outstanding abilities in bed that she stays asleep.

I pick it up to silence it just as the call is taken to voicemail and abruptly ended. The caller ID says it was Chris.

Chris.

Too good to be true

My mind rushes to locate the information associated with the name.

She had a text thread with him.

But it was nothing exciting, I tell myself, then frown, remembering.

Nothing concerning other than the fact that there were a number of deleted messages that I've been unable to recover. But Aurora had deleted messages in several other conversations, too. Not just with this guy.

The line of thinking doesn't make me feel any better.

My cock softens as my mind pulls all the necessary blood flow to work the problem.

No. It's not a problem.

I'll just ask her who it is when she wakes up.

I'm in the process of setting her phone atop the dresser when it buzzes again in my hand.

I wish I could say I hesitated before looking at the message that flashes across the screen, but I don't. I bring it closer.

My ears ring as I read the single sentence.

Chris: Did you get in?

My mouth is dry, and the blood in my veins freezes to ice.

I look at her again, facing away from me, asleep in my bed.

Who is this?

Did you get in?

Did she get in where?

Here?

My grip on her cell tightens enough that I'm shocked the glass doesn't crack. I flick the screen up to open the conversation, but it attempts to use Face ID, fails, then

CHAPTER 49

requires a PIN code. I don't know it, but I still have her phone mirrored on my desktop.

I tug my jeans on and am up the stairs before I even have them zipped all the way up.

My body hums with latent energy, and I can't hear a fucking thing over the buzzing drone in my ears. I had to take a piss a few seconds ago, but that urge is gone now, replaced with an ugly flutter in the pit of my stomach that tells me something is very fucking wrong.

How could I be such an *idiot*?

I shake my head hard, trying to rattle it back to rights, but the spike of testosterone raging in my blood is poisoning every thought with worst-case scenarios. Twisting her—*twisting me*—until I don't recognize our shapes anymore.

Chill. I need to fucking chill.

I shove my chair out of the way when I get to my office, slamming Aurora's cell down on the desk to fire up my monitor. My hands shake as they fly over the keys, bringing up the application that mirrors her phone. I haven't looked at it in days. *Why?*

Why haven't I looked at it in days?

My teeth grind as I click through to her messages and bring up the conversation with *Chris*.

I see the message he just sent, but the text before it is one I've already seen and dismissed as inconsequential. Besides, it was sent a while before she even came here. So either there's more deleted messages I'm missing, or this is in response to something else. Something they discussed before she came here?

A phone call, maybe?

I click over to her call log, but don't see anything from him in recent calls.

Too good to be true

There are a few unknown number calls, though. I run the numbers through Google and two other less legal search engines and come up with nothing. I could call them, but I'm not sure I want to hear whatever is on the other end. And if Aurora is...

Fuck.

Fuck, fuck, fuck.

I growl through my teeth and slap my hand to the side of my head like I can dislodge the thought, but it's already there. Already spreading seeds and growing roots.

If Aurora isn't who she says she is, I don't want to give her or anyone else the heads-up that I know.

Always keep the upper hand, Julian used to say. *Don't show your cards.*

I fucking *told* myself this was a bad idea, that I shouldn't let her get close. Shouldn't trust what I don't know.

But I let her in anyway.

No. No, I didn't. It was just sex. She said it herself, she still thought I was a dick. It was just...just fucking. Just fucking.

I didn't let her in.

I don't let people in.

Think!

What could she have to gain from...

Everything slows to a crawl as it dawns on me and I sink heavily into the chair, dropping my face into my hands.

Of course.

He planted her here.

I laugh hollowly, bristling when my skin suddenly feels too tight over my bones and my world starts to spin and spiral.

Ambrose planted her right in my path. Just like he

CHAPTER 49

planted himself among us eight years ago. I didn't see what he was then and we all paid the price for that mistake. It's not one I'll ever make again.

I push the heels of my palms into my eye sockets and mutter a curse under my breath. Fuck, I knew it seemed too good to be true.

From the goddamned start, I thought it. A girl who matched the description Ambrose put out a couple of months ago, alone in the mountains with a single suitcase and nowhere to go. No one who would miss her.

He *knew* I'd jump at the chance to use her. That we'd walk right into his hands if she sang the right lyrics to lead us there. Like the pied piper and her rats, hypnotized by false promises and an alluring song.

I could see Eli falling for that. Maybe even Seven. But *me?*

How did I not even consider this as a possibility?

I fucking slept next to her last night? *Slept.* I was entirely at her mercy for at least six hours. She could've done anything to me.

God, and the girl can shoot, too. She 'saved' Eli in Paris. Who was the poor sop that Ambrose sacrificed to make sure we would fully put our trust in her? He probably didn't even know the guy's last name.

He's sacrificed more and worse to get what he wants.

Fucking hell. Is *he* 'Chris'?

I rack my brain, discovering and discarding and forming new connections with every potential threat.

I should've seen all the red flags for exactly what they were. I should've listened to my gut.

It makes me sick thinking that she's still in my bed. That I had my cock in her just hours ago. Probably right where Ambrose wanted her. What did he promise her? Money? *Art*?

What was the going rate to seduce every last one of us?

FUCK!

I gag as I shove away the emotions trying to expand in my head like hot air. In my chest like toxic fumes.

My thoughts jar and race. Crash and burn.

Confirm. The word crackles in my mind with the whisper of radio static, and I'm back in uniform with a gun and blood on my hands.

Yes. I need to confirm.

Not wasting another second, I make three calls, barking down the line as I call in three favors I've been saving for a rainy day. Information is power and I am about to take back every ounce of it that she stole from me.

By the time I'm through, I'm panting. Pacing. Waging war against the dark thoughts trying to creep in like shadows at the edges of my vision.

Not again. *I won't let it happen again.*

I just have to wait. They'll get back to me soon and then I'll know what I need to know.

Who 'Chris' is.

Where Aurora really came from and whether she has any tangible ties to Ambrose.

If my buddy Angelo from sniper training still has that tech contact, I should also be able to recover every message Aurora ever fucking deleted from this phone.

I just have to *wait*.

I stop pacing, remembering the time.

Damn.

The guys will be back soon. Within hours.

I can't...

CHAPTER 49

I can't fucking watch them go all googly-eyed over her. I can't give her the opportunity to sink her claws into them any deeper than she already has. I need to protect them. Protect *us*. That's my job. The last promise I made to Florence.

And I don't intend to break it.

I failed them once. *I won't fucking fail them again.*

Flexing my jaw, I let the rage move freely in my blood, carrying me like a voyeur through a nightmare as I unlock my safe and take out the M18.

The fury floats me on a red cloud through the eerie silence of the cabin and down the stairs. It enters the bedroom and locks the door behind it, and I let it take control.

50

THIS BITCH BITES BACK

AURORA

I reach out to the other side of the bed, my fingers brushing nothing but smooth sheets and empty space as I wake up. Sighing, I press my face into the pillows, inhaling the warm scent that I think will now be forever imprinted in my mind as *Atticus*.

There's a whisper of shifting fabric behind me and I blink to clear the sleep from my eyes as I roll over and find him sitting a few feet from the bed. He's pulled the armchair close, and he's leaning over his knees, watching me intently.

God, how long has he been doing that? "What are you doing?"

There's laughter in my still sleep-toned voice as I stretch again, "Please don't tell me you've been sitting there watching me sleep."

I can't decide if that would be creepy, or kind of cute.

"Atticus?"

I prop myself up on my elbows, looking at him more closely in the warm orange glow of the lamp. His eyes flash

CHAPTER 50

like reflective stone, and there's something between his hands. Hanging loosely from his grip. What is that?

Is that my cell phone on the arm of the chair?

I sit up, pulling the sheet with me to cover myself. My skin prickles as I swallow, casting my gaze around the room, trying to find what I'm missing.

The door is closed, and I don't hear the guys in the house or Ellie. Atticus must've let her out. "What's going on? Is everything okay?"

I swing my legs off the high king bed, looking for my clothes on the floor, but Atticus's cold voice stops me.

"Stay there."

"What?"

He inhales audibly, leaning back in the chair. As he moves, the object in his hand catches the light, and my heart stops.

"Why do you have that?"

"I have some questions," he says in a dead monotone, angling the weapon atop his thigh so it's pointed at me.

My skin flushes with heat, and I clamp my jaw, glaring at him. "What the fuck is this?"

His grip on the weapon flexes and his next words come out through his teeth. "That's exactly what I'd like to know."

I shake my head, scoffing as I get up to collect my pants from the floor.

Atticus is up in an instant, making me flinch as he stands over me. "Sit the fuck down."

My heart pounds hard in my chest as I hold my ground. I don't know what this is about, but he needs to check himself. I glare up at him. "Why are you being such an asshole?"

"As if you don't know."

When I go to grab my pants again, and he tries to block me, I duck and scramble out of the way, picking them up anyway.

His hand comes down on my shoulder, and I whirl with venom in my throat, knocking him off. "Don't fucking touch me."

I don't know what kind of bullshit he's trying to pull, but I am *not* interested.

"Did you wake up on the wrong side of the bed or something? *Jesus*."

I *knew* this was a bad idea. Why didn't I just walk away last night?

Turning away from him, I drop the sheet and pull my pants on without bothering to locate my panties, searching the floor for my shirt. Atticus doesn't stop me as I snatch it from the edge of the bed and pull it back over my head. He doesn't stop me as I storm toward the door and go to wrench it open so I can get the hell away from whatever fuckery this is.

But the handle doesn't budge. I try again, twisting harder, searching for a lock.

Beside the door, partially hidden behind an the ancient-looking bust I almost knocked over yesterday, is a fucking keypad.

Was this his plan all along? Get me to come down here so he could, *what*? Hurt me? Keep me down here and have his way with me for as long as he damn well wants? I am into some kinky-ass shit, but I've never had a fantasy of being fucked by a total asshole while he holds a gun. I'm not one of his 'playthings' and I didn't sign shit that said he was allowed to lock me in here with him.

"What's the code?"

"Why are you really here?" he counters.

CHAPTER 50

"Atticus, what is the fucking code?"

He steps forward, coming slowly around the bed like a shadow in the desert of his room. He adjusts his grip on the gun in his right hand, and it makes a metallic sound as it rubs against one of his rings.

"No one is going anywhere until I get the answers I want."

"What the hell are you talking about?"

I want to tell him he's scaring me so that he'll stop, but I think he already knows. I think that's exactly what he wants to do. And it makes me so angry I want to scream.

"Why are you here?" he repeats, stopping a few steps away, standing so still he could be a fucking statue. It's unnerving.

I frown. "You brought me here."

"But that's exactly what you wanted," he snaps back, agitation in the set of his jaw. "*Wasn't it?*"

And I see what this is now. I recognize his expression. It's one I've seen in the other men who've inserted themselves into my life from the time I was old enough to remember.

This is someone who's already made up his mind, and nothing I say, no matter how rational, is going to change it. Not while he's like this.

I could do what I always have—agree, apologize, and live to deal with another day...*but to hell with that*.

"I'm sorry, Atticus," I sneer. "But you're going to have to be a little more fucking specific with your accusations because I don't speak jackass."

He lurches forward a step, and I'm proud as fuck of myself when I don't shrink back.

I clench my fists and lift my chin.

"You really had them fooled," he seethes. "Shit. You almost had me, too. I actually thought..."

He laughs hollowly before his eyes narrow again. "Did he pay you extra to spread your legs for all of us, or did it just come naturally?"

Atticus ducks as the bust of some ancient philosopher's head flies toward him and smashes into the wall, raining bits of ivory stone over the floor. My shoulder aches from the heft of it. I look at the pedestal where it just was and blink. I don't even remember making the decision to throw the fucking thing, but you know what, I'm only angry it didn't hit him.

Is that what he really thinks of me? That I'm some whore who's only sleeping with them as a means to whatever ridiculous end he's just come up with.

"You *bastard*," I seethe.

Atticus stares, gaping at the now half-faceless bust on the floor by his feet, slowly dragging his gaze up to lock back on me. My throat goes dry at the look in his eyes.

"That was from the third fucking century."

I cross my arms over my chest and eye him down.

"Well, now it's trash."

He snarls as he storms over to me, getting right up in my face.

I clench my fists and jut out my chin, refusing to be cowed by his size. I'm calling his bluff. If he were going to hurt me, the fucker would've done it already.

"I *never* should have brought you here," he shouts into my face, and I stand my ground even though it feels like it's shifting beneath my feet.

I say nothing, and my silence only seems to rile the malice in his stare. He snarls as he pulls himself back and

CHAPTER 50

stalks to the chair to snatch my phone from the armrest, bringing it back to shove it into my hands.

"Open it."

"What?"

"*Unlock. It,*" he says like he's talking to a complete idiot who doesn't understand basic English.

"No."

I'm too slow to stop him before he gets his arm around me, holding mine down as I thrash against him.

"Atticus!"

He flips me around and my chest hits the wall.

"Atticus, *stop!*"

He presses me harder into the wall to keep me pinned.

Panic rises in my throat when I realize I can't move. He brings my phone up to my face where it's squished against the wall, unlocking the screen and letting me go as soon as it's open.

"*What the fuck?*"

I hate how my throat has started to burn. How speaking feels like pushing words through razor blades trapped in my windpipe. I shove him, and he doesn't react. Doesn't even shift on his feet. I shove him again, but he stops me, grabbing my wrists, spinning me into his chest to grip me tight. "I asked you nicely," he snaps. "Twice."

Managing to get my wrists free, I twist myself out of his grasp, dizzy on whatever chemical is making my world feel small and suffocating.

I force the air into my lungs. "Let me out of this room... *now.*"

"Tell me who this is," he says, ignoring me, shoving my phone screen in my face.

It takes me a second to see the jumble of light and letters for what it is. A message.

Chris: Did you get in?

"Chris?"

Oh my god, what is this about? Is he...is he *jealous*? Does he think Chris is another ex?

"Chris is my dad, you prick."

He snorts derisively. "Your adopted father's name is Melvin Davis."

I never told him that. How does he know that?

"You know that it's pretty easy to tell when someone deletes messages from their phone, and there are a *lot* of deleted messages in this conversation. In a lot of your conversations, actually."

My mouth falls open.

"Oh, come on," he says, waving the gun around in his hand like it's the most obvious thing in the world. "As if I didn't look into you. It was the first fucking thing I did when you got here."

My chest hollows, draining away the panic to make room for the rage to return.

He hacked my phone. I want to laugh at myself. Because of course he did. The guy I *gave* my phone to literally to check to make sure it *wasn't* hacked in Paris was the one doing the hacking all along.

What else did he see? The messages between Jesse and me?

The video he sent me?

After Jesse and his goons fucking drugged me and watched while...

My stomach sours, and bile hits the back of my throat like boiling acid.

"Don't look so surprised," he says, patronizing. "You're the one with all the secrets, aren't you, *Aurora*—if that's even your real name."

CHAPTER 50

He's really fucking lost it.

I would feel sorry for him if I wasn't so fucking angry.

"His name," I start, shivering even though I'm hot all over. "Is Melvin *Christopher* Davis."

I need to get out of this room before I do something I might regret. Before I set something into motion that can't be stopped. Because I want to hurt him.

The feeling creeps over me like a living thing, rearranging my wires and filling my head with poisonous whispers.

It's every time I hovered over Jesse with a pillow, ready to push down and hold until he stopped breathing.

But I already unleashed that part of myself in Paris and I don't think there's a way to get it back in its cage.

"It's his *middle* name."

Atticus's brows lower, and he shakes his head. "I'm not buying it."

"I don't give a shit. Let me out."

This time when he steps forward, I step back, giving him a warning look that I think the predator in him recognizes because he stops, cocking his head at me.

"Just tell me the truth. How long have you been working for him?"

"Working for who?"

"Tell me what I want to know, and I'll let you walk out of here."

I gape at him.

"Did Ambrose tell you to—"

"*Ambrose?*"

"Don't fucking play with me! I don't want to have to hurt you."

Hurt me? He can fucking try it.

Covertly, I scan my surroundings for a weapon in case I

need one. If I'm fast, I can probably get to the acoustic guitar in the corner. There are pens on his nightstand that could also do some damage if they're jammed just right into his jugular.

I decide to try reason one more time. Not for Atticus. He can suck a fucking dick. For Elijah and Seven, who wouldn't condone this. I try because they care about him. I'm not sure why I ever thought I could anymore. Some people are too fucked up to fix.

"If I was working for Ambrose, why the hell would I have saved Elijah's life in Paris?"

"He's sacrificed dozens of his men trying to get to us. What's one more to cement you as an ally?"

I roll my eyes.

"What about this house?"

"Not following."

"You said he didn't know where it was. So, how could I have been in exactly the right place at the right time?"

I'm shouting, but I can't seem to stop. Can't seem to rein in my fury.

Atticus recoils from the question, eyes shifting as he considers it. "I must've fucked up somewhere. Maybe the meeting we crashed was a setup and you tailed us all the way from Jonesville."

I laugh derisively at him, and he doesn't fucking like it, but that only makes me double down. "Now you're really reaching, *Atty*."

His returning grin is full of malice.

"Am I? Let's call 'Chris', shall we?"

He tosses my phone to me and I catch it on instinct.

He gestures with his gun. "Go ahead. Call him."

"Hell no. I'm not bringing him into whatever fucked-up delusion this is."

CHAPTER 50

"Why was he asking you if you got in?"

My face falls. Why *was* he asking that? I rack my brain, but it's like trying to grasp at leaves in the wind. I can't catch the thoughts before they're carried away. God, why is it always like that when you're on the spot?

But you know what? I don't owe Atticus an explanation because I've done nothing wrong.

I'm not working for Ambrose, and if he opened his eyes for one goddamned second, he'd be able to see that himself.

"That's what I thought." Atticus's tone turns deadly. "Call him."

"*No.*"

A vein in Atticus's temple stands out blue beneath bronze skin as he clenches his jaw...and raises his gun.

"Make the call, Aurora."

My heart hammers in my chest.

He wouldn't.

"They'll never forgive you."

"Don't!" he yells. "You don't talk about them. Do you think you're special? You're just a warm cunt. Another backstabbing whore digging for gold in the Ashford coffers. I'm not fucking having it."

The knife in my gut twists, opening a hundred old hurts.

Not good enough. Not nice enough. Not pretty enough.

Just another warm cunt.

I gasp when he twists his fist into the front of my shirt, shoving me back into the wall. I can't fight him. I don't know where the rage went. My body feels too heavy to move.

"Make the call."

He shakes me, and the cool metal of the barrel presses to the bare skin where my cropped shirt ends, just to the right of my belly button. A bullet there will kill me slow. It'll hurt.

With shaking hands, I lift the phone and find Chris in my contacts through the blur of the searing tears welling in my eyes.

I hate him. I hate him. *I hate him.*

When I hesitate too long with my finger over his name, Atticus takes the cell and taps the call button for me, turning on speakerphone as he pushes the barrel of the gun harder into my stomach.

It rings twice before the line picks up and a sob grows in my throat.

"There she is," Christ says warmly. "How are you, kid? Did you get into that course you were talking about?"

I choke on another sob, remembering. I told him I was applying for an Intro to Music Business course in Boone so that someone would know where I was headed.

And I deleted the messages in case Jesse caught me. Like I deleted all the messages I didn't want him to find and exploit against me.

Atticus taps me with the barrel of the gun.

"Yeah," I manage, trying so fucking hard to make my voice sound normal. They don't need to know how much of a screw-up I am. Not after everything they did to make sure I turned out differently. "It—*uh*—it starts next week."

"You okay, hun?"

Atticus looks at the phone as if he doesn't understand the meaning of the words coming from the speaker.

"Aurora? You sound like you've been cry—"

He taps the button to end the call, and I sag against the wall.

"Must suck..." I mutter. "Being such a monumental fuckup."

CHAPTER 50

My phone buzzes with Chris calling me back, but Atticus doesn't answer it, just watches it go to voicemail.

The sound of a door opening upstairs proceeds heavy footfalls and the tapping of Ellie's paws on hardwood.

I bat his gun away from my belly and bang hard on the locked door before he can stop me. "Down here!"

Atticus gives me a hard look, and I swear to god, if he comes one more step in my direction, I will rip his dick off with my bare hands.

It takes seconds before the whole damn cavalry comes stampeding down the stairs.

"Aurora?" Seven's voice comes through the solid metal pane and I want to cry when I hear it.

"Could you open the door?" I ask, swallowing the gravel in my throat.

There are four chirping sounds as he puts the code in on the other side, and the handle turns in my grip.

"Ro?"

I shoulder past him, unable to meet either of their eyes as I take the stairs two at a time to escape the terrifying version of myself that still wants to make Atticus hurt.

Ellie whines, trying to get my attention with little jumps that almost knock me off my feet as I trudge up the stairs.

"*Aurora*," Elijah calls after me.

"What happened?" Seven demands, following me up the stairs.

When he tries to grab my hand to stop me, I rip it away. I don't want him to make it better. I want fucking blood.

"Ask *him*."

Seven's blue eyes harden to ice.

"He's the one who thinks he fucking knows everything."

51

WHAT DID YOU DO?

ELIJAH

Seven shuts off the engine in the drive, getting out to greet Ellie, who chased us almost all the way from the front gate.

"Hey, pretty girl," he says, going to a knee to let her attack his face with kisses.

I give her a little pat when she comes to greet me, but I'm still trapped in my own head. We stopped to rest for a few hours at a truck stop in the night, but I couldn't sleep. It's been a while since I've had to see Dad that way—talking nonsense and acting like a completely different person than the man who raised me.

I should have been there for him through the worst of it, but I was off on a fool's errand, letting Ambrose steal time I can't ever get back with him. He's fucking right to blame me. I was there, *right there*, where Ambrose was keeping our family collection and not only did I not get it back, I came home broken and empty-handed.

He's right about that, too. His son never came home. Not really.

CHAPTER 51

Elijah Ashford died in that room. I'm just his ghost.

Sev leans against the front of the Jeep, taking a cigarette out to put it between his lips and light it. Atticus will have his head for it, but Sev doesn't care. Every time Atticus finds his cigarette stash and trashes it, he just buys more and finds a new hiding place.

"What are you thinking?" he asks after he inhales. "You've hardly said two fucking words since we got in the Jeep."

My gaze lands on the front door of the house. It's still dark inside. Quiet.

"You really think Aurora is going to say yes?"

He nods. "I do."

I drop my head.

"I don't think you should fight her on it if she does."

My teeth click as I clench them. "You would really want to send her right to him? You know what he's capable of."

"I wouldn't fucking want to," he snaps at me, ashing his cigarette. "But it isn't about what *I* want."

When I realize what he's saying, I feel like an asshole. "Because it's her choice."

It's not a question, but he answers it anyway. "It is. She's not yours to command. She's not mine, either. Ro belongs to herself."

He's right.

As much as I want to keep her as far away from Ambrose as possible, it's not my call.

I've been back and forth with it in the car for hours. I made a promise to my dad that I would set things right, and Aurora might be the key to helping me finally keep that promise. It feels fucking wrong to use her like that. To use her in *any* way that would result in my own personal gain.

What did you do?

But is that what this is if she *wants* to do it?

Mom would throw her arms up and say it's a moral dilemma, and then she would probably agree with Seven.

Let her decide.

I made Aurora aware of the risks. Now it's her call.

"If she does say yes," I have to grind the words out, "I won't try to stop her."

But I will do absolutely everything I can do to help her succeed and make sure nothing happens to her in the process.

Seven crushes the remains of his cigarette beneath his boot, and when I look up, he's frowning at the house. "Let's head in. Something's off. It's too quiet."

My stomach turns. "They're probably just still asleep."

He gives me a dubious look. "When's the last time Atticus slept past six in the morning?"

He has a point.

I waffle with going back to the Jeep to grab my gun, but Sev has his and he's already halfway up the damn stairs. I rush to follow him, taking the short blade from my ankle as we step into the tepid silence of the house.

Ellie gives a little growl as she enters behind us, her nose going to the floor like she can smell whatever Seven sensed was wrong.

"I'll check Aurora's room," I mutter, moving through the entryway, but a loud pounding stops me.

It's coming from the other way. Seven and I share a look before rushing through the dining room.

Where the fuck...

"Down here!" Aurora's voice is far away and muffled, coming from down the stairs that lead to Atticus's room.

Seven flies down them with me and Ellie on his heels.

CHAPTER 51

Atticus's door is closed, and when Seven reaches for the handle, it doesn't budge. "Aurora?" he calls through the door.

"Could you open the door?" she asks, and even muffled, there's clear panic in her tone.

I jam the code into the reader and the instant it lights up green, Sev wrenches the door open.

"Ro?"

She shoves her way out, pale and frantic as she brushes by Sev and ignores my outstretched hand to rush past us both up the stairs with Ellie barking the whole way after her.

My chest goes cold.

"Aurora?" I shout after her, rushing to follow.

Where the fuck is Atticus? Did she get herself locked in down there?

"What happened?" Sev's voice is deadly, and I feel the violence of it in my own chest. He grabs her hand to try to stop her, and she rips it free with an animalistic sound in her throat.

"Ask *him*!" Aurora all but screams, my angel looking more avenging than I've ever seen her, with true fury and pain in her watery eyes that makes me want to smash and *kill*.

Him? My head whips toward the stairs as a searing sensation crawls up my spine.

What the fuck did he do?

"He's the one who thinks he fucking knows everything," she spits before turning on her heel to stomp through the house.

Seven and I share a look, and I find the same rage I feel mirrored in his hard stare.

I take a step toward the stairs, but stop myself,

What did you do?

clenching my fists. Not sure if I want to throttle Atticus or run after Aurora.

"Go," Seven says, making my mind up for me. "Go talk to her. I'll handle him."

He fucking better.

52

PAYING THE PIPER

ATTICUS

I still have her phone, and Chris is still calling.

When it goes to voicemail for the third time, a message pops onto the screen.

Chris: Is everything all right? Is it that guy you were seeing? I can come and get you. Just say the word and I'll leave now. I can be in Amherst by three o'clock.

There's no way this is legit, right?

They could've planned a cover just in case she was made.

Upstairs, Aurora shouts at Eli and Sev about me fucking knowing everything.

I usually do. I'm never wrong. There's no way we got that lucky to have run into her on the road. A girl who's a near-perfect physical match for Ambrose's lost daughter, with a legitimate history that we can use to our advantage. Alone. With nowhere to go. There are just too many coincidences and if life has taught me anything, it's that if something seems too good to be true, it's because it usually fucking is.

CHAPTER 52

Her phone vibrates again and I check the screen, but it's dark. It's not her phone. It's mine.

Juggling my gun, I tug it from my pocket, seeing the name of one of my contacts light up the screen.

Sev's heavy footsteps pound down the stairs, and I shut the door, jamming the lock hold button to keep him out while I answer the phone. "Go."

Sev tries to punch in the code and the door beeps angrily at him, not allowing him entry.

"That number you sent is a cell. It belongs to a Melvin Christopher Davis."

A sensation like nails on a damn chalkboard scrapes down the back of my neck until I shudder.

"Born May 18th, 1968. Wife is Grace Davis. He lives in..."

He rattles off more information I can barely hear over my blood rushing in my ears.

"Atticus!" Sev bellows through the door, pounding louder. "Open the fucking door!"

I drop to a crouch, dropping Aurora's phone to clench my hand into a fist against the floor, searching for stability while my contact continues shattering every narrative I constructed.

"Any connections to Ambrose De La Rosa?" I demand, interrupting him.

"None that I could find, and I checked everywhere. The girl was declared a ward of the state at three years old. She bounced around from foster home to foster home until she was about sixteen, at which point she was officially adopted by Melvin Davis and his wife. She has some priors but nothing major, and all committed while she was still a juvenile. Petty theft. Vandalism. Truancy. Trespassing. Normal shit given her circumstances. Looks like one of her fosters was recently booked for sexual assault against four kids in his care. There are also some child pornography charges pending for the fosters she spent a year with when she was—"

"That's enough," I grit out through my teeth. "Thanks."

I end the call with shaking hands, unable to listen to another word. Sexual assault? Child pornography?

Christ.

There's a gaping hole in my chest, and I rasp when I try to breathe as if it's fucked up my lungs.

This contact has resources I could never get my hands on. It's a favor I haven't called in for years because of its innate value. If he says it checks out, then it checks out.

Which means I was wrong.

There's acid in the back of my throat, and I bite my clenched fist, hoping the pain will make it recede as I remember everything I said to her.

Fuck.

FUCK!

My skin heats and prickles as I push back to my feet, distantly hearing Seven trying to literally break down the fucking door with heavy, angry thuds that echo in my skull like gunshots.

Sweat beads over my chest, and I let out a shuddering breath.

I shouldn't have...

If I'd just waited, I...

I remember her face last night before I woke up and handed the reins to my demons.

I recall her smile. How she felt in my hands. It wasn't just fucking. Not entirely.

And she wanted to stay here. With *us*. Aurora wanted to help us.

And I...

CHAPTER 52

There's a metallic *chink* and the metal door yawns and smashes against the wall as Seven breaks through, crazed and breathless.

His blue fire eyes find me and zero in. "What the *fuck* is going..."

His gaze drops to the gun still in my hand, shifts to the messy sheets. To the shattered third-century bust of Aristotle, and then locks on her panties next to the bed.

"Atticus." My name is a warning dripping from his mouth like acid. "What did you do?"

"I..."

"*Atticus!*"

He comes over, shaking me violently until the words are dislodged from the chaos in my skull to fall onto my tongue.

"I...I fucked up, Sev. I *really* fucked up."

53

OFF LEASH

SEVEN

"What do you mean you fucked up?"

The blood in my veins turns to fucking battery acid, corrosive and leaking so much poison into my bloodstream that I can taste metal on my tongue.

I shake him again, trying to rattle him back to the present moment when he looks like he's a million miles from here.

"Atticus, what the fuck did you do!?"

He shrugs hard to get out of my grip, whirling to kick the already broken bust of Aristotle into the wall.

"*Fuck*," he hisses, gripping either side of his head like he wants to rip his hair out, knocking the barrel of his gun into his temple. "I thought she was a mole, man."

I gape at him openly. "What?"

"It didn't make sense," he rushes to say, pacing three steps away and back again. "It didn't make fucking sense that we just found her, and she was perfect for the role of Ambrose's daughter, and she had the right history and no real ties to anyone, save for one asshole ex-boyfriend and... and then the text message and I just—"

CHAPTER 53

"You're not making sense," I growl, trying to find the end to the fuse that set him off because my own is growing shorter by the second. "Slow the fuck down."

He gestures wildly at me, his eyes wide like I haven't seen them in years. "The text message," he snaps. "She got this fucking text from 'Chris' and it just said, 'Did you get in?' *Did you get in?* Just that, and I knew she'd been deleting messages, and I thought maybe Chris wasn't Chris, you know?"

No, I fucking don't.

"And then—"

"Atticus, *stop talking*."

"No, you don't get it. I was wrong, man. Fuck, I got it all wrong and—"

"You think?" I bellow, and mercifully for us both, he shuts the hell up.

Why couldn't he have waited to have a paranoid freak-out until we got home?

Fuck.

I force a slow inhale, trying to remember how Ro looked before she ran off. I didn't see any wounds, did I? I don't want to accuse Atticus of something he didn't do, because if he did...

I would protect my brother from any enemy, but that doesn't mean I won't kick his fucking ass if he deserves it.

Her neck, I remember. There was something on her neck. A mark. *A bruise?*

I level Atticus with a venomous stare, waiting for him to see it. To see *me*. And to understand that I am not fucking around.

"I'm only going to ask you this once. Did you hurt her?"

His lips part, and there's a knot between his brows that tells me he's disgusted by my question, but then why the

Off leash

hell isn't he answering it? Dread sinks in my gut like an anvil.

"Brother, I told myself I'd kill any man who tried to hurt that woman." I gesture out the door, my chest getting hot, my skin itchy. "Don't fucking put me in this position."

"No, man." He shakes his head. "I didn't hurt her, but I was...rough. Rougher than I needed to be."

So help me...

"*How* rough?"

"I said I didn't fucking hurt her, Sev. Jesus, do you really think I would?"

Right now, I'm really not sure, and I hate that I'm not.

I wave to the offensive weapon still gripped tightly in his hand. "What about that? Please fucking tell me you did not pull that on her."

He adjusts his grip on it and lifts his chin. "I did what I had to, to get the answers I need—"

I punch him so hard in the face that blood splatters over his carpet as he staggers sideways and falls to a knee. I have him disarmed in the next instant, but I can't keep the gun. I can't be trusted with a weapon right now. Not when my own fucking brother is the cause of the rage burning in my blood.

"Fuck!" I shout, chucking the gun into his music room and kicking the door shut after it, flexing and clenching my hands to get the feeling back to my extremities.

It's Atticus.

It's Atticus.

I shudder.

"*Why*, man?" I whisper-shout because I don't trust myself not to scream, and I don't want Ro to be any more afraid than she might be already.

"I was trying to protect us!"

CHAPTER 53

I give him a sarcastic, slow clap that has the intended effect. "Well, good fucking job, Atty."

I lift my arms, gesturing to the wonderful ambiance in this room. "Look how much safer we are. I feel safe. Do you feel safe?"

He shouldn't.

"You don't get it."

No. I *don't*.

I hope she held her own. I hope she told the fucker exactly where to go and how to get there. Did he think *at all* before he jumped to a thousand conclusions and pulled the gun from the safe in his office?

"*Christ* man, she *saved* Eli! Did you forget that? She fucking..."

I trail off, hating the sick feeling in my stomach, unable to say another word, or something might come out that I can't take back.

Atticus spits bloody saliva onto the carpet, reaching into his mouth to pull out a tooth.

Guilt and satisfaction face off in my chest, and I shove down the former. He's lucky I only hit him once. Depending on what he says next, I'm not writing off the possibility of knocking out a couple more of his perfect teeth.

No one gets to hurt Ro. And no one gets to scare her. Least of all my fucking brother.

I hope he sees the line I am drawing in the sand here because if he *ever* crosses it again, I don't know what I'll do.

"You don't have to tell me how badly I fucked up," he says. "I know, okay? *I know*."

"A lot of good that does us now."

It doesn't fucking matter now. What's done is done. There's no taking it back.

What if Ro leaves because of this? What if she never

comes back? My guts twist and my chest hollows. I wanted her to stay from that morning she bared her soul to me at the shed, and now I just want *her*.

But what if she doesn't want us anymore after this?

"She said yes."

"*What?*" I snap.

He looks up, and I feel no sympathy when I find the guilt and sorrow in his broken expression.

"She said yes to helping us."

"Of course she said yes. She was always going to say yes, you fucking idiot."

He drops his head in a nod. "And after she agreed, we..."

I find her panties on the floor again, and I think I can fucking guess.

"So let me get this straight. You *fucked* her...and then you *threatened* her. Is that right?"

When he doesn't answer me, I see red, and my breaths come in hot pants.

"Seven..."

"Don't you fucking come near me, Atticus!"

I corner myself into the wall, bending over my knees to try to lower my heart rate before I fucking kill him.

"I let her in, Sev. I didn't even realize it, but I did. I just... *fuck,* and then this morning, when I saw the message, I thought..."

"Not everyone is out to get us, Atticus!" I growl at him, lifting my head. "Not everyone that isn't us is *bad*. You fucking get that, right?"

We were all fucked up after Ambrose showed us where trust could get you, but that didn't mean we could never trust anyone again. And Ro? She's perfect. She's fucking *perfect* for us.

Why can't he see that?

CHAPTER 53

He nods to himself, the spot on his lower left jaw already swelling and turning red.

My stomach turns.

"I can understand not fully trusting her," I grit out. "But don't you trust us? Don't you trust *our* judgment?"

"Of course I do."

"But you just proved that you don't."

His jaw flexes. "I'm sorry, Sev. You know I—"

"It's not me you owe an apology to."

He sags, roughly shoving his hair from his face. "She won't want it."

"Do you fucking blame her?"

He's silent for a minute and I'm able to collect the still seething parts of myself and push them back into the black box just beneath my rib cage.

Atticus's Adam's apple bobs in his throat. "I like her, Sev."

I laugh. Actually laugh. "That's fucking rich."

His cheekbones flare. "I'm serious."

"You might like her, Atty, but you don't *care* about her. If you did, you never would have pulled that weapon on her."

He has nothing to say to that and halle-*fucking*-lujah because if he tried to rationalize it, I might've had to open that box back up and knock out another few teeth.

"I know it scares you," I push the words out, trying to listen to the tiny part of my mind that'll always be in his corner no matter what, even when it's being drowned out by the full stadium of hell beasts feral with the urge to protect their queen. "That she might...*fit* here, with us. It would mean things change. It would mean *you* have to change. But she's already changing Eli, and it's a damn good thing for him. She's changing me, and I think I'm pretty fantastic as I am."

He lets out a short, hollow laugh.

"You don't like change, and I know that," I add. "But not all change is bad."

He nods like he understands, but I'm not sure he does.

"*I* like her," I tell him. "I more than like her, man. That girl belongs here. She belongs with us. And if you ruined that..."

"I can fix this."

I give him a look that says he's done enough.

"*I can*," he presses.

"There's no way she's going to help us anymore if that's what you mean," I scoff. "I'd be surprised if she isn't already packing her damn bags to leave."

And fuck if it doesn't feel like she's ripping my guts out to take with her.

Atticus shakes his head and gets unsteadily to his feet. "No. It's not about that. This is *my* mistake, I won't let it mess shit up for Eli, or you. I can fix it. I can make this right."

His expression hardens when I say nothing. He might feel confident in his ability to do that, but I sure as hell don't.

"I *promise* you, I'll fix it."

I sigh, already turning to leave. I'm done in this room. I'm done hearing him make promises he has no way of knowing he can keep.

"For your sake, Atty, I really hope you can."

Because I don't want to live with the alternative.

54

UNMASKED

AURORA

"Tell me what he did."

Elijah and Ellie chase me through the house, all the way up the stairs into my room.

I shove through the door and meet the dead end of space and wonder why the fuck I even came in here. It feels small, tight, *asphyxiating*. I turn around and go the other way, almost tripping over Ellie in my haste to rush right back down the stairs and out the front door on my bare feet.

"Aurora," Elijah calls after me as I storm down the drive, spotting the Jeep parked out front. I make a beeline straight for the driver's side door as the buzzing in my ears grows louder, overtaking every other sound.

Throwing myself into the seat, I reach for the keys in the ignition, but my hand comes up empty.

"*Fuck!*" I slam my palms against the wheel.

Elijah opens the door, raising his hands as if I might shoot. "Hey, it's okay. Whatever happened, we can—"

"*What?*" I snap, hating myself. "We can *what?*"

God fucking dammit!

CHAPTER 54

Elijah needs to leave. I don't want to take this rage out on him. There's something building just beneath my breastbone and I'm not sure what will happen when it bursts, but I don't want him or Ellie in the blast radius.

I grab the door from him and shut it, locking myself inside the vehicle as Ellie tries to claw her way in one side, and Elijah presses his hands to the window on the other.

"Just go!"

"Please." Elijah's breath fogs against the window and his soft, gentle tone makes me want to cry and scream all at the same time. "Please just talk to me, Angel."

I drop my head to the wheel, trying to steady my breaths, but they only come harder as the back of my neck boils to an inferno, and I think I might pass out from the heatwave racing over my body.

Elijah tries the handle, and I flinch.

"Please," I shout against the steering wheel. "If you aren't going to get me the fucking keys, just *go*!"

I need everyone to leave me the fuck alone. I need to think. I need to calm the fuck down.

"I can't let you drive, Angel. And I'm not going to leave you like this," Elijah says quietly. "So I'll just be right here when you're ready."

The gravel shifts under his feet as he moves away from the Jeep and calls Ellie with him. When I look out the window, I find him sitting on the ground outside the Jeep, trying to get Ellie to sit patiently next to him.

A sob tries to swell in my chest, but it evaporates in the inferno still coiling through my lungs, making me want to spit fire. I curl my fists around the wheel until my fingers strain and hurt.

How fucking dare Atticus say that shit to me? And *after* I agreed to help them?

A raw shout pushes from my throat, an animalistic sound.

There's an engine trying and failing to turn over in my chest, sputtering as it floods over and over again.

I let that bastard touch me. But that's not even why it hurts so much. It's not where I let him leave his marks on my body; it's where I didn't realize I was letting him leave his mark someplace deeper.

Even if I didn't want to admit it to myself, I wanted what I thought someone like Atticus—someone completely unwilling to compromise the safety of his family—could give me. Like a pathetic moron, I actually woke up this morning thinking that I could really belong here. *With them.*

For one fleeting second, I believed it.

I wanted it so badly. More than I've ever wanted anything. And now it's ruined. It's all fucking *ruined*.

My rage focuses to a dangerous point as I remember the moments before I let him have me. The vulnerability I felt with one of my favorite songs echoing in the record-filled space around us.

Did he already know music was one of my passions? Did he really hear from one of the guys that I like Sleep Token, or did he stalk my Spotify while he was ravaging through my phone?

Was it all a manipulation?

I can see why they like you, he said.

Was it all a lie?

...you could stay. If that's what you wanted.

You wouldn't mind that?

No, Trouble.

Liar.

I don't think I would mind that at all.

CHAPTER 54

Fucking. LIAR.

I need to get out of here.

With trembling hands, I lift my head and flip down the visor, looking for a spare key, but finding my reflection instead.

I gasp at the girl in the mirror, my pulse skittering in my chest like a caged thing.

My eyes are a violent red. The pupils dilated so big that I look like a fucking monster. Black drips down my face from the ugly streaks of yesterday's mascara standing out in heavy contrast with my pale skin.

I want to look away, but I don't. *I can't.*

Because there she is in brutal, blinding clarity—the Aurora that I've hidden from the world for as long as I can remember. She stares back at me with cruel venom in her eyes. With a sort of certainty that I didn't know I had.

She tells me I was right to want Atticus to hurt.

He *deserves* to hurt like *I* hurt.

I promised myself never again. *I promised.*

I shiver as I slam the visor shut. *No.*

Stop.

Stop, stop, *stop*.

Keys. I need the keys.

I pop the glove box open.

I need to get out of—

As I search for the spare keys, my fingers clasp something solid and cool and metal, and I pull out a gun instead.

Fuck.

Oh fuck.

He should know how it feels.

No.

He should *hurt*.

No.

I can hurt him.

Yes.

I feel nothing but cold conviction as I step out of the Jeep.

Elijah launches to his feet, sighing with relief he shouldn't feel. "Oh, thank god."

There is no God.

"Aurora?"

Ellie whines as she pushes her snout into my shin. "Sit," I command. "Stay."

She gives me an anxious bark but does as she's told.

"Aurora, what are you doing with that?"

Did he say something? All I can hear is the echo of my own heartbeat.

Hurt him. Hurt him. Hurt him.

"Hey," he says, racing ahead of me to stand in my path. "Angel, hey, look at me. Look at me. You don't want to do this."

He's wrong.

"Move."

Elijah makes a move to take the weapon from me, and I snarl at him. "*Don't.*"

I don't allow myself to understand the look on his face. What it means that his eyes are wide and he can't seem to catch his breath.

I shoulder past him, up the stairs and through the open door of the house.

"Wait," Elijah says, frantic as he shuts the door behind him to stop Ellie coming in. "Aurora, just wait for one second."

Atticus appears at the top of the stairs, coming from the hall to the left. Was he in my fucking room?

The gun comes up all on its own, and Atticus freezes

CHAPTER 54

between the landing and the top step. He knows I have him dead to rights.

His jaw snaps shut.

"*You!*"

"Aurora," he says in a pacifying tone that makes my blood spike with something that tastes like power. It's fucking *delicious*.

"You bastard!"

The gun shakes in my grip.

"You don't want to do that."

"Don't tell me what I want!"

Elijah comes closer, and I jerk away.

"*Eli*," Atticus snaps. "Back away. This is between me and her."

Seven enters through the dining room, coming into the entryway to lean against the banister at the base of the stairs. At first I think he's going to try to stop me. Block my warpath. But he crosses his arms over his chest and just… watches.

"Let her pass," he says to Elijah, picking something from his thumbnail.

"Seven, *she has a gun.*"

"I can see that."

Atticus stepping down another stair draws my attention back to him, and the rage sparks back to a full burn.

He raises his hands, slowing his movements as he drops down another step.

My chest squeezes when I remember the feel of those hands on my body, and I almost gag.

I flick off the safety and Atticus flinches.

God, I want to shout at him. There are a thousand curses poised at the tip of my tongue, but none of them will hit as hard as this bullet will.

"I was wrong," he says, and my vision narrows. "I never should've accused you without having more facts."

Seven scoffs.

"I never should've accused you at all," Atticus amends, and my palm starts to sweat against the gun in my grip. I didn't anticipate this, but it changes nothing.

Atticus comes down another step, and I bare my teeth.

His jaw is red and swollen, I realize. And there's blood at the corner of his mouth.

Did Seven hit him?

When I meet Seven's blue eyes, they hold mine steadily.

He isn't trying to stop me. He only watches. And something tells me he is going to let this play out no matter what I do.

My throat goes dry as my adrenaline-addled thoughts race to find the reason why.

He doesn't think I'm wrong?

He doesn't think I'm crazy?

He doesn't think I'm bad?

I read the words in the fine print of his stare.

They tell me it's okay. That he understands.

Seven sees my monster, and he doesn't want to tame it. He wants to free it.

My arm feels heavier, and it's a fight to keep hold of the rage.

A broken sob escapes my lips, and I sniff hard to try to pull it all back in.

While I've been busy looking at Seven, Atticus has reached the bottom stair.

"Stay back!"

I adjust my aim and his hands rise higher in submission.

Elijah lets out another string of expletives somewhere

CHAPTER 54

beside me, and I sense his anxiety like tainted fingertips brushing against my resolve.

Atticus doesn't listen to me, and I shift my grip, moving my finger to poise it next to the trigger as he comes even closer.

"Fuck, *fuck*," Elijah curses as he spirals, shifting on his feet, making me fucking shifty. He can't stop me. I won't let him.

No one is taking this from me.

This is *mine*.

It's mine.

Atticus stops with only a breath between himself and the gun at his throat.

I could erase him with a flick of my finger. I could blow a hole through his windpipe and watch him choke as he dies. *I could.*

But I can't ignore Elijah next to me, no matter how hard I try to. Or the way Seven is starting to stiffen where he leans on the banister.

Are they as afraid as I am that I might do it?

"I was wrong," Atticus repeats. "And I'm sorry."

He's sorry?

He's fucking *sorry?*

I growl through my teeth, unable to find words strong enough to tell him how little I care about him being *sorry*.

"I did what I did because I thought I was protecting my family," he adds. "I need you to try to understand that."

"Fuck you."

His jaw flexes and his next words come out harsh and blunt. "It's the truth. I might've gone about it in a fucked-up way, but I will always do whatever it takes to keep them safe. I made a promise to Florence—that I would always protect them. *Always* put them first."

The angry thing in my chest twists.

He may not have said the exact words, but Atticus threatened to kill me. Implied I was a fucking *whore* after he manipulated me into his bed.

"And I promised myself I would *never* let anyone threaten me again, and I actually keep my fucking promises."

Rage and hurt flicker over his face at the insult.

"You *left* them."

His cheekbones flare, and I don't give two shits if I'm not being fair. I hope my words hurt him. I hope they slice right through his facade of self-control. I don't think I've ever met a man with less self-restraint than Atticus.

Fuck him.

Fuck. Him.

"That's not fair." His voice is a low rumble.

"None of this is fair!"

"Fine," he says through his teeth, and I gasp when he wraps his hand around the barrel of the gun and presses it against his chest, right over his heart. It thuds into my palm through the metal. "You want to hurt me, then hurt me."

"*Aurora*," Elijah breathes, and I shiver.

"If you want it to hurt the most—" He aims the barrel down toward his kneecap. "Take my knees."

My ears ring and pins and needles spike along my arms.

"If you want it over quick," he jerks the barrel up and holds it to the space between his eyes, "plant your lead right between my eyes."

My breaths falter and my mouth goes dry.

"And if you want the pain to last before I'm gone..." He lowers the weapon and plants it against his stomach—mirroring where he pushed the barrel of his own gun into me. "Then shoot me here."

CHAPTER 54

I'm shaking and I can't seem to make it stop.

"I won't apologize for protecting them, but I am apologizing for hurting you. I can see now that you aren't interested in hearing that, so accept it or don't, but either way don't take it out on Eli and Sev."

I *hate* the guilt in his eyes. It has no right to be there.

It doesn't matter now, anyway. Elijah and Seven won't want me to stay after this.

"What the hell did you do, man?" Elijah demands, his voice cracking. He should be yelling at *me*. I'm the one with the gun to his best friend's stomach.

Atticus replies to him while never taking his eyes off me. "Something I'll be regretting for a long time, Eli."

My stomach aches.

"Bull*shit*."

Somewhere behind me, Ellie barks. Hear her claws scratch at the door, and I lose another inch of my edge at the knowledge that I'm scaring her.

"She said yes, you know," he tells Elijah. "She was willing to risk her life for our vengeance before I fucked it all up."

Elijah comes into my line of sight, his brows low over his eyes, haunted. "Is that true?"

There's a tremble in my throat. A quiver in my bones. He looks so hopeful. I thought he didn't want me to help them. Did he change his mind?

"It doesn't matter now."

Elijah won't want a crazy bitch living under his roof.

"It does," Atticus argues, and I realized I said the words aloud. "But I don't care if you help us anymore. Just don't let what I did ruin things for my brothers. They really care about you, Aurora."

Atticus closes his eyes and breathes out slow, releasing

the barrel of the gun to lower his hands to his sides in open-palmed surrender, handing me back the power.

"You do what you need to do. They'll forgive you."

He waits, and I can't seem to move my finger. Did I want him dead? I wanted to hurt him. I still do. But then why can't I move my finger the five millimeters to the left to exact *my* vengeance?

"Aurora." My name is a plea on Elijah's lips. "Please. I can't lose anyone else."

My heart cracks, *bleeds,* and as the rage pours out, a sob escapes with it.

At the door, Ellie barks and whines and my stomach hollows.

"Let me take the gun," Elijah whispers, and when he comes closer, I don't have the energy left to stop him. Everything feels so heavy.

When his fingers brush against mine, my hand reflexively releases the weapon, and he takes it, pulling me hard into his chest. "I've got you, it's okay. *It's okay,* Angel."

He plants a kiss on the top of my head that makes my eyes burn like hell. He isn't angry? How can he not be angry?

Atticus doesn't deserve him.

I don't, either.

I cling to Elijah, and I swear he's the most steady thing I've ever held on to. An anchor in the black sea of my mind. And I don't ever want to let him go.

Please don't make me let you go.

"I'm sorry," I cry into his chest.

"I know. I forgive you, Angel." He strokes his thumb against the side of my neck. "It's okay. I'm not angry."

"I'll find a way to make this right, Aurora," Atticus says,

CHAPTER 54

and the last flickers of my rage rip me out of Elijah's arms, away from the calm they provided.

I shove Atticus as hard as I can, making him knock back into the stairs.

Seven steps out of the way, watching Atticus grimace when his spine connects with the edge of the bottom stair. I need to make this absolutely clear if there's any chance I can salvage a little piece of what I found here—with Elijah and Seven.

"You don't get to talk to me." The words come out eerily calm. Venomous in the dead silence. "You don't look at me. You don't say my name. Do you hear me?"

He recoils, unable to meet my stare.

"Do you hear me?" I shout, my voice blaring like a siren now, shrill and demanding attention.

A vein in his temple throbs as he clenches his jaw. "I hear you."

"I'm doing this for *them*," I scream. "Not for you."

That gets his attention. He looks up at me in unreserved shock. "You'll still help us?"

"*Them*," I correct. "I'm going to help *them*. I don't exist to you."

He snaps his mouth shut. Looks down.

I can see the fight in his coiled muscles. He doesn't want to respect my wishes, but he will, only because he doesn't want to risk me backing out. He doesn't care about me, he just doesn't want to be blamed for the missed opportunity only I can give them.

Atticus says nothing. He doesn't look at me.

It's just like I told him: *like I don't exist.*

And when I spin on my heel to go back outside with Ellie, I decide he doesn't, either.

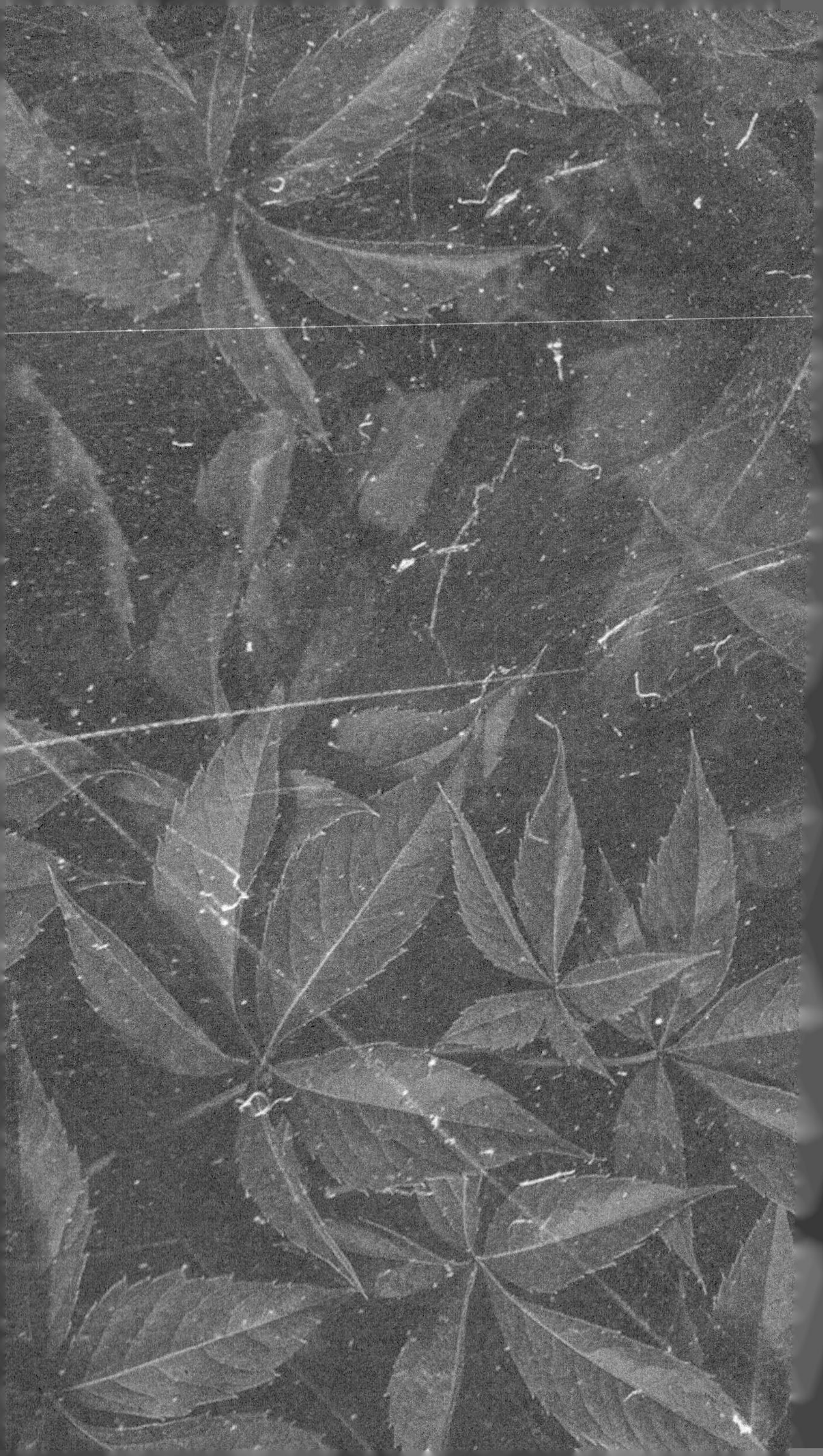

THANK YOU

Thank you so much for reading! How are you holding up? 👀

This one was an absolute *ride* and we can't wait to show you where the story is headed in book two! For bonus scenes, NSFW character art, and other exclusive content, subscribe to Elena's newsletter, join her Facebook group, or follow her and Blake on Instagram!

@authorelenalawson
@blakelawsonauthor

https://www.facebook.com/groups/elenalawson

ACKNOWLEDGMENTS

These characters absolutely stole our hearts. From day one Blake and I could feel we were making something special. It was in every late night plotting sesh and in every new idea that wreaked havoc on all our best laid plans.

We needed this book. I sure as shit know I did. I wasn't sure I'd ever feel that ✨spark✨ again after I finished with the Crows (IYKYK), but I found it right here, with these Painted Sinners.

This book wouldn't have happened without the closest people in our lives. So a big thank you to my husband for picking up the slack during late nights spent writing to meet our deadline (I am so sorry you have a do-everything-last-minute-wife😅). And to our Mom, for helping out with babysitting our young ones while we schemed and plotted over a few bottles of wine.

To our alpha readers, Kelly, Anita, Chrissy, Laura, Morgan, Kristina, Leslie, and Sierra—thank you. You helped us find the souls of these characters and polish their story into something that really shines. Special mentions go out to Kelly—for saving the bacon. To Anita—for #Daddicus. And to Leslie—for going above and beyond after the book was finished to make sure no errors snuck through.

This book wouldn't be nearly as flawless without the help of Rumi Khan. It was our first book together and we can't wait to work with you again. Thank you for taking us on 🥰

We also need to send a big thank you to my PA, Paige Jenkins. When things started to fall apart for us, you stepped up and filled in all the gaps. I can say with 100% certainty that if you hadn't, this release wouldn't have gone even half as well as it did. Thank you for being someone we can count on—and for being more organized than us every day of the week and twice on Mondays.

To all the incredible ladies who read and reviewed an ARC or joined our masterlist and helped spread the word for *White Rose Painted Red*—you really do make the book world go round. I hope you know that, and see your value. I know we do.

Last, and possibly most important, thank *you*. Without you, dear reader, none of this would be possible. Without you, I wouldn't be living my dream, and I wouldn't have been able to share a slice of that dream with my little sister. It's an honor to write for you. One that neither of us will ever take for granted.

ALSO BY ELENA LAWSON

BOYS OF BRIAR HALL

a dark enemies-to-lovers why choose romance series - now complete!

Crooked Crows

Wicked Trials

Twisted Games

Warped Minds

~

KINGS OF KILBORN UNIVERSITY

Soulless Saint

Ruthless Reign

Made in the USA
Middletown, DE
20 July 2025